Lg.Print MA‾

Mapson, Jo-.

Shadow Ranch

3205ØØØ2745252

Y0-BCU-702

WITHDRAWN

SHADOW RANCH

SHADOW RANCH

Jo-Ann Mapson

East Central Regional Library
244 South Birch
Cambridge, Minnesota 55008

BEELER LARGE PRINT
Hampton Falls, New Hampshire, 1999

Library of Congress Cataloging-in-Publication Data

Mapson, Jo-Ann.
  Shadow Ranch / Jo-Ann Mapson.
      p.   cm.
    ISBN 1-57490-176-1 (alk. paper)
    1. Aged men—California—New York—Fiction. 2. Family—
California—New York—Fiction. 3. Children—Death—Fiction.
4. Large type books. I. Title.
[PS3563.A62S53 1999]
813'.54—dc21   98-48129
                                                                        CIP

Copyright © 1996 by Jo-Ann Mapson
All rights reserved.
No part of this book may be used or reproduced in any manner whatsoever
without written permission except in the case of brief quotations embodied
in critical articles and reviews. For information address:
HarperCollins Publishers, Inc., 10 East 53rd Street, New York, NY 10022

Grateful acknowledgment to Linda Pastan for the use of her poem, "Shadows."
Reprinted from *A Fraction of Darkness* by Linda Pastan. Reprinted with
permission of W.W. Norton & Company, Inc. Copyright © 1985 by Linda Pastan.

Published in Large Print by arrangement with
HarperCollins Publishers, Inc.

BEELER LARGE PRINT
is published by
Thomas T. Beeler, *Publisher*
Post Office Box 659
Hampton Falls, New Hampshire 03844

Typeset in 16 point Adobe Caslon type.
Printed on acid-free paper and bound by
BookCrafters in Chelsea, Michigan.

In memory of
Donald Leslie Mapson
8/25/05 – 5/17/95,
but especially for
John Mapson,
brother, bluesmeister, and incomparable friend:

A whole bushel of wheat is made up of
single grains.

—THOMAS FULLER, M.D.
GNOMOLOGIA, 1732

ACKNOWLEDGMENTS

SO MUCH HELP GOES INTO THE MAKING OF A believable book. Again, let me extend thanks to my language experts, Gil Carrillo y Martin Nava: *Quien sabe dos lenguas vale por dos*—and then some. For medical advice on the stages of grief, mitral valve prolapse, gestation, and the inner workings of ultrasound technology, I am indebted to Lois Kennedy, M.F.C.C., Daisy Tint, M.D., M. E. Brownell of UCI Medical Center Radiology/Ultrasound, and Gerry C. LaJeunesse of Advanced Technology Laboratories.

Once again, Camp Pine listened to every chapter and delivered honest, supportive, critical care.

My friends, family, and animals generously allow me to enter their private universes, probe their hearts, and borrow their stories, and for this unselfish gift remain forever in their debt.

To Robert Dees, Division Dean, Department of Literature and Languages, Orange Coast College, for allowing me flexible scheduling to accept the gift, and to Lori Wood and Villa Montalvo Center for the Arts for the month of September 1994, thank you.

Janet Goldstein and Terry Karten's wise hands edited and shaped the final manuscript, and Deborah Schneider, my exceptional agent and friend, managed with her abundant grace and endless patience to keep me on track.

Shadow Ranch, the town of Harper, California,
and all the characters herein are imaginary.
Though some actual places
and names occasionally occur,
be assured they are used fictitiously.

SHADOW RANCH

PART ONE

THE
EGGSHELL
CRUST
OF EARTH

Last night as I was sleeping,
a dream—the image remembering *us*!
—of a beehive, real and alive
inside my heart. And here,
where I had hid my bitterness,
a swarm of golden, stinging bees
building combs of snow-white wax,
filling them with sweet, sweet honey.

—Antonio Machado, Untitled Poem,
TR. M.R.CHAPMAN

CHAPTER 1

THE MEN IN HER LIFE

THE TIGER LILY BOUQUET ON SPENCER'S GRAVE could have been left by any one of a number of people. During his brief hospital stay, Lainie Clarke's four-year-old son had charmed every nurse, orderly, and janitor on the pediatric cardiac unit. Three years later, a few of them still sent Christmas cards, and from time to time Lainie received those little computerized notifications in the mail indicating that someone had made a donation in his name. But there was only one kind of individual on earth who would purposely abandon his 100X Resistol beaver-felt cowboy hat on her little boy's marker because he despised the brass angel.

That two-hundred-dollar hat, with its frayed brim and braided horsehair hat band, rested upside down next to her on the passenger seat of her 1982 Volvo sedan. At every stop light, Lainie flipped her wind-knotted long brown hair out of her face, nudged her sunglasses back up the bridge of her narrow Carpenter nose, and stared at the hat, getting madder.

Without examination, she knew it was a size eight, the satin lining worn dull and thin where her grandfather's forehead perspired against it, from years of riding horses in full sun and barking out orders. On his more benevolent days, Bop Carpenter was a man who sported a kindly, Robert Duvall smile. People—no, *women*—would do just about anything he asked when he smiled that way. On his mean days, a chilly grimace

1

told the real story. He was wealthy. He was about as powerful and as wealthy as a man could be in this Southern California beachside county. He could well afford to replace a hat. But eventually, because of its history, the memories connected with it, he'd miss this particular one. Maybe not today, but in a day or so, when he automatically grabbed for it from the moose antler coat rack near his custom-made redwood front doors and found it missing. She knew how it would go: Not finding it, he'd walk outside on his deck, gaze out over the sun-dappled harbor water he'd paid a fortune for, his old blue eyes squinting against the almost unbearable brightness. In his mind, he'd slowly retrace his steps from Whistler's stables to his great-grandson's grave, and start to cry.

They all grieved. In grief they were partners, equals, a cohesive tribal unit. In every other way they were a distant, estranged family, full of blame for each other. She wanted to stamp her foot and holler, but just now her foot rested on the accelerator and stamping didn't seem like a good idea. She was thirty-five years old, once again up to 120 pounds, six months out of the psychiatric ward, and determined not to go back. It was probably as wrong not to return the hat as it was for Bop to leave it at Spencer's grave. Any halfway decent great-grandfather wouldn't make a stink about what marked his great-grandson's grave. Any halfway-sane granddaughter could find ten minutes in her schedule to drive over, drop off said hat, and tell him—politely, without an undue emotional display—to mind his own damn business when it came to angels and headstones.

At Beach and Adams she pulled over, got out of the car, opened the Volvo's trunk, and threw the hat inside. There was space for it between the toys she'd meant to

2

take to Children's Hospital and the box of baby clothes she had—for a year now—intended to give to Goodwill. In fact, that hat looked like it had joined a little in-between club of Spencer's things. They might make it secretary or, given its original cost, treasurer.

Lainie tucked a gold sweatshirt with the Santa Fe train logo back into one of the boxes, bit her lip, and slammed the trunk shut. Then, determinedly, she got back in her car and drove on home to her husband and dogs, to all that was left of her life.

CHAPTER 2

Mo-Tel Ro-Mance

THE BEIGE SONY CORDLESS ON THE PATIO TABLE was ringing like a hive of angry bees. Charles Russell Carpenter II, Bop to his friends—and enemies—studied the instrument, weighing his options. More than likely, it was one of those nineteen-year-old telemarketing saleschildren, hoping to talk him into buying two million bargain trash sacks. But then again, this was the 1990s, the age of miracles, and a day didn't pass that he didn't hold out the hope one of his grandkids might call and invite him to Sunday supper. Roast chicken, creamy mashed potatoes, new baby peas, a slice of lemon pie—that was the menu from the old days, when everybody was friendly and forgiving.

The intelligent choice was to let the answering machine pick up, but lately the gizmo had a mind of its own. It cut off his attorney, silenced his stockbroker's tips, yet every idiot caller it fed generous tape. In his opinion, ever since they relaxed the fair trade laws, and

3

electronics started getting too affordable, things had taken a hefty downslide.

Curiosity won out. He lifted the receiver, pressed Talk and held it to his ear. Across Huntington Harbour, a sliver of early morning sun struck the water through a haze that wouldn't lift before noon. He was an old man. He could say anything he wanted. "This better be worthwhile. You're interrupting my morning swim."

"We're conducting a survey, sir, and require only a few moments of your precious time. Today's question is: If you could bring a famous person back from the dead, ask him one question, who might that person be?"

The voice on the phone was tauntingly familiar, and Bop did not hesitate with his answer. "Alexander Graham Ding Dong Bell."

A muffled snicker preceded the next question. "And your question for the man?"

"What's the big idea, inventing machines to make it easier for a hack reporter to invade the privacy of a law-abiding taxpayer?"

Now the voice broke into creaky seasoned laughter. "Howdy, Bop."

Bop joined in. "MacLellan Henry! The prince of yellow journalism. Ain't you pushing sod?"

"Oh, I'm a young colt compared to you, Carpenter. If I'm not mistaken, you've got a birthday coming up next month. The big eight-O, isn't it? That's a herd of candles. Hope you've got smoke detectors in that claptrap barn of yours."

Bop set his beach towel down on the table. "Mac, I'd hardly refer to Casa de Carpenter as a barn. Speaking of barns, how's your wife?"

There was a small silence before Mac responded. "Gloria is a fine woman."

"Oh, sure, if you enjoy daily hysteria and maximum credit card debt, she's about as good as they come and she's all yours. 'Course, after I got done with her she wasn't good for much, was she?"

Mac cleared his throat. "What do you want this year—big feature story on the house, complete with tawdry family history and rattling skeletons, or will this be the year I rate a personal invitation to your birthday bash?"

Bop waited for a cabin cruiser rumbling down the harbor channel to motor out of sight before he answered. "Neither option sounds all that attractive. Hadn't planned on a party, Mr. Henry, but if I did, I'm afraid you'd only make the B list. It's not just me you've been offending all these years. There's family to consider."

"And like it or not, you and your family are news, old man. You going to give my photographer a break, let him shoot some new stills, or do we have to raid the morgue?"

"What part of no don't you understand? Every year I tell you I'm not interested in pictures old or new, and I don't want a story. You must be as hard of hearing as you are hard up for news. Let me give you the number of the audiologist fitted me with my Belltones. Remember to ask for the senior discount."

"You take them out when you do your little morning doggypaddle, Charles Russell? Doesn't that make it difficult to hear the barracudas?"

"It's the prehistoric land sharks I have to worry about. Say, why haven't they revoked your press pass, Mac? You're almost as old as that fish wrapper you work for. They running low on gold watches?"

"Old man, those are fighting words to a professional

journalist."

"Professional pencil chewer is more like it."

"I'd watch my mouth, Carpenter. Some of us can't depend on money gleaned from the sweat off our parents' backs. We do it the old-fashioned way. Earn our paychecks."

Bop pressed his lips together and waited. He and Mac Henry went back thirty years and one woman: Gloria, who had been Mac's steady girlfriend before she became Bop's second wife. The reporter had never gotten over losing Gloria to his old rival, and married her when the divorce ink was barely dry. This business about a story on the Carpenter family was a front; Mac Henry was holding out on something much more important. Bop wanted whatever it was out in the open as soon as possible so he could get to the pleasant sensation of salt water pickling his skin as he peeled off his laps. "All right, Mr. Team-Effort Pulitzer. Let's cut to the chase. Why the call?"

"Nothing important."

"Tell me anyway."

"A human interest item from the *Blade Tribune* popped up on my screen this morning. Seems the town of Shadow is for sale, lock, stock, and lemon crate."

Immediately Bop suspected a lie. "That so?"

"Yep."

"Not that I care diddly, but how much are they asking?"

"Two and a half million. That's pocket change to you, isn't it? Maybe one of your grandchildren could give it to you as a birthday present. Oh, wait. For a moment there I forgot you spent all their inheritance."

"I hope you choke on your pencil lead, Mac."

"Charles, Charles. We're in the nineties now. Pencils

6

are a thing of the past. We use computers."

"None of that fancy crap has managed to teach you to write any better. Well, I've got a date with some seawater. *Adios.*"

Bop pressed Talk again, set the phone down on the table top, removed his hearing aid, and walked a few steps down to the dock's edge. His sailboat, *Shadow IV,* was algae-covered up to the deflated bumpers, the aluminum mast pocked and crusted with salt. If he turned his head and looked at the house, he knew he would see the same kind of damage mirrored in the copper roof and stone face of Casa de Carpenter. If you could bring someone famous back from the dead, Mr. Frank Lloyd Wright would about run him down asking what in hell Bop thought he was doing, letting his ex-wives paint over the earth tones. He'd undone most of the damage after he gave Gloria her walking papers, but Casa de Carpenter would never be the pure architectural vision it once was. Bop shut his eyes, pressed his hands together in a gesture common to prayer, arched them above his head, and executed a reasonable swan dive into the water.

At seventy-nine years and eleven months, these swims were vital. As long as he was able to perform his morning constitutional, crawl back and forth twenty laps from his mooring to his neighbor's across the bay, his body felt nearly as youthful and supple as it had at fifty. Only back on earth did gravity assure him he was growing older, rapidly approaching the status of fossil. That was old age—sure, you still wanted to do it all, you just had to do it in slow motion.

He lapped to his neighbor's dock—the snobby Englishwoman he suspected of poisoning the ducks—turned and stroked back toward his own house.

MacLellan Henry's phone call was no more troubling than an ordinary bee sting. Scrape the stinger free and it'll only hurt for a day at the most. The town of Shadow for sale. What horsepucky! The weak-fingered writer would lie about nuclear war if it might net him an inch of column space and his John Hancock in italics. Bop completed the remainder of his laps, breathing every other set of pulls, and in his mind, hummed an old Hank Williams favorite, "I'll Be a Bachelor Till I Die."

In contented weariness, a rejuvenated Charles Russell Carpenter II climbed out of the water with the steady grace of a sea turtle. At the turn of the century, Shadow, California, consisted of one dirt-floor hacienda and a small orchard of trees. His parents' ranch. The only thing they ever had in great supply was Meyer lemons.

To this day, he began each morning with an array of citrus: half a pink grapefruit, no refined sugar or that fake sweetener—when his horse refused NutraSweet he took it to be a sign—a peeled tangerine when they were in season, navel oranges when they weren't, and his tumbler of what had come to be known in the family as Carpenter punch:

Take the juice of one freshly-squeezed lemon,
mix in tap water (none of that store-bought fizzy crap),
stir in a tablespoon of honey,
a dash of Angostura bitters,
then wedge the whole business with lime, or maraschino cherries for the ladies.

Drink it down everyday to avoid colds, flu, and the

8

achy-breakies to boot. Too bad he couldn't feed it to his house.

In Los Angeles, Frank Lloyd Wright was a god. In Orange County, where homogenized art reigned supreme, you mentioned his name and people thought maybe he was a car dealer. The fact that the designer of his house bore those famous initials had been a burr under his saddle from day one. Odd years they were putting him in the guide to the city, even ones they came after him with fistfuls of ordinances. His neighbor's was a watered-down Frank Gehry—nice enough, but common as church mice. The poor fellow had passed on, his wife shortly after, then their ungrateful children sold it to new-money yuppies who partied hard the first six months, scrambled to make the payments the next six, then let it get run down enough to just about qualify for public assistance. Recently, it had sold again, this time as a fixer-upper to that unfriendly Englishwoman who had it in for the duck population.

Not a week went by he didn't scoop up two or three of the wobbly necked dead, their white feathers tainted a pitiful green where they hit the waterline. From laying hens to halfway decent horseflesh, Bop Carpenter had seen enough of the animal world to reason that ducks hardy enough to find a food supply in a fouled harbor channel ought to maintain a little longer lifespan than seven days.

Of Irish-Welsh stock himself, he'd never mustered much reason to trust the British accent—fired the first doctor set up to do his angioplasty soon as he heard the man's fussy high-pitched whine. *Send me somebody who wears a cowboy hat*, he'd bellowed, *even cowboys deserve a second opinion.* And they had, hadn't they? Boom, boom,

boom went his patched-up old heart.

Mac Henry's words echoed in his head as he fitted his hearing aid back into his ear canal. Voices could tell you all about a person. Take Lainie, his granddaughter, who had given him the nickname, Bop. In the old days, why, her singing voice was about as pretty as hammered silver. Now, well, she hadn't sung a note since her breakdown—or spoken two words to him, for that matter. Okay, so he had told the doctors the crazy things she did. Pressed for her hospitalization when everybody else was waffling. But damn it all, that was part of the responsibility of loving someone. You did what was best for them. And she was better now, wasn't she? Back at work part time, doing fairly well. He still had a few willing spies in the county.

His son Chuck's daughter, and his first grandchild, Lainie had been unable to pronounce the traditional "grandpa," or its simpler cousin, "pop," which he was secretly hoping to be called. But she had her *b* sounds down good, and "bop" seemed close enough for government work. When, as a one year old, she first toddled toward him on those fireplug legs, calling, "Boppa, Bop," his heart was hers as surely as if she had sunk a pitchfork into the muscle. The nickname made him sound like a character instead of the old fart he was. Everyone, including his enemies called him Bop. Lainie-gal.

Sometimes he spent whole afternoons out here on the graying redwood deck in the shadow of the old house, thinking, sorting out the decades in his mind, puzzling over the larger picture they produced. Somewhere in all those jigsaw pieces, there had to be a kernel of wisdom. Too often, all that consideration simply ended with the sun at the waterline bobbing like a lost tennis ball, and

Bop's sudden astonishment at how much time had passed without him saying a single word.

He rubbed himself dry with a once-fancy but now quite faded beach towel. "Never wash these in anything but cold!" one of his three wives had carped, but faded seahorses dried you about as well as vivid ones, and faded things went with an aging house, even an aging monument. He knew the gossip: The foundation wasn't up to code and he'd paid off the county to overlook it; Bop Carpenter had built his fortune atop others' misery; inside the stone and cement walls people believed he wasn't above thumping his wives.

He blamed the house. Like a gothic soap opera, its oddness fueled newspaper stories from the moment the first bag of cement tasted water. All he wanted was something modern near the ocean, so he could sail his boat and, when the notion struck him, catch a fish. Was it his fault the Harbour had turned into prime real estate, a playground for the rich? Far as he was concerned, those Cheez-Whiz brains down at the city could send him warnings and fines every other week for something that didn't meet with the new codes—the roof, the deck, some new business he didn't quite understand about the glass in his windows—he didn't have to give them one squat inch. Casa de Carpenter rested in the loving embrace of a grandfather clause. Tough titty for the inspectors the Harbour had ushered into the fold in 1960.

He stopped swatting away the water caught in his silver chest hair and glanced at the upstairs bedroom windows with their famous vanished corners. Shut, there was little to distinguish them from modern-day inventions. But on a bright summer day, fully open, they became two stories of beveled glass wings spreading to the east and west, hovering suspended in the air. The house was designed to appear as if that particular corner rested on a geometry never to be found in compasses and equations. Rather, they were the byproduct of a concept consisting of space and faith.

In its day, the redwood a bright blood-orange, the copper roof shining like a newly minted penny, the *casa* seemed to be pure magic. Now, all the silvering wood and crumbly stone was like some broken-down old man, continuously in need of hammer, nail, and Metamucil. But finding someone honest and intelligent enough to attend the architectural vision turned out to be about as easy as losing the ten pounds he wore around his middle like one of those dopey fanny packs. No doubt, food made amenable company when all three of your wives had either vamoosed or gone on to play bridge with Jesus. He folded the towel over the deck railing to dry and caught a glimpse of that skinny Englishwoman coming out onto her deck with her bag of Weber's bread.

He waved broadly and called out, "Hi, neighbor! Come on over! We'll have us a wee cuppa tea! Or how about a little *Cold Duck?*" And he mimed a little cup coming to his lips, his pinky finger extended in what he surmised she would find good British manners.

He chuckled at her hasty retreat and watched the drapes in her front window slide shut on a motorized track, heartened clear down to his toes. He didn't really care one nit if old bony butt ever answered him back; he intended to defend his ducks. Something about ducks struck him as downright American. With ducks around, an old man felt less lonely, though when you got this old, loneliness wasn't something you made public knowledge.

12

Of late, he'd found company in those talk shows. Couldn't stomach Señor Geraldo, however. Now there was a young man not bright enough to open a matchbook unassisted. Oprah covered some whimsical subjects, among his favorites the episode "They Fell in Love Over the Fax Line," where she went around gathering up couples who advanced from thermal print to thermal undies.

But if it was his last day on earth and he got to watch only one, it would have to be Sally Jessy in her maverick red-rimmed glasses and smart assortment of suits whose skirts showed athletic leg all the way up to the knee. He'd read in the tabloid headlines at the supermarket checkout that Sally was single again, and had considered calling her up to see if she might harbor any interest in becoming the fourth Mrs. Carpenter. In the end, however, he went against the idea. He couldn't stand behind bi-anything, not even those in-vogue bicoastal marriages, which, given his attachment to Southern California, and hers to her television show, their union would surely become.

But dreaming was free. Bop dreamed quietly, pining for someone to share the last few years of his life. *It may just be I have stayed overlong in this world,* he admitted on his bluest days, when he spent too much time thinking about the dead—his only son, Chuck, and his great-grandson, Spencer. Some history, like theirs, continued to rewrite the future.

He'd flat out quit thinking about women after Helene, his last matrimonial mistake. For all her gallery openings the woman had no conception of the value of art. Why, she had gone so far as to line up a museum donation for his Maynard Dixon painting when he wasn't done looking at it! Women were difficult, cyclical

13

creatures. But the idea of a warm female body next to you at night—no getting around it—heaven lay between soft, pink thighs.

As much as he sometimes craved eternal rest, he knew he wasn't deserving of Forest Lawn just yet. There was still something left on this earth he needed to do. If only he had a clue as to what that was. While he waited for this enigma to reveal itself, he did what he could— reminisced about better times, tried to forget Mac Henry's resurfacing into his life talking trash about Shadow, and surfed the channels as ably as old Duke Kahanamoku.

Today Sally Jessy, in her navy blue suit and smart white pumps, which made the best of her ankles, was featuring a panel of ex-burlesque artists. He'd plugged high-resolution tape in the VCR for this one. If *TV Guide* wasn't lying, it had the earmarks of a classic.

Sally was quick to pitch her no-nonsense voice over her audience's immediate sarcastic groan, insisting these women were not topless sluts in pasties and G-strings doing the lap dance for a gin-damp five-dollar bill, they were *ecdysiasts* (ek-diz-e-asts, he pronounced silently), a dying breed who once practiced the graceful art of divesting clothing in combination with dance. Ostrich feather fans were employed. Dance moves choreographed. The beauty of the human female body hinted at, revealed layer by shell-pink layer.

All the ex-strippers were over the age of fifty. Three had been beauty queens, born in Kansas. A couple were really getting up there in terms of the tree rings: Miss Cara Mia, now in her eighties, appeared to be drooling down her dress front. Work With Me Annie sat in one of those armless athletic wheelchairs since her skiing

14

accident, and in between them perched this cute little pixie of a gal who piped right up saying, "I'm in my sixtieth dee-cade and proud to say so!"

Bop laughed. She looked damn good for six hundred years old. He swore he heard Texas Gulf Coast in her cheery voice. Chinaberry trees, trips to the Washerino, bad weather, bowling alleys, waitressing jobs—that tiny gal had one meaty history. Trim and sharp, the platinum blond had about the sunniest smile he'd seen since he buried old Alyce, his first horseback ride on the marriage-go-round.

Everyone, himself included, had kidded Alyce something fierce when she started putting her brassieres in the freezer and the ice trays in her underwear drawer. Yes, it was all one big joke until she started forgetting who she was. Nowadays they called it Alzheimer's disease, not losing your marbles, but that sure as shingles didn't mean insurance would ever cover it. It had taken Alyce seven years and 210,000 U.S. dollars to pass from this world to the next, though her mind had departed long before she moved to the small room off the smelly, dark hallway in the convalescent hospital. He still missed her.

On his Sony wide screen, Miss Earlynn Sommers, who was "retired from the profession," was telling Sally Jessy, "I have performed for heads of state. Once this Saudi prince proposed marriage to me. Give me a ruby the size of a Florida grapenut!"

"You couldn't possibly mean—grapefruit?" Sally politely inquired, a smile playing at the corners of her mouth.

"Oh, no. Grapenut, ma'am. There'd be a world of difference between the two."

Sally pursed her lips indulgently and went on. "Well,

15

can you tell the audience why you said no?"

"I'm old-fashioned," Earlynn answered. "Myself, I like an earthy man. One who can ride herd and mend fence along with the hands. Plus, I feel certain the good Lord didn't intend for men to wear bedsheets, except for maybe in motel rooms and romance novels."

Mo-tel. Ro-mance. Bop's smile widened.

The audience roared with laughter and Miss Sommers, who had "performed" under the name Early Summer, as the caption overlay informed, looked straight into the camera and blushed from the adorable gap in her own front teeth down to the ample cleavage at the top of her gold lamé pantsuit. Bop cranked the volume on his hearing aid, adjusted the BarcaLounger, and checked once again to make sure he'd punched Record on the VCR.

CHAPTER 3

CHARLIE, DON'T SURF

FOUR P.M. THE ARSENIC HOUR. NOTHING ON TV and two full hours before a single man could sensibly put together supper.

Bop got into his Ford one-ton truck, fired up the horses, depressed the Stanley opener, and drove across busy Algonquin with its hairpin turn to Warner, flooded with July beach traffic. Hardly paid to live near the water when all those inlanders invaded from May to September, and they were just as likely to be armed with spraycans or Saturday-night specials as they were surfboards. Across the boulevard, he boarded his horse at Whistler's Stables, a few dirt acres that butted up

16

against the marshlands preserve where Ash Builders was arguing with the city about whether to build two thousand custom homes immediately, screw the migratory birds, or five hundred and screw them more slowly.

Independence Day was next week. Though the city had long ago outlawed fireworks stands, people still managed to drive over to Harper and buy them by the crateful. In the middle of all the popping, whistling, and sulfur stink of matches, Whistler's was a little bit of all right, smelling nicely of sun-warmed horse buns and ocean breeze.

If he shut his eyes and managed to drown out the traffic and boomboxes, Bop could almost remember the world of sixty years ago, three hours south and twelve minutes inland to the town of Shadow, where the packing house his parents built had shipped thousands of crates of lemons every month, eventually filling his pockets with so much money he had to start emptying it out or drown under the weight. When he'd sold Shadow Ranch Packers, the very first lemon packing plant in the state, back in 1957, he'd expected it to continue on, the town to thrive under the profitable industry. He imagined the Carpenter connection an important footnote in California history. Instead, industrialization moved the operation out of the county, and the once-lush groves had passed through a series of hands, and now the whole town was up for sale.

Bop had used the lemon money to grow his own kind of family fortune, a legacy to bequeath to Chuck and the grandkids. His investments paid off so handsomely it seemed almost criminal for business to go that easy. Thanks to a posse of lawyers and accountants, the legacy remained airtight. As for the inheritors—well, your only

17

son wasn't supposed to pass through the exit door before you did. Dying at thirty-seven, leaving behind half-raised kids, that wasn't the natural order.

One of those silent heart attacks, they called it. A perfectly healthy thirty-seven-year-old man, walking up the same flight of stairs he did every day, on his way to teach mathematics to ungrateful teenagers. Chuck keeled over dead, slipping the cotter pin of the Carpenter family, so that all that was left of them was odd wheels, bent axles, and a puddle of slippery grease. Then last year, Lainie slipped in it but good. At least Chuck was spared seeing his daughter in restraints.

A flurry of preteen girls in riding habits rushed by, fearlessly leading tall, nervous thoroughbreds. "Hey, Bop," one of them called out. "How's it hanging?"

"Well, darling, it's a-dangling. That's about all I can say for it. And hey yourself," he answered, giving her a wink as he waited for them to pass safely by. Women and horses—as natural a combination as salting fried eggs. Just like salt, and most everything that tasted halfway decent, eventually, you were supposed to do without and keep smiling.

The trouble with poking around in the past was that once disturbed, it wanted to rear up in every corner, Bop decided as he unlatched the stall catch in the breezeway barn. Behind the bars stood the ugliest Appaloosa stallion ever to set hoof on the planet. Whereas the breed standard featured solid color in the front and a blanket with a spotted rump, this horse was splattered indiscriminately with fist-sized black spots, like the loser in a mud fight. One fat tear-shaped blotch lay directly between his pig-eyes, where some days, Bop was convinced, every last one of his brains had leaked out. Tio Tonto Son of a Dancer, was his papered name;

18

Tonto Son of Bitch was more like the truth. The feisty offspring of his brilliant third stallion, Tonto's Sun Dancer, this devil on hooves would be his last steed, because with a partnership like this, sooner or later one of them was bound for the bone pile.

Tontito nickered in a combination of brute animal panic and nameless delight at the sound of the chain coming up. It was always thus. You could work the animal into a lather for three days, put him back in his stall, open it ten minutes later and his hooves would go right into that little war dance. His current state, however, involved heaving his bulk at the bent bars of the gate, which indicated once again that the horse hadn't been exercised this week. Bop was paying an extra fifty dollars a month to a flock of teenaged girls to school the rankness out of the beast. This wasn't the first time he suspected they took his greenbacks and ran straight to the mall. Couldn't get enough of those blue slushy drinks or those cropped blouses that hurt a man of any age to look at.

One of the Mexican stablehands working nearby stopped his raking. "Need help?"

"*A pesar de gracias,* Mr. Alejo. The *caballo malo* that could take down a Carpenter male has yet to be invented."

"Whatever you say, Señor Bop." Alejo continued, from a safer distance, raking up buns.

Carefully, Bop threaded a brass stud chain through the nose band of the halter, giving it a sharp tug to let Mr. Ants in the Pants know rebellion versus metal was useless. The horse quieted to a satisfactory degree, but down the length of striped green lead rope, Bop could feel tension and a very low IQ humming.

They made it as far as the turnout arena, creaked the

19

lopsided gate open, and were halfway inside before the Appy exploded like a M-100 dropped in a toilet bowl. "Ho, there!" he cried. "Quit now! I say, quit!"

The animal paid no heed. People came running from every direction, more anxious for a good show than they were to lend a hand. It was not unlike one of the crazy multicultural modern dance ballets his last ex-wife, Helene, had been fond of buying tickets for: wild spotted horse rearing up, old man taking a rear hoof in the forearm, his own demented dance of pain, the unbreakable chain snapping, lead rope burning through fingers, dust clouds, horse snorts and swear words filling the air like shrapnel. All the while in the arena alongside, a dozen girls in English riding habits kept their legs correctly positioned—heels down, posting the trot with a collectively correct seat for the afternoon group lesson.

"I don't think that horse ought to go on the hot walker," one of them had piped shrilly the first time Bop had tried to cool the horse out. No, but it might make for a fine equine suppository, Bop considered as the beast ran in wide circles, dragging the motor and two of its mechanical arms behind him. The machine was designed to walk a horse slowly until it was quiet— not incite it to riot.

"Don't suppose they let any of you fellows pack a gun?" Bop asked the paramedics who insisted on taking his vitals and giving him a ride to the hospital. "I've half a mind to shoot him. Never once in my life have I owned a horse that reared on me. Crazy Indian acts like someone stuck a wedge of ginger up his ass."

"Sir!" The paramedic yelled. "We're taking you in for X-rays! Do you understand!"

"Ease up there, partner. My Belltones are working

20

just fine. I'm not senile yet, and I imagine I can drive myself to the sawbones."

Of course, that would never do for these twenty-two-year-old milk-breathed paramedics, so rather than create any more of a scene, he accepted their ride, but he drew the line at lying down on the damn gurney. It made for a cramped fifteen minutes, everyone hunched back there like that, nothing much to talk about except the medical equipment.

As soon as they turned him loose at the hospital, and the nurse who assigned him to his bed went off to attend more pressing concerns, he got up, put on his pants, and called Yellow Cab for a ride back to the stables. He didn't need an X-ray, but a certain spotted horse might need one later on.

The victorious Tontito did not appreciate being yanked away from his dinner flake of alfalfa and at once pinned his ears. This time, Bop ran his back-up stud chain *under* the horse's lip. As a result, man and horse walked in a very orderly procession to the exercise arena, where the teenaged girls gathered to watch him hobble his horse in order to saddle him.

"Hey, Bop! Hey, Grandpa!" they cried. "Are you gonna ride him?"

"Yes, ma'am."

"Doesn't your arm, like, *hurt?*" they asked.

"No more than your average bee sting," he answered, then immediately thought of Henry's phone call, and got irritated all over again.

"That's a cool bruise you're getting."

He tightened his cinch. "A little ice and it'll be history by morning."

And from the smart one, with the sunburned breasts spilling over her yellow bikini top, "Isn't that the horse,

21

you know, that like, tore the hot walker out of the ground?"

A brief moment of shame flooded though Bop before he answered, "It's on his résumé."

"Guy, mister. You're *way* brave."

"Now there's a statement I believe to be about as true as turkey turds."

They laughed. Everyone loved Bop. The horse show mothers sent him their toddlers, and he'd gather them in a bunch and read *Misty of Chincoteague*. Teenaged girls cried on his shoulder about their boyfriends' betrayals and he bought them Cokes, bags of cheese curls, told them there wasn't a man fit to walk the planet who deserved their beauty. Everyone loved him, that is everyone except his grandchildren and his son's widow, Meridel. Them you couldn't buy anything.

While the sins of a horse were often visited upon the owner in a mostly financial way—the hot walker had dented his pocket to the tune of two grand—money meant little when your blood kin refused it.

Really, what had he done that was so terrible? All right, he'd embarrassed them now and then fighting with City Hall over the house, but was it his fault lazy reporters like MacLellan Henry found Carpenter life made for easy journalism? Admittedly, those last two divorces had been rather public undertakings, but he'd given them three clean years. What was so appalling about sending your grandchildren checks to buy new cars when they drove around town in embarrassing rattletraps, or trying to get Russell lined up with a halfway decent job? He was thirty-four-years old, for Christ's sake—Bop doubted Red Lyzyrd Vynyl Records was providing his grandson a retirement plan, even if he had worked there since high school.

It had been Chuck's decision to opt for a working-class life, teaching school, raising a family in the tract housing on the cheap side of Harper. He'd wanted no part of family business. His insurance policy transformed Meridel into a wealthy widow, and instantly imbued her with status. After Russell graduated high school, she'd high-tailed it out of Harper and bought a place in Carmel Valley. Now she had her wine-tastings and horse races and golf tourneys, plus enough pocket money to buy one new antique geegaw a week from now until Judgment Day. All that beat motherhood, apparently.

With her children, Russell and Lainie, the issues were at once simpler and more complex. Bop had Russell's plan all figured out: Trust fund looming the moment his grandfather checked out, there was no particular reason for him to get overly ambitious. Lainie, he knew, took a broader view. She held her grandpa accountable for every weed in the world's garden. From gang warfare to earthquakes to bad hair days, all of it was his fault. These crimes boiled down to one fairly logical conclusion, one that he shared: Lainie blamed him for having the audacity to live longer than her little boy, his only great-grandchild, Spencer.

It embarrassed Bop to have to use the wooden stair steps to mount his horse, but his hips weren't as trustworthy as they had been thirty years back, when he used to trailer out to the canyons and ride fence with the Portola boys. He gathered his reins in his left fist, checked his wristwatch, and held that bastard on the bit at a dead walk for a solid hour.

During this retraining period, people came and went. Girls finished their lessons and cooled out the horses along the marsh path.

Alejo finished his mucking, leaned on his rake and studied Bop's progress. "You worry me, Señor Bop. Thought that crazy *demonio* was going to kill you."

"Do I look killed?"

"No, sir. You look damn foolish. I look at you, I look at this rake, think maybe Alejo got easier job down here with horse caca."

"Entirely possible, *amigo*. You want to trade places?"

Alejo shook his head, smiling under his handlebar mustache. "No way, *viejo*. I want to live. Plenty beautiful women on earth, but in heaven? Only angels."

Eventually, the little girls got bored and went off drinking sodas, giggling and shrieking about whatever they found funny besides the prehistoric cowboy. For every shiny horse one of them led by, there was a lifting of tail, a small plopping sound, and job security for Alejo. Pretty soon, Bop rode alone in the ring, just him and his wild horse, his arm smarting in rhythm with the four-measure hoofbeats.

"Okay," Bop said, returning Tontito to his half-eaten alfalfa. "Are we in agreement as to positions on the food chain?" The horse didn't answer, just greedily attacked his hay. Bop bolted the stall and walked to his truck, rubbing his arm. In his absence, one of his little girls from the Old Man Fan Club had stuck a "Charlie, Don't Surf" decal on the rear window. He inspected it, decided that yes, indeed, it appeared to be a silk-screened likeness of Charlie Manson, and yes, chances were Charlie wasn't doing much surfing in prison except maybe in his mixed-up head. He left the sticker where it was and started the engine.

Because his throbbing arm had gone unusually numb, he drove to the walk-in clinic. It hardly paid to get a

24

regular doctor when they kept getting old and dying on him. From the clinic's melting pot he drew a girl who hardly looked old enough to wear a brassiere, let alone hang a stethoscope between her upright little bosoms.

"You fractured your ulna," she told him, pinning the X-ray up to the light box in the office.

"No, honey," he corrected, "my brainless horse did that for me."

She smiled. Light and health bounced in her ink-colored hair. "You're going to have to wear a cast for six weeks, Mr. Carpenter. At your age, possibly even longer."

He groaned. "How'm I supposed to wash my hair? Fix my three squares? Can't you just throw some tape at it?"

"Sorry." She took down several boxes and showed him pink, purple, and lime green waterproof casting gauze. "But you do get a choice of colors."

He pointed to the green. "That color puts me in mind of Popsicles. Lime green always came partnered with root beer, which after banana flavor was about the best-tasting frozen confection on a summer day—that is, after Shadow Ranch lemonade. Why, time was, I'd fight the grandchildren over green Popsicles."

"You know, Mr. Carpenter," the doctor said, "maybe you should hire a housekeeper, or ask one of your grandchildren to temporarily help out."

He winced as she wiped down his arm with gauze and alcohol. "Honey, housekeepers steal your coin collections for drug money. Good towels, too. They're as dishonest as crows."

She laughed. "And grandchildren?"

"More like woodpeckers," he said, sighing at the thought of Lainie and Russell, ten miles away in

25

Harper, tucked into their own shabby lives. "Besides, they all got troubles of their own. What do they want with a broken-down old gomer like me? Maybe what I ought to do is sell that white elephant of a house and move into one of them old folks' apartments, get me a Life Alert, so if'n I fall, someone can get me back up."

The girl doctor didn't smile, and he wondered if the silence indicated she thought his joke a sensible idea. He prided himself on keeping young women amused and was disappointed to have skunked out without rousing so much as a grin.

"Maybe what you ought to do is consider selling your horse."

"To my own worst enemy," he finished for her, then exclaimed, "Ouch! Jesus Christ, honey, you got to wrap that around me so tight?"

"Only if you want it to heal straight."

He ordered Chinese food, tipped the delivery boy, threw the complimentary chopsticks in the trash compactor, and sat down in front of the TV with a fork and the VCR remote. There was nothing halfway interesting on any of the 120 channels, so he reran the tape of "Sally Jessy Raphael." All the strippers except the drooler were still a little bit pretty, considering their ages.

Something about that Sommers woman, though. She had a glow, the aura of years' worth of consecutive sunny Texas days and church picnics. *Mo-tel ro-mance.* He froze the frame on her smile and cleavage while he ate up the last of his sweet and sour pork.

His arm throbbed, and he thought about taking one of the pain pills the girl doctor had foisted on him. Pills clouded the head, and in truth, they didn't really do much for pain except chase it to a far corner. It was nearly midnight in New York. He decided to call the station that ran "Sally Jessy." "I need to get hold of one of those women on the show today," he told the switchboard operator.

"You and ten thousand other well-meaning individuals. Sorry. The best I can offer is our address."

Bop wrote it down in spidery left-handed printing. He hung up and called FTD.

"And a pleasant good evening to you, too. I'd like to order two of your finest arrangements for delivery Monday morning."

"Birthday? Graduation? Get Well?" the clerk droned, as if he had come to his job straight from the DMV.

"None of the above."

"Well?"

Such an impatient young man. Didn't he realize that one day he too would be old and lonely, trying hard to burn up his Friday nights instead of working them? "No special theme. Something with a lot of red in it on the first one. But none of them cheap dyed daisies, you hear? Big flowers, tropical ones. The kind with the little yellow dingle hanging down in the middle."

The clerk cleared his throat. "I believe you're attempting to describe the Hawaiian anthurium."

"That's the ticket, son. Not pink though, I need a true red." The same red as Sally's glasses.

"And the second arrangement, sir?"

You could cut molars on the young man's voice. This one had to be extraordinary. "Got any peach-colored flowers this time of year? Anything real frilly?"

"Tiger lilies, snapdragons."

"Nah. Both smell too funereal for my taste. How about orchids? Surely a big florist like you with

27

television commercials got peach-colored orchids."

"An arrangement featuring more than two orchids would be cost prohibitive, sir."

Bop laughed. "Forget the money, son. See if you can get your hands on exactly sixty peach-colored orchids and maybe throw a couple of peach-colored fans in there, to boot." This far in, he had a sudden brainstorm. "Listen. Hold off sending that out until you get a package from FedEx. Inside will be a first-class plane ticket, and I want that to be part of the peach arrangement, not the red. You got that?"

"Sixty peach, not red, orchids." The clerk sighed. "Your credit card number, sir?"

"Hang on." Holding the phone under his chin, Bop unfolded his wallet with his good arm. He spread his various credit cards out and from the lot extracted the American Express Platinum. The clerk was oily as focaccia after he ran the credit check. "Anything else we can do for you this evening, Mr. Carpenter? Reactivate your corporate account, perhaps?"

"Well, you could send someone over to help me wash my hair."

Thursday of the following week, he was sitting out on the deck spying on the Englishwoman with his binoculars. Typhoid Mary Queen of Scots was pretending to be reading a mystery novel at her patio table, but Bop knew better than to go by appearances. Number one, she was wearing a long-sleeved blouse and long pants—an unlikely costume for a July afternoon of sunning. Number two, she had a loaf of bread and pink rubber dishwashing gloves parked on the table next to her. All she had to do was make her move and this could be paydirt. He zoomed his Nikon telephoto in on the scene when the cordless rang. Mac Henry? He ignored the first three rings, then when the answering machine didn't pick up, swore under his breath and reluctantly set aside the camera.

"Hurry it up," he said into the receiver. "I was about to gather some serious evidence regarding a duck poisoning."

"Who on earth would want to murder a cute little duck? One of God's own perfect creations?"

"My thoughts exactly. Now let's have it, sweetheart. What are you selling that I can't live without?"

There was a small pause, during which Bop considered those telemarketers pushing newspaper subscriptions had bribed the phone company into giving out his unlisted number again. "Is this Mr. Charles Russell Carpenter the second?" a girlish voice trilled in his ear.

Here came the pitch. "Well, it was this morning."

"You sent me the pretty bouquet. Thanks."

His heart did a little Tontito dance against his ribcage. "Miss Sommers?"

"That's me."

"Why, you're welcome. The color suit you?"

"Only my absolute favorite! How'd you know?"

He thought of the peach-colored fans she'd demonstrated on "Sally Jessy Raphael." It didn't exactly take a rocket scientist. "Lucky hunch. Any chance you might consider using that plane ticket?"

"Well, sir, right now I'm putting it to good use as a bookmark in my latest Elisabeth Ogilvie."

"Your what?"

"It's a historical romance novel. Dark-eyed Scotsmen and peat fires. Love on the moors. That's kind of like mountains but not exactly."

Her Texas accent gave the skirted Scotsmen a more masculine twist. "That ticket's first class."

"I noticed. Either you broke the bank trying to impress me or money don't matter much to you. But I'll still have to give some thought to using it. I just wanted to call and say thank you for the flowers. So, thank you." She laughed. "Guess I said it twice now."

Bop squinted up at the south face of Casa de Carpenter. Constant sun had split the copper at the roofline, and the metal had turned motley blue from the elements. "I'm a gentleman, Miss Sommers. Got a big old house here I'm rattling around. You struck me as both a lady and an optimist. I'd enjoy some happy company, that's all. Maybe share a meal. Talk about gardening. Take walks." He listened to the silence hum on the wire between them. She didn't believe a word he was saying. "No funny business. Honest. If it'll help, I'll sign a bond."

"There's some people waiting here to use the phone."

"Give me your number so we can talk again."

"It's better if I call you for now. I'm traveling."

"Any chance you might travel out my way?"

She laughed. "Mr. Persistent! You never can tell. I might call up someday and tell you I'm standing in the luggage claim of your airport."

He pictured the retired stripper among battered Samsonite circling the rotating carousel at John Wayne Airport. "That's news I'd be heartened to hear."

"Well, bye-bye for now."

"Good-bye."

He set the phone down and smiled so hard he believed he heard unused face muscles creak and strain. One minute you were playing lonely Sam Spade and the next a beautiful woman was calling you on the horn.

Hooray for the red, white, and blue. Sun was shining all over this holiday weekend. Surely a cure for cancer was just settling in some lab worker's test tube. Old Mother Earth was duct taping over the ozone. Lemons were growing into juicy yellow globes fatter than a man's fist and any minute one of his grandkids would drive up the driveway. The only disappointment was that somehow when he'd gotten distracted with Miss Sommers's call, that wraith of an Englishwoman had managed to accomplish her dirty deed and disappear. In front of her house, a line of doomed white ducks swam away from the dock, a trail of telltale soggy white bread crumbs floating behind them.

CHAPTER 4

SUNBOUND WITH EMMETT LAWLER

WITH HIS CAST SWATHED IN HANDI-WRAP, BOP could manage a shower, as long as he kept his arm stuck out the open door. However, while his arm stayed dry, his body chilled, the draft settling most prominently on the old rainbow tree snake and his tropical cousins, the brothers coconut. It beat trying to best the gamy smells with a washrag and a bar of Irish Spring.

The instant he soaped up his head with shampoo, he heard the phone ring. The remote possibility that it might be the ex-stripper calling drove Bop naked and dripping from the bathroom to the bedroom, where he hastily fitted in his hearing aid, simultaneously swiping the phone from its cradle. "Hello?"

"I swear that's the first time I've ever heard you answer the phone properly in ten years, Bop Carpenter.

31

You must be in love."

Bop wiped away the suds dripping down his forehead and held his broken arm aloft so the shower water wouldn't trickle inside and stink up the already-funky cast. "Mac, don't you have anything better to do than annoy the retired? Isn't there some kind of little old lady poetry reading you ought to be covering? I have to go now. Say hi to each one of Gloria's personalities for me."

"So you're not interested in what I just learned regarding a certain Slab City. Come to think of it, why should a professional journalist waste valuable time giving an ungrateful bourgeois lizard free news regarding his homeplace? I've got to go check my mail. I expected that party invitation yesterday. Maybe it'll come today. If not, I've got some writing to do."

"Now listen here, Henry—"

The dial tone hummed in his ear and Bop sat down on his bed. Around him, the first wet spot to dampen this mattress in quite a few years began to seep into the bedspread. He touched it idly with his fingertips, thought about the ex-stripper's voice, and hung up the phone. "Well, goddamn it all to crazy," he said out loud, and picked up the phone, punching in 411.

"What city?" the operator asked in her unemotional monotone.

"Harper. See if you can locate a number for MacLellan Henry, *Los Angeles Times,* county edition."

"Do you know the department?"

Bop wiggled water from his right ear. "No, ma'am, I surely do not. But if it's any help, he writes those trashy stories that intrude on people's privacy and get all the facts wrong."

"I'll give you the main number."

Eventually they switched him through to Henry's extension, but of course, the bastard wasn't about to pick up. His nasal message on the voice mail recording insisted he was "out on the beat, covering the county's late-breaking news."

Not likely. Mac Henry hadn't gotten a decent byline since the early eighties. College students wrote everything now, not that they were any more polished at journalism than Henry. He'd have trouble getting hired on at the *National Enquirer*. Bop left him a message. "Mac, you got me out of the shower. I haven't even had my grapefruit yet. I'm running errands around lunchtime, then I'll be in the rest of the afternoon. I'd appreciate a call back sometime today. I can't promise nothing but I'll try to be civil. Appreciate that call, buddy."

Buddy. The word stuck in his throat, dry as toast, but as hard up as Henry was for anybody to listen to him, it just might fool the idiot.

Behind the sweating glass of the florist's case, larger in circumference than a regulation basketball hoop, waited fifty dollars worth of fat orange tiger lilies surrounded by deceptively fragile baby's breath. Tiger lilies were a man's flower—tough, not overly frilly. Why, back in the twenties, hadn't his own father grown a mess of them in the shade of the ranchhouse? Flower gardens were a rarity in Shadow. Come spring, wildflowers blanketed the hillsides, and as a kid, Bop had thought nothing of riding his horse over them. Every drop of irrigated water, dew, and human sweat was siphoned toward keeping the trees hydrated so they would spill forth Meyer lemons. Fat and juicy, they fell into the workers' hands. From there, they were packed into wooden crates, and eventually made their way back to the ranch in the form of cash profit that his father counted and pocketed. When his mother wanted a flower garden, she made do with dishwater. A little cake soap seemed to sit all right with the lilies. These days people were stricken with environmental awareness, paying out good money to have graywater systems installed. When those buds burst into bloom, his mother's once-in-awhile smile transformed her face from the everyday determination of a grower's wife to a wistful longing for the soft things she'd never know. Those were the only kind of gifts they could afford. Lilies—Alyce had carried them the day they married.

Bop hadn't always been an only child. Large families were expected, and in his birth year of 1914, babies didn't cost much either way to keep or to lose. His sister got sick with pneumonia and passed on swiftly. Sad as that was, burying a dead baby was priced fair.

Not exactly the case with his great-grandson, Spencer. For what it cost to try to save his tiny life then put him in the ground, Bop's granddaughter could have bought herself a brand-new Ford dealership. It had taken some sweet-talking, but he'd finally gotten the receivables clerk at Children's Hospital to reveal the balance of Spencer's bill. God almighty, three years after Spencer's death, Lainie and Nick owed six figures above and beyond their pitiful insurance coverage. Though his offer to clear the debt wouldn't make much of a dent in his estate, bullheaded Lainie refused to take so much as a dime from her grandfather.

The flower shop clerk snapped her purple gum. "Hope they like the arrangement! Come again soon, sir!" He handed her a crisp, folded five, then exited through the crowded parking lot, the flowers cradled as preciously as he'd once held little Spencer, his first, and if things kept on the way they were going, only great-grandchild.

As usual, kids in four-wheel-drive Toyotas so tall they probably needed stepladders to climb into the driver's seat were smoking asphalt at sixty miles an hour down Beach Boulevard toward the sand. He waited for a decent space, braced himself for the moment of fear that would flood his pores at joining this madness, and made a right back onto the busy street, heading south. He inched his way over three lanes to the left, where he needed to be if he wanted to turn into the memorial park without having to make a messy U-turn. He breathed a sigh of relief and gunned the motor to keep up.

The fact was, a little speed helped an engine this large blow out the carbon. Originally, the dealer had only been able to partner him up with a 460 V8 dually, but Bop had scouted around and located a willing mechanic. The guy had flame tattoos crawling out from under his T-shirt sleeves, no more than eight teeth to his grin, but he lovingly installed a stroker crank and rods to boost the cubic inches to a more desirable 570. Technically, the truck was street legal, but come smog check time, Bop knew he was in for a battle royal. Now when he pressed on the gas pedal, he loosed 625 horses, all of them stallions, charging at a furious gallop. In theory, their titanium hooves tore this flimsy asphalt down to honest dirt. At eight-hundred-pounds per foot of torque, a man could feel safe no matter who drove around him, and in this vein of confidence he found himself well into the stream of traffic, stroking through yellow lights along with California's other legally licensed sinners.

A dozen hurriedly plastered strip malls flanked the boulevard, shoved in between import car dealers, their cheap plastic flags fluttering like ladies of the night waving in the customers. The town was jammed with specialty shops: tennis shoe outlets, lamp stores, imported clothing boutiques. Those two matrimonial mistakes since Alyce, Gloria and Helene, more accurately named Gluttony and Excess, looked down on local clothing stores because they didn't sport the mandatory designer labels. Alyce had sewn her own clothes in a room he fixed up for her off the laundry. Why couldn't any decent human being, male or female, get along just fine with new underwear once a year? A pair of Levi's (which lasted two years, minimum) and a clip-on necktie or hair bow for funerals? Gloria had the eye for labels, her closet alphabetized from Chanel to Vittadini. Helene's wardrobe peculiarity was store-window mannequins. If she liked what she saw, from scarves to shoes and whatever lay in between, she said, *I'll take that. The blouse, ma'am? No, the entire ensemble. Wrap it up and charge it to my darling husband here, Hopalong Generosity.* Paying off Helene had cost him more than the stock market scandal.

"Jesus!" A battered red Yugo zoomed illegally out across the double yellow from a liquor store, and Bop eased his horses back toward the corral. His turn signal indicator already flashing for a left, he wondered what addle-brained designer had come up with all these paper cars, none bigger than a footlocker. Junk heaps in the making. When he turned his Ford truck through the tall iron gates into the cemetery parking lot, his jaw tightened in anticipation.

The sullen young attendant who always insisted on seeing his ID probably suspected he was spray-painting

Gray Panther graffiti on mausoleums. Bop rolled down his window and handed him his license before he could ask. "Here to visit my great-grandson, just like every month."

The boy inspected his license, turning it over to read the donor card information, flipping it back and forth in the sunlight. Why? To make the hologram of the California seal shimmer? Maybe dancing decals constituted his thrill of the day.

"See here," Bop said. "It's not like I'm underage trying to buy liquor. What's the problem?"

"New rules." The boy smiled and handed him back his license along with a sheet of paper. "After you read them, I'll lift the gate."

Bop scanned the typed nonsense. There were three spelling errors in the first paragraph, some horse caca about not leaving breakable vases on "loved ones' rest areas," a new rule revoking the old one about playing portable radios and in large, block type: NO PICNICKING. "No picnicking?" Bop said aloud. "Who wrote this crap? Chairman Mao?"

The boy stared at him blankly.

Bop sighed. "All right. You got your way. I've read the damn paper, now will you let me in?"

The boy pressed whatever button caused the gate to lift and Bop drove through. Perhaps, when it came to repeat visitors, this fellow's drug-fried brain possessed no long-term memory bank.

Bop proceeded at the posted ten miles per hour toward the rear left corner of the cemetery, past the cheaper plots where the traffic noise threatened to deafen even those enjoying eternal rest. Here lay the earthly remains of his poor demented Alyce, though it was a mystery where her once-sharp mind had gone to so long before her body finally wore out. A little ways off slept his son, Chuck, whose bad heart had skipped his own children, but come back to haunt them. He hadn't come to see either of them today. Today he was after a nice, long summer afternoon with Lainie's son, Spencer, whose egg-sized heart hadn't skipped much at all for his brief, four years on earth.

Somebody had taken his hat. Once again, on the small brass headstone, Bop was forced to endure the smirk of that stupid angel. Rendered in three-quarters detail, as if he were trapped half in the stone, half out, the smart-aleck cherub squinted up in celestial joy toward the presumed kingdom of heaven. Lainie, claiming it wasn't practical, wouldn't let her grandfather buy any larger a monument, so Spencer had to make do with this middle-class seraph you could find cloned all over the whole damn park, probably a sale item from Angels R Us.

Brass versus marble. On a purely elemental level it bothered Bop. He picked up the tea roses Lainie'd undoubtedly left, their pink blossoms gone as dry and smelly as that costly potpourri crap Helene had used to stink up every room of Casa de Carpenter. (It smells like *leather* in here, Charles. I just can't bear it.) Damn it all, Lainie paid all this money, they were supposed to cart the dead flowers away, keep this place looking halfway decent. Nobody took pride in a job well done anymore, not even when it came to respecting the dead.

He set down his lilies and paused a moment to rub his face. He'd shaved at six this morning and already his cheeks were grizzled with whiskers. It was like some crazy second go-round with puberty, his body hair taking off this way. Maybe he could donate some to Russell, who, except for that girly ponytail he refused to

38

cut, was going balder than a newborn chick. Russell, as moored to adolescence as if he'd dropped his anchor. Was he waiting for a rebirth of the sixties, so he could strum folk songs in coffee houses for a living, grow a goatee, take up professional finger-snapping?

Bop recalled Spencer's hand rubbing against his beard and giving the child sandpaper kisses. Holding hands when they'd take walks, Spencer's entire hand would circle one of Bop's fingers.

"Grip like that, you'll make a ball player," he promised him, imagining the lengths he'd have gone to in order to buy him decent equipment. Lainie would never have stood for autographed ash bats and good leather gloves. Over time the baby fingers had lost their tenacity. Spencer's focus turned inward, urging the muscle to beat out the necessary tune of his heart. Then one day he went into the hospital and never came out.

By then Lainie hardly let anyone see him. She was so afraid of letting one second of his life pass with someone else, she kept him all to herself. When the boy's heart finally stopped in the hospital room—doctors and nurses shouting "code blue" and those screaming machines determined to jump start what was beyond repair—Bop realized he'd never gotten the chance to say a proper goodbye.

For the last three years he'd gone over it in his mind, imagining what he might have said to the boy, had there been a time slot allowed for great-grandfathers. Spencer'd had enough of tears, of adults pretending they weren't unraveling in grief before him. The boy was wise. He knew his ticket had been thoroughly punched. Bop would have sat him down and talked straight, no beating around the bush whatsoever.

"Okay, son. It's time for your big journey. Got both

shoes tied? There's a good boy. Now listen to your great-grandpa. Up there in heaven, first thing, I want you to introduce yourself to your grandpa and great-grandma. You'll recognize them right off. They'll be the handsomest folks in the place, and they'll be waiting for you. You need to keep an eye on them for me, savvy? They're good people, and they'll show you the ropes. Spencer, all that business about the roads being paved with gold and the pearl gates, well, that might be a load of horse poop. But you won't be lonely and you won't feel any more pain. That much I promise."

But Bop Carpenter had said none of those things. He'd stood alone in the hallway and run his thumbnail into a groove in his best hat, separating the felt at the brim, ruining it for anything but maybe a Halloween costume. A month ago he'd set that same hat atop the irritating angel and said, "Boy, I would have built you a monument, but your mama's hard."

He couldn't forget Lainie's wails echoing in the hallway. She sounded like a dog getting beaten by a once-trustworthy master. Even Russell, who'd been finger-picking *Here Comes Santa Claus* practically nonstop for the boy—that tune was little Spencer's choice, no matter that it was ninety degrees outside—left the room without acknowledging him, walked down the hall, and smashed up his prized Western Orange Gretsch Rancher guitar on the nearest water fountain.

"Where the hell's the reason in tearing a four year old from his goddamn family?" Bop hollered, then cleared his throat loudly.

Two elderly women weeding their own loved one's resting place shot him withering looks.

"Sorry. Caught an angry bullfrog," he called out, but the fussy women, their cream-colored Lexus parked on

40

the nearby asphalt path, only gave him unfriendly glares and resumed silent weed eradication. Dried-up old harpies—their husbands were probably delighted to keep company with the worms.

Once on *Oprah,* this panel of hired guns explained why it was folks chose certain colors for their cars. Champagne, which used to be called beige, was now referred to as "mocha frost," and white, which now went by "winter morning clearcoat," indicated you believed yourself superior, but not only to other drivers. He had waited the duration of the show for them to explain what driving a two-tone nonmetallic blue-and-green bored-and-stroked Ford dually meant, but it turned out no one except the poor cared for the two-tone paint job anymore.

The Lexus Sisters were behaving like they owned the whole damn cemetery, and therein lay one of the fundamental problems to be found with California in the 1990s—everyone ran around trying to act like old money, when the green ink on their bills hadn't even dried, and wouldn't in this lifetime. True old money in the state was unrecognizable, mostly because it looked, smelled, and tasted a lot like dirt. Land—that was where the value lay. Land like Shadow—acres of rich earth that promised crops. What was it Henry said they were calling it—Slab City? What on earth did that mean? Had some idiot gone and paved over the orchards?

From his truck bed, Bop unfolded a ratty horse blanket Tontito had chewed the ass out of and settled his creaky knees down, opening the book he'd brought along.

"Today, my young buckaroo," he said aloud as he adjusted his other hat over the bronze angel, "we are

41

going to introduce you to Mr. Jim Tully. I know, I know. Will James provided you with timeless examples of courage and adventure, and you don't need me to tell you no man can ever get enough of horses and adventure, but unfortunately life's not all about adventure. It's time to move on to larger concerns. Love, forgiveness. Human compassion."

He paused a minute as his words sank in. Love, simply put, had become a seller's commodity. Oh, it was purported to be the tender sanctuary you could enter when you were downtrodden, where forgiveness waited in clear pools for you to jump in and drink deeply, like some lucky camel. But Lainie and Russell wouldn't forgive him his sins, no matter how wide or sturdy beat their Carpenter hearts. He didn't know how to explain that to Spencer.

His arm in the Popsicle-green cast ached. He flipped pages, remembering his son's admonishment twenty years back: *Dad, if you ever want to know your grandchildren, you need to quit letting them down. When you do manage to show up for a birthday party, there's a phone attached to your ear, or you have to leave early for some big bucks deal. You're what they call a workaholic. Sure, they'll inherit big time, but Lainie and Russ will never know the difference between their grandfather and a fifty dollar bill.*

Hard as that had been to hear, he had let a few of the deals go, trying to create a balance in his life, but damned if his own son and the grandkids didn't end up lost to him in spite of the sacrifice. With Chuck it was a shock, and a funeral within a week. With Spencer, things dragged on until hope unraveled like string. Once those heart valves went and they started putting in the synthetic ones, it was really just a matter of time. One tragedy per family seemed fair. Their tragedy had been Chuck. It was unthinkable that young Spencer had inherited the bad heart, but he'd been such an active little tadpole no one noticed his problem until it was too late.

Well, this self-indulgence was about as comfortable as a soggy old Band-Aid, and it was not getting Spencer his story read. "'*Emmett Lawler,* the first episode,' " he began. "That means chapter one, Spence. There's some of that damn poetry business to start it.

"'Lord, give to men who are older and rough/ The things that little children suffer/ And let keep bright and undefiled/ The young years of a little child.' " He read on. "'The child had arrived a month too soon.' Like you, Spence, eager."

He squinted up at the July sun and felt healing shoot across his broken wrist bone like a sideways bolt of lightning. If you wanted them to turn out properly, children deserved consistency. If your children were dead, some might call you three bales short of a truckload, sitting in a California graveyard reading them stories, but you played the cards life dealt you or you folded your hand. "We'll read a chapter today and then you can think about it, store up some questions for me, Spence. What do you say?"

Above him, the forty-foot sycamore tree he'd paid a thousand dollars to have the cemetery plant so his great-grandson could rest in shade rustled its dried-out leaves on sturdy branches. The cheap bastards didn't water it deeply enough. Until they partnered up with the water table, new trees required that. Overhead, dirty city birds chattered and fought with each other over who got which insects. Bop Carpenter possessed a deep, steady voice that he had used to lull three generations of

43

Carpenter children to sleep. Due to family history, he felt loath to stop with the funeral chapter, so he continued on through the orphanage episode to "A New Life," which was upbeat and enough of a teaser so he could quit on a positive note. He set down the book and ran his fingers through the grass covering the grave. Grass so green it made his eyes water. From the tiger lilies he freed two flowers and set one each on his wife and son's graves.

"Alyce," he said. "Neither one of those women could hold half a candle stub to you. Some days I wake up feeling pretty bad. I know, you never did cotton to couples shacking up, so I suppose I did right by marrying them, but I hope you can forgive this old mule when we meet up again. Can't help but get to wondering sometimes. Can you see down into my life here, all the bad ideas I come up with, the foolish acts of an old man? Tell me what to do, honey."

He'd always had trouble with the concept of heaven. Years back, he'd put a picture in his mind of her and Chuck, sitting at an oak kitchen table, sipping cups of tea that never ran dry, spicing them up with juicy lemon wedges. Now he saw them taking turns at rocking Spencer, or watching the boy run free with all of God's favored dogs. Let it be something like that, he hoped. Something like that would be reward enough.

A burst of rap music came thundering from the boulevard, then disappeared as quickly as it had arrived, and off in the distance he could see the never-ending traffic blur. It was easy to speak to an Alyce who didn't answer; he'd done so for years when she sat mute in her other world. Chuck presented more of a task. To Chuck he spoke his thoughts silently, afraid if he said them aloud, his son would turn a deaf ear.

Chuck, about this Shadow business. If I sold Casa de Carpenter, I could give the money to Lainie and Russell right now, dole it out in tax-free parcels yearly, amended trusts, fix the government's wagon. Russell'd buy more guitars, no doubt. Someday I expect the Health Department is going to get wind of Russell's living situation and there'll be a bigger scandal than any of my shenanigans. But Lainie and her headshrinker husband, I'm telling you, Chuck, those medical bills are going to choke the life out of them. They're living in a cracker tin. Prisoners get a bigger bathroom. 'Course, our dear Lainie'd undoubtedly buy up one of those court injunctions and keep me in the next county until I'm ready for the bone pile. I know where I'm not wanted. So can you explain to me what staying away's solved?

Chuck, you probably don't remember Shadow Ranch. The purple flowers, the smell of the blossoms late at night. I don't guess I've ever smelled anything to beat those lemon groves on a summer night. One of those nights Alyce and I made you, son, way out in the grove, rolling around in that rich, soft soil. We were barely twenty. I loved her so damn much my ambition was to plant one baby a year in her belly. Lemon blossoms and a good woman. These days, everywhere you go it's car exhaust and Carpet Fresh. Reach doesn't even smell fishy. Suntan oil and crazy people begging on the pier. I'm telling you, son, you wouldn't have liked the nineties any better than the eighties. You were smart to check out early.

Overhead, the chattering birds continued their commentary.

The answering machine light was blinking when Bop returned home. He pressed Play and listened to Mac Henry's message.

"'The Kuneyaay band of the Southern Diegueño Indians have put in a rock-bottom bid for the town of

Shadow. They discussed the possibility of filing suit in federal court for permission to use the 614 acres as commercial landfill. Slab City residents are up in arms. McCormick Farms, which leases the few remaining lemon groves, admitted the necessity of cutting trees to clear the way for the facility.' That's straight off the board, Carpenter. I'll expect that invitation in the mail or you'll be priority number one for my feature stories. Count on it."

The answering machine rewound. Bop threw his car keys on the counter and listened to the metal clatter across stainless steel.

When the lonelies hit, the only logical course of action was to get busy. He watered the garden in the steel and glass atrium—a few spindly orchids left over from Helene's tenure and his personal army of pale-looking cactus. The damn door was sticking again. It had been cranky the last twenty years, and planing it seemed only to encourage it to warp.

"Open up, you nickel whore," he swore at it, and stood there a moment, letting the oxygen-rich air float over his face. Like him, this house seemed to be growing as it aged. In carefully planned corners such as this one, impish spirits not only prevailed, they prospered.

He used his nail clippers to remove the nastier spines on his barrel cactus, never again wishing to experience the infection and fever those little bastards had inflicted upon him in a single, unfortunate scrape. He sanded a mere millimeter off the door, retrieved his hammer and nails and went off in search of what he could repair that the fanatics down at Conservancy wouldn't notice. They wanted everything architectural to stand still.

The downstairs bathroom cupboards were looking a

little cockeyed. All it would take to set them straight was carefully placed biscuits and judiciously applied hammering. He had a shoebox full of shims, but hammering left-handed seemed it might require more dexterity than a man with a broken ulna possessed.

He was an old man surrounded by the sarcophagus of a house he couldn't care for properly. He set the hammer down on the kitchen table, next to his portable phone, and looked out at the channel seeing nothing but dull green water.

"Hello?"

It was well after midnight. But with Mac Henry his only source of information on Shadow and the ever-dwindling possibility the ex-stripper might call back, Bop wasn't sleeping, he was catnapping.

"Charles Russell?"

It hit him as sharp as spring rain—that Tinkerbell voice, the tentative question mark with which she punctuated his first and middle name—Miss Earlynn Sommers. "Yes," he answered. "It's me, Earlynn. Where you calling from this late, honey?"

She laughed. "Seems like only a couple of hoot owls should be awake this late, but that ain't the case. I'm in Las Vegas, Nevada, where decent people pay no nevermind to the moon or the clock."

An image of those peach-colored fans revealing strategic parts of her trim body flooded his mind. "You working again?"

"No, when I say retired, I mean retired. Nothing sadder than a dame past dancing age up there shuffling her saggy skin for drunks. I just came here to bridesmaid for an old friend. Imagine, me in a wedding at my age. Isn't that a laugh and a half?"

47

"It's not so strange an idea. People get married for all kinds of reasons, Earlynn. Love doesn't skedaddle when you start in getting Social Security."

"Well, I'm telling you true, there's more whalebone than lace under this dress."

He heard her deposit a few coins to appease the operator. When the clinking stopped, he said, "Honey, television is supposed to add twenty pounds to a person, and I saw you looking trim on Sally Jessy. Why don't you leave the whalebone to the poor endangered whales?"

"Aren't you a nice man."

"So I keep trying to tell you."

"You and all these flowers you keep on sending! Mr. Moneybags. Do you own a florist?"

He pictured that nasty-voiced FTD clerk in chains, working off an indentured lifetime to Charles Russell Carpenter II. "No, sugar, but I might just buy one."

"Charles, think what would happen if every time you got the urge to send me flowers you donated money to something decent, like, say for instance, the ASPCA?"

"I'm guessing the dogs would eat better."

"That they surely would. Think about it, them poor homeless doggies getting canned food for a change. I guess that's what they call a random act of kindness. It's popular to do these days; someone even wrote a book on it. I admire kindness. In my opinion, the world could do with more of it. Well, I guess I better hang up. I'm running low of quarters I won in the slots. I always make myself spend my winnings right off, don't you? Otherwise it feels too much like stealing. All that dirty money."

"Don't hang up."

"I've only got enough quarters for just a few more

minutes. Talk fast."

"Tell the operator to reverse the charges. Hail a cab on over to McCarran Airport and charge yourself a first-class seat to John Wayne on my card. I need you."

"Now, Charles Russell, how can you know a thing like that? Except for these phone calls I can't seem to stop myself from making, and you watching me on TV, why, you don't know me from a bank robber."

He smiled in the dark, imagining five-foot-nothing Earlynn in gold lamé, tennis shoes, telling some bank suit to "Stick 'em up or else." "Call it Carpenter instinct. When's this wedding?"

"Over the weekend."

"How about I come sit in the back of the church? Help you throw rice at the bride." That timeless word shimmered and echoed into his hearing aid. He envisioned all the brides of his life—Alyce in her good white suit; Chuck's wife, Meridel, in her low-cut satin; Gloria and Helene in outfits so strange they almost seemed like twin nightmares with hoop skirts; deliriously happy Lainie in her Mexican wedding dress, drunk on good champagne and anticipating all that sex she was now legally entitled to enjoy.

"Smokey's never been what you might call traditional. I guess it wouldn't hurt."

"Smokey?"

"Oh, that's not her Christian name. But I've called her that so long it might as well be. She danced under 'Smokey the Bare,' b-a-r-e, not the kind that *grrrs*. And had about the cutest little ranger outfit you've ever seen. She'd put out the gentlemen's cigarettes with her holstered water pistol, and that was way before the surgeon general had any hard words over smoking."

"She's a stripper, too?"

"Why, the whole wedding party is, Charles! Six bridesmaids behind Smokey making that long hike to the altar. The newspaper is going to do a little story on us. We're taking over the Little Chapel of the West. It's historical. Movie stars get married there all the time. Richard Gere, I think. Of course, it's very sad what happened to him and Cindy. But a whole bunch of others tied the knot there also. The reception's going to be held at the Dunes, kind of for old times' sake, seeing as we all of us danced there at one time or another. You know, they're tearing it down next month. I think that's such a shame. Perfectly good hotel. Seems like nobody holds much interest in the past anymore. Why right now, outside my hotel room, it sounds like a hillbilly circus going on next door. I can hear the MGM log ride going full blast, even though it's a hundred and ten degrees out, pitch black and nobody's riding the darn thing. You know what I think? This town is bound and determined to set a world's record with the electric company."

He smiled, plucking the covers away where they'd caught on his cast. "I think they likely control the utilities, Earlynn. Where do I meet you and when?"

"Just leave a message for me at the Carriage House Inn. I'm in room two-seven-four."

He turned over in his big, empty bed. "Did I tell you that two-seven-four is my lucky number?"

"Charles, lying disappoints me like no other vice."

"I'm not lying. Just this second it became my lucky number."

The operator interrupted. "Please deposit—"

"I'm out of money. I'm hanging up now."

Before he heard the flat buzz of dial tone, he managed the "good" half of good-bye.

50

CHAPTER 5

ALWAYS ROOM FOR JELL-O

"I WANT YOU TO ENVISION ANGER THE WAY YOU might one of Nick's woodworking tools," Dr. Annabelle Mapp suggested.

It was Friday, 4:45 P.M., and Elaine Clarke sat across from her therapist in the overly soft upholstered chair reserved for clients, trying to visualize this atypical concept. Whatever did Dr. M mean—a hammer of hate, a router of rage, or perhaps something simpler, like a file of frustration?

"Nick keeps all his tools hanging on individual hooks in the garage," Lainie said. "They have spray-painted outlines on the pegboard, each one assigned to a specific place. He gets upset if I forget to put them back."

"They don't have to be your husband's tools, per se. Just pick a tool. Any one that comes to mind."

Lainie played along. "Okay, how about an ax?"

"An ax is good! Now let's take a close look at that ax and define its capabilities."

Keeping her eyes shut as instructed, Lainie listened to Dr. Mapp's soothing voice, and as they too often did, her thoughts—those shape-shifting, perpetually in-motion clouds—began once again to drift away from the subject. Axes. Firewood. Campfires. Once she and Nick had taken Spencer camping in Big Sur. Every morning, they crawled out of their tent to blue skies under a canopy of redwoods. Framed like a snapshot in an album under that same blue sky, she saw her boy's skinny back in a plaid flannel shirt, the angel wings his shoulderblades made as he bent forward, helping his

51

dad chop kindling to feed the campfire.

In one week, coinciding with the day after the Fourth of July, it would be the anniversary of her child's death. Three years with no yellow dump trucks spilling dirt in the hallway. No bathtime serenades, no oxygen tanks. The wound was closing over but still tender. Just like losing her grandmother and father, Lainie fully accepted that the echoes of those aches were hers to carry into eternity.

"An ax," Dr. Mapp was saying, "can be useful, or it can be used destructively. That is the nature of tools. What they are used for depends on the state of mind of the person holding them. Now I want you to take hold of this imaginary ax, Elaine. Heft it. Tell me, how does it feel in your hand?"

"Well . . ." The talking part she did all right with. It was this other, this pretending thing that made her squirm in her chair. What kind of medical doctor asked her patients to grip imaginary tools? Did Nick ask such questions of his clients as he logged in hours on suicide watch? Was the tool thing so obvious a metaphor she was missing the point? "Oh, it feels manageable. Not too heavy."

"Does the ax bring up any feelings of anger?"

Lainie pictured a cartoon ax wearing a steel sneer, chasing trees. She suppressed a grin. "No. It's fairly content, as axes go. It watches the Turner Broadcasting Station. It reads thrillers late at night, makes itself too scared to sleep. Its secret vice is counted cross-stitch embroidery of dancing unicorns."

Dr. M didn't laugh. "Suppose you were required to assign an emotion to it. Quickly now, without too much thought, what comes to mind?"

"Pride, I guess. Yeah. Like my brother's old Boy

Scout ax. It was an optional part of the uniform, but it looked so authoritative strapped to Russell's belt, so prepared. Good Lord, what could a kid ever hope to accomplish with that dull a blade? It's that sort of pride you soar with at ten, but laugh about at thirty-five."

Dr. Mapp sat quiet. Lainie could feel her watching behind the owlish eyeglass frames. *Your therapist looks like Joyce Carol Oates on steroids,* Lainie's best friend Candace had said once, when they met at the hospital after one of her Friday appointments. *Perpetually startled by something Heidegger might have written.*

Lainie knew her smart-ass answer was a cop-out, but part of her couldn't help hearing every tick of the Buddha clock on the table second-handing its way toward the hour's close. Time, ticking away in the eternally peaceful Buddha's belly, had them all in its grip. Why get into something heavy in the last five minutes? What was this sudden subject change from sadness to anger anyway? For three solid months, they'd talked losing Spencer into the ground. *It's like I have a perpetual case of the blues,* Lainie told Dr. Mapp when she came slinking back, asking to resume their sessions. Maybe that was the reason Dr. Mapp bought Kleenex in the man-sized boxes.

Last winter she'd lain in front of the refrigerator in her kitchen for hours, tracing patterns on the cracks in the floor tiles. She'd cried so hard and long she'd lost her voice. How could you ask for help if you had laryngitis? Nick found her, called Bop, and against her protests they'd driven her to the hospital. But Nick wasn't responsible for signing her in. *This business has gone on long enough. See what you boys can do with her,* her grandfather had said, then cut a check, cocked his stupid hat on his head, and walked out the glass doors, leaving her alone in that awful place.

Lainie couldn't really afford therapy. But its effects allowed her to work part-time again at Public Assistance, and after three months, she would requalify for complete insurance coverage and sick days. Work made her feel she wasn't imitating life, but nearly living it. But come on, what did losing your child have to do with emotional tools? A child's death was a fact, one you certainly didn't *elect* to have become a part of your history. One day you looked up and found it attached to you for good, the way a remora plugged into its host shark. Besides, she wasn't here because she had a problem with anger. She was here because every day, at least once, from out of the blue she would start out doing one thing—say typing intake reports, or baking the Spago meatloaf recipe, which required mincing an entire head of garlic—then find herself completely transfixed by a shred of last night's dream or some vague childhood memory, the garlic half-chopped, her task abandoned, with no clear idea where the transition between the real and imagined lay.

It wasn't anywhere near as bad as last winter when, upstairs in the psych wing, deciding which flavor of Jell-O she wanted for dinner presented a major brain strain, but it was troubling enough that when she resumed these appointments she'd kept them a secret from Nick. Irony of ironies—her once-union carpenter husband was studying to be a psychologist. He worked much longer hours than when he was building cabinets and stair banisters. He fitted in seminars and reading when carpenters slept. The last thing he needed was to worry about his wife losing the grip again. She was doing him a favor not telling him. This wasn't denial, it was more like the reality principle.

54

Axes. Lainie sighed. Maybe she was failing to grasp the larger picture, but today was not turning out to be one of her more enlightening therapy sessions.

"Do you hear what I'm saying, Elaine?" Dr. Mapp continued. "Anger is a human reaction to feelings of hopelessness, of not being heard. It's normal, not some kind of mortal sin, and until you slog your way through it, you're not going to heal."

Heel! Lainie heard, the continual command she gave Oddjob, the untrainable Pomeranian who had been a gift to Spencer from her grandfather Bop's last and ickiest wife, Helene. Eighty dollars for obedience school—a waste of money, because Oddjob, an eight-pound terminator when it came to destroying the yard, was unstoppable. To him, "heel" meant scarf down half a loaf of her homemade bread, quick, before anyone noticed. Their other dog, Shaky Jake, the shepherd mutt she rescued from the pound, was quiet and grateful. In a perfect world all dogs would have been cloned from Jake. Wars would end—a canine détente immediately in force. People liked to smugly infer owners resembled their dogs, but as far as Lainie could tell, Oddjob, balding in patches, overweight, an asthmatic purebred, resembled only their exterior lives. If Dr. Annabelle Mapp had a dog, Lainie bet it was an English bulldog, a graceful dowager sporting a velvet collar.

"You did some good work today," Dr. Mapp said, as she almost always did when the Buddha clock read five minutes until the hour. "You can open your eyes now."

"Thanks." Lainie blinked, then dug in her purse for her wallet. Dr. Mapp opened her appointment book and studied it, as if she'd somehow goofed up and given someone else Lainie's time slot. This gave Lainie time to count all her saved fives and odd ones, and Dr. M time to pretend she wasn't giving her an embarrassingly low cut-rate on therapy.

She'd chosen Dr. Mapp for three reasons: She was twenty pounds overweight; she never, ever, not even to the staff Christmas party, wore high heels; and, totally contrary to her masculine exterior, her right hand was graced by a marquise-cut diamond solitaire the size of a raisin. Lainie loved how it shimmered in the lamplight, casting rainbow prisms over the tweedy hospital furniture.

Choosing such a therapist held advantages over the more perfect, go-to-the-gym-everyday ones. A Dr. M workout was internal, like spending fifty minutes on the NordicTrack for the soul. She had so many initials after her name that the "Mrs." she lacked before it seemed superfluous. Nick said there were undying rumors around the hospital that the woman was lesbian, but whatever she was or wasn't, for one hour every Friday, Lainie felt safe sitting across from her in the tiny office. She sat in her creaky gray secretary's chair and smiled at Lainie for all kinds of reasons that seemed to make no real sense. Whether Lainie was explaining the teensy problem of her dreams bleeding over into the waking hours—which Dr. M called "a loosening of associations"—or her real work dilemmas of dealing with drug-addicted clients and the frustrations of the system (Lainie called this "my crappy job"), Dr. M smiled equitably. She was like one of those ancient stone goddess figurines, fertile with acceptance, all breasts and belly.

Lainie pressed fifty-five dollars cash into her hand. They'd maxed their insurance coverage after Spencer's death and she'd lost her hospitalization when she quit

56

her job. At the close of every session Lainie stated the same request: "Please, even if I go crazy as Corn Flakes, don't tell Nick about our appointments."

Dr. Mapp smiled. "Elaine, you're not crazy, and how many times do I have to tell you what happens in this room remains confidential?"

"I know. It's just . . ." She thought of her grandfather's hat on the angel and felt the resentments stack up inside her. "I come from this family where everybody knows everybody else's secrets. They hear them whispered in the breeze. Seeping through our genes. I don't know, maybe we sense them in our dreams—some kind of astral eavesdropping thing. Listen to me blather! It must be a glucose drop. That will teach me to skip lunch. Have a nice weekend, Dr. M."

"You try to as well, my dear."

"I'll try."

Here it was—that long terrible moment stretched out before them like an empty clothesline. They both stood there, knowing what needed to come next. Lainie was supposed to head back out that door into the real world, to shoulder her way down the hospital hall like an arthritic wolf, trying to fit unobtrusively into the swiftly moving pack, avoiding running into Nick. Dr. M needed to straighten the throw pillows Lainie'd mashed, dispose of any dropped Kleenex, collect her thoughts so she could convince her next patient to heft his or her emotional ax.

Before she could open the door, Dr. Mapp stopped her. "Since I'll be away next week, I have some homework for you."

"Homework? Like what? Vocabulary words? Algebra formulas? Or do you want me to weave lanyards?"

"Nothing so taxing. I'd like for you to come up with a list of five things that make you feel angry."

"Five things?"

"Yes, my dear. I know you'll find this hard to believe, but most people have trouble stopping at five, I feel certain you're ready to do this for me."

Lainie knew the translation of that phrase: *You wouldn't want to disappoint the good doctor.*

"So," Candace said on her end of a very scratchy telephone connection, "what did you and the divine Dr. M dissect today?"

Lainie stood in the back door frame of her Wisteria Street house throwing a damp tennis ball into the backyard for Jake. Candace had been her confidante since third grade, when they both decided trading Trixie Belden mysteries beat the hell out of Barbie dolls. "Axes and anger. It was an A kind of day, I guess."

"Interesting. What did all these As signify?"

"I'm not really clear on that, Candace."

"Maybe it's an alphabetic approach to . . . ."

Lainie felt herself beginning to drift as Candace chattered away, her mind's eye traveling from the Big Sur campfire to Nick crumpled in grief over the still body of his son. The hospital bed seemed too large to hold such a tiny person. Say good-bye, someone was telling him. But whether he couldn't or wouldn't, male grief was harder to endure than watching a puppy get flattened by a car. Do not get started on this, she told herself. She made herself rejoin the conversation. "Are you still coming over for Fourth of July fun?"

"I want to. But, um, I might have a date."

"Darn. Holidays are boring without you. But far be it from the Fourth of July to begrudge you a chance at romance. How soon will you know?"

"Well, as soon as this 757 lands and the pilot decides whether or not he wants to follow through on the wink he gave me."

"Pilot? Candace, where are you?"

"Approximately thirty thousand feet over the Rockies. There's snow on the mountains. In June, no less. I suppose I like Denver well enough to attend conferences and go shopping, but I don't think I could live there. Too many yuppified cowboys for my taste. Whoops. They just told us to replace electronic instruments since we're heading into turbulence. Gotta go."

"Yeah, it's always one sort of turbulence or another," Lainie said. "Call me back."

"Love you, Lainie. Kiss Russell for me."

"I will not. You want to kiss my brother, do it yourself," Lainie said, but the connection was already broken.

Lainie gave the subject of anger serious consideration all four days of the long holiday weekend. Her dad was dead, and that made her mad in a primitive, walk-me-down-the-aisle kind of way. Seventeen years seemed way too long to be mad about the accident of his Carpenter heart, so she scratched My Dad off the mental list and kept searching. She missed her grandmother Alyce's kind words and comforts fiercely; did fierceness qualify as anger? Bop, on the other hand, made her furious, but what did you expect from the king of selfishness? He wagged his wallet and expected her and Russell to jump like trained dolphins. If there was anyone who used anger as a tool, her grandfather qualified. When one of his ex-wives took him back to court for more alimony, which actually happened quite

59

often, he bellowed and hired hammerhead lawyers. He'd offered to help her and Nick pay off that mountain of debt they owed the hospital, but for every dollar Bop spent on you, there was a chunk of your soul expected in return. When she said no, he got all huffy and threatened to spend his estate on floozies so she and Russell would inherit nothing but bills. *Go ahead,* she said, *who needs a man who'd let a hospital staff put his only granddaughter in restraints?*

Her words never fazed him. Bop was always trying some new tack. Last year, he'd planted some massive tree at Spencer's grave. Of course it was the only one in the entire cemetery that tall, which made it visible from the street, an arrow marking the spot: *Right here! Here's where we buried your son!* He means well, Nick said, defending him, just let it go. She tried. Since her release six months ago, Bop had been pretty quiet. Then the cowboy hat appeared on Spencer's angel. Now it lived in her Volvo's trunk. Well, it was just a hat, not a wrist cuff or a sedative injection. Dr. M, I'll bet I've grown out of this particular emotion. It sounded so plausible that she tried it on the dogs.

"Boys, you have an anger-deficient mistress. What do you think of that?"

They cocked their heads momentarily, then slid back into stuporous naps in sunny spots on the kitchen tile. Jake, tennis ball between his front paws, was a professional sleeper, traveling instantly into pleasant dog dreams. Oddjob, on the other hand, slept lightly, ready to shift into gear in case some event, like the plum tree dropping a single leaf, required ten minutes of commemorative, high-pitched barking. Lainie looked out the window to where the tree stood, its few offerings turning from sage green to the blue of a bruise.

60

This Dr. M homework was sounding a whole lot like the town of Harper needing a toll road to the beach: Residents could bitch that it wasn't necessary, but it was getting one, just as sure as Dr. M wanted her list.

She noticed the blinking light on the answering machine and listened to her mother's latest message: *Hello, Precious, I can't believe I've missed you again. You're probably out shopping with your girlfriends, buying cute little summer tops and Bass sandals. Just wanted to let you know I'm going to Healdsburg for a wine-tasting over the Fourth. I knew you'd worry when you tried to call me. Happy Birthday, dear America. . . .* her mother sang breathily, trying and failing to sound like Marilyn Monroe. Meridel was stuck in a late-fifties time warp. One day she was Jackie in a size-four Chanel, the next, the Kennedy brothers' bimbo.

The only sandals Lainie owned were some Zories borrowed from Russell's closet over five years ago. Ever since she was old enough to abuse her own MasterCard, Lainie'd bought all her clothes from catalogs. Her mother disapproved of this facet of her personality. For one thing, it prevented them from mother-daughter shopping trips. Catalog shopping was a grand invention. Lainie ticked her favorites off on mental fingers. L.L. Bean's for blue jeans and T-shirts, Land's End for their affordable, durable soft wool blazers, and 100-percent-cotton undies through the Vermont/Cumberland. "Why can't you just be a mom, tell me you know the anniversary is coming up, and be done with it?"

Jake, on the verge of a trembling fit from the tone in Lainie's voice, got up and came to her, nudging her knee with his wet nose. She stroked his wilting ears. "Sorry, old soul. Didn't mean to scare you."

Since their father's death, Lainie's mother had kept

mentally polishing a high school portrait of Russell and her, ages sixteen and seventeen, dressed in school colors, clutching notebooks, just emerging from a pep rally. What was truly odd was they hadn't ever been those people. Russell had spent his junior and senior year as a *Consumer Reports* activist on the varieties of marijuana, and Lainie was more interested in accruing as much sex as possible with her boyfriend than passing economics. They were adults now—Russell thirty-four and herself thirty-five—much of the sting of their bad behavior had dissipated over time. When it came to Mother's way of thinking, Lainie almost understood this false portrait-making. In order to keep her own marriage tilting authentically on its fragile axis, now and again she practiced a little fakery herself.

It was six P.M. She gathered up leashes from the key rack and both dogs immediately rose and began stretching in happy anticipation.

Half a mile from her house, on the bluffs overlooking the flood channel that led to the Pacific ocean, Lainie unhooked their leashes and let the dogs run free. From a morose, spit-colored mutt, Jake transformed into a silver streak of muscle, moving fleet-footed over dirt hummocks in search of any faint scent of rabbit. He pinned his ears to streamline his body, and she thought a person could certainly do worse than stand there forever and watch a good dog run himself tired. Even Oddjob seemed calmer out here, though his staccato lope was punctuated by periodic episodes of digging. When he encountered freshly turned earth, he became fixated, digging with his tiny rat paws, then biting at the damper dirt, determined to uncover a gopher that would undoubtedly outweigh him, happily getting nowhere.

Lots of people walked dogs here. Every once in a while a horseback rider trotted by, leaving C-shaped hoofprints in the hardpacked dirt. There wasn't a proper stables in the town of Harper, just this one last house with falling-down stalls.

Having a horse again would be nice, Lainie thought. *I wasn't so bad at riding.* She remembered the hours she'd whiled away her grief on horseback after her father's death. But the nearest public stables anymore was Whistler's, which she could not afford, and that was where her grandfather kept his horse. Imagine boarding next to Mr. Know-it-all: *You use that bit, you're going to spoil that horse's mouth. Run your irons up, young lady, and another thing. . . .*

She walked swiftly, the leashes gathered in her right hand, the dogs a good twenty feet ahead. Whenever another dog walker passed by, their dogs had to stop and sniff each other, urinate to establish territory, and she had to smile and make eye contact with the owner. She could do it naturally now, only occasionally having to force her mouth to turn its corners upward. They'd taught her that in the hospital—to form a quick smile, make brief eye contact—a pretty simple trick for most people. There were still times, however, alone out here, thinking, of nothing, she found her face suddenly awash with tears, her ears filled with a great human howling only she could hear.

She looked out over the cliff, imagining the Lukup Indian village of centuries ago. The ocean had slapped right up to the cliff's edge. Chiefs and shamans, grandmothers and children lived here. They dug up clams and caught fish for dinner, in awe of that clear blue water continually unfolding its plenty. They told stories and loved one another. This was the last wild place left in Harper. Everything else was asphalt and minimalls. Walking here felt like balancing between worlds, a kind of meditation in motion. She worried what would become of the land. The toll road, okay, maybe as a source of revenue it made sense, even if it did seem unfair to inlanders seeking a day at the ocean. But if the city ever got a wild hair about developing this place, planting grass and scratching out soccer diamonds, well, Dr. M, you want anger, Lainie thought, I imagine I can muster a little in honor of this dirt.

Just then, the six-noted cry of a meadowlark rang out, trilling over the weeds. The pure song, sung for no other reason than the ability to do so, made Lainie stop, shiver, and catch her breath, all at the same time.

While painstakingly pouring quarter-inch thick layers of raspberry, clear, and blueberry Jell-O into a copper lobster mold that usually hung on the wall above the kitchen sink, Lainie listened to Bob Wills and his Texas Playboys. The recipe for the striped Jell-O was customized from a back issue of *Gourmet*. The *Gourmet* chefs boiled cow hooves to create their gelatin base, but Lainie didn't know any cows personally willing to donate theirs. Her cupboard was jammed full of these three-year-old packages of Jell-O, butterscotch pudding, and cocoa mix. Might as well use it up as throw it out. In a spasm of country fiddle and steel guitar, Bob sang out about Mother Nature and forgetting and time changing *ev'rythang*.

She felt the jiggling begin in her left foot, the desire to sing congest her lungs, an almost mandatory yearning to add her voice to the chorus. When she and Russell had first gotten interested in Western Swing, they learned all the cuts on this old record. "Stay a Little

Longer," "Deep Water," and Russell's perennial favorite, the "Brain Cloudy Blues." Russell had laid the Dobro guitar on his lap, and hunkered down into his homemade slide. All Lainie needed to do was raise her head and belt out her own smoky tenor. Russell was shy of his singing voice, but it wasn't so bad, just a more thinly poured version of hers. When they harmonized, no question, they'd made music.

Russell still played. Guitar strings beneath his fingers were as mandatory as breathing to Russell. But Lainie did not sing anymore. Since losing Spencer, she couldn't raise more than three notes to whistle her dogs back. The time for singing was past. There were bills to pay. It wasn't fair to expect Nick to shoulder the whole burden. Being back at work at Public Assistance wasn't that awful, unless she focused on people who found joy in making her job difficult, like rat-faced Elizabeth Friedman from the county, the social worker who looked on children as ticks. Assistance was a privately funded, public regional planning body, a sorting house, responsible for shuttling clients to the correct departments. Battered wives went to Casa Esperanza, abused children to Sunshine House, drunks and junkies to College Hospital. Their motto was "Always, always, as a last resort, call the County." Unlike the County Services, Assistance was totally dependent on rich people's donations and their few grants. As a result they were swifter, kinder, and gentler of heart. Lainie wrote reports on intake interviews, handed out Care packages, and scheduled return appointments. She had a way of gaining kids' trust, and her boss, Irene, liked to send them to Lainie's office to calm them down. Irene was great. They took turns boxing with meanies like Elizabeth Friedman.

Her life kept her busy. She did laundry on Thursday mornings, mopped the Mexican paver tiles on Fridays, and without fail walked both dogs in the bluffs every afternoon. In the hospital they helped her make out this schedule, and she'd stuck to it like a twelve-step program. She tried to cook every night, but at Dr. Mapp's request, only to cook things she felt like cooking, such as this striped Jell-O mold for the Wisteria Street Fourth of July block party she had no desire to attend.

It was already noon, and outside the neighborhood kids were racing up and down the sidewalk, lighting packages of snakes on the curbs, performing artful dances of anxiety, trying with little-kid-faith to turn the sky from bright blue to dark. In the kitchens of her neighbors, Lainie could predict the fare under construction: A slightly tipsy Mrs. Andrews was boiling brisket and cabbage they all would take polite helpings from, but not really eat. Next door, Martin and Uté Fuentes were wrapping corn husks around the more popular pork and green chile tamales to serve alongside Martin's smoky chipotle salsa. Two doors down to the left, Mr. and Mrs. Karponi would be cooking up a restaurant-sized batch of homemade resentment.

Today, like most days, they kept their daughter, Ruth, and son, Aaron, captive indoors, convinced that somehow this whole fireworks thing had to be the work of the devil. Before the night was over, Mrs. Karponi would call the police, and one of Harper's men in blue would drive by to try to settle the imaginary dispute Mrs. Karponi had spent all day stirring up in her head. The dark the children had waited all day for would be violated by headlights and civil codes and the paranoid fantasies of Edna Karponi.

66

Talk about anger—Edna should be in Dr. Mapp's office, Lainie mused, not me. Russell loved a good Karponi story almost as much as the television show "Cops." After an incident when Mrs. K had called the police over a supposed lot variance with the Fuentes— two inches of flower bed—he renamed Lainie's neighbors the "Cranky Ponies." Consequently, whenever Lainie saw them venture forth from their shuttered house to the cars they parked across their driveway so no one could drive in, she envisioned them thus: Edna, a Shetland pony with a bad back; Nino, a long-jawed rent-string horse who raced around the corral to see who he could bite. Their handsome, dark-eyed children were as innocent and doomed as feedlot horses, adolescent bundles of energy just aching for a weak spot in the fence. A pair kept that long and that hard on the bit couldn't help turning nasty.

Lainie'd watched them grow up. When they were tiny and Edna allowed them a brief foray into the real world, such as running through sprinklers with the rest of the neighborhood children when the temperature hit one hundred degrees, she insisted they both wear shower caps. She dressed them like Sears catalog models. In the neighborhood hierarchy they had cooties with a capital C. Now they wore teenage self-doubt like acne. Lainie wanted to steal them from the undeserving Karponis, give them crimped oats and blackstrap molasses and the whole wide world in which to run.

Nick said in all his mountains of counseling textbooks he'd never come across a family who could out-dysfunction the Cranky Ponies. Russell, more objectively, and perhaps because he lived three blocks away, believed that one day they would see Aaron and

Ruth on national TV, famous, just like the Menendez brothers.

All the houses on Wisteria were 1940s Spanish-style stucco, built by some visionary contractor who made everything look quaint as old Mexico from the outside, but who turned blind when it came to interior design. Hadn't she and Nick done the same—fallen in love with the three-inch-thick, red-painted arched door, the curvy tile roof, the tall green hedges that formed a natural fence? Ten years ago, it hadn't mattered to them that the bathroom only sported a stall shower, or that counterspace in the kitchen couldn't hold a phone book and two dinner plates at the same time. Someday, when they'd paid off Spencer's bills, when Nick's job at the hospital was a sure thing—if they didn't lose the house—they planned to remodel. Add a second story with an overhanging balcony, put in a restaurant cookstove, and repair the fireplace so they could burn real wood in it. Someday always seemed just over the horizon, but eventually, payment by payment, the American way, Lainie figured they'd get there.

The high-pitched whistle of a Piccolo Pete sent Oddjob barking and scrabbling across the tile and Shaky Jake into his trademark tremble. Before Lainie knelt down to soothe the old shepherd, she got down the bottle of tranquilizers the vet prescribed for Oddjob. Poor dogs—this was no holiday for them. She plugged the pill into an inch of nitrate-free turkey hot dog, whistled, and Oddjob inhaled it. Jake, out of fairness, she gave a hot dog placebo. In an hour, Oddjob would be snoring on the bathroom rug, and hopefully stay that way until morning.

The final layer poured, she set her Jell-O into the fridge. Out of nowhere, one of those bad moments hit her, as of she'd received a swift kick in the backs of both her knees. *You're nobody's mother. Your husband can't look at you without thinking of what you lost. You spend three-quarters of your time wandering around your head thinking crazy thoughts. Who do you think you're kidding?* That carping voice inside her head continued, and she took ten deep breaths the way Dr. M had taught her. She had been married twelve years to a faithful, gainfully employed man who in his spare time counseled the needy for free. She'd had a good-hearted grandmother who taught her to make Waldorf salad. Being a mother for a short period of time was better than not being one at all. Her own mother chose to communicate with her via answering machine tape, and as smarmy as some of the messages could be, that sure beat having her live next door.

Given national averages, Lainie figured she had at least thirty-five more years ahead of her in which to live out this adventure called life. Those were verifiable, countable blessings. Her hands gripped the counter tile, and she thought maybe she would make bread tomorrow, all that kneading and rising helped steady her. Then she remembered something cheerful and felt instantly calmer.

Margie Lomanto had to work the Fourth, so there really was a kind of independence to celebrate. An entire evening alone with her brother Russell not having to endure a single crack from his girlfriend about why was it that Lainie's house, while decorated very cute considering what she had to work with, always smelled a little like wet dog?

This party's only a matter of hours, she told herself. You will be fine—not great, but fine. Just take things one Buddha-ticking minute at a time.

CHAPTER 6

NOT SINGING THE BLUES

RUSSEL TOOK ONE LOOK AT THE PATRIOTIC JELL-O resting on the bed of wilting butter lettuce and said, "Excuse me, Lane, but why exactly did you make us a Jell-O dick for Fourth of July?"

Lainie watched her brother poke an index finger at one of the testicle-claws. This caused a shimmy to resonate through the lobster body and the lettuce to sway slightly, like a close-up in a JacquesYves Cousteau documentary. Because gelatin didn't carry off the definition of the copper mold, the final product did resemble a phallus more than a shellfish, one with big droopy testicles full of sugar and impending dentist visits. "Nick signed us up to bring dessert to the block party. Don't regular people eat Jell-O?"

"How should I know? I've never been a regular person. Regular people wisely shun Carpenters."

"It's too bad Margie had to work."

"Yeah, her boys love Jell-O. So long as there's Cool Whip, those two can really put it away."

Lainie bit her tongue, hoping to drive away her question why lately every mention of Margie made Russell immediately change the subject and start talking about her boys. Russell was an adult; he could make his own romantic choices, even if his girlfriend sometimes said mean things and didn't like his sister. She changed the subject. "Did you bring a guitar?"

"Duh. Of course."

"Which one?" she asked, knowing it wasn't going to be the ruined Gretsch Spencer loved, though she remained eternally hopeful her brother might repair it.

"My Gibson Southern Jumbo. Why?"

Because when you play that one I can still hear him, and when you play any other one I can't. Tiny footsteps racing down the hallway. The splash of bathtime carried out in the kitchen sink, plastic boats and suds flying every which way, spotting the barking dogs. *Mama, Mama, I want my truck pajamas.* Those rhyming songs Spencer invented when he was thoroughly ensconced in his own world, where every organ beat properly and nobody doubted for a second it wouldn't continue.

"Lane? You with me?"

She smiled. "Sure. Just asking. Hey, play me something totally un-Fourth of July, Russell, please? Nick, Russell's here."

Russell frowned and Lainie peered out the glass doors at the rear of the house. Born one year ahead of her brother, she knew what his frown meant. His mind was a player piano, scrolling through the tunes he knew until he came up with exactly what he sensed people needed to hear. They'd been able to read each other that way since they were toddlers. Their mother would open the widest bottom drawer in her kitchen, take out the measuring cups and baking tins, and wedge the two of them inside to keep them occupied. Then she could paint her face, play bridge, or watch "General Hospital" uninterrupted. Their brother-sister communication was innate, the way some twins developed their own language.

Russell loosened the catches on the brown Lifton case and unwrapped the instrument from its flannel sock. He cradled the Gibson in his arms. As his fingers hovered over the metal strings, tuning it by way of harmonics, Lainie felt archaic emotions rise up inside her. He

71

noodled around awhile, then settled into "Sugar Moon," a Bob Wills tune.

We're still on the same wavelength, she thought. Dr. M, who among us could possibly be angry? "Nick," she called out, "Where are you?"

Nick, manning the barbecue in a borrowed hospital lab coat, stuck his head in the back door. "I'm right here. Hey, Russell."

"Whoa, check out the Master Chef."

"No, that's my wife's title. I'm only barbecuing because on the Fourth it's a societal expectation."

He set the chicken breasts on the barbecue grill and Lainie flinched, hearing the tender flesh sizzle. Her forty-three-year-old husband was tall, straight-backed, and handsome. His graying temples and beard provided a vision of the physical attributes every soon-to-be psychologist formerly employed as a union carpenter should possess. Five years ago, he'd decided wood wasn't enough—he wanted a "real" career. She'd supported his decision, and he'd dug in, working two jobs, studying every spare moment. Neither of them suspected the irony life held for them tucked in its tight little fist.

Nick understood all that textbook stuff. Whatever the books said worked, he tried. Once, he'd made her go with him to a support group for parents who had lost their babies in various awful ways, but thankfully that disaster ended with that one time. They were a couple, but they handled their grief in quiet and individual ways. Sometimes, when he'd suggest some new tactic, he reminded her of Bop. Nick and Bop got along. When the whole family was afire with conflict, Nick could always reason with her grandfather.

While the food cooked, Russell sat down in the

wicker rocker and played all the songs he knew with the word moon in the title. "Blue Moon of Kentucky," "Shine On, Harvest Moon," "It's Only a Paper Moon," and an opened slide guitar ditty he'd written himself, "When the Moon Gets Under Your Skin, Time to See the Dermatologist."

Lainie took inventory: Candace was on her date with the winking pilot. Mother was in Healdsburg. Bop, who knew where. In the fridge, her Freudian Jell-O waited for presentation. On the bathmat, Oddjob snored and shed long strands of black fur. Shaky Jake balanced on the precipice of trembling under her eternally stroking hands. She watched Nick turn the chicken breasts, sprinkling them with spices and olive oil, and listened to Russell strum as Nick chatted about his latest woodworking project. "I'm book-matching the grain," he explained, and whatever that meant, Russell seemed impressed.

There was ideation and plan present, Lainie knew, though Dr. Mapp would say, *Now Elaine, life is only a series of random events human beings spend far too much energy trying to organize into a meaningful pattern.* Okay, so maybe not, maybe this was just a ritual concocted to keep that tricky randomness at bay. Whatever it was, she saw clearly that they were all performing their tasks admirably, each doing exactly what each was capable of, what needed doing. As far as happiness went, they were managing. Still, all the while, that hole in her heart glowed and burned at the edges, like Nick's barbecue coals, cooking at something that never seemed to get quite done.

Suspended halfway between the block partiers and her own front door, Lainie waited for enough time to pass

73

that she could politely sneak back indoors. Russell had offered to forego the pyrotechnics, presumably to comfort Jake, but Lainie suspected his altruism had more to do with the "Cops" marathon on TV.

Fireworks time—sulfur and smoke assaulted her nostrils. The older children lit the fountains and cones, running back toward the crowd of onlookers while white ash sprayed over the street in two-foot arcs. Every now and then, one delivered its money's worth, shooting three different colors, or those coppery, falling-star-shaped sparks. But most seemed to fizzle out so quickly it was kind of embarrassing.

She abandoned her plate and watched the Fuentes kids squabble over whose turn it was to hold the ubiquitous California candle. Like the Olympic torch, the brief honor was not without an uncomfortable responsibility. Lainie remembered that it had taken her biggest alligator tears to get Grandpa Bop to hold onto it until it burned out. Bop used to motor them slowly around the harbor in *Shadow IV* to watch the displays. If they tossed sparklers in the bay water, Grandma Alyce make them dive in and retrieve them. Twenty-five years ago, diving in the Harbour was no chore. You could still see the bottom, there were still fish.

In an effort to appease her disgruntled brood, Uté Fuentes passed out sparklers. Their youngest, Isa, complained in Spanish that her brother had the *verde* sparkler she wanted. "*Cayate, mija,*" Uté stage-whispered. "Don't call your brother a *puto.*"

Nick set his plate down next to Lainie's. "Mrs. Andrews's boiled cabbage tasted a little like red wine this year."

"She probably got too close to the pot when she was enjoying her afternoon tea. I can't believe you ate it,

74

Nick."

"It's all fuel to me." He patted the front of his T-shirt. "The original iron stomach."

"Even the patriotic Jell-O appendage?"

Nick grinned. "That did require a bit of a leap. I waited until the scarier pieces were taken." He set a hand on her knee and began stroking upward with his thumb toward her thigh. "Listen, this isn't so bad, is it? The whole neighborhood, all of us together in the dark."

It was eighty degrees out and she felt an instant chill travel her spine. Nick's roundabout approach to foreplay was generally doled out over several hours in the form of small gestures such as this. Lainie felt every muscle tighten in defense of tomorrow, the anniversary of Spencer's death.

"You know, it's getting kind of smoky. I think I'll go inside now and check on Jake."

"Russell's with him."

"I still want to check."

"What'd I say, Lainie? What was it this time?"

Brightly she answered, "Nothing. You didn't say anything."

"Bull."

"Come on Nick, it's not like anyone's going to notice one less body."

"I will."

"Then come in with me."

She felt his resistance as strongly as she did his resolve. "We have to learn to get through holidays."

She sighed and stood up. "We are. We did. I made Jell-O and small talk. You burned chicken."

He stood up too, his clean plate and her uneaten one at their feet. His mouth was tucked up in one corner as

75

he studied her, and he knew what that meant: Nick worried that her antisocial behavior was the first curve of the spiral that had landed her in hospital. Only by staying at the party could she prove otherwise.

"Nick, I *want* to go inside now."

"All right. Go."

But it wasn't all right. This holiday wasn't over; he intended to see it through, by performing all the required steps. As Martin came over and offered him a Bud Light still dripping from the cooler, a big false grin emerged from Nick's trimmed beard. Lainie felt frustration rise up like a rash. He'd already made plans for their Christmas, a trek into Mexico to watch *La Posada*. For Lainie, the holiday usually meant an obligatory call to Mother, a quiet dinner with Nick's elderly parents, and, thanks to Margie, *not* getting to see Russell. The only anticipation involved in the holiday was wondering what totally inappropriate gift Bop would send to appease his guilty conscience.

Sometimes she imagined pinning her husband down like Gulliver, so securely that he couldn't move, then whispering into his ear, *Nick, we have to face facts. I love you. You love me back. No problem there. But we're both sleepwalking our way down some freeway that has no offramps. Our lives now are like leftover Chinese food. Even people with really good taste can get a little sick of eating Mongolian beef three times a day. If you want togetherness, can't we just cry together, instead of hiding behind bathroom doors to do it in private?*

But she was afraid if she told him that their marriage would blow up like one of the fireworks. So instead, come December, she would pack her Samsonite, her salt pills, her bottled water, her *Feliz Navidad y Prospero Año y Felicidad*. She shut the front door behind her, inhaled

76

the familiar doggy aroma and immediately began to relax.

Jake and Russell were on the couch, Jake stretched out across her brother's lap, his front legs and back end spilling over onto the couch. Normally, "on the couch" wasn't allowed, but today all canine rules were suspended. The cathode glow of the TV turned both Russell and Jake an alien shade of blue. "What are the 'bad boys' up to tonight?" she asked.

"Mugging most of the population of Miami, Florida. What a deceptive climate those poor Floridians have. Their weather is warmer more days out of the calendar year than ours, they can practically walk out the front door and fall into crystal sea water, and they have the citrus industry by the short and curlies, not to mention Epcot. But for what? So they can get gunned down by some Samoan gang that just wants to borrow the car for a drug deal?"

"Russell, would you ever consider smoking pot again?"

He pressed the remote control's mute button, momentarily silencing the Florida night. "Hell, no. I did so much of that stuff in high school I'm sure if I took a drug test today I'd come up positive. Why?"

"No reason. Sometimes these thoughts just attack my brain without warning."

He pointed the remote at her. "Lane, don't even *think* about starting that crap. I mean it."

"You said 'drug deal,' pot is a drug, I asked a perfectly normal question. That's called linear thought progression, Russell."

He eyed her. "Why don't you try that reasoning out on Dr. Mapp? Might be fun to watch her drive several big rigs through it."

"Let's just watch TV, okay?"

"Whatever you say. It is rather patriotic of us. 'Cops' and all. I mean, it's not like we're watching *Smiles of a Summer Night* on cable. We're taxpayers. Crime is very American. Where's the Nickster?"

"Watching the fireworks. He'll be in soon."

Russell delivered her a half-smile. "Give him a break, Lane. Guy's trying so hard somebody ought to give him a medal."

She crossed her legs. "I know he's trying. You don't have to tell me."

"And you?"

"Duh, Russell. Back off."

"Duh yourself. Nice Jell-O."

"Fireworks evader."

The day ended predictably, she and Russell sitting out back on the swing, him strumming the Southern Jumbo through the intriguing starts of all the songs he knew, both of them trying not to flinch at the louder booms, which sounded suspiciously like gunshots. After each one, Russell'd say, "That was somebody slamming a car door."

"Play my favorite," she nudged her brother, and in the darkness saw only the glint off his John Lennon glasses as he sighed before complying. She knew what he thought—that the title alone said it all, but Melvin Endsley's "Singing the Blues" was too short a song to satisfy Russell. She longed to hear the song suffuse through her the way those neighborhood children out front were absorbing every spangled explosion into their young memory banks.

"I'll play it," Russell said, "if you sing with me."

"Come on, Russell. Just play the song."

"Nope."

Lainie drew her knees up and hugged them, traveling to that numb no place that seemed to have a shorter and shorter access path these days. Where in the first year there was a constant aching and sobs that came out of nowhere to contend with, the second year was more of a frantic reordering that had not worked too well until she landed in the hospital. But this third year was starting out long and hollow, like a cold wind at her neck. It wasn't weather, though, it was determination. Grief had hold of her leash. She shut her eyes and let her mind drift to her grandfather's hat on the grave marker.

Galloping horses. The rows of trees on the Shadow Ranch. Aisles of trees, dwindled to a few scraggly survivors. The ground was thick with rotted lemons. The ghostly white-painted tree trunks and rusty smudge pots had gone so long without fire that the ash fused to the metal and seemed a testament to failure. Even dead, the trees stood waiting to bear, to once again be productive. The relics opened their branches, urging her to join them, saying it was much easier to stand dead than endure this tough business of living. Part of Lainie ached to go to that place. If she could be certain she'd see her grandmother, rest in her embrace, make peace with her dad and cuddle her son—why the hell not? Nick, Russell, and Candace would disagree. She tried Dr. M's way, raising her Boy Scout ax, feeling the heft of the blade sink into the dry wood of the trees in her mind. For every chunk she cut loose, the tree grew a thicker girdle, became twice as impenetrable. These were the kinds of thoughts she was afraid to share with Dr. M.

Another car door—gunshot rang out and Russell said, "Buick. Four-door caliber. Damn, it's hotter out tonight than fried peas. That's a sign of global warming, you know. This planet is ticking like a bomb on a seven forty-seven. Hear it? It could blow any time. I wonder where we'll be when it happens? I hope to Jesus I'm not at work. If I'm at work selling Dave Clark Five albums to some gumhead blowing Daddy's money, I swear—"

He tucked his chin down and began to play the theme from 'Jeopardy,' and Elaine started to smile. "Russell, do you ever think happy thoughts?"

"Hey. These are my happy thoughts."

"You want some patriotic penis?"

"No thanks. I can live without eating anything that has a layer of blue in it."

"In high school you used to drink mouthwash."

"Yeah, but that was different. I assumed I could be done with halitosis for life if I built up a reserve in my gut."

"Instead you got an ulcer."

"Which I only did to copy my sister."

"Russell, don't you think Tagamet's a brilliant invention?"

"One of the seven wonders of the pharmaceutical world."

Their comfortable darkness was suddenly broken by lights—Harper police lights—Lainie recognized the trademark orange and white swirl. Edna Cranky Pony, serving up her dish of neighborhood discord. She and Russell looked at each other and started to laugh. Pretty soon Nick would step in, try to facilitate. At their feet, Shaky Jake lay quietly, only the risen hackles on his neck giving away how much this holiday business didn't fool him, not one bit.

CHAPTER 7

WHEN LIFE HANDS YOU LEMONS

"YOU WANT TO GO OUT TO DINNER TONIGHT?" Lainie asked Nick that morning at breakfast. "Fish tacos down at the beach?"

"It's volunteer night at Teen Outreach."

"Oh." Lainie knew the pro bono work was important, no matter what the anniversary of this day meant. She didn't blame him; after three years it was time to relinquish this day to ordinary status.

Nick stood there finishing his coffee, watching her cut the few remaining zinnias from the backyard planter, and said, "He loved to crash his trucks into your garden."

Her fist was full of woody stems. "Russell always warned him that someday the Harper florists were going to form a militia and repossess his fleet of Tonkas."

Nick touched his beard and looked thoughtful. "I wonder just how many of those teasing threats shape our adult personalities."

"I don't know."

"Are you going to the cemetery today?"

"I might."

His eyes darted away from hers. "Well, I'll see you about nine then." He gave her a dry kiss and was gone.

Lainie couldn't help seeing double meanings everywhere—in a handful of zinnias, a husband's tally of how often she visited their son's grave, even the vitamin-fortified messages on the cereal box. Dr. M said even the most well-adjusted people spent their lifetime seeking answers, and questions weren't accusations. After Nick shut the front door, she stood at the window watching Oddjob furiously dig yet another hole leading to nowhere in their pathetic lawn. Balding in patches, urine-browned in others, the divot-ridden expanse was beginning to resemble the dog himself, though on a much larger scale.

An hour later, at work, she'd routed a pregnant woman whose husband had blackened both her eyes to a halfway house where she could sleep safely for one week. When that week was up, the woman had to start the process all over again, make an appointment to come back to Assistance, see whether another shelter had room, show her restraining order. What she would likely do was find a way to bail him out, and the cycle would start all over again.

"Maybe," Lainie'd suggested softly, aware she was overstepping the boundaries of her job description, "you might want to think about divorce. I know it's hard, but do you really want your baby to go through what you have?"

"I love my husband. This never happened before. He has a hard job and sometimes he just . . ." The woman, her hair the bright brass Spencer's angel statue had originally been, stared right past her, as if Lainie's words of caution were only a no trespassing sign on a private beach. She accepted her plastic grocery sack containing the essentials Assistance provided- toothbrush, miniature tube of Crest, two pairs of J.C. Penney's underwear-and marched with dignity toward a privately funded single bed.

After she'd gone, Lainie pressed her cheek to her desk blotter, trying to quell the despair she felt for the woman's unborn child. Nick said all the books insisted heredity was only one factor in determining personality. Environment, the biggest crap shoot of all time, could undo generations of heredity. You couldn't predict anything, you had to wait and see it played out over a lifetime. Lainie wondered where exactly, in a psychologist's estimation, environment began. Within those first blinding moments inside a hospital delivery room, when those medical cheerleaders urged you into a momentarily safe, sterile world? Or did it begin long before that, in the pulsing dark of the womb, when the blows your father delivered your mother sent the first bubbles of panic into the saline of the fetal aquarium? She could envision this woman's fetus as clearly as the coffee cup full of number two pencils on her desk top: a dark-haired, dark-eyed boy, his starfish hands already curling into fists.

Sometimes, when Russell was going too far with the smart remarks, her dad had smacked her brother, but afterwards he'd taken him right in his arms, apologized, and hugged him. He'd never hit Lainie, not even when she deserved it, or her mother, who Lainie sometimes thought might just be the walking argument for justifiable attitude adjustments. Grandpa Bop, who admitted he'd been too free and easy with the belt on Chuck, had spent the remainder of his life attempting to make up for it by spoiling his grandchildren and pinning his highest hopes to Spencer. To Lainie, the idea of striking her son seemed about as plausible as interplanetary travel. More than anything, Lainie had wanted Spencer to know he was loved. What worried her was that maybe he'd left the earth uncertain and afraid.

The pregnant woman was her last scheduled interview. Friday, generally jam-packed with clients, was so bereft of appointments that Irene told her to go on home. The afternoon and most of the evening were hers, so why not sneak off to the cemetery for an extra hour? Nick didn't have to know how long she stayed. She'd stayed away almost one entire month. He'd approve of that. At least she couldn't come across the damn hat twice.

She sat at his grave under the tall tree and told Spencer about the block party. "Uté made tamales, Spencer. Every family pitched in ten dollars and we got the Freedom Assortment fireworks. My favorite was the Spinning Flowers. They're new. You set them on the ground and they pinwheel and make a furious noise, like the Tasmanian Devil in the cartoons. The Cranky Ponies started a ruckus and the cops came, but they were cool. They let the Fuentes kids sit in the squad car before they left."

She ran her fingers through the grass, combing the grave, getting dirt under her nails. The brass angel squinted and leered and her boy was dead. Damn Bop for ranking Spencer's angel. She came here expecting peace only to be reminded of a larger war.

It was too hard to say good-bye, so she said, "See you later, honey." She pointed the Volvo toward Pacific Coast Highway, taking the long, scenic, think-it-over route to her grandfather's house.

Bop's gardener was out front, trimming the ever-advancing bamboo and fertilizing the herb garden. "Hey, Tony," Lainie called out as she parked behind his white Toyota truck.

"Hey yourself. Haven't seen you around in a long while. What did he do this time? Buy your street and

84

condemn all the houses?"

"Don't give him any ideas." She held up the cowboy hat. "He . . . I'm just dropping this off." She eyed the house nervously, afraid any moment now her grandfather would snap open the redwood front doors and bark her name in his creaky bass.

"Garage's open. Why don't you go on in and set it on the dead moose head? I'm sure it would fit."

Bop's truck was parked in the garage. "I was hoping maybe you'd take it inside for me."

Tony wiped his forehead with a dirt-stained hand. Twenty years ago, when he was nineteen and she was nearly fifteen, Antonio Navarro had given Lainie her first kiss, in the front seat of another truck, perfumed by the heady aroma of grass clippings and motor oil. Shortly after, he'd wisely delivered her first brush-off. The embarrassment was short-lived; the friendship persisted.

"I don't think he's home, Lainie. He sure hasn't come out and told me which direction to rake the dirt, and next to interfering in your and Russell's lives, that's about his favorite pastime."

She nudged her red tennis shoe toes into the soft, rich earth. Anything could grow here, anything Tony planted and tended and Bop granted permission. Bop had trucked the top soil in all the way from the Shadow Ranch himself. All around him, his neighbors made do with minimal plantings in the native clay soil, artfully arranging rocks when their plants came up spindly and disappointing. It was hard work maintaining a waterfront property and a traditionally landscaped yard. Some went so far as to give up entirely and put in decorative rocks. Not her grandfather. To the left of the property, a hedge of Chinese bamboo separated Casa de

Carpenter from its nearest neighbor. Below, rounded river rocks wide enough to sit on offered sunny surfaces for lizards and various insects to practice solar gain. Lavender, rosemary, and sage snaked around the boulders. Once she'd naively asked Bop where he'd gotten them, as if they might go check out this rock-forest themselves.

"Pennsylvania," he'd told her. "That's Mill Run River rock from just north of the Fallingwater site. Had to buy an entire truckload. Criminals charged me a small fortune, but it sure enough did the trick to give this house a taste of Mr. Wright's most famous project."

In elementary school geography class, Lainie'd traced her finger across the states between Pennsylvania and California, picturing the boulders plucked from some secret woods another family had claimed as their own, the dents left behind in the earth like chicken pox scars. Charles Russell Carpenter the second laid down his money and Pennsylvania rocks became transplants to his California front yard. *I want, I buy*—her grandfather's lifelong credo. Did rocks ever feel homesick? Her fingers danced nervously on the hat's felt.

"Listen," she said to Tony, who leaned over his shovel looking attractive and outdoorsy in a white T-shirt and cut off jeans that made the best of his muscled legs. "Play your cards right, there's a loaf of homemade bread in this for you."

Tony gave her a patient look. "He's just a lonely old man in a big house, Lainie, not some poisonous snake. He rides that stupid horse, swims his laps, and watches Oprah."

"Keeps him in shape for meddling."

"Shoot, you're more stubborn than he is. Drop the hat and run, why don't you?"

"All right, all right. I'll do it." She squared herself and took a deep breath.

"Wait." Tony clipped a sprig of rosemary from the fat bush he'd been trimming. "For luck."

He tucked it into her shirt through an open buttonhole, and as the aroma tickled her nose she remembered Tony's kiss all over again—the surprising softness in his mouth, but a sharpness there, too, a good kind of edge she leaned into with eagerness. At fourteen, you leaned forward; at thirty-five, you spent so much time and energy leaning back the deed wasn't worth the undertaking. "Thanks, Tony. You can still have the bread if you want it."

"Sure do miss seeing you around, Elaine . . ." His voice trailed behind her.

And Spencer, she knew he wanted to say, but wouldn't. No one felt comfortable saying the child's name, which was perfectly understandable. Dead children make for a difficult topic. But what they all failed to see was that it didn't matter to his mom. She didn't need anyone to say his name aloud. It beat in her blood, pulsed through her serviceable heart every four minutes, making its way through her body, lightly renaming each cell before it coursed back through her heart muscle again. And again.

Between the three-car garage and the living room, which faced the deck and all that costly, polluted water, lay Bop's workshop. Here, radial arm saws and drill presses stood gleaming as clean and well-oiled as the day Sears delivered them. Even the scrap wood box was neatly kept. No splintered chunks of cheap plywood sticking out to catch yourself on, no piles of sawdust in which to track footprints. Here, once they'd mastered the safety rules, she and Russell had spent hours

87

constructing sailing craft from scrap teak and those heavy tenpenny nails—a wicked combination doomed to rust. They'd perfected the art of carefully peeling labels from empty liquor bottles to create their sails. Russell preferred the ship motif of Cutty Sark; Lainie favored rum labels with their coconut palms and sleepy pirates.

The fieldstone fireplace at the far end of the living room always surprised her. It had been designed to appear to grow organically from the stratified rock walls into the massive hearth, a consensual marriage of concrete and layers of stone evolving into redwood flooring. It had taken a team of stonecutters two attempts to get it right enough for her grandfather. Larger chunks of fieldstone jutted up from the diagonally laid redwood floor, just inches at the lowest point, over four feet at the highest. The rocks had been carved into formidable seating, chiseled to graduate fluidly into the hearthstones. She ran her hand over the waist-high one and shut her eyes.

In the old days, Lainie helped Grandma Alyce keep them lacquered smooth with coats of Johnson wax. Now they felt rough and dingy. She'd been posed atop them for countless family pictures—Lainie in her good dress and Russell in his vile boy's suit—Christmas eves, birthdays, Easter Sundays where a round of Bloody Marys—Virgin Marys for the kids—preceded the egg hunt. The day of Spencer's christening, Bop had once again set his Nikon on the tripod and taken portraits. Carpenter children framed against American stone. Those memories were all about Bop at his best, a slide show she used to rerun as she fell asleep in the backseat of her parents' car on the drive home. Every now and then, unbidden, the carousel flipped to a different picture. When she'd come into this room to find the reel-to-reel tape puddled on the floor like brown fettucini, her grandfather passed out on the sofa, reeking of booze. Or just in time to hear one of his wives in the middle of a departure speech. Significant learning had taken place during those lectures. The definition of certain cuss words had been made undeniably clear.

Once, Gloria—she was pretty sure it had been Gloria—used Bop's Remington bronze of a tired trail horse to hammer out every window on the first story. Beveled glass panes didn't shatter into nicely rounded pieces like safety glass. Gloria went to the hospital in an ambulance hanging onto that bloody horse statue while she and Russ, just back from sailing the Laser, scrubbed down the driveway with Tide.

"Why bother?" Russell wanted to know, and Lainie remembered her fevered response, "You want to look at that the rest of our lives? Blood stains!"

Once begun, the flood of bad memory wouldn't stop—screaming matches Bop got into with her father while she and Russell sat on the couch pretending to be upholstery, waiting for a clear escape route to show itself. The hot August night Bop had taken the three-tiered birthday cake intended for his retirement party— glittering marzipan lemons and dancing red horses on a field of creamy buttercream icing—and pitched it clean off the deck into the water. He was sixty years old. She was seventeen. Far away from this family war, two U.S. soldiers out pruning trees on work detail had just been killed by North Korean troops. Was that why he had gotten so angry? She honestly could not recall political discussion, just the swift arc of his throwing arm, the glint of his wrist hair caught in the band of his gold watch, the way the cake had disassembled, tier by delectable tier, just before it landed in the water, a floating plastic horse and clots of foamy icing to mark the spot. The "toys" he'd sent them a few days later were supposed to induce filial amnesia: hefty shares of Coca Cola stock, a cruise to Hawaii. If her dad had still been alive, Chuck would have let them keep the stock, but would have insisted they send the cruise tickets back. Her mom let them go, but hula skirts and watching in fear as Russell surfed the North Shore had only made Lainie remember the birthday debacle forever.

The heat of those memories loomed before her like a bonfire, causing real and past time to shimmy in confusion. The crazy house was at the root of the family. The bizarre magic it was capable of working never stopped. Its trick was to remind every Carpenter who entered it that the past was a powerful force. And as haunted as the house seemed, she adored it.

She laid his cowboy hat upside down on the scarred mission oak table. *Ye old brain bucket*—Bop's term for it. Here in the wealthiest corner of the county the westernness of his hat set him apart. Even without it her grandfather looked different, his trademark toughness of voice and skin hearkening back to early years of broken saddles and manual labor.

"Well, Elaine, I see you've gone and cut your hair."

Her grandfather stood at the sliding glass doors on the deck, dressed in his tan swim trunks, an arm-length plastic glove cinched around what seemed to be some sort of lime-green cast. He was dripping water on the floor, unconcerned.

"Hello, Bop."

"Hello back at you."

For a moment, the two stood and surveyed each other, mentally circling, taking inventory. In a year, he

90

hadn't changed much. His handsome face was all hard planes and steel jaw, his thick silver hair clipped short as a drill sergeant's. Deep inside that grin she could see an echo of her dad's, Russell's, and sometimes, when she was able to let go, her own face.

Bop's steadfast conviction was that unless she had hair falling halfway down her butt, a woman's gender was in doubt. She touched the shoulder-length ends. "It's not as if I shaved my head. I only chopped a foot off. It gets hot in the summer."

He dismissed her logic with a wave of his hand. "You know how I feel about that. I see you've brought me my hat."

"Apparently you forgot it."

"Girl, I didn't forget anything. That goddamn angel gives me gut cramps."

"Grandpa, can we not get into this?"

"Get into what? This is my house, I'm just stating my opinion."

"I *know* how you feel about the angel. Everyone knows how you feel about the angel. What are we supposed to do, blow it up with dynamite, let you build my dead son the Trump Towers?"

"Cut that out, Elaine. I don't appreciate that kind of talk in here."

"Well, you want your stinking hat back or don't you?"

He looked away. "It's probably for the best you fetched it. Hard to resist leaving presents, isn't it? After a few hours, these bright ideas we have seem like such prideful failings."

Now it was Lainie's turn to look away, her heart tripping as nervously in her ribcage as a hummingbird. She allowed her eyes the luxury of running randomly over the dozen or so framed crate labels that hung on the wall, their bright colors a sharp contrast to the silver-gray stone and concrete. At the end of the line of the others hung Shadow Ranch Packers. The artist had gone to the Art Deco shading school of design. He gave the lemon trees a forest-green cartoon roundness they never possessed in real life, but neither their painted insect-proof trunks nor their abundant foliage was the focus of the label. The shadows on the hills behind them and the dark spaces beneath the trees themselves were what stood out. He must have been an odd sort of painter, she'd always figured, to take the company name to such metaphorical levels. In the foreground, a single Meyer lemon glistened beneath cellophane wrap, a globe of Carpenter gold. In wide yellow type below, the label insisted: *Grown on the Shadow Ranch, Hand-packed by the Shadow Ranch Co-Operative, Shadow, California.* Next came the company motto: *Citrus followed the Cross.* Maybe Charles Russell Carpenter I had darkened a church once in awhile, but aside from his own weddings and two family funerals, to her knowledge Bop hadn't made worship common practice. As Russell once pointed out, *It's simple—Bop figures there isn't a religion big enough to hold him and a deity both.*

"Was there something else you wanted, Lainie?"

She felt the weight of his words press her neck like a heavy necklace. "No, not really."

Her grandfather set his bunched-up beach towel down on the table top. Immediately, salt water began to seep into the dry wood, and she wanted more than anything to snatch up the towel, take down the lemon oil, and rub away at the spot that would surely remain there for all time, another historical stain she or Russell would inevitably inherit.

Bop caught her looking. "It's just a table, made out of

dead tree, honey. Who gives a shit if I stain it? Someday it'll all be firewood." He opened his arms. "Come here, Lainie. Come on, let your old grandpa give you a hug on this hard day. You can even hug me back in secret. I won't tell."

As determined as she was to resist, she went. She felt his strong arms, one with the familiar leathery, always-tan skin, the other with its weird rubbery plastic, close around her, his sharp pipe-tobacco scent enveloping her safely. He was six feet tall, barrel-chested, as handsome and dishonest as any government official could strive to be. He was also the closest thing to a father she had known for nearly twenty years.

"Sugar, you can just hold on here until you feel like letting go, then we can go right back to the way things were."

"Sworn enemies?"

"No. Family."

Can we turn back the clock and do this over, paying closer attention this time? Have barbecues and birthday parties, Daddy and you not fighting, Grandma Alyce in the kitchen, teaching me how to cook? Somewhere in there, can you locate a healthy future for my baby? Aloud she said, "Whatever that means."

He hugged her tighter. "Don't have to mean anything more than hugging."

"I miss him so much, Bop."

"Me, too." He patted her shoulders. "It's going to be all right."

As always, the largest part of her heart wanted to believe him. She studied the room from the vantage point of his arms. Once it had been an ultramodern castle, all impossible angles, broad beams, clear redwood, cantilevered glass windows opening out over

93

the water with no visible means of support. Every room had a built-in strangeness, the figured wood creating loony shadows, the rocks concealing like an indoor forest. The secret panel he swore was there, just so they would never stop looking. The shelves so high and sturdy they provided perfect kid hide-and-go-seek places. Entering it had been like going to a skewed Disneyland, where they served whiskey and filet mignon instead of hot dogs and Coke. People used to drive by on Sundays, whole carfuls of families pointing out the "gem of the waterfront." Now its magic was threadbare. Like finding a fossil encased in a wall of stone, a museum curiosity that no longer caused so much as a shiver of awe, it reminded her of when scientists had discovered the bones of that walking fish, millions of years old, changing all the theories with that single skeleton. After all the flurry of discovery settled down, the skeleton became a part of history—like it or lump it—it had to be integrated into a larger picture in order to preserve what was vital to keeping science pure—the truth. Casa de Carpenter had become relegated to tawdry history, as much a natural resource as broken seashells on the beach.

Bop cleared his throat. "Damn it, Lainie."

She could hear how close he was to tears. "Damn what?"

"Just when I about got used to not seeing family, you show up and upset my applecart. It'll take a glass of Carpenter punch to help me get my bearings. How about you?"

"Okay."

He released her, stepping into an awkward little dance, the same goofy steps he'd used when she was a kid, and he was trying to make her forget her troubles.

He sang, "Oh, you Froggie boys can keep your French champagne, your Arabica coffee from the Costa Rica plain. I don't want Perrier with my sandwich for lunch, but you can pour me a glass of Carpenter punch."

His awful singing voice made her smile. She watched him unwrap his arm. Under all that rubber there was a cast, a lime green one. He patted it dry with a dishtowel, bustled around his stainless steel kitchen gathering ingredients. The metal cupboards and countertops gleamed like tarnished silver, only a little dented in spots from thirty-five years of use. It was too small a room to go with the rest of the house, but that was because the man who had it built never planned on cooking for himself. If she were to open a drawer, all the utensils would be lined up, graduated in size. The dishcloths and dishes were always bright yellow—next to gold, the color her grandmother had believed closest to celestial harmony. On a laminated wood cutting board he'd made himself, Bop sliced six lemons into halves, then commenced squeezing.

When the juicer was full, he had half a lemon left over, and while the machine whirred, he absently picked it up and bit into it as easily as if it were a sweet orange. As far as she knew, he was the only man on earth who could do that and not wince. He added crushed ice, a shot of grenadine, and a sprig of mint to her glass and set it on the counter in front of her.

"Drink up, honey. Drown your troubles."

She toppled the mint leaves into the drink, then lifted the glass to her lips. While her grandfather sponged up spills, she tasted her childhood.

"Forget the bubbly glee of orange soda, the unnatural sweetness of Kool-Aid, even the summer-day refreshment of fresh-squeezed lemonade. Carpenter punch is 'a superior beverage invented for superior people.' How's that sound? Would it make a slogan?"

"Maybe." She was a kid again; this feud had never happened; Russell was plunking out "Reuben, Reuben, I Been Thinkin' " on his very first guitar, a Harmony Singing Cowboy he'd bought with his own money through the Sears catalog.

"I'm telling you, we should've marketed this like punch that Paul Newman boy with his salad dressing. Snapple stock's up ten points. Nabisco's going to buy them out—you just watch the *Journal* and tell me I'm wrong. Hell's bells, we could still give this a go. Set you and your brother up with a future instead of those go-nowhere jobs you got. Let me juggle some figures at my accountant and find out what the damage'd come to for R&D."

Any other day she would have argued they were honest jobs. "Grandpa? Let's go ride horses."

He chuckled. "Now there's an idea. Can't hardly think of a better way to waste a summer afternoon than sitting horseflesh alongside my favorite granddaughter."

"I'm your only granddaughter."

"Well, blame your mother."

She took another sip of her drink. "I'll race you down the marsh trail. I'll even give you a head start. Think Eddie Whistler still has that paint horse?"

"Jon Gnagy? Shoot. That old nag couldn't hold a candle to Tio Tonto. Ed's riding a real nice blood bay now, goes by the name of Type A."

"Think maybe he'd let me ride him?"

"I've no doubt he'd be glad to see a decent rider atop him. But I can't, today, honey girl. I'm headed out of town for the weekend and I want to get under way so I can cross the desert before dark."

Lainie's face fell. "The desert?"

He nodded. "Say, why don't you look in on Uncle Stupid for me? That gray bastard is getting uppity as a liberal, so I'd use a stud chain, hell, while you're at it, two of them." He showed her the green cast. "It's not that I doubt your horsemanship, you understand. Just makes me feel better if you keep his butt in check so you don't end up with a cracked arm yourself."

"Is that how you broke your arm? Oh, Bop—"

"Now Lainie, don't look at me like that. It was a stupid accident, my own fault for trying to take a shortcut, as most horse wrecks turn out to be, so back off. You ain't yanking the reins from this old man yet."

"You're almost eighty."

He bristled. "I believe I know exactly how old I am."

"That horse is untrainable, even you admit it. Geld him and be done with it."

"Hell, no! His blood lines are stellar. His kind of madness is a once-in-a-lifetime fluke. He's saddle broke, he'll make a trail horse yet, and when we find a worthy mare, he'll be a daddy. These things take time. He's just a little Roman when it comes to the nose."

"How much time and how many broken bones can you afford?"

Her grandfather pursed his mouth, as if the lemon's sourness had finally caught up to his taste buds. "I can still swim my mile, young lady, even with this fiberglass fishing weight."

"Whatever that's supposed to mean."

"It means get your nose out of my business. You haven't cared one nit for a year; why start now?"

"Fine with me if you want to go out bleeding to death in a pile of fresh horse manure." She picked up the crushed mint and squeezed until green bled from the

97

torn leaves. "Where exactly is it you're going that you need to cross the desert in July, Bop?"

"Las Vegas, Nevada."

"Vegas in July?" She set her half-empty glass down on the counter with a resigned thump. "You're gambling again."

Bop slapped the counter. "I swear, you and your mother could play for the NBA. You're a pair of kangaroos when it comes to jumping to conclusions. It just so happens I am going to a wedding chapel, not a roulette table."

"Sure you are."

"What? You think I'm so old and pitiful women no longer find me attractive?"

"Well, they find your wallet attractive."

"I never said it was a woman."

"Then what are you saying?"

"I'm not saying anything to a young lady who can't find it in her heart to be polite to her elders."

"How long have you known her, Bop?"

"I never met her before in my life. She's a telephone woman. We talk on the telephone now and then. She sells me magazine subscriptions I don't need and we have us a little phone sex, all nice and tidy."

Lainie sighed and shook her head. Her grandfather would walk into a national forest, find the shade irritating, and pick a fight with a redwood. She walked out of the kitchen toward the deck. Sea breeze blew in the open doorway, and she stopped there, crossing her arms in front of her, the same girl at thirty-five she had been at ten, mystified by her hard-headed grandfather, who was right on her heels and up to no good. "Bop, here I'm trying—"

"Trying to what? To say you forgive me now, a year

98

down the line, when I never did nothing wrong in the first place except love you enough to tell some doctors you needed lockdown time to straighten out your head?"

He was backing her into a corner, the way he always did, a rodeo bull considering his options, nostrils flared. "I could have checked myself in." Her voice shook. "I wasn't so far gone you needed to call the goon squad."

"Look, the important thing was to get you safe before you did yourself harm."

"I'd never—"

He wagged a finger. "Now, Lainie. Don't fib. You were inches away from a real bad plan. The signs were there. Ask Russell if you don't believe me."

She forced herself to stand her ground, her voice to come out steady, to give away nothing. "I should have done the Mexican hat dance on your stupid sombrero."

"And after I uprooted that chintzy angel I should have sold him to a junk jewelry outfit. Go on, you drank enough to be polite, nothing holding you here. You're free to go."

"Damn you, old man!" Lainie wheeled and faced the window, biting her lip to keep the words in.

"Come on," he wheedled, stepping toward her like a boxer. "Why don't you just give me the verbal thrashing you want to and make yourself feel better? I'm a tough old buzzard. Whatever you dish out, I can handle it." Bop picked up her glass from the counter, rinsed it, set it into the narrow Swedish dishwasher rack and once again the kitchen was pristine and empty.

"You're fussy."

"And you're a headstrong Carpenter female."

"I'm half LeVasseur."

Her grandfather's smile returned full force. "Half LeVasseur, my butt. Meridel only carried you around.

99

You're pure Carpenter, better thank your lucky stars about that."

"At least bring this woman home out on a trial basis before she has you in court."

He chuckled. "Now isn't that my Lainie, always looking out for my money?"

"I don't want your stupid money. I've never wanted your money."

"Don't I know it. All my dollars got the herpes. Well, the truth is, I'm going to meet the woman, not marry her. Why don't you call up your mother and tell her all about it, let her chew on my sex life for a thrill?"

CHAPTER 8

THE PERFECT REPLACEMENT FOR LETTERMAN

"BOP'S GOT HIS EYE ON ANOTHER WOMAN, ALEJO," Lainie said to the stablehand who years ago had taught her the difference between running and standing martingales as she helped him polish tack. "Here we go again."

Alejo leaned on his rake, nodding sympathetically. "*A buey viejo, cencerro nuevo.*"

"Um, since high school, my Spanish has kind of dwindled down to *como esta.*"

He clucked his tongue, chiding her. "Young women keep old men sharp, Elena. Your grandpapa one lonesome *viejo satiro.* He likes the *fuego* of younger woman."

"He's a lonesome prune head, that's what he is. All his brains are located in his balls."

Alejo looked away, and Lainie knew this frank talk

100

embarrassed him. No matter how far back they went, or how many times they'd had this particular discussion about her grandfather's appetites, Alejo retained a formal respect for the man. "*Lo siento.* Just forget I said anything, okay?"

Alejo nodded. "Try to remember for me, something my *abuelo* said."

"What's that?"

" 'Love juices the old fruit.' "

A picture of Bop's wooden fruit bowl full of bright yellow lemons came immediately to mind, gold-digging girl fruit flies buzzing wildly above them. They were smart flies, and each one of them had an even smarter lawyer representing her. "Sure, Alejo. I'll try."

"Bueno. Now be careful that *caballo. Volverse loco para diverterse.*"

Lainie rolled his words over in her mind while she saddled the gray beast, who stood quiet and compliant, as if all this talk of sex in the summer sun had struck him into stuporous obedience. "This time he's probably going to marry a showgirl," she informed Tontito, who took the news soberly. With the ball of her foot, she tapped the horse's barrel so he'd release his breath and she could tighten the cinch. "He'll end up with some rode-hard bimbo who will squeeze him by the *cojones* until she's buried in nickels. Then there'll be another big divorce, smearing all our names in the paper. Mother will fly down and make it all worse and Russell will get a new allergy. Will someone please tell me why I couldn't have been born an orphan?"

She sat down in the aromatic cedar shavings that lined the stallion's stall. It was twice as wide as the other horses', and lined with plywood four feet from the ground up to accommodate Tontito's penchant for

101

kicking. She stared up at the Appaloosa who'd broken her grandfather's arm. "Your aim's worse than his manners."

The horse looked at her nervously.

She breathed out her hot air in a huff. *Young lady, when you get on a horse's back, you leave your bad mood back at the tack shed, you hear me?* It was sensible advice, no matter who delivered it. She rechecked the horse's bit, an eggbutt snaffle she'd chosen instead of that hideous twisted sweet iron gag her grandfather used. She tightened the headstall a notch to create the double wrinkle at the corner of his mouth, and shouldered open the stall gate.

There were mares in both arenas, so she decided to warm him up on the marsh trail. After ten minutes of walking, she legged the horse into a trot. She posted for another ten minutes, made a seated transition into a slow jog, keeping his head slightly bent so that he was concentrating on more than one task. The more she asked of the stallion the more dramatically her chances of emerging from the ride intact increased. Like his owner, Tontito was a hard-mouthed puller. If he felt so inclined, he could clamp the bit in his teeth and run for the border. Anyone else would sell a horse this rank, pay the money, and get a push-button animal. But Bop had a hard-on for bloodlines. Rather than give up the legacy of Sun Dancer's frozen semen he'd gamble breaking his own neck.

Beneath them, the sandy soil sank a couple of inches with each strike of horseshoe. Horses didn't scare Elaine the way they did Russell. Put Russell on a carousel pony, he'd fall off and whimper all night. *I can't trust anything that doesn't come with handlebars, brakes, and a kickstand*, he insisted. Her father had been the true rider of the family—Chuck Carpenter could place in an equitation class on a pack mule. Lainie'd seen him dredge talent from the trashiest bloodline. With a well-placed command and hands so quiet they hardly moved, he'd taught her the art of equitation—though he'd often let her know that her minimal style never quite measured up. Bop had come along afterwards with sympathy and trade secrets—*Here now, no tears. Hook your keys on your belt loop, Lainie. Horses associate keys with the* jefe. What her dad began and abandoned in frustration, her Grandpa Bop finished with patience and secrets. When she rode alongside him, she felt included, worthy of the Carpenter name. But when Grandma Alyce died, and Lainie'd outgrown being his sweetie-honey-granddaughter-girl-child, he'd turned his attention to the cheapest kind of women, marrying whatever slid a lotioned hand down the fly front of his Levi's.

For an hour, she rode loose-legged, watching seabirds hunt food in the muck, listening to the sounds of the marsh vie for room against the steady highway traffic drone. When the sunset began its descent over the Pacific, streaking the washed-out blue sky with orange and amber, a trio of pelicans flew across the earthy palette like paper silhouettes. Smog was the reason it always looked so beautiful. But why couldn't it be child-angels armed with paint pots and giant brushes, racing each other across the atmosphere, creating a different mural nightly, Spencer among them? Why the hell not? Scientists rewrote science all the time. *Sesame Street, Mama. Big Bird gots a cookie for the Cookie Monster and Grover want some, too. We make cookies now, Mama?* She let the memory of his voice fill her up like an unglazed clay pitcher accepting water, let it fill her, seep inside, and overflow, gorging and dripping until her cheeks grew wet.

As if to remind her self-pity was a worthless endeavor, Tontito chose that moment to spook at something or maybe nothing in the marsh, rearing up as high as if he'd been an understudy to Trigger. Lainie pitched her body forward, grabbing mane to steady herself—the classic emergency grip—and, as he jerked his head forward, she felt the ominous burn of reins slipping through her hands. My fault, she thought as she leaned into him, forcing her center of gravity to meld with his, as he galloped straight across the trail toward the million-dollar houses. I asked for this, she thought, me and my big mouth about taking Bop's horse away from him.

A ride on a runaway horse got the heart pumping. She smacked her chin hard on his crest and saw stars. Clenching his mane between her fingers, she heard the following commercial featuring her father's voice: *Never ride alone; don't ride an untrustworthy horse after dark; even the greats like Bill Shoemaker wreck, and always, always remember to wear your helmet.* Every rule she'd ever learned came flooding back to taunt her. Then Tontito started to buck, at first frisky experimental kicks with his rear legs, then deeper ones, his engine coiled down low to the ground for optimum upswing.

She fumbled for the saddle horn with her right hand. "Settle, easy," she crooned, trying not to shout, but Tontito was at maximum oat-drive, hearing only his jolly brain waves cheering him on. Along the curve of his spine she felt him round and call forth every muscle, and with a single notion of dread, she realized there wasn't even time enough to be frightened. One moment she was clinging to him for dear life, the next she was

104

airborne, an angel herself, wings snapped off and discarded, a bag of human bones flung down in the dirt. Landing took all her breath, and she heaved to pull air back into her lungs; Meanwhile, Tio Tonto had taken it into his mind to go wading, and there he was, sunk up to his hocks in mud, munching up state-protected marshland at five hundred dollars a mouthful.

Among the crowd at Whistler's, there were stories galore about the wetlands swallowing up horses. Right now, she wished they were true. The most persistent legend involved a wealthy matron who dressed a money thoroughbred in a thousand-dollar (the amount varied) heavy silver show saddle, decided to take a shortcut across the marsh to the beach, and ended up losing both horse and tack in a fight against gravity. The stable boys used to take Lainie down to this same spot at dusk, tell her the story, then try to feel up her breasts. That was men, certain all stories of treasure, buried and female, were equally enthralling. Nick, eight years her elder, hadn't touched her breasts until the third month they were dating. The first time she brought him to the stables, walked him down this path, she'd had to practically shove his hand under her shirt for him to get the idea.

She bent her legs experimentally, somewhat surprised to find they still worked. Her head spun dizzily, and both arms were bruised, but the powerful ache in her behind convinced her that her butt had taken the brunt. She'd limp the rest of this weekend. Brushing off dirt, she got to her feet.

"Tio Asshole," she called to the horse, who trotted a few feet off, his entire body held stiffly, poised for more nastiness. If she moved toward him, he sidestepped a few feet closer to the asphalt. She'd have to wait it out, pray for other riders to arrive or else a swift impact on the highway; that was the way this day was going to come to its crescendo.

"Get back here, you gray bastard," she crooned sweetly, picking long stems of grass and pretending to eat them in case he might be fooled into investigating. So far, he remained satisfied with the marsh grass.

"Here, you walking bag of Purina's cheapest," she trilled in her most sensuous voice, as close as she could come to singing without Russell behind her strumming a G major. But just like his owner, Bop's horse possessed a savage breast no music could soothe.

Eddie Whistler was too old to ride in the dark, so Lainie wasn't all that surprised he'd sent his granddaughters out to search for her. The skinny girls had horses permanently affixed to their bottoms. Lainie saw them come riding up in the shadowy dusk, lengths of rope coiled in their hands, already anticipating how to drag the unwilling Appy back to his stall. They rode bareback, their braids flying out behind them, echoes of their own horses' tails. Bless their brave hearts, she thought. Tonto, no doubt bored of the marsh, wanted nothing more than to join in this dance, and as he emerged from the mud Lainie caught him on what was left of a short, businesslike rein. "Hey, girls. Been looking for me very long?"

They giggled. "Grandpa said he wouldn't be surprised if Tontito had thrown you in with the mudhens and mud and took off swimming for Catalina."

"Well, be sure and tell Ed I send thanks for the escort. I'm a little stiff from Buck Owens here. Could one of you dismount and give me a leg up?"

More giggles, then one of them slid to the ground as

106

easy as syrup down a buttered pancake. "Sure."

Ahead of her, little ducks leading their crippled mama, they rode confidently through the dark to the stables. Out of the corner of her eye, Lainie watched the last brilliant display of sunset before the muddy dark overcame the sky. The hues—maple, fiery brass, burnt sienna—could have come straight off the fake spruce face of Russell's old Harmony guitar. To complete the picture all that was needed was five cowboys stenciled in silhouette. Two drinking coffee, one roasting a weenie, two more playing guitars and looking skyward, their slope-front Stetsons covering their craggy faces.

Sleep tight, my angel, she sent forth to her boy on the anniversary of his death, to a vision of Spencer apple-cheeked and laughing through the space where he was growing his permanent front teeth.

When both dogs stopped barking their justifiable complaints at no walk this afternoon, and no dinner on time, either, she fed them kibble and listened to the messages on the answering machine. The first two said basically the same thing—it's a crying shame this day has to be part of our family history and after three years why hasn't it gotten any better? Lainie nodded her head into the bag of crushed ice she was holding. What part of her body hadn't the fall bruised? She didn't have any answers for them. Her mother was brief; Candace sounded drunk. When life overwhelmed Candace, she drank Greyhounds and rambled. Russell had waited for the beep, then laid the receiver down and played Lainie a medley of blues: Ray Charles's "Sun's Gonna Shine Again," the Stones' "You Can't Always Get What You Want," and a five-note riff of what it hurt her most to hear, but what he knew she was hearing all day in her heart anyway: "Here Comes Santa Claus." She cried a little, which Dr. M said was perfectly acceptable, even healthy, and did not indicate she was headed for inpatient status. She stood in the shower for a brief scald, then dragged herself to bed.

An hour later, Nick undressed and slid in beside her, trying to do so stealthily, so as not to disturb his sleeping wife. Lainie pressed her naked, sore body up against his smooth back, and trickled her fingers across his chest.

"Oh. You're awake."

She stroked his stomach in silence.

"Why is it that no matter how I engineer it, this day always turns into whipped shit?"

Lainie thought of her stand off with Tontito. "I know what you mean."

"All I want is to go to sleep."

"Me, too."

"So why can't I?"

"Because it's never that easy. Tell me what else happened today."

"Besides Spencer's leaving us?" Nick blew out a ragged breath. "Well, that Frampton kid at Teen Outreach isn't having much luck."

"His mom's still using?"

"Drugs are the least of it. You know how he said she was losing so much weight?"

Lainie nodded.

"Two weeks ago she lets drop she has full-blown AIDS. Doctor said she's got three to six months."

"Oh, Nick. That poor kid. He spends half his childhood watching her get carted away by cops and now he gets to plan her funeral. What's he going to do?"

"Well, one of his many stepfathers offered to take

him back, but only if he gets a job and pays rent."

"Did you help him feel better?"

"I said everything you're supposed to. That it's important not to leave behind any unfinished business. That the number of years a person lives doesn't necessarily have anything to do with the quality of life. Textbook logic doesn't exactly repair a sixteen year old who never got to be a kid."

Lainie turned Nick's face back toward hers, rested his head on her shoulder, and touched his cheek. "Sometimes the best thing you can do is listen."

"If I was still a woodworker, I could teach him how to install crown molding. But I'm not, and no amount of listening's going to unravel his messed-up life."

"Hush. Let's just hold each other and—"

"And what?"

She pulled back. Apparently still stung from her behavior of the previous evening, Nick wasn't about to help her finish the sentence. Despite the rigors of his job, life seemed easier for Nick. Whatever he wanted, he just came right out and asked. Meat loaf for dinner, for Lainie to go to parties and chat with his incipient colleagues, for his patients to want to live as much as they wanted not to. It was even easier for Russell, who strummed his feelings, and made his living selling vinyl records in an age of plastic CDs. But for her, nothing came out that fluidly or that fluently. At work, it was always difficult, and when it wasn't, charming Elizabeth Friedman from the County stepped in and made certain it was. Getting pitched off her grandfather's horse was the easiest thing Lainie had done this year.

"Take me to that other place," she whispered, the words sounding false and fragile to her ears.

"Show me what you mean."

These were *her* tools: a mother's empty hands, a dozen years of shared memories, and the ghosts of far too many spent tears. Through all that history, a flicker of renewed human desire sparked. With it, she did the best she could.

Things went so well at the start. She could feel Nick starting to loosen up, leave behind his difficult day. The heat rising from them both, collective breath quickening, the commingled rush of their blood joining as he entered her and began to move. It had been a long time.

Then Oddjob decided they weren't making love, they were fighting, and leaped out from under the covers and bit Nick on the ankle.

"Ow!" Nick shook the dog loose. "What the hell is it with these dogs? Isn't anybody entitled to a little humping besides them?"

Then good guy Jake, who always tried to lie quietly at the foot of the bed no matter what his masters were doing, began trembling so vehemently the whole bed began shaking, and Lainie felt like they weren't two married people trying to remember how to have sex with each other, they were two idiots engaged in an obsolete occupation, centered in the main ring of the Ringling Brothers circus. Together, but more apart than a few minutes earlier, she and Nick held each other, their mutual sighing eventually giving way to laughter.

"*Caninus interruptus*," she said.

Nick nodded his head, his beard scratchy against her cheek. They held onto each other and eventually Nick slept. Lainie stared at the night sky coming in the gap of the curtains. It was dark blue outside and silent, like an empty movie screen. Eyes open, she waited out the remainder of the night.

CHAPTER 9

A SHOOTING STAR IN THE DESERT

WITHOUT CRUISE CONTROL, BOP KNEW HE wouldn't have lasted two hours on the interstate. As he blessed Ford Motor Company for the option, he wondered what had become of the leisurely art of road trips, the romance of Route 66. These sons of bitches were all driving ninety, hell-bent for early graves, behaving like bratty children playing freeway tag. He set the reins at sixty-five and let them all pass. No point in hurrying just to end up in a fridge with a tag on your toe.

He couldn't gather much in the way of a radio station other than a fundamentalist preacher who believed like so many before him that the world was a done deal in terms of sin and corruption. Old news, scare tactics. The world would continue on long after people did each other wrong and dirtied the oceans. He locked onto a faint Mexican station playing *banda,* hoping to practice his languages. Once a week he got to chat with Alejo over at Whistler's Stables, but the Spanish Alejo spoke was *calo,* tainted by so much American slang it hardly provided a challenge. The last time Bop had spoken any kind of authentic *Español* was back on the Shadow, just before he moved Alyce and baby Chuck north.

In its heyday, Shadow Ranch, located so close to the Mexican border, had employed many nationals and always a few Chinese. The latter had been imported to finish the Arizona-California railroad, and gravitated toward the orchards in search of kinder work out of the blistering sun. Bop recognized these thoughts convicted

111

him of old-world thinking and inherent prejudice. All those years back it was still permissible to refer to your employees as "my Mexicans" or "my Chinamen" without finding yourself in the middle of a lawsuit. Nowadays—and wouldn't Miss Lainie Complainer be the first to tell him—saying *Mexican* out loud made you out to be some kind of whip-toting slaveowner smoking cigars on the verandah, not a butt-busting farmer who'd brought in a necessary crop. One that kept the children of the free world from dying of rickets and guaranteed certain individuals a decent inheritance, he might have added. Now you had to choose from a list: Latino, Chicano, Asian, Asian-American, African-American. Plus, they could change it at any time! Very confusing. Whatever name you designated them, the Shadow workers had been solid people, trustworthy, often second-generation to parents who'd worked the ranch while raising their families.

A youthful Charles Russell II had harvested and packed lemons right alongside them. His father didn't believe in any kind of favoritism when it came to the division of labor. Charles I approved of family. The Shadow workers' outlook seemed to be the more children, the better the family you were likely to assemble. Bop labored under the only child's pressure, trying to walk tall, but somehow always coming up short in his father's eyes.

As he headed into the Shadow Mountains, he wondered what had become of the workers' lives when he sold the ranch. The Chinese-Asians, he prompted himself—had headed in a steady stream toward Los Angeles, as had most of the Mexicans. California was what they called bilingual these days; if you didn't know some *Español* you were shit out of luck, but Spanish wasn't the half of it if you went by voting ballots.

If some people resented his talking like that, hell's bells, let them carp. They sure enough sported better-looking families than he did. He wondered if their stateside-born children grew up to sass their elders, if it was some kind of American failure that crossed the racial barriers. Did they get to a point where they too, found family so irritating they just up and quitclaimed the whole tree? In his estimation, Mexican children knew their station, particularly females. You sure enough wouldn't hear any granddaughter of Alejo's throwing him dating tips.

Bop felt himself bristling with disapproval, way out here in the middle of the Egyptian nowhere. That visit of Lainie's had him so worked up he needed cruise control just to pretend he had some kind of governance on this planet, the gray freeway stretching across it like an endless rubber band. Lainie—his pretty little angel with the pink hair ribbons and rosy cheeks—had grown up more headstrong than Tio Tonto on his worst day. When Lainie reared up on you, it wasn't your arm that got broken, it was your heart.

He punched up the volume on the fading radio. So many oompaahing trumpets he couldn't make out a single word the girl was singing. Well, as Alejo was fond of saying, *las mujeras, la femininidad, todas decir ton tonterías*—women, womanhood in general, every one of them talks nonsense. That was about all the Spanish a man needed to know. And here I am, headed once more into the breach, he reminded himself, dreaming of Earlynn's gold lamé cleavage while keeping my eyes peeled for crazy drivers.

Forty miles from town, he slowed for a long line of cars checking out a wreck that had the cars messed up

113

pretty good. A white Nissan looked about totaled, but that was what you got for buying foreign—when you needed bulk for a buffer, there was nothing but aluminum parts and a car loan holding your ass together. The other guy had an airbag. Like Paul Bunyan's condom, it swung huge and skin-colored out of the driver's side of his BMW. All the victims had managed to get out whole and stand there yelling at each other, throwing lawyers' names and accusations as to who was at fault as easily as wedding rice. As Bop idled there, waiting for the rubbernecking to cease, he spotted a desert tortoise perambulating slowly alongside the freeway beneath the light poles, a good two feet from harm's way. Nice-sized fellow, accomplishing a little travel in the cool of the evening. You and me, buddy, Bop mentally sent to the tortoise. Brothers in this game. Here we go, no fuss about it, just quietly making our way past the madness.

There'd been significant change to the strip. The boulevard was thumping, exploding with carnival lights, banked with luxury hotels like a hot game of Monopoly, but now the MGM Grand flashed emerald neon, 5,005 rooms guarded by an eighty-eight-foot high lion. Bop tried to imagine a nonunion outfit in a town where old Norma Rae was almost as popular as Jesus. He passed hotel after hotel, simmering like mirages in the summer heat, their garish color schemes designed to keep even the weariest gambler on his hind legs, tossing chips at the felt. The stage-set glamour tempted him to pull over and go exploring. But in sunlight it would all look different, a shadow of desperateness hanging over the humans who tried to outrun the numbers on the clock.

Somewhere out beyond the glitz lay the real Nevada,

114

mountains with bighorn sheep, desert sunsets. It put him in mind of the Shadow Ranch again, and Mac Henry's message regarding the potential sale. No federal court judge with half a brain was going to rule they could use Shadow as a trash dump. These were the days of recycling, use-it-up, wear-it-out in the name of votes. Even politicians were stacking newspapers and saving their soda cans. Maybe McCormick Farms next door would win the lottery and add Shadow to its orchards. He'd been hoping for years somebody would. As Alyce used to say, *Hard work accomplishes, Charles. Hope is a chest you tuck heirlooms inside.* Be that as it may, whatever potential buyer went after the land would only have to run a fistful of earth through his fingers. He'd be plowing rows and sowing seedlings by sunrise.

The turn for the Carriage House Inn was off Tropicana, but the sight of all this well-manufactured happiness was distracting, causing his businessman's heart to pump in double-time. If there was anything left to be surprised about at the tail-end of age seventy-nine, it was that organ's inherent hopefulness. Toward the middle of the boulevard, things grew less colorful. Traffic thinned down to a more reasonable flow. These older hotels were mere sandcastles in comparison to the Grand. On a couple of the marquees, whole sections of lights had burned out. Pedestrians wandered the streets in the relative cool of the evening, and more than a few women waited patiently in the dark of bus stop enclosures, undoubtedly professionals hoping a car would pull over to ask for a "date."

When it was considered bad form to divorce and your Mrs. had locked up the Love Tunnel, tossed the keys into the ocean, there were willing ladies who would gladly ease your pain for a fair price. Sometimes Bop thought about one particular woman who had soothed his aches, and wondered whether or not she didn't have the right idea keeping it all business.

The perpetual loneliness of the human race crawled over him like the skin inside his arm cast. Bop didn't want a "date." He didn't even want to imagine what people did on one. The idea of making love began to weigh on him heavily as he made his way amid the billboards of busty showgirls. There were droves of women right there for the taking, and if that didn't do it for you, another kind of billboard sported homosexual magicians with Cover Girl complexions and penned-up miserable albino tigers. They were all selling the same thing: s-e-x. Out front of the Mirage the volcano spewed its gasoline-fired fake lava every twenty minutes, just like any able-bodied man should be able to. It was a city of beds. Charles Russell Carpenter the second could swim miles in the Pacific ocean, jog along the beach, and leave the Nancy boys in the sand; given a few months and a modicum of luck, he could turn a hundred thousand dollars into a neat million. But when it came to what fell below his belt buckle, something once proud and intrepid was irretrievably lurking in permanent retreat, shamed.

Oh, he'd had his share of successes. He'd learned the art of love with Alyce. There was nothing terribly adventurous about their conjugal nights, but plenty of warm memories to recall. She still found her way into his most erotic dreams. He'd managed, for a while, with Gloria, who had her black belt in Kama Sutra. Lord, he had to turn to hippie yoga just to keep in shape for those positions she was so fond of trying out. They fought like dragons, and he might have driven her to the nuthouse at the end of the marriage, but damn it all,

116

he'd watched Gloria slide into her pillows at night with a satisfied sigh.

It wasn't just Helene who'd affected him; it was a whole line of events leading up to the mistake of marrying her. Chuck dying, the stock market dive, losing a fair chunk of cash in divorce court—all that combined drove his abilities into the doldrums. He'd tried taking the pills his doctor prescribed, but they kept him from thinking straight. He was capable then and again, but not studly enough to suit Helene. Before she bailed out, she flipped his switch to off extinguishing his manly abilities the same as capping off a gas line. She was the last woman he'd bedded. Even now, whenever she came high-heeling into his memories with her sarcastic laughter and pointy fingernails, he made himself recite the varieties of fruit-destroying insects, the names of every stock he held in the Dow Jones, until her ghost took the hint and high-heeled on out.

Sex wasn't all there was to being a man. There was word and deed to consider. In the presence of a pretty woman, however, such thinking became a wobbly justification.

He spotted the Carriage House Inn, nine stories, its quiet beige stucco and unassuming plastic sign with the single rose offering cut-rate rest for the casino-weary. This was a businessman's hotel, typical box construction, a place to close a deal without running interference with the temptations of gambling. He pulled up to the front, parked the truck, and stretched his stiff body in the night, the heat chasing the soreness out of his muscles faster than an experienced masseuse.

"Reservation?" the clerk at the desk asked.

"Carpenter. Charles Russell. That's a nonsmoking room, son."

"Yes, sir." All business, brass key, calling for the bellman, he wanted the valet boys to park Bop's truck for him. "There's no charge."

"No thanks."

The clerk, now fielding an incoming phone call in addition to running the registration receipt through his computer, seemed to hardly have a spare second to process the refusal. "Valet parking is included, sir."

"And I appreciate that, young man. What you're offering is the last vestiges of the American way. But these days anyone could take a fancy to your car, late model or beater, pull a gun, use it for criminal activity. They'll crack your skull over a Yugo. It lays you wide open to lawsuits and the costly whims of the legal profession. While I can still do it, I figure it's best to park the monster myself."

From behind him, another senior, equally anxious to register answered, "Amen to that. Now can I get a room?"

Unhappily, the clerk relented from his corporate manners. Bop tipped the persistent bellboy two dollars to carry his single duffel from the elevator. In his room, he stared at the cream-colored house phone on the table between the beds, anticipating the call he'd driven three hundred miles to make. Miss Earlynn Sommers was here in this very hotel, one floor below, with her own faded burgundy bedspreads and complimentary cable television. Basically, what he knew about her was her telephone manners and that tape of Sally Jessy he replayed too often for his interest to be ordinary. She seemed sensible. She was as careful about revealing herself to him as he was about letting strangers park his truck. He tried to imagine her sitting next to him in his Ford, so new it hadn't yet taken any women for rides.

In 1934, he motored around Balboa Park with Alyce, her raven black hair curled into a tight page boy under a patterned scarf. That summer people were saying the Depression was coming to an end, something the growers hadn't felt quite as painfully as other businessmen because they always had food on the table. They'd thrown in the towel on Prohibition. Bop suspected if anything could take them back to the status of a profitable nation, it would be the liquor industry. Alyce. That milky skin and shy smile convinced him they would marry, have a passel of children. But after Chuck there were a couple of miscarriages, and then something inside her had busted. Three different doctors shook their heads.

He figured they'd spend a lifetime feathering a comfortable nest for their grandkids, attending each other with love and respect. Some things a man just knew in his heart, or so he had believed, until Vietnam, and President Nixon shaming them all by telling lies, and Alyce turning fifty and growing forgetful. *There are men in the floor,* she came and told him one afternoon, a funny kind of smile playing across her pretty face. He stayed calm, asked her, *Show me these men,* taking notice of the childlike concentration in her face as she traced the shadows cast from the fieldstone onto the varnished redwood. Men—they tried to laugh about it.

He remembered what it had been like when they stopped making love, that gradual cessation of bodily closeness. While he puzzled out how to care for Alyce, he thought very little of sex, and began to imagine he could get along without it. Then four years after Alyce died, Gloria came charging into the foyer of Casa de Carpenter. It was Christmas, and he'd opened Casa de Carpenter for some architectural firm's fund-raiser. Mac

119

Henry was covering the story for the *Times*. His girlfriend was all cleavage and perfume, bored to death. She marched right up to Bop, took his cowboy hat off his head and put it on her own, starting swaying her taut little hips to the music, crooking a finger, saying, *My name's Gloria. Want to dance?* Well, his answer was pure penis talking: I *want in, I want in now, I'm willing to pay cash money.*

And he had. When Gloria departed wedded bliss for Mac Henry and the team-effort Pulitzer he earned, Bop said good riddance. He was in his "horndog phase" (so Russell had informed him). He charmed the ladies wherever he could find them—benefits for the homeless, fund-raisers for the Performing Arts Center, all that pious charity work was full-to-bursting with an abundance of willing females eager to hook up with a fat wallet.

What had he been thinking marrying Helene? That a matronly, cultured, well-mannered lady could at that late date wring the rotten cowboy out of him? All that had gotten rung was wedding bells and his bank accounts—wrung nearly dry. And talk about stingy in the bedroom. The night she packed her Louis Vuitton and checked out for good, she'd told him, *You're a terrible lover, the worst I've ever endured. I'd sooner bump my pudenda up against a doorknob than have your droopy flesh within a continent of mine.* He'd answered her, *Honey, making love is like a good painting—without inspiration it ain't no better than dipping your brush into numbered paint pots.* That got the harpy where she lived, her being head of the Harbour Art League, fancying herself some kind of holy authority.

But in truth, back then he wasn't much good in the boudoir. He was drinking too much, and Señor Love

120

Muscle was always weary. When he did manage to rise to the occasion, he'd flake out short of the finish line, even after forty minutes of hard running.

For all her daydreaming and bellyaching, Lainie was right about this. Coming here was a mistake. He should buy a gun, put two bullets in the chamber, one for Tio Tonto, the other for his own hard head. What good was an old man?

Now that he longed to put his back into some work, his was too worn out for more than an hour of anything half-assed at best, be it housework or hoeing. The government was digesting his estate in tidy chunks with every passing year. His hearing aid worked well enough, but once your hearing started going, there damn straight wasn't any turning back the clock. Even his eyesight was the result of a skillful surgeon and lens replacement. He could remember both world wars, not getting to fight in either of them, those shameful skirmishes from the Falklands on down to the current situation in Haiti, the first nuclear test explosion, a bunch of no-good presidents playing too much golf, and that remarkable moment when the commies had stood and shook hands with the United States, everyone agreeing to dismantle the bombs and try and get along for a change. A linear memory bank and three forays into marriage did little to erase the need for human companionship. Damn it all—he was getting as introspective as headshrinky Nick. Well, he still had balls, even if they were good for nothing. He picked up the phone, dialed the desk, and asked for her room.

"Yes? What is it?" She sounded a little perturbed.

"Miss Sommers? This is Charles Russell Carpenter, upstairs in lovely room 387. How are you today?"

"Oh, you're here already! You'll have to give me a

121

while."

"No trouble at all. You want to meet a little later in the lobby?"

"I guess that's a good place."

"Okay, then. I'm looking forward to it." He heard her sigh before she replaced the receiver. This was not one of their usual conversations, where the phone lines stretched and relaxed like two old cats sleeping side by side in the sun. There wasn't even enough time for him to tell her that in honor of the hotel's logo, he'd wear a rose in his lapel, to locate a rose or a lapel for that matter. She needed a few minutes—he'd be generous and give her ten.

While he waited, he studied himself in the bathroom mirror, looking for areas of possible improvement. A seventy-nine-year-old man in a cowboy hat wearing a Hawaiian shirt patterned with tiny gray airplanes and yellow leis, Levi's, Lucchese boots, and an old leather belt with a horsehead buckle probably older than both his grandchildren combined—Earlynn would take one look, cut and run. He ran the Remington cordless over his whiskers, slapped Lemon Water on his skin, welcoming the sting. He had no idea what sort of clothes were appropriate to meet a retired stripper, and quickly peeled off the shirt, flinging it over the towel rack. He scrubbed with motel soap from the waist up, creating a generous lather and rinsing. Then, following a swipe of unscented deodorant beneath both arms, a quick search of the duffel, which offered nothing suaver, he put the airplane shirt back on, tucked it into his pants, picked towel lint off his cast, and patted his pocket for his keys. Perfect—nine minutes wasted. Even if it was going to be a colossal disappointment, it was time to go down the elevator to meet the ex-stripper.

A number of women came and went as he sat next to the coffee machine, holding his gift-shop bouquet of peach-colored roses. Some of these ladies looked as young as the stable brats, leaning on the arms of men that he wished like heck were their fathers. There were elderly women as well, using wood canes or those chrome walkers with the fork-shaped tip, their bodies too spent and buckled for Carpenter punch to make any kind of appreciable difference. One woman wore a hot pink minidress so tight he could plainly see the springy outline of her pubic bush. Given the direction the man was leading her, undergarments were probably a waste of time. She was a tired-looking pro of about fifty, but her line of work had aged her ten years further. His heart fluttered, worrying that Miss Sommers—should she ever show up—would sport that same tuckered-out face. They had professional make-up crews on those talk shows, lads so clever they could probably outfit Russell with hair.

He'd read *USA Today* clear through twice and learned nothing he didn't already know. Young Mr. Saxophone was in hot water with his liberals now that he'd put the kibosh on the Cuban refugees, throwing them in with the Haitians on Guantanamo Bay—summer camp for Castro's boys. It was time to face up. Miss Sommers had changed her mind. He dialed her room from the house phone, muttered "Nevermind" when the desk answered. Well, he was all paid up for the night and it was funny how this three-hundred mile disappointment set atop his others made such a neat stack. He didn't foster much interest in the way of venturing downtown to gamble. He might run into Helene, first in line for Barbra Streisand's next show or hunting down David Copperfield, hoping he could turn her tongue back from a venomous asp into something nice. Maybe he'd check out the dining room, drink something bad for him, then sleep a few hours before heading on home.

"Nice roses," his waitress commented. "You want me to put them in water until she shows up?"

"Well, I don't know, honey. Looks like she ain't showing up. I was thinking about sticking them in my ear."

"Waste of good roses in my opinion." She was plump and acne-scarred, her legs thick as sugar pines from this punishing kind of work.

"Why don't you take them? If a pretty girl takes them home, then I haven't spent in vain."

Her tough face softened. "Isn't that sweet of you! I will. Seafood buffet tonight. All the crab legs you can eat. Salad bar, dessert island, eleven ninety-five, coffee and tea extra."

He smiled. "You're too young to remember this, but a long time ago, before this town started tying ribbons in its knickers, you could get stuffed like a Thanksgiving turkey at the El Rancho for the sum of one single American dollar."

She laughed. "Well, times change, but people don't. You look thirsty. What can I bring a handsome gentleman like yourself in the way of refreshment?" She glanced backward for a moment, taking inventory of those legs, turning one ankle prettily. The gesture looked old enough to come out of one of Meridel's antique stores.

It stabbed him, how she was throwing on the charm, flirting so hard for a twenty-dollar bunch of hothouse roses. Over the edge of this smiling and polite talk, Bop knew she would be his in the bedsheets the moment she knocked off work, without so much as an exchange of surnames. It was what the world had come to, strangers screwing themselves into a sweat, looking for passion in friction. That particular realization made him feel all the more desolate at this neatly set table. The best thing was to pull back, keep the exchange simple. "Any old bourbon will be just fine."

She sashayed toward the bartender, one heavy-hipped mama with moonlight on her mind. Beneath the poundage and support hose, he could almost make out a thinner version of her, just aching for company, but presently it was being held inmate in a fat holding cell. Not so different really from his own needs or his own failures, she just wore hers on the outside. At the thought of his limp member he grew anxious for the alcohol.

"Here you go. Anything you want you don't see, just ask. My name's Tonya."

"Thanks. I believe this'll do me."

She went off to seat a raucous party of twelve who weren't at all in need of spirits.

As he swirled the drink with his forefinger, tasted it and felt the fire seep down his throat, he could once again recall the attraction of drink. Through it, life looked pleasantly swirly, like sitting atop a carousel pony, reaching for the gold ring. Pony rides were easier on the soul than feeling let down. Even overweight, rode-hard women like Missy Tonya grew soft and kind through the arc of a wet glass. He placed the rim to his lips and felt a tap on his shoulder.

This time it wasn't the waitress. It was a tiny platinum blond, ninety percent of her head covered by a red bandanna, the same cotton material the Mexicans rolled into headbands and wore to keep the sweat from their eyes on the Shadow Ranch. It hadn't kept her eyes safe; she was obviously fighting tears. He set the drink down and politely rose to his feet. "Ma'am? Something I can do for you?"

She gestured for him to sit down and sniffled. "Smokey insisted we all get our hair done by this makeup artist she's good friends with. Well, I always do my own hair, and I'm particular about how I get it cut. I tried to explain that to him, but he got to chatting about his boyfriend problems, and what with chopping here and perming there, I ended up looking like a French-fried poodle. I been in my room three hours trying to fix this mess up with nail scissors." She threw her arms up in exasperation. "It's hopeless. And on top of all that I made you wait so long. Can you forgive me, Charles?"

Earlynn—her voice all shimmers and high notes—she was one long country road prettier than television had given her credit for. Dressed in a white T-shirt decorated with gold glitter and yellow paint-tube hibiscus flowers and tight yellow stretch pants, at once she lifted his spirits. He waited for her to slide into the booth next to him. He smelled a clean, womanly smell, backed up by something soft that could have been baby powder. "There's worse things need forgiveness than arriving late, Earlynn."

She patted the bandanna self-consciously. "Oh, you're kind to say that. But you must've thought I had the manners of a wild dog, leaving you sitting there almost an hour, not answering my phone."

She looked about as wild as a lap dog hand-fed gourmet biscuits, and so adorable he could hardly get his words in order to make a sentence. He touched her hand with his forefinger. "Let's just put those forty minutes in the past. You're here now. Are you hungry?"

He called the waitress over. Miss Tonya hid her

disappointment as she listened carefully while he explained the drinks he wanted the bartender to make—how it was most important to roll the lemons across the counter a full 360 degrees before squeezing them. "Might as well take this," he said, pointing a finger at the bourbon. "Toss it out with the dishwater."

The smile the waitress gave him was part of a patented expression, one with a wealthy bank of happiness reserved for other people's lives. He'd tuck a twenty dollar bill under his plate for her. It wasn't a date, but it would buy her a couple of hot fudge sundaes while she waited for her prince.

CHAPTER 10

SIN AND BUSYWORK

BELLIES FULL OF CRAB LEGS, BOP AND EARLYNN walked the hot July night, circling the hotel grounds, watching late-model cars race in and out of the parking lot. "Look at them go," Bop said, "Everyone's in such a rush."

Earlynn smiled at him. "Missing what's important and wasting fossil fuel."

"What do you find important, Earlynn?"

"Life. Every single breath of it. If I had my way, I'd slow it down to a crawl."

"Really?"

"Well, not all the time, but when it feels this good, yes."

They stopped alongside the rectangle of turquoise hotel swimming pool, its surface unbroken by bathers or wind-driven ripples. The steaming whirlpool was shut down for the night and the glow from a hundred television sets lit the hotel's windows.

"Feel like sitting awhile, honey?"

"Why, that'd suit me just fine, Charles."

Bop drew two chaise longues close. Unlike at home in the Harbour, he found little peace by this water. The racket from the MGM Grand carried so far it felt like they were two crash-landed aliens, the carnival in the near distance their worst nightmare. His hearing aid could hardly keep up. If the noise bothered Earlynn, she didn't show it. She settled herself and tucked her feet up daintily on the chaise. Pink toes glinted from spaces between the gold-strap sandals, featuring toenails painted a signature shade of peach.

"I was wondering if you'd mind telling me something. If it's none of my business, just whomp me upside the head."

Earlynn laughed. "There's nothing secret about my life. Anybody who goes on a TV talk show might as well turn her IRS records over to the newspaper."

Bop shuddered, imagining Mac Henry's palpitations if he heard that one. "Well, I was wondering how it was you got into stripping. I mean, not to stand in judgment, not that at all, Earlynn. It's just not your regular career choice."

They were at that point in their conversation. He'd told her about most of his successes and a few of the failures, how the specter of death seemed to sting the Carpenter family every time it made a whisker's width of progress. He'd told her how Spencer had gone and left them and how it seemed like there was nothing much left to call a family except his grandkids' lack of ambition and his glut of the same. Now it was her turn. He knew however she responded would spell out the future of their relationship. Either she'd wade through the truth and they'd become friends, or she'd sidestep, insist she "preferred to dwell on happier days," they'd mutter their polite good-byes and she would fade from this bright night to unreliable memory by morning.

Earlynn took off her scarf and ran her fingers through her cropped hair. It had dried into soft waves in the heat and, besides being too short, didn't look all that bad, in his estimation.

"Well, after Wayne took off on me, I had the two boys all to myself," she explained. "They still needed blue jeans and sneakers, cans of spaghetti, pencils, notebook paper, and puppy shots. All that about cost an arm and a leg to a five-and-dime clerk. Not to mention medical bills for little Dewayne! I worked the hot nuts machine and stocked sundries. I had aspirations of making head cashier, but probably would've had to wait for the owner to die for it to happen." She shook her finger at him. "You try finding a job that pays a gal more than minimum wage in Fort Worth. I dare you. There wasn't no choice for me but to dance or give up my sons. I always called it 'dance,' Charles; I figured that made it sound a little more respectable to the boys. I started local, and then I made my way to the bigger cities, Tulsa, Dallas, Cleveland, Chicago, Miami, Vegas. My sister Carol watched the kids when I traveled so they could stay at the same school. Always told them, 'Mama's got to go on a business trip now, boys. Ya'll behave for Auntie Carol.'" Her smile tightened, and she stopped talking long enough to touch up her peach-colored lipstick. "I never did any of that other stuff that usually goes along with it, but there was times I came close. But skip to the bottom line! I was a stripper. I was pretty good at it, too, not to brag on myself or nothing.

129

I kept my dancing very artistic and tasteful, using the fans after everyone quit using anything. And I never touched drugs. That's about all there is to it, Charles. The grand finale was some college kid calling up asking me to fly to New York and be on Sally's show." Her eyes teased. "I'll have you know yours wasn't the only bouquet I got sent."

"No doubt. What made you call me?"

"For one thing, you didn't talk dirty in your card. They weren't just generous flowers, they were thoughtful. And I'll admit, the plane ticket trick impressed me."

"Wasn't a trick."

"I know that now."

"What then? Why me and not the other guy?"

"Just a feeling I got."

"I'll be damned. For once in my life I suppose I'm grateful for women's intuition."

"So now you know my life story, Charles. Funny how every time I tell it, it gets a little bit shorter. That's what happens when you grow old, isn't it? You can leave more out and still get the job done."

"You're right. Where's Dewayne and his brother now?"

She tilted her head and looked wistful. "Frank's wife moved him to Abilene to be nearer her folks. She's a nice gal, real Christian. They did good with their lives. I got me two granddaughters in college, do you believe it? Smart girls, going far in the world. Frank lives in a red brick house with a wrap-around porch. That's what he does, brickwork. We don't see each other much. Not since his wife took up with this strict church."

She faced him and Bop saw her mouth quiver a little. He guessed the daughter-in-law's church didn't have

130

much to say about retired strippers. "It seems to me you did pretty well by those boys. Nothing beats good masonry. Getting to be a lost art. And Dewayne?"

She waited a moment, and it seemed to Bop her smile struggled to gather itself. "Down's kids don't live a regular life span. The doctors all told me he was just some kind of a miracle baby, hanging on until twenty-five. I buried him next to the prettiest oak tree in the entire cemetery. Lightning hit it a few years back, split it right down the middle. But I kind of think Dewayne would've gotten a kick out of that. He wasn't the brightest Crayola in the box, but he sure loved life. And bad weather. Always running out in storms without his galoshes, tilting his mouth open like a turkey, drinking rainwater, catching himself these terrible colds."

Bop touched her hand. "I'm sorry."

She patted his hand back and he could hear the clatter of her plastic bangle bracelets. "Don't be! He might not've had the longest life on earth, but we got a few good years in, especially when he was little. Lord, he was just precious, the happiest boy. After he came of age, things got a little rough for me to manage. Nature's urges don't skip over the retarded, you know. Eventually I had to put him in the hospital, and I don't know which one of us hated that more. He's with his maker now. That's got to be more peaceful than anything here on earth."

"So they say. I mean, that's how I try to look at Chuck's and little Spencer's passing. The only trouble I have with that line of reasoning is believing there is a maker."

"That's a whole other can of worms to cut open some other night. Think how hard it must be for your granddaughter, Charles. Poor Elaine, losing Spencer so

131

sudden."

"Nothing easy about it for any of us."

She looked directly into his eyes. "But a mother takes it hardest. After all, that baby started inside of her. She felt his little arms and legs grow and push at her and she went through the pains of labor to give him life. Then poof, all of a sudden, nothing to hold except pictures and memories and baby blankets. Cold comfort when your arms are empty."

"My head knows you're right, Earlynn. Wish it'd explain it to my heart."

She put her other hand on his face. "Oh, Charles. You poor, sweet man. Believing is so much easier than you make it out to be. Accept what's happened and go on."

"How?"

"Faith in your higher power."

"I got some trouble with that particular concept."

In the distance, Bop could hear the whoop of some happy hotel room party. It was past midnight. The anniversary of his great-grandson's death had officially concluded. He could spend 364 days working up to another night like this, and higher power or not, it wouldn't go any easier. Despite all that, he didn't think he could feel any better had he spent the day buying the grandkids U.S. Savings Bonds. "It's late. You getting tired?"

Earlynn shook her head. "I ought to be, what with Smokey's dress fittings and this rat's nest they made of my hair. I'm just a mess of coffee jitters and I'm not even the bride! Tomorrow will be a long day, but I know if I go to bed now, I'll just toss and turn. You go in if you want. I might stay up a while."

"Why don't we go on up to my room and watch some

132

of that free HBO? I could order room service if you're hungry."

She laughed. "Charles, this late there's nothing on that channel but dirty movies."

He stammered. "That's—that's not my intention, honest. Christ, I couldn't even if I wanted to." Somehow the confession had just blurted itself out, and he wished he could redo the last few minutes of his life.

Earlynn eyed him primly. "Is that the way it is?"

He wiped his forehead and grimaced at her straightforwardness. "It's not important. And I sure didn't ask to meet you expecting a cure." He looked up at the desert sky, pleading with the few visible stars to rescue him. "Can we start this conversation over again?"

She patted his knee. "I've got a better idea. Let's go watch us a movie."

"Earlynn, I told you on the phone, I'm not like that. Besides, I like you too much to disappoint you."

"How can you disappoint me? I'm not talking about sex, sugar, I'm talking about going to sleep. Right up there, in that king bed together. We were put here on earth to comfort one another, Charles. That can be a two-way street."

Her knock at his door coincided with first light. Wordlessly, she crawled into the sheets first, her satin peach-colored nightie wafting that same pleasant, powdery female scent. He got in after, his striped boxers looking almost too festive for slumber. They lay there side by side, Bop so nervous that if this pounding in his chest didn't let up he might need to go to his shaving kit for heart medicine.

Then Earlynn turned to him, lifted up his left arm, snuggled herself in the crook there, and laid one hand

133

across his hairy chest. He curled his arm around her, feeling her solid warmth, her petite body melding itself to his side. His fingers accidentally brushed her breast, and before he could mumble an apology, she reached up and cupped his hand around the soft mound of flesh.

"We're adults. Nobody in this bed's taking the slightest bit advantage. We'll take things slow and just see what develops. We won't expect anything magnificent right off." She kissed his fingertips one by one, holding on to the lime-green cast. "Isn't kissing nice?" she whispered. "People are so eager to get to the elephants they don't spend enough time in the petting zoo."

Kissing was nice. But in his mind he could see the awful pamphlet the doctor had given him explaining the Osbon pump, this awful plastic cylinder that was supposed to fluff up his member to a weak facsimile of an erection. Bop thought he might die of embarrassment if he tried taking things further and couldn't follow through, so he just held her there, rubbing the fingers of his hand up and down the small of her back, feeling the evenly spaced bones of a dancer's spine.

"Good night, my friend."

"Good night, Earlynn."

Then the room was quiet, and they were both breathing deeply, arms around each other, aiming toward sleep.

"Charles? I'll be going now."

Going where? From a rustle of peach silk, Earlynn's voice tunneled into Bop's dream, where at ten years of age, he'd been driving his father's Ford from Shadow Ranch to San Diego for the first time, solo. They were horse-trading that day, as well as stocking up on supplies for his mother. It was necessary to have two cars to haul back both the horse trailer and the foodstuffs. Necessity dimmed all other concerns, a method of rationalization Charles senior regularly employed. How shaken Bop had been, gripping the oversized steering wheel in his long fingers for the first time. His father had taken for granted that a boy could perform this task without rehearsal. A nervous Charles had barely slept the night before, picturing how he'd handle passing trucks, which abounded on the road, and now here he was seventy years later, hardly any more rested, Earlynn's soft hand pressing what had evolved into an old man's shoulder.

He blinked as past melded into present—hotel room, pervading scent of room deodorizer competing with the slight tartness of his unwashed body, this new woman about to leave his bed. "Don't go, honey," he told her. "Stay. We'll order breakfast."

Her smile was honestly regretful. "I'd like to, but there's too much to do for the wedding. I promised Smokey I'd help her paint her face on. Besides, look at your watch. It's afternoon, and as my Texas daddy used to say, past time for church or second thoughts."

There was so much more he wanted to learn about this little blond. In an earlier dream, they'd moved into each other's bodies as easily as shadows on the sidewalk. Bop seated himself on the edge of the bed now, and though there wasn't anything particularly pressing he needed to hide, covered his lower half with the quilted spread. "I don't know about your daddy's clock, Earlynn. If there is an almighty, and notice you don't hear me saying there is, I kind of doubt he'd care what time of day you practiced worship or fried your bacon. But I do know one thing. If this Smokey's half as pretty as you are, she won't need paint to make a handsome bride."

Earlynn laughed, a deep well-water splashing against stone sound, as direct and startling as it was refreshing. "Fact is, Charles, at our age we need all the paint there is. Add it up, old women give the circus clowns a run for their money. Go have some fun around town. This here's Vegas. Sin and busywork on every corner."

Fully awake now, he watched her move toward the hotel room door, an anonymous beige portal that eventually spilled out into the oven of Nevada's summer heat. Before she could shut the door, he said, "I'll only be looking at you during the wedding."

"Then that'll be your loss. Smokey's going to look just beautiful." Earlynn tsked at his expression. "Stop looking so glum. This bridesmaid will save you first dance."

You'd better save them all, he wanted to say. But Earlynn might interpret that remark as overbearing, possessive, an attempt at claiming territory to which he held no paper. Women—no matter how many you had known—trying to speak their language was a trepidatious business. The door clicked shut. Everything was still save for the air conditioner's faithful hum. Well, he could sit here thinking about his poor limp dickens or he could find himself a distraction. He slapped his hands down on his thighs. Time to set aside these thoughts and move out among the natives.

Still damp from his shower, Bop leafed through the guide on the desk. Choices: gamble, eat yourself sick, go gawk at Liberace's thirty-pound rhinestone tuxedo. The ExCalibur hotel advertised horseflesh on the premises. Royal Lipizzaner stallions, no less. It seemed doubtful

136

you could do much with horses in 120-degree heat except hose them down every two hours in an attempt to avoid heatstroke, but he decided to check it out.

Now he sat in traffic, waiting for an opening, nosing the truck forward by inches. Old age wasn't boring—if you weren't happy where you were, all you need do was focus your thoughts and wham-bam, there you were, two-and-a-half decades earlier, plunking down eleven hundred American dollars for Lainie's Banjo Man, a strawberry Appaloosa Pony of the Americas. Chuck'd about had a litter of puppies, as if the occasion of a granddaughter's tenth birthday wasn't deserving of anything more elegant than a new Schwinn bicycle.

"You're spoiling my kids, Dad," Chuck had said, standing there in his white short-sleeved shirt and J.C. Penney slacks. "You want to explain to me how us getting Lainie a new Barbie doll for her birthday is supposed to measure up to you giving her a pony?"

"What's a grandfather supposed to do? Hold back while they're young, have them inherit a bushel basket of moldy cash when they're too old and world-weary to have any fun on it?"

Chuck had set his jaw, shoved his fists into his pockets. His teacher's salary barely covered cube steak and Keds. Chuck could have opted for an office next door to his, read the *Wall Street Journal* instead of trudging off to back to school night, his arms full of math books and hope. "Don't do this, Dad."

"This time you can bark until you're blue in the nuts, Chuck. I'm not sending him back. Lainie keeps the goddamn horse and you can learn to live with it."

The reward of thirty years' perspective was the luxury of certain moments like that one, laminated for all time. What had Bop done besides smother those kids, even if

137

he'd done so in the name of love?

From Eddie Whistler had come word of a stout little Appy sporting no outward faults other than some idiot had gelded him. Lainie's pony was "made," possessed even gaits, and was "horsey" in stature—none of that blocky pony build and accompanying snotty attitude.

He'd never forget her face when he handed her the reins. She was too Carpenter to resort to a girlish act like crying over her heart's desire. Lainie went straight to the pony's legs and ran her stubby fingers down every inch, checking from cannon bone to pastern, using her developing horsewoman's eye to measure proper angle and ample bone mass. Only when the legs passed muster did she untie the ribbon from his halter and say, "Thank you, Bop, oh, thank you, thank you, thank you!" He collected a kiss, and she set to exploring the rest of him, stroking, crooning, memorizing his sturdy body, digging her fingers into his neck, lacing them in a possessive lock around the swanlike crest. That lucky horse had checked into a permanent suite at the Hilton. Bop and Ed Whistler sat on the fence smoking their pipes.

Ed, who hardly ever said anything much at all other than "Your rent check's late," remarked, "Seeing equine love visit your own issue almost beats a day's ride."

Bop agreed. "Except for those times we rode fence with the Portola boys."

"No, you couldn't beat them days," Ed concurred. "Or playing Knickerbocker Glory balancing beers instead of the ball. Shitfire, Carpenter, appears we've turned into old men."

"Giving our grandkids horses isn't so bad a way to wind down the clock, is it?"

Ed, who'd had some trouble with his grandsons using

138

recreational drugs and was always emptying his pockets to make their bail, smoked a while before answering. "I guess it's preferable to sprouting a boil on my hinder."

Bop shifted against the custom upholstery in his truck. Traffic was thinning. At this rate he might make the ExCalibur by dinner, just enough time to turn around and head off toward the chapel to meet Earlynn—wearing these same dirty blue jeans. What a shame she'd had that Down's baby. Seemed almost worse than what happened to Lainie, but when you lost them, all tragedies were filed under the same heading. He made his right turn and finally got to check out the slow corner. Well, hell's bells. A mime in a shiny black' suit was performing some silly antics that would have gotten anyone else locked up. Hope it nets you a nice bout of heat prostration, Bop thought, and turned into the parking structure of the ExCalibur.

He collected his ticket and started across the cement, slowing his pace as the heat rose up in thick, choking waves.

By comparison to Lainie, Russell ran around tripping on the laces and bloodying his nose, a permanent grape-colored Type-O stain marking the front of every T-shirt. In third grade, some bully had taken a fancy to chasing Russell home every day after school, just so he could have the pleasure of throwing the slight boy in the ivy. Chuck said, "Ignore him and he'll get tired of it," but Bop took the boy aside and taught him to make a fist. "Next time, pop him one in his smart mouth." Russell elected to jump in the ivy on a voluntary basis.

Lainie was full of pure Carpenter willingness, daring failure by always trying. Russell honed to an art avoiding confrontations. His sister bent poles and ran the cloverleaf around barrels while Russell amused himself

139

putting together a splinter collection culled from fenceposts. Of course, since Spencer, Lainie's instinctive abilities had about dried up. And Russell? Well, he would always be handy at selling old records and plunking guitar. Lainie was good for nothing lately except emotional outbursts like that business back at the house.

He worried constantly she'd land herself back in the hospital. People understood breaking down—once. They made allowances, but not forever. Get the crazies again, she might as well file a change of address. Lainie spent half her life dreaming who knew what, doing crazy things—like cooking up twelve loaves of bread at a time, just loading them up on the kitchen table and letting them set there molding—so Nick had said the day he called asking Bop for help. And that husband of hers! Foregoing his trade as a woodworker for the loony idea of psychology being mankind's Band-Aid of the nineties. How much good had it done his wife?

Part of her strange behavior had to do with genetic bad luck on the LeVasseur side, but at least she wasn't an antique hound like Meridel. Rooms full of ceramic statues, ugly vases—now there was a valuable pastime. Maybe Earlynn was right. Grief had hold of his granddaughter by the neck, not unlike Russell's elementary school bully.

"Which way to the horses?" Bop asked as he entered the ExCalibur hotel lobby, raising his voice above the chatter of happy gamblers.

A generic young man enthusiastically pressed a color brochure into his hands, automatically opening his own for a tip, as smoothly as performing a card trick. Bop passed him a folded five. Sometime today, that fiver was on its way to the slots, the blackjack table, or craps,

140

because here in Lucky Town, money was more recyclable than aluminum soda cans. He tipped his hat to some pretty tourist women, standing aside so that they could go first into the sightseeing queue, and opened the brochure. "The Royal White Stallions of the Spanish Riding School," it insisted, then in fine print, the inevitable disclaimer: "In actuality, only two of our horses descend from that particular line of breeding; however, the maneuvers all the horses perform are identical in nature to the Vienna Riding School's 'Airs Above the Ground.' "

"Hope it don't smell like horse plop in here," one lady in a sparkly sequined American flag T-shirt confided to her tour mate. "This heat coupled with horse doo, I'm done for."

Bop couldn't resist a reply. "I heard they spray the horses with cologne."

The woman lifted her oversized sunglasses and peered at him while she decided whether or not he was telling the truth. She looked like a shabby owl.

Widows traveled in packs, dressed in high-collars that denied their bosoms. They were permanently hungry for the early bird dinner specials and discount tours. So few sexy women of a certain age left in the world, he mused. After fifty, most packed the old libido into mothballs. Earlynn seemed an exception.

"In a moment, we'll step up behind the golden ropes for a closeup view of these magnificent creatures," the guide intoned, "however, under no circumstances feed the animals. This includes popcorn, candy, gum, and gambling chips, folks. Let's save the latter for the casino!"

The small crowd, or at least those who hadn't yet lost all their money, cheered like good little cattle. My great

141

good fortune continues, Bop thought. I get to be part of yet another slow-moving line.

Chuck had grown up riding borrowed or rented horses, but that was only because the Carpenter coffers weren't quite so full when he was Lainie's age. Was the tradition of middle-class poverty any reason to continue to behave selfishly?

Charles senior had lived like a pauper and expected Bop to wear high-waters Levi's with Calvinist pride. He'd never found an act important enough to impress his father. The only natural talent Bop could claim was his innate ability to cull decent horseflesh from ordinary. His father'd let him ride any horse he wanted on the Shadow acreage, but as soon as Bop and the horse were of a similar mindset, his father would up and give the animal to one of the Mexicans, who'd ruin it rodeoing every weekend over the border. *Charriada*. He could still hear the sound of the whips they used. The great inhumane thuds when they went to tripping the horses. They called such cruelty tradition. *Mangana* was outlawed now. But those long nights they practiced, he'd put his pillow over his head to muffle his sobs. Feather ticking didn't shut out the vision of his father putting a bullet in the head of one mare gone lame. He could still hear the horses' pitiful whinnying.

Gentling was a simple art, but nobody wanted to take the time for kindness when it was easier to corner a horse's spirit and beat it to death with a length of rawhide. At Bop's argument, the old man went to fists and he got a black eye. Horses got beaten until the day Charles I died. The Mexicans wept like it was one of their own saints passing. They brought armloads of flowers for the grave of a man who'd begrudged them a small amount of pay for working very hard making him rich. Bop stood

142

alongside his mother at the funeral, feeling like some big old dirty Santa Ana wind had finally blown the whole mess out and away toward the Pacific.

Just like Patton helping free the Lipizzaners, his first official act as ranch foreman was taking back the horses. From that moment forward, there would be no rodeoing over the border with Shadow animals. Next, he built a fire, stoked it high, tossed in every last whip in the barn, and sat watching the flames, taking comfort in the smell of burning leather. He gathered up spurs, dug a grave, and buried them six feet underground, same as the old man. Then he tucked his son into bed, made love to his wife, and went out to check on his lemon trees.

Here came the tour guide again, a big smile on her face. "Ladies and gentlemen, there'll be a short delay while we move our previous tour group out through the gift shop. If you'll just be patient . . ."

She'll herd us to the feed troughs next, Bop sighed. Watch me get ponied alongside the widow women and force-fed a generous scoop of senior-discount gruel.

Lainie could shinny up her pony's tail and lie across his back drinking a Coke, the horse so used to her weight he'd nod off, dreaming of sweet oats. When her legs practically touched the ground as she straddled him, Bop retired the animal to a ranch in Santa Barbara, and bought her Habañero Chili Pepper, a hotblooded sorrel gelding with one white sock that looked as if it was falling down over his hoof. Nero challenged her. A summer of pole bending, cutting cows, and then the worst imaginable struck—thirteen-year-old Lainie caught the National Velvet bug, the itch to ride those tall, nervous hunter-jumpers over the highest fences she could find. Then Chuck died so unexpectedly, changing everything. Nero jumped puddles for Lainie, because in his mind water was untrustworthy. But unable to see any good reason to jump fences when it was safer for all concerned to walk around them, he refused to go along with this nonsense, twisting his tail into a figure eight the moment she buckled that half-assed Crump saddle across his broad back. All Bop could think was, What if she broke her neck, that pretty white neck bent at a wrong angle forever, his tough-talking Lainie-gal lying still under a cold gravestone same as his son. Without explanation, he'd cut off her request for a thoroughbred. It was Nero or nothing. "You're mean," she cried. "You don't want me to be a better rider than you are."

"Nonsense," he'd fired back, hearing Chuck's early concerns come back to haunt him. "Quit acting like a spoiled brat and be thankful for what's been handed you."

She'd lumped along, never once letting the horse down in terms of proper care, but doing far worse by him by withholding her heart. Then a solid month went by and she hadn't taken the horse out once to ride, so Bop sold the horse to Eddie, whose granddaughter was looking for a roping horse. Lainie wouldn't speak to him. She stayed clear of the stables altogether. She was sixteen, getting into that stage when she wore so much eye paint that every time she blinked she looked like a startled iguana. It was a stage, and stages passed, but never quickly enough. After the bad news from Santa Barbara came, the failed colic surgery on her pony, he'd thought about waiting to tell her Banjo'd died, then decided no, death was part of the package.

He showed up in her living room after school one afternoon, sat down on the couch to wait, hat in hand. She came in the door, a child in a skirt too short to be legal. Flat out, he told her, "Got some real sad news, honey. Your old Banjo Man has lit on out for the great

144

hayfield in the sky."

Her tears came in a flood, as much for her daddy as that first horse. The only gift of this shared sorrow was that it sent her into his arms. Meridel stood in the doorway, polishing some hideous old vase bought on Chuck's insurance money, observing her weeping daughter, never once coming over to pat Lainie's back or say she was sorry.

Bop lied. He told her it was a quick, painless passing, mumbling something about the old pony going to sleep and not waking up, the only way he ever wanted Lainie to hear about death again. They made up—temporarily. Such was the case in all Carpenter family alliances. A week later he bought the sailboat, taught Lainie port from starboard, watched her tan deepen as she sunned herself on the dock, frying the grief out of her. Sometimes they ate pepper and tomato sandwiches, or steaks slathered in yellow mustard. She'd take the photo albums of her father as a child into the living room and study them all day long. One more season of childhood. Then she was lost to her grandpa for good.

Death was like a paper wasp's nest, growing so quietly under the eaves that you never noticed. The insects perpetually aimed their stingers at the Carpenter clan— all of them seemed to come together only when they had to bury someone who wasn't supposed to die that early. You could set out Big Stinkys, plug in a king-sized bug Zapper, spray the sons-of-bitches with strong poison, but the larger insect remained immortal. To spare his grandchildren pain, he would have gladly given himself in place of Chuck and Spencer. Such bargaining fell short. What could an old man do besides distract himself with women?

"Ladies and gentlemen," the tour guide announced—

and from her expression Bop thought, Well, finally, looks like I might get my five dollars' worth—"may I present the Royal Lipizzaners?"

She gave a slatted sliding door on a well-oiled track a shove. Suddenly, a half-dozen pale noses were peeking over stall doors, curious, wondering whether this latest intrusion meant food or work. The horses' stalls were five feet back, designed to keep the tourists' cameras at a safe distance. Thankfully, someone'd had enough sense to insist that no flashbulbs were allowed. Nevertheless, clicking shutters and speedy film went to work recording as the guide rattled off her rehearsed spiel.

"Just fifty years ago, these magnificent animals were on the verge of extinction, exiled during our Second World War. Originally trained to perform the airs above the ground for dexterity in battle, Vienna's national treasures were secreted away to the village of St. Martin. After the Hungarian Riding School was destroyed by bombing, villagers and horse lovers alike conspired to reunite what remained of the Spanish Riding School. Thanks to the American forces' intervention in Operation Cowboy, these lovely examples you see standing here today directly descend from those same fortuitous animals.

"Born a pewter gray to almost black, they develop this distinctive silver-white coloring as they age. This mare is twenty-seven, and last spring she gave birth to her seventeenth foal . . ."

As if cued, a wet-eyed baby face looked up from his mama's flank. The cameras clicked in triple time and the widows in the sparkly T-shirts shoved their hands into their purses for something, anything they could feed this bright-eyed darling.

Bop stayed a good pace behind the tour, picking out

the noticeable idiosyncrasies common to the breed. Patton's remark regarding crossing the line of demarcation to free the horses went something like, "No sense letting the Russians have 'em."

War cleaned house, made equals out of every man. All these stinking weekend wars had no use for courage. Nowadays they built costly bombs, sneaked in germ warfare, lied about it, and took their conscienceless revenge on the next generation of babies.

In his spine he felt the unnatural chill of the air conditioning begin to collect, and as the tour moved ahead, he took advantage of the lull to push aside the chain and take a closer look at the horses. He held up his hand to feel the exhalation of the nearest muzzle against his flesh.

"Aren't you boys something to look at," he whispered through the stall bars. Then, not wanting to shun the mare, he added, "Ladies, too. I wonder if I bought you and trailered you home with me whether that would put the smile back on my granddaughter's face."

"Sir?" the tour guide prodded. "Are you keeping up with us? We're walking."

"Oh, yes, ma'am," he said, reluctant to move on at all, "I'm walking, too."

CHAPTER 11

THE LIFE YOU SAVE MAY BE YOUR OWN

THE SAXOPHONE PLAYER STUBBED OUT HIS cigarette to blow the first few notes of "Fly Me to the Moon," which coincided with Earlynn's dainty steps down the chapel aisle. Leave it to retired strippers to hire the best jazz quartet in all of Vegas, then find a church willing to substitute jazz for old-woman hymns and organ.

Earlynn's French-fried hair teased out in a white-blond halo couldn't help but remind him of the Lipizzaner baby's mane. She wore a red sheath dress slit clear up to her thigh, and every time she baby-stepped forward in time to the music, leg as taut and interesting as a female leg of any age could ever strive to be shone through. Beneath all that Texas hardscrabble, watermelon rind, and perfume, Bop thought, there lies undeniable class. She held her bouquet of wilting lilies in front of her, as poised as the queen of England.

Apparently he wasn't the only impressed onlooker—the horn player went off on a crisp little tangent at the "in other words" section of the song, giving Earlynn a solo. She dissolved in breathless laughter as she stood in place, waiting him out. The other attendants were nice enough. Tradition was important, but following the rules got you folks like George Bush.

Greatness, Bop decided, came from thumbing your nose at the status quo. His stripper had more class than an ivy league college. And last night they'd slept in the same bed—Bop couldn't wait for the I do's to be said to see if that miracle might repeat itself. He checked his watch—ten minutes already, and still more bridesmaids coming, in more red dresses. There was an abundance of fine leg to be found under them all.

The fellow next to him in the pew poked his arm, whispering, "Smokey's marrying some big-ass cop."

"Is that so?" The groom stood at the altar, smiling at the bridesmaids, looking like your typical nervous groom. Bop checked the man's tuxedo to see if he was packing a firearm. "Looks kind of soft for an officer of

148

the law."

"You're telling me. Got this plum desk job in Houston. They're flying out tonight. I just hate the thought of never seeing that tall redhead naked again. Damn. I'd marry her myself, but she can't stand my face."

"Puts a damper on the situation."

"Here she comes now. Look at her. You ever seen any woman so pretty?"

Bop shook his head no to make the guy feel better. The bride wore a white dress and rose-bedecked cowboy hat. As the jilted seatmate insisted, she was pretty, and Bop appreciated her bow to the western tradition, but she remained a far cry from his type. He whispered to the broken-hearted man, "Doesn't this wedding strike you as moving a tad slow by Vegas standards?"

He sighed. "Guess they wanted a day to remember. I know I won't be forgetting it anytime soon."

They wanted Earlynn to ride along with the wedding party from the chapel to the Dunes, so Bop drove along behind them, watching through the rear window of the limo as the laughing bridal attendants popped the cork on a bottle of champagne. He took back his earlier thoughts concerning widows and marriage. They looked so happy. Maybe happiness was as simple as Earlynn claimed—you just accepted things on faith and went about your life.

While the jazz quartet set up at their new station inside the hotel, and guests nibbled on thumbnail-sized sandwiches and guzzled oysters, Earlynn shook hands in the receiving line. She had a genuine interest in whichever guest stood before her. Her attention focused on that person 100 percent. Alyce'd had a similar way with people. She was a wonderful hostess, even if the people she was entertaining might decide *not* to drop a lawsuit against her husband. She cooked authentic Mexican food long before it was popular. *The true test of a Mexican cook is in her chile rellenos,* Alyce always said. Hers melted on the tongue like spicy little clouds.

In his mind, he tried fitting Earlynn into Casa de Carpenter, just to see what the combination might deliver. Just tiny enough that she might not bitch about the lowered ceilings, Texas enough she might appreciate the rough stonework in the living room. He was curious what her preference leaned toward in the way of art, and tried as he had many times before to imagine parting with his beloved western art. To hang some washed-out watercolor of street urchins where Maynard Dixon's herd of wild horses brought tears to weary eyes.

The saxophone may have set the mood for all this pondering, and music could go a long way in creating ambiance, but he guessed what had made him finally tip from a prickle of intrigue to the undeniable pinpricks of love was the sound of an ambulance siren. Smokey's brother, a rather portly fellow who looked less than pressed in his rented tux, was line-dancing with the young girls, making a total fool out of himself.

"Pay no attention to Jimmy Lee," Smokey apologized as she passed by Earlynn and Bop's table. "However, when he gets to clogging, that's when I start asking for volunteers."

"Count on us," Earlynn said and hugged her friend.

"An enterprising endeavor, that line dance," Bop commented when Smokey had moved on to warn her other guests.

"Well, I don't know," Earlynn answered. "All it looks like to me is some kind of crazy exercise routine. I'd sooner slow dance. Less chance of pulling a muscle, you can snuggle up to your sweetie, and when nobody's looking, maybe steal a kiss."

"How about I ask the band to play something slow?"

"That would be nice, Charles."

Bop was on his feet, threading his way through the crowd, now involved in some triple-time cowboy dancing that required footstamping and slapping the person nearest you on the posterior. It wouldn't go far around horses, Bop was planning to tell Earlynn when he'd finished his errand—the perfect opening line to introduce an important subject. But then Jimmy Lee, his face a florid pink that rivaled the contents of the punch bowl, started moaning about chest pains, and before anyone could say put your head between your knees, he was down on the dance floor, clutching his left arm, looking seriously gray.

Bop tried to get to him, but half the guests were still whooping it up, dancing that crazy dance, blocking his path. While everyone else was gawking, Earlynn toed out of her pumps, threw herself onto Smokey's brother, and began delivering the breath of life. She pounded her clasped hands into his chest. In between breaths and counting out loud, she took a moment to call, "Anybody else here know CPR?"

Bop knew CPR. After Chuck, a Red Cross class had been his first attempt at atonement. As he bent over the man, a vision of Spencer in his hospital room, blue-faced, laboring for every breath, flooded his mind.

"One, Mississippi, two, Mississippi, three—come on, Jimmy Lee, don't you dare wreck this day for your sister," Earlynn counted.

As Bop pressed the heels of his hands down, his broken wrist smarted inside the cast. Their rhythm

151

quickly synchronized. Perhaps up to now they'd been wandering the globe, rehearsing for this particular moment. She continued to blow, and he to push the heel of his good hand down hard, sending an urgent message through the layers of fat. How could he let a woman this determined go?

"I think we got a little bit of a pulse here," he told Earlynn after five minutes, and she sagged with relief, lipstick smeared all over her face.

"Well, thank God."

"We'll take it from here," the paramedics said, and Earlynn and Bop stepped away from Smokey's brother and back into their ordinary lives.

"He breathing on his own?"

"Yes, ma'am."

"I didn't break any ribs with my cast?"

"Doesn't look like it, sir. You two did everything just fine. Good teamwork."

IVs were duly hung, the gurney loaded into the ambulance, and the paramedics were on their way to the hospital. Smokey and her cop husband rode along. "Stay and dance," she urged everyone. "Earlynn, make sure somebody cuts the cake and here, you take this for me."

Bop watched as the bride tossed her maid of honor the bridal bouquet. Earlynn's face grew wistful and embarrassed staring at those pretty flowers tied up in white lace and baby ferns. She caught him watching. There were tears in her eyes.

"Oh," she said, touching her mouth. "Where on earth's my handbag? I need my lipstick. I'm sure I look like the original sea hag."

"You don't need lipstick," Bop said quietly to the bridesmaid who stood there in her stocking feet. "You're beautiful. Come home with me to California, Earlynn. I know, it's not much of a state anymore, but there's a few good spots left and we can make it our life's work to search them out. Come on," he urged her, "say you'll do it."

She fingered the baby's breath. "Charles . . ."

"Hold on a minute." He cleared his throat. "I've done a lot of bad things in my life, Miss Sommers, but never once have I stooped to kidnapping a beautiful woman. Of course, I've never been so sorely tempted as right now. Say you'll give us a try."

She fingered the rose petals with her polished fingernails. "We're too old for this. We make good telephone friends, but we're long past this other."

"Long past this other what?"

She looked downcast, as if the fading high drama of saving a life was being replaced by something almost too dull and painful to bear. "Romantic talk. This idea that between the two of us we got half a future."

The turn surprised him. He gave her words a moment to sink in and thought fleetingly of Jimmy Lee giving a weak thumbs-up sign on his way out strapped to the gurney. "Lady, the future might be marked out in weeks, not decades. Hell if I know what I'm supposed to be doing with it all by myself. I picture us at some kind of crossroads, Earlynn. We can turn down one road or another. Last night sleeping alongside you felt like I'd finally come home to something I been missing for years. You'll break my heart if you say no. Marry me."

She cocked her head, stroking the rose petals, considering his words. After a long moment, during which her sunny face turned sober and then downright sad, she said, "Well, all right then. But kiss me first. I've got to know how a man kisses before I go make his breakfast for the rest of my life. And I really do need some lipstick."

He bent and recovered his hat from where it had fallen onto the carpet during the CPR. Lainie was right; he needed the hat. Across the room, the saxophone player trilled the first few notes into "Birdland," a song Bop admired but hadn't heard played live in thirty years. Toucans and parrots were taking wing throughout his blood, swooping every which way, with their brightly colored beaks pinning his worn-out heart up into well-toned muscle certain it still had a flex or two left in it. In his mind's eye, he reached out and grabbed one of the birds, held it in his hands just long enough to feel a throbbing breast beneath his fingers, then he let it go.

Earlynn screwed her lipstick shut and turned to him. "Ready."

First kisses formed a crossroads, too, separating a man's life from outgrown boyhood. Now in the twilight of his seventy-ninth year, kissing seemed once again just as monumental. He tried to remember the last time he'd kissed a woman with passion and honestly could not recall. He stammered, "You—you do understand that's about all I'm good for, kissing. We're crystal clear on that?"

She sighed. "Charles, to tell you the truth, it's kind of a relief. But hurry up and do it. Don't make an old woman beg."

Her mouth was soft, warm, and sweet, like fresh-from-the-oven lemon meringue pie, sugar spun into egg whites piled high as sand dunes, browned to a crispness on the edges. Her skinny arms around his neck felt as grand as the time he'd stepped off the plane in Hawaii and the nearly naked hula girls had heaped flower leis over his neck. W-E-L-C-O-M-E, her kiss spelled out in capital letters, written in a script so tall it covered

154

acres. On the flip side of that same banner was written: *Buster, I'm holding you to your word. Don't you dare let me down.*

Even before he let go and gave her room to catch her breath, he knew he was going to marry Earlynn Sommers, ex-stripper extraordinaire—with her taped-together sandals and Red Cross certification for saving lives and wholly unique Texas grammar—in front of what was left of his family, whether he had to hog-tie all of them to get them there or not.

PART TWO

THE
SHADOW
RANCH

The great epochs of our lives are at the points
when we gain courage to rebaptize our badness as
the best in us.

— FRIEDRICH NIETZSCHE

CHAPTER 12

A Batman Complex

"IT SAYS," LAINIE COMPLAINED HEATEDLY INTO the telephone receiver, "'You are cordially invited to celebrate Charles Russell Carpenter II's eightieth birthday. Festivities include an evening harbor cruise, California-style barbecue, dessert and dancing. Formal wear requested. RSVP to Miss Sommers,' and then it gives his phone number—like we've forgotten—that's what the cream-colored envelopes in each of our mailboxes says!"

"So, Bop's throwing his own birthday bash," Russell answered back. "Big effing D. It's not like he's squelching our surprise party. I quit sending the old man cards same time he quit sending them to me. He wants cake and cheer and as many presents as he can wrestle out of us—why are you flipping your wig?"

"Formal wear?"

"He probably thinks it'll minimize fights."

"Cordially?"

"Lane, you have to admit, for Bop, a cream-colored envelope is cordial."

"Well, who's this Miss Sommers bimbo?"

"A secretary," Russell offered. "Or maybe some nubile nurse hired to massage away That Which Is Painful."

"Russell," Lainie said. "Bop's never been sick a day in his life. I'll bet you a thousand dollars she's stepgrandma number three, and this is some ploy to get us all there for a wedding."

"Lane, A, you don't have a thousand dollars to bet. B,

Dr. M would call that kind of thinking parataxic distortion. Just because certain events played out that way in the past doesn't necessarily set a precedent for the future."

"Well, aren't you brilliant and psychological today."

"Saw Dr. M yesterday. The effects usually fade in twenty-four hours. Talk to me tonight and I'll be recognizably neurotic once again."

Russell was at work, leaning on the register at Red Lyzyrd Vynyl. While talking to his sister, he observed two teenaged girls dressed in extremely new wanna-be biker regalia. If at thirty-four his instincts hadn't completely forsaken him, they were going to try to shoplift the store's only mint-condition shrink-wrapped copy of *Led Zeppelin*. Since the MTV Blues Retrospective, they couldn't keep the album in stock. Rich boys from the community college came in and threw down money no matter how high Farmer, the store manager, raised the price. People looking for it called from as far away as Louisiana. Shipping costs be damned, they wanted an original pressing of *Led*. The girls were wearing leather flight jackets, which ordinarily wouldn't have raised any eyebrows among the staff at Red Lyzyrd, but the AC was on the blink today and, nearing high noon, it was a full-bodied eighty degrees. A junkie in the throes of drug rush would have taken off his leather jacket.

On the other end of the telephone, his sister sighed.

"Nick will want you to go," he said.

"Nick wants a lot of things he doesn't necessarily get. You're not going—are you?"

"Hey, I just might," he tried kidding her, hoping an injection of humor might torque this whole party nonsense into perspective. Thus far, it seemed only to be digging him an Oddjob-sized grave. Determined, he wrung the joke dry. "Free food, a boat ride with the rich and infamous—those items are pretty high up on Margie's list."

"Oh, screw Margie's list, we're talking family loyalty, Russell. . . ."

While his sister railed on, he thought about how he definitely screwed things up on a regular basis where Margie was concerned. The thing was, what made her happy one week made her angry the next. And as much as Lane tried to pretend otherwise, he knew she didn't like Margie. They were equally strong women, equally bullheaded. At least with Margie you always knew what you were getting: *It's like you two are twins or something,* she'd said. *The creepy way you talk on the phone every day and have breakfast together all the time. It's not natural, Russell. Normal people don't do that.*

No one could accuse Carpenters of normality. Where Bop was concerned bigamy was a possibility, and sanity was a fine line they all walked, not just Lane. Russell craned his neck to keep the dressed-in-black girls in sight as they disappeared down aisle four. Aisle four, more commonly referred to as "Strange Brew," collected everything noncategorical and downright weird, from Brenda Lee to Herb Alpert and the Tijuana Brass to Benny Hill albums.

"Russell, if we go to his party, it's like we're condoning his behavior."

"Really? I thought all we were condoning was an old man's birthday."

"He doesn't need us there to turn eighty."

"True. What are we but fragmentary reminders of his flawed DNA? He can party down with the cleaning lady, or failing that, converse with his photo albums."

159

With the latter, Russell knew he'd strike a nerve. Bop had an album of Spencer Lainie wanted. *He's my only great-grandson, damn it. I'll hold onto these pictures until you have another baby.* Like procreation was replacing a carburetor. Chilly silence echoed in his left ear; a burst of Ray Charles blistered his right. Farmer had cued up "Do the Mess Around," and the potential shoplifters apparently found Ray's request as offensive as Easy Listening, because they emitted twin screeches and cupped their pale hands and black fingernails over their multi-pierced ears.

". . . fair he gets an eightieth birthday and everyone forgives him like we're all amnesia victims while the rest of the world. . . ." Lane was saying.

Lane, Lane, Lane. Since her breakdown, his sister had developed what he'd come to think of as a Batman complex—justice at any cost, potential villains lurking around every corner. Any minute now, she would promote their grandfather from the heinous crimes of multiple marriages, withholding baby pictures and foisting valuable stock certificates on them to the savaging of South American rainforests.

"How about the time he was divorcing Gloria, and that awful photographer followed us around. Or when that reporter Mac Whoever published those pictures of Daddy in the paper on the anniversary of his death?"

"You're right. That sucked. All of it." Their whole lives, Lainie'd rooted for the underdog. When they were just kids, she befriended the tall girl in the back brace no one would speak to. Now Candace was Lane's best friend, closer than a sister, and drop-dead gorgeous. Lane had the instincts. But since Spencer died, it was as if her mind loped a dog track aimed toward gleaning

160

revenge for Bop's crimes. Indeed, the old man had been instrumental in his sister's hospitalization. That whole deal had taken things too far. Had it been up to Russell, he would have flown Lane to Hawaii, let her cry her head off in salt water, and talk to fish. Sand and salt water always worked for Russell.

Margie didn't like it when he went to the beach. She recited skin cancer statistics on green-eyed individuals, but Russell knew she was really afraid he was looking at bikini-clad women. Margie's mantra read: *I am all you need. Therefore, no other people matter including sisters.* In the early days, when Spencer was alive and she was in a good mood, exclusivity had almost worked for them. The kids went to their dad's and he and Margie spent hours studying each other's skin. Now, if Russell zoned out in front of the TV from six P.M. to midnight, Margie watched, too. If he commented on a commercial touting cherry-topped cheesecake, Margie made it for him the next day. If he dropped a hint about time alone or a night out with Farmer, she cried. Russell's brain throbbed with indecision. How could you break up with a girlfriend who anticipated your junk food desires, voluntarily cleaned your bathroom, and had two wonderful boys he was teaching to surf? Though his own EKG said normal, his heart felt as doomed as his father's, the final spasm out there lurking, waiting to claim his breath in one quick squeeze.

"Russell, are you telling me you forgive him for cutting your hair short when you were sixteen and sleeping off a hangover on *Shadow IV*?"

"Lane, it was hair. It grew back. Now it's falling out. Should I sue the hair gods?"

A few months back, Margie had—no kidding—hinted broadly about him investigating the Hair Club for Men. That was when Russell had started seriously examining things. In the nearly four years they'd been together, why was the first year the only one that seemed happy? Margie had just cut loose of her ex, Ethan and Seth were in preschool and first grade, and she weighed 127 pounds. She was broke and her ex played roulette with the child support, but somehow they were always laughing. Now she slugged through graveyard shifts at the hospital so she could attend nursing classes during the day and never seemed entirely rested. Anyone in her position would turn to food for solace. Christ, look at Lane with her cooking fixations.

These days it seemed like the relationship lay at the bottom of one of those deli pickle barrels, flotsam floating in brine. He suspected it had something to do with the lack of a gold wedding band to grace Margie's left-hand ring finger. The idea of marriage was about as appealing to Russell as undergoing bone marrow biopsy. He needed to do something soon, before he woke up one morning with all new rules—she didn't even like it when he turned on "Baywatch."

"When I was sixteen he sold my horse without even letting me say good-bye. Maybe I did a pretty good job messing up my life, Russell, but half the reason I'll never get out of therapy is Bop Carpenter and you know it."

Into the phone Russell said, "Listen, Lane. This is too complicated to hash out over the phone. Go walk the pooches or something. I'll call you back. Right now I have to go shake down some shoplifters."

"Some what?"

"Shoplifters." The Zeppelin album wasn't deserving of the $175 price tag by a long shot, but it was worth more than these two Harley babes sneaking it out under surplus-store flight jackets they had somehow managed to pay for. "This isn't for the good of American profit, you understand, it's a matter of giving unto Farmer that which is Farmer's."

"Russell, what are you talking about? What's Farmer's?"

"Zeppelin. Nevermind. I'll call you back, I promise." He set the phone down in its cradle, where it promptly rang again. "Red Lyzyrd Vynyl. We draw the line at Lionel Ritchie. If you wish to speak to a human being, please hang up and dial one—"

"Don't start that pretend voice mail business with me, Russell Carpenter. We were supposed to meet for lunch in the park. I packed us a picnic with all your favorites." Margie paused a moment, then recited the list: "Albertson's barbecue chicken, cole slaw with fresh pineapple, banana bread *without* walnuts, K.C. Masterpiece barbecue chips, lime Popsicles and mango iced tea Snapple. I've been waiting here for twenty minutes and you know I don't have a very long lunch hour. The Popsicles melted."

Russell winced. To Margie's way of thinking, every minute alone with her meant one less he spent with Lane. They got together a couple of times a week, but in truth he disliked eating lunch anywhere except in the dark of the office, where he could pore through *Guitar Player* magazines and think of nothing except how much sense music made versus the needs of the women in his life. "I'm sorry, Margie. I'm all alone here so I can't get away."

That was true. Farmer had just stepped outside to smoke a cigarette.

"You would not believe my day. We've had two Elvis sightings, and now the Traveling Wilburys are in here

163

looking for Jimmie Dale Gilmore's *Flatlanders* album. I have to go wait on them or lose my one chance to meet famous people."

"Did Farmer call in sick again? He's such a total faker. Is he surfing? Tell your boss in two more semesters when I get my LVN, I can prove he is as well as the next person, just lazier."

Russell laughed. "I'll inform the faker his sick days are numbered. Meanwhile, why don't you share my half of the lunch with some very lucky pigeons? I have to hang up now, Margie. Hug the boys for me. See you this weekend." He replaced the receiver, punched all four of the store's lines onto hold, and yanked the CLOSED sign in its metal holder across his register.

The pseudo biker girls were almost to the double glass doors. Red Lyzyrd didn't make enough money to install those coded strips to protect the stock or metal detector gates. Farmer was a hanger-on to the Flower Children generation. Idealistic and foolish, he trusted everyone not to rip him off. Keeping his faith intact made for security work for Russell. "Ladies?" he called out. "You mind coming with me a moment?"

"Why?" the thinnest one answered. "You so hard up for company you date children?"

Her front teeth, long and horsey, were so thin the blue of the enamel showed through.

"Setting aside the dating question a moment, it's my suspicion you're about to shoplift store merchandise. You walk out that door, I have no choice but to call Harper's men in blue in their shiny Crown Victorias, and then we can all spend our lunch hour down at the lovely city facility, ironing out the question of possession."

"Possession? Are you, like, inferring we're carrying

164

drugs? You're the one who looks like a pothead, Mr. Grateful Dead ponytail."

Just about everything else disappointing in life he could take—the dwindling lack of enthusiasm he woke with each morning, Lane's periodic harangues, lunch in the park—everything except when something young, female, and attractive called him mister. "I think it's in your best interest to voluntarily come with me. Then again, I am so old I could be senile. Yet note I am not senile enough to forget how to punch up the cops and describe you and your little white BMW 2002, license plate METLBCH." Knowing he had them with his photographic recall, he grinned. "It's your call."

The slightly less-thin one pursed her black lipstick, reached into her jacket and handed him the Zeppelin album. "Oh, take your stupid fucking record back. We only wanted it because of 'Traveling Riverside Blues,' which happens to be the coolest blues song of all time."

Russell accepted it gratefully and thought about how far he'd have to travel to educate those bullet heads who'd assembled the MTV retrospective. "*Au contraire*, ladies. Zeppelin had their moments, but I'd hardly categorize them as master bluesmeisters. For blues, particularly the 'Traveling Riverside Blues,' one must consult the early pressings of Robert Johnson. If you'll be so kind as to step into the office, I'd be glad to give you a small but sufficient lesson."

"You're not trying to, like, pick up on two girls at the same time, are you? You're not the kind of freak who can't do it with only one person?"

Russell set the album on the counter and showed them his empty hands, bare all the way up to the arm of his Blistering Rockets Guitars T-shirt. Because the only addiction he called master was music, there were three tattooed musical notes at the bend of his right elbow. Such subtlety was wasted on girls who no doubt had frightening tattoo art in considerably more frightening areas.

"I'm simply here to educate when possible, smile when not, and continually hump Red Lyzyrd along toward meager profit. My office?"

Red Lyzyrd's office was a closet with smeary one-way glass looking out on the merchandise floor. For seats, there were a broken-down secretary's chair, a couple overturned orange crates, and three or four years' worth of *Guitar Player* magazines stacked into a three-foot-high pile. One of them took the secretary's chair and began rocking back and forth in it, giving him the evil eye.

Russell took down his listening copy of the Robert Johnson recordings, touching only the edges of the brittle record with his fingertips, which were hardened by years of pressing steel guitar strings. He cued the record on Farmer's old Magnavox turntable. The girls traded smirks. Then one old man gathered his misery, boll weevils, and the color of his skin into his fingers, strummed them across six strings and delivered the world a gift.

"See what I mean?" he asked them after the Riverside cut had finished playing. "Need we play the Led to compare?"

"Sounds like some old gomer," one said. "All scratchy and faint like it was played through a blanket or something."

"It was played through something," Russell said. "Through slavery and picking cotton and hardship.

166

Why do you think they call it the blues?"

"How should we know?" They laughed, and he shook his head sadly.

"Now girls, what truth can we glean from today's lesson?"

The thicker one said, "Well, if you're going to steal something, you might as well steal something really valuable—like Robert Johnson. But don't expect to dance to him."

They weren't as young as they looked. And it seemed there was no question of right or wrong here. It was a distinct possibility that smartness was being bred out of women. Lane was smart, but push smart up against difficult times and all smart netted you was the ability to more sharply feel the sting.

The thinner one bought a Robert Johnson priced at $175, paying for it with her American Express. "I'll give it to my dad or something," she said. "He likes really old stuff that's worth a lot of money."

Russell called for a credit line verification. However much she'd already charged, she was still good for a low five figures. Five figures? At this discovery, he blew out a breath, considering that very possibly, except for the guys pushing the *menudo* carts around the neighborhood because they lacked green cards, this information might qualify him as a lower class wage earner. Well, his grandfather was always telling him he'd come to nothing.

He tucked the record in its red recycled plastic bag and wondered sadly if it would warp on the back seat of the Beamer, forgotten in the heat of some larger adventure. "We buy back," he told her, "should you ever decide to return this."

CHAPTER 13

WHEN THE CACTUS ARE IN BLOOM

RUSSELL'S MAILBOX STUCK OUT LIKE A METAL tongue from the hedge of four o'clocks that buried the front fence. He was no gardener; the flowers thrived on the few inches of California rainfall they gleaned all on their own. In spring, college kid came by to take photographs. The vines set prettily against his small white clapboard house as if the entire business had been uprooted from Cape Cod. Mornings when Russell went out front to retrieve the newspaper, the flowers were a pure winter Pacific blue. In the summer heat, by evening, they turned a red violet that reminded him of the bruises on his arms when the bullies ganged up on him in grade school. *Russell, Russell, ya big corpuscle!*

His mail was minimal: a bill from the electric company he could write a check for and be done with and his grandfather's party invite, which unfortunately would exact more effort. He fumbled for his keys thinking of Lane's questions. Miss Sommers—hired help or the new squeeze box? The old geezer had some kind of magic hoodoo going with the ladies. They were always coming and going, suing and screaming, but their first stop was Bop's bedroom.

Russell sympathized with his sister's frustration. There were plenty of lessons Bop had delivered him that kept Dr. Annabelle Mapp busy on the days Lane didn't. He had been seeing Dr. M almost as long as Lainie, but for much less dramatic issues. Russell, Dr. Mapp had often said, *I want you to think of your grandfather as a resolute force with whom we need make an appointment to reckon.*

168

Russell envisioned Bop's craggy jaw up there alongside the presidents at Rushmore. He couldn't have that many years left on earth, but he still had his hair. Sometimes Russell felt his ponytail might consist of a few hummingbird feathers. The minute you checked into your thirties it was all there waiting to get you: male pattern baldness, his own ever-expanding list of allergies, girlfriends tapping their feet and holding out the ring finger. Lately life resembled a crud sandwich, grilled on Satan's barbecue, a little picnic in hell designed for you personally.

Shoot, he'd forgotten to call his sister back. Lane's mood would only darken. Well, they had their standing breakfast date for Sunday morning. He'd speak to her then, try his best to cheer her up. He ran the edge of the envelope under his thumbnail before he opened the front door.

Why not go to this party and watch Bop make a fool of himself one last time before the lights went out? The year his father died, Bop had set up his estate so that he and Lane received yearly dividends. It was almost enough cash to live at the poverty level, which meant the old man intended they bank it. But coupled with his job at Red Lyzyrd, that money made a fairly comfortable life—as long as he drove an old car and liked thrift shop decor. The big *dinero* was eventually headed their way. What was the point of getting ambitious? Didn't they owe their grandfather something, even if only for investing wisely?

Just inside the front door, the overpowering stench of potpourri assaulted his nostrils. Margie'd let herself in to clean his house again. His eyes began watering in histamine protest. There was the culprit—a china bowl on the coffee table filled with mummified flowers. She moved furniture, laid his *Guitar Traders* in a fan shape on the coffee table, left her mark everywhere. *It's no trouble, Russell. I like making you happy.* He prayed that she'd stayed away from his vintage guitars. Pledge and French polish did not mix. Breathing through his mouth, he quickly emptied the contents of the bowl into a Baggie, cinched it shut with an old bread tie, and took it out back to deliver it to the giant plastic trash can the city of Harper insisted all residents use then, for the privilege, charged them $7.50 a month.

He'd dropped the too-large hinged lid on his forearm once and still felt the twinge of injured muscle whenever he reached for a diminished chord. Any sane person would sue the city and retire, but Russell'd had enough of his grandfather's lawsuits to last him a lifetime. He stepped back and the lid fell with its usual boom. His neighbor's husky started barking.

"Easy, Porkpie. That's just the sound of a satisfied trash can digesting some frilly girl bullshit. No reason for you to hack up a hairball."

He went back inside and made himself a sandwich of avocado slices, purple onion, and cheese. He put in on a clean plate, took it out back to the postage-stamp yard, stooping to lift up a soccer ball the kids next door had lost again. He tipped it over the back fence, a wobbly structure composed of rotted and cracking boards, fronted by cactus so tall and prickly the kids were afraid to scale it. In the morning, the kids would holler out, "Thanks, dude!" and high-five each other, start the game all over again, lose the ball by nightfall, give it up and go play Mortal Kombat on their Sega systems. Russell found this predictable chain of events comforting.

The six-foot-tall hedge was night-blooming cereus. Three of the cacti were going to flower tonight. The purple buds were already opening at the tips. Anywhere from ten P.M. until midnight, they spilled waxy yellow flowers the size of dinner plates. By morning the flowers would blacken and fall off. This late-night event never failed to make him sit there in the kind of stupid awe only humans are capable of experiencing, wondering at this skewed plan of nature producing such transitory beauty.

He could hear the kitchen phone ringing inside. It was probably Margie or Lane, and more than they needed to talk at him, he needed some time alone to watch the flowers.

Lane was after him to get an answering machine. Margie wanted him to get one too, then a color TV to replace his black-and-white tabletop Sony, a top-of-the-line VCR, a fancy microwave, and an engagement ring, size eight, but all the items didn't necessarily need to arrive in that particular order. Ignoring the phone, he ducked inside to the spare bedroom, where guitar cases were organized one atop the other in stacks.

He'd begun collecting in high school, thanks to Bop's checks. Lane had ordered Dehner boots and a new saddle; Russell bought a Triplate steel body National from a methamphetamine user low on cash and bereft of long-term logic. On the bottom left, the steel section proper, followed by the subset of finger-picking steel—all small-bodied guitars. Next came the Dreadnought steel, flat-picking guitars commonly used in Country and Western music, the large body bold in tone and show, aptly named for the large ships that possessed such cutting power they were said to fear nothing. In the middle stack were seven "parlor style" guitars, including an original 1897 Washburn and three copies fabricated in the late 1920s through the '30s. Girlish in appearance, they produced a large sound he enjoyed, as

171

well as the idiosyncrasy of silk-wrapped steel strings, which were easy on the fingers. A pair of mandolins hung on the wall above them, along with a war-era Gibson decorated with mother-of-pearl and one hokey Middle Eastern job.

The stack second from the left were his classicals—not an area of expertise, but one he was unwilling to ignore. He had a Martin, similar to the style Joan Baez strummed her little 1960s protest songs on, a Hernandez, a showy Ramierez, plus one new Tokai that, according to structure and price, should never have played even half as well as it did, but that, when it came to tone, was actually a stellar little monkey-biter.

The final stack consisted of his two resophonic guitars, a Dobro wood-body he played lap style, and the one he feared most might be stolen: the National with its etched chrysanthemum back. When he played that guitar, his hand cupping the rounded neck, he felt something close to mother love. It increased in value with every chord change; it was the only insured guitar in his collection. Russell would take up residence under a freeway if the circumstances directed, but he'd be sleeping with his arms around the National.

He owned one electric guitar, a 1950 Fender Broadcaster in butterscotch, the Country-and-Western god of guitars. There was another he wanted: the Gretsch 6120 Chet Atkins model in Pumpkin orange—a hue so remarkable the collector's book likened the shade to "the color of a Flagstaff sunset."

It was Margie's birthday. He knew no one was going to give her a present, so he'd taken the boys to pick out a card, paid for it himself, then passing by the travel agency, seen a poster for a Mexican cruise in the window. The day the tickets arrived, a guy showed up at

172

Red Lyzyrd with the Gretsch 6120, said he'd heard Russell was in the market. Due to limited funds, Russell had to let the opportunity pass.

All by itself, the guitar he'd played at Lane's on the Fourth, the Gibson Southern Jumbo, sat snug in its brown Lifton case, last week's favorite. *Play me "Singin' the Blues," Russell. . . .*

What would become of his sister? Would she ever learn to balance her menus? Was she headed back to a single room on the nutsy-bobo floor of the hospital? Could Dr. M effect a magic cure or, now that he was about to hang up his shrink shingle, did that miracle fall on Nick?

At the far right of the small room, under a shuttered window he rarely opened, a hollow-core door rested atop two file cabinets. In addition to his woodworking tools, the table held the ruined Gretsch Rancher he'd been repairing for the last three years. Had it been intact, there would have been no more perfect choice for a July evening and flowering cactus. He'd loved that ax passionately, the fiddleback flame maple sides and back bookmatched as if grown for this guitar. Sometime this summer he'd crossed a line—gone from browbeating himself for ruining the instrument on the afternoon of his nephew's death to a commitment to repair it. At this stage, commitment consisted of building a jig and comparing samples cut from the wreckage to the Polaroids sent him from Luthier's Mercantile.

He'd known the moment he saw the Gretsch in an Atlanta pawnshop that it was worth five times what the guy was asking. Not many people would fly eight hundred miles on a rumor to look at a guitar. Russell closed his eyes and saw the arc of the instrument coming down on the hospital water fountain, the only way an uncle knew to release the pain of his nephew's death. *What do you want me to play, buddy,* he'd whispered at Spencer's bedrail, and had to strain to hear his answer for all the oxygen tubes and IV lines.

Spence had batted left-handed, quoted "Sesame Street" philosophy, and his favorite food was whatever Uncle Russell was having. Spencer was dead.

Russell sighed, pushed cases aside, and took out his newest acquisition, an Everly Brothers model replete with the "That Girl" plastic pick guard, so named for the Marlo Thomas-style flip haircut shape. That large a chunk of mother-of-toilet-seat cut down on the soundboard's ability to resonate, but tonight he didn't want loud. He took it outside and faced the cactus.

From the Robert Johnson riff he'd played for the shoplifter girls, he segued into "Will the Circle Be Unbroken," using a cycle of fifths, a way to change keys as the song progressed, of which the challenge was to move forward from no one particular tonal center. Improvising as he went, he played his cacti "Blackberry Blossom," "Beaumont Rag," then the more rhythmically challenging "Red-Haired Boy." By playing the fifth of every root, the entire piece became a tricky, taut endeavor commanding all of his attention, keeping his mind off the picture of the red-haired lad struggling for breath in that hospital room. He'd tried explaining it to Dr. Mapp once, how if you did it right, the notes stacked and played without error, it created in his mind's eye an impenetrable fortress. Conversely, they shattered when he couldn't keep up the demanding spiral of changes. He'd been coping with this particular medley for three years. Tonight, the fifths lined up for him, good little clothespin soldiers who fell to their musical deaths as his fingers dictated.

Before him, the flowers were opening. He played hard but methodically, as if a metronome beat out time in his blood. When his B string broke, he quickly tuned down to an open D and continued playing, moving fluidly into a bottleneck slide using a half-full bottle of Tabasco he'd stolen from his sister's kitchen on the Fourth. Next time Lane went to make jambalaya, she'd be scratching her head, but then, given her thought progressions, she'd find some way to blame Bop for taking it.

He set the guitar on his lap to watch the moon-faces of the flowers bobbing toward him in the slight breeze. The cat from down the block leaped over the fence and came to sit at Russell's knee. In companionable silence, they listened to yuppies speed up to beat the light on South Burton, to the Mexican kids playing Hide and Seek, their cries of "ai, ai," every time a hiding place was discovered. Their fathers never came out to holler at them, to insist they wash up and go to bed at a halfway decent hour. If they had fathers, they were the kind of men who would rather watch *boxeo* and drain tall cans of Bud than look out for their kids. Dad had croaked before he or Lane could become pals of any kind with him. His grandfather's checks couldn't fill that particular gap. He heard the jingle of his front gate and stopped playing.

"Hi, Rusty."

"Hey, Margie. This is a surprise."

"We have a whole night alone together."

"Nice dress."

"Thanks."

He took a breath. "Please don't tell me you left those boys alone again," he said into the dark of the small patio.

175

"God, Russell, aren't you the cranky one this evening? Ethan and Seth are spending the night with their dad."

"Oh, wonderful. That's just great. Mr. Personality, whom we all know gargles with 151 rum, is watching the children."

Margie pulled at the wrinkle-pleats on her black and white granny dress. "They'll be fine. And it's not like they have any other real father figure in their lives."

He knew where this was heading. "A lousy drunk is better than no dad?" He regretted the words the moment they shot from his mouth. "Look, forget I said that, okay? It's been a long day. Not an altogether pleasant one. You want a Coke or something?"

Margie followed him into the kitchen. "Only if it's diet. Did you catch the shoplifters?"

"Yes. I even made a sale in the process. Farmer will probably give me a bonus."

"Well, that's great." Margie smiled and popped the tab on her soda. "Russell, the next time you get shoplifters you should call 'Cops.' I bet they'd send out a crew and film it and everything."

"Maybe." He put the guitar away. "How's Seth's ankle?"

"Fine. It was just a little sprain." Margie held up her straw purse, big enough to hold encyclopedias. "I packed you a surprise."

Another picnic? One of those gargantuan vibrators? It wasn't big enough to hold a guitar. "Well, don't keep me in suspense."

She lifted a dark blue bottle of scented massage oil from the purse's depths. "Today in class we learned the major muscle groups. I can do my homework while I give you a backrub."

He eyed the bottle. "I'd love a backrub, but I'm

176

probably allergic to that."

"Russell, it doesn't have any walnut oil, or raisins, or apple skins, or bee venom in it. I checked the ingredients."

"Truthfully, I don't feel all that tense."

Margie began unscrewing the cap. She took a patchouli-scented candle from her purse, set it on the coffee table and lit it. Russell tendered his shirt. "Don't go overboard on the oil, please? You never know. I might have developed an allergy to something new in the last fifteen minutes."

"You are the original worry-wart. Lie down."

He hugged the couch, his right arm extended just enough to press the buttons on the TV remote. Letterman wasn't on for another hour. He settled on a rerun of an earlier 'Cops.' Some good old boys were rousting youthful car thieves and lecturing a crying lesbian about using her lover's car to transport drugs. Now the flame-red Firebird was the property of the Louisville Police Department, but just to be fair, they were going to let the girl keep up the car payments. For a brief moment, Russell pictured his lost Chet Atkins Gretsch 6120 in the arms of some geek who locked the instrument behind hermetic glass. The small of his back seized.

"See," Margie said, and her hands went to work, sliding his ponytail to one side, where the few hairs could dangle over his shoulder. She kneaded like a baker, yanking and pulling while Russell watched the men of law and order perform what seemed like a fairly straightforward job. He hated it when they digitized the criminals' faces. He kept imagining he recognized people he knew. He tried to appreciate the backrub, but the truth was, he and Margie were so far apart that he mostly felt the film of grease on his back. Margie snaked her fingers over his shoulder, then she was rubbing his front, tickling his hairy nipples with her fingertips, and beneath the guilt, he felt himself responding,

He sighed and turned over, glad it was dark enough that he didn't have to watch her face, that look of possessive adoration he could no longer return welling up in her eyes. He shut his eyes and tried to make her happy. Was that what his grandfather did, right before he strode into divorce court, arm-in-arm with his lawyer? How did you go about divorcing someone you'd never married?

Somewhere in the back of his spinning thoughts, he thought he could hear the flowers dropping unceremoniously to the cracked pavement outside, each cactus already sending out instructions for the next impending bloom. He wondered what kind of music Bop had planned for the party, because bitch as Lane might, they were all going. He prayed it was going to be live, not some DJ with a shag haircut and a slinky jumpsuit.

Lane expertly folded the edge of the ham and pineapple crepe in her skillet, then slid it onto Russell's plate. "There's a pitcher of sauce on the table."

Ever watchful for anaphylactic reactions, Russell queried, "You mind my asking what's in it?"

His sister rubbed her forehead with the back of her hand, the metal spatula in her fingers catching the sunlight from the open kitchen window. She smiled, her hair still funny from sleep, that ratty blue bathrobe tied around her skinny body nearly twice. "Let's see. Apple peel, I think, raisins, walnut oil, and ground-up bee stingers."

"Ha ha. Very funny. You can watch me die laughing while you punch up 9-1-1."

"I was just trying to 'inject a little humor into each and every day,' a la orders from Dr. M, Russell. I used fresh papaya, a few drops of sesame oil, strained orange juice, and a half-cup powdered sugar. You should be okay on everything. If the sesame oil bothers you, there's Benadryl right here in this cupboard. Prozac, too. I'm going to take a shower. Would you mind telling Nick breakfast's ready?"

"He's your husband. You call him."

Lane frowned and he could tell they'd had a fight. "You're closer."

"No problem." Russell patted Shaky Jake's head, which rested on his knee every Sunday morning while he read the *Calendar* section, waiting for Lane to lay down the feed bags. "Take a hike, Jake," He pushed open the screen door and walked to the garage, where Nick was clamping together his scrap oak. "S'up, Mr. Villa?"

Nick returned to earth, his distraction the trademark of a carpenter puzzling out a problem with infinite patience. "Just gluing up the sides and sanding. I've got the drawers laid out. Come take a look at this bird's eye maple and let me know what you think. Found this in a scrap box at O.C. Hardwoods. I think I can get enough straight grain out of it to cover the fronts."

Russell laid the pieces out on the sawhorses. The tiny figuring was choice. These days people opted for the durability of oak or for soft pine that looked more trendoid the more dents it acquired. "Maximum usage, for sure. What's your plan for the drawers?"

Nick swept sawdust from his graph paper, uncovering

a sketch. "I was thinking a pyramid arrangement, then on top attaching this. Doweled from underneath." He held out a carved wooden horse, its features crude but charming.

Russell nodded. "She'll like the horse."

Nick slipped a square of fresh sandpaper into a block, handed it to Russell, then loaded up one for himself. "She talks about that pony every once in a while. About learning to ride when your dad was still around. Grandma Alyce and the cooking lessons."

"What do you think about this party thing?"

"I think it's a good idea."

"So you got Lane to agree to go?"

"Not exactly." He tucked an errant corner of sandpaper back into the rubber block. "Shit, Russell. We spend all this time groping our way past the gaping hole Spencer left in our lives. We have to start trying to sew the bastard back together. Maybe this party will help."

"Well, I applaud your attitude, but certain others may resist."

Nick frowned. "She can't stay locked up inside this house forever. That's no better than her being in the hospital. She can dream all she wants, Russell; Spencer's not coming back."

They began sanding.

He felt for Nick, the rock of the family, a man who gave every word serious thought before speaking. His sister had a decent marriage. It held together during a time when anyone else's would've blown up like a car bomb.

They worked in silence, the susurrant paper chasing minute imperfections from the wood. Russell ran his thumb across the dovetail joints Nick had made with his router. His brother-in-law did precision work, creative,

180

original, and surprising. If he made half as decent a psychologist as he'd been a carpenter, he'd kick posterior at his new career.

At the kitchen table, Nick poked a finger into the crepes.

"Cold?" Russell asked.

"Some of my mother-in-law's finer moments come to mind."

"Think Lane would mind if we nuked them?"

"You're talking about tampering with my wife's art."

"Well, give me yours, we'll do them both on one plate. Limits her opportunity to hear the microwave bell."

While they waited for the crepes to heat, they threw the ball out back for Jake. The happy mutt made wider circles with each consecutive pass, hoping to complicate the game while Oddjob, Olympic spoilsport, nipped at his heels. Nick smiled. For Russell it was a relief to see a natural expression on his face instead of the stock therapist's mask.

From the open bathroom window, over the sound of the shower, they heard Lane start singing. Russell recognized the tune at once: "Tweeter and the Monkey Man," off the first Traveling Wilburys'. "Whoa," Russell said. "Will you listen to that."

Nick knitted up his brow as if it were up to him to explain the sudden change of behavior.

It seemed like even the pooches were transfixed, their heads cocked at the perplexed angle dogs assume will illuminate something out of the canine ordinary. Nick held on to Jake's ball and looked intently at his calluses. "I miss hearing her sing."

"You're hearing her now."

He shook his head. "It's not a conscious effort,

Russell. Now and then she lets herself slip for a minute. She'll stop as soon as she remembers."

Lane continued to belt out the dark tale of love and betrayal, her voice as strong as it was four years earlier, as full of honey and longing as her life had once been. Then it snapped off, a compelling narrative torn in two, no resolution or explanation.

Nick let the ball drop to the ground. Jake knew better than to go after it. They went inside to the crepes, unable to find anything to say to each other regarding what they'd just witnessed.

"You want some of this sauce?" Nick asked. "It smells really good."

Russell nodded. "You want the *Calendar*?"

"Okay."

Nick handed the pitcher over, and Russell met his eyes for a moment. "Hang in there, dude. It'll take some time, but she'll come back."

"Yeah."

Then Lane was standing in the doorway, rubbing her hair with a towel. "So, what do you guys think of this recipe?"

With both of their mouths full, they nodded enthusiastically.

CHAPTER 14

THE BELLY SPIN

SETH LOMANTO SAT ON THE TOP STEP OUTSIDE HIS mother's duplex, a bucket of water and an oversized sponge clutched between his thin, splayed legs. He smiled a wobbly smile at Russell, who was coming up the pathway. Russell squatted down on one knee and smashed an ant with the Fender pick he always carried in his change pocket. It was tear-drop shaped, used primarily for jazz, but worked okay on insects.

Seth was an eight-year-old byproduct of an alcohol-related divorce, and Russell couldn't have loved him more if he was his own son. He handed him the pick. "Dust an ant if it'll make you feel better."

"Is killing bugs murder?"

"Not in America. What's with the bucket?"

Seth pursed his lips thoughtfully. "I'm supposed to wash the car. Then I'm supposed to wax it. I'm in trouble."

"Trouble, huh?" Russell looked down at the dead ant and felt guilty. "What'd you do, rob a second-grader or something?"

"Way duh, Russell. It's *summer*. No school, remember?" Seth dipped a corner of the sponge into the bucket and dribbled water over the ant corpse. "I didn't go off the high dive."

Russell sighed. "The high dive? You couldn't make me go off one. Not even if there was a naked girl in the pool ready to catch me."

Seth gave him the big brown cow eyes, the one heart-breaking feature he'd inherited from his mother. "Really?"

"No shit, Sherman. Those things shrivel my pickle."

Seth grinned. "You're lying."

"Would I lie to you?" Russell took the sponge, loaded it up, and squeezed it out on the hot cement. "You call Wavetrak this morning?"

"Yeah. Before she got up."

She was Margie, who had given birth to these fine, honest boys with whom she was always finding fault. If

183

they weren't doing some pointless chore like washing the Buick, she had them grounded to their room. Every time Russell tried to put in his two cents' worth, she told him to butt out.

"Well? Do I have to give you a quarter or something? What'd it say? The ocean dry up, or is today whale humping day, no surfing allowed?"

Seth started to giggle, then laugh, showing his maverick teeth, each going its own direction. He needed orthodontia. He wasn't going to get it unless Margie went to work for an understanding dentist.

"Four foot, south swell."

Russell stood up, wiped his pick on his jeans, and put it back in his pocket. "They're breaking, dude. What do you say?"

"She won't let us go."

"We're manly men. We going to let some skirt tell us how to spend our Sunday?"

"She'll start yelling again. I don't like it when she yells at me and Ethan."

"Seth my lad, when women start yelling, the smartest thing a guy can do is go dead silent. Not only does it drive them crazy, it's rather entertaining to watch them spin their wheels trying to get a reaction. Kind of like those shows in Spanish on cable. Who cares what they're saying? The best part is how the ladies' faces pinch up. Come on, let's get this over with. We don't want to miss any good waves."

Seth reached up for Russell's hand, then, perhaps realizing holding hands was babyish, stopped in midair. Russell tickled his fingers, high-fived him, and opened the front door.

Margie was folding laundry on the couch. Great piles of frilly nylon and satin underthings mixed in with her

184

boys' socks and T-shirts. Russell gave her a peck on the cheek and started helping her fold. "Hey, Margie. My back has never felt so relaxed. Whatever you did to it the other night really worked."

Her smile thinned out as she watched Seth drag the bucket into the kitchen. "Seth, you finish the car already?"

"Lay off, Margie," Russell whispered.

"Russell, he has to face up to his fears and go off that diving board someday."

Russell pushed aside a stack of shirts. "Will it keep him from learning higher math?"

Margie folded her arms across her breasts. "Since you're not a parent, you can't possibly understand."

Ouch. Hardball. If they wanted to go surfing, he'd have to dismiss logic, go straight to plan B, compliments. Seth stood in the door frame between the kitchen and the tiny living room. Russell could see the lump of swim trunks wadded into his shorts pocket, his hand hovering there as if he knew he would have to take them back out. "Where's Ethan?"

"Ethan has a fever. I'm making him stay in bed so he'll be well for day camp tomorrow. I can't miss any more school and I can't take off work."

"Mind if I stick my head in and say hi?"

Margie shook out a violet teddy. Russell's eyes widened at the sheer fabric and lace.

"He might be contagious."

"That's okay. I'm invincible."

He opened the door to Ethan and Seth's room, which was decorated with blue ripcord bedspreads and a horrible clown lamp he knew both boys detested. On Ethan's wall were posters of the Mighty Morphin Power Rangers. On Seth's, a *Surfer Magazine* foldout of

185

the Wedge King, Dan "the Man" Taylor, whitewash spraying like a rooster tail behind him as he flew off the lip—with air, no less—of a fifteen footer. "Yo, Spud Monkey. Are you faking?"

Ethan put his toy race cars down and squinted at Russell. "I feel great. Mom says I gotta stay in bed anyway."

The boy had a lisp; getting two consecutive sentences out of him was hard work. Russell felt his forehead. It was a little bit warm, but he suspected all little boys ran their engines hot. "Your head ache, throat hurt, something like that?"

He scratched his leg and grinned, "No."

Seth spoke up from behind Russell. "He threw up on the bathroom rug last night after Dad brought us home from dinner. Mom went *off.*"

"I see. Couldn't quite catch the porcelain bus, pal? What'd he feed you guys? In 'n' out burgers?"

The boys giggled.

"Russell?" Ethan said.

"No, I won't read you *Snow White*, so don't ask."

"Would you light a fart for me?"

"Jesus, Ethan, be quiet about that. Your mom finds out, we'll all catch hell." Sticking his hand under his armpit, he delivered the boys a few pseudo-fart noises. "Gentlemen, this stunt was performed by a trained professional. Do *not* try this at home."

Ethan threw himself forward on the bed, rolled over, and started laughing. Seth did, too.

Margie called out, "Are you getting him all stirred up in there? I want him to take a nap!"

Russell mimed her words, shaking a finger at each of the boys in turn. "Why don't you take off and go shopping, Margie? You deserve a break. I'll watch these evil children, make sure everyone takes naps."

She came into the room, opened their dresser drawer and separated the piles of clothing, Seth on the left, Ethan on the right. "Oh, sure, that's a great idea. The minute I leave you'll have them running around the living room making a mess, watching Arnold Schwarzenegger movies and eating candy."

He feigned shock. "I never."

"Russell, you know you do. Every time."

"Not this time. I give you my word. No running, no movies, not so much as one stick of candy. Only restful rests."

The boys froze into statues as she thought it over. Russell could feel them willing her to go. "Well, there's a close-out sale at Ross Dress for Less I've been dying to check out. But it's all the way over in Westminster. It would take me three hours to drive there, take a quick took at everything, and drive back."

"Three hours isn't nearly enough time to fully relax, Margie. Take five hours, no less. I'll even start dinner if you tell me what you have planned."

She touched his cheek. "God, Russell, this is so sweet of you!" She walked briskly to the kitchen, already grabbing her purse and keys. "There's frozen chicken and macaroni and Brussels sprouts. . . ."

He and the boys made gagging motions. "Okay, we can handle that."

"And," she said, her hand on the door knob, pointing at Ethan, under no circumstances is that one to skip his nap."

"No problemo." Russell gave her a kiss good-bye.

The door shut and the boys looked at him. He kept his face deliberately solemn, walked back to the living room, sat down on the butt-sprung couch, and opened a

Lillian Vernon catalog. Margie had circled the things she liked. Yikes, lace curtain ties, bouquets of dead roses, ceramic rabbits strangled with wide, pastel ribbon. He could hear the boys whispering in the bedroom.

"Ho, hum," Russell yawned loudly. "What a lovely, hot, sunny day. Why, July hardly gets better than this. Ah, summer! So much to do, how to choose? Perfect for a two, no make that three-hour nap. It's too bad I feel like—" he drew out the silence as long as he dared, stretching their hopeful agony to the breaking point. "Going surfing!"

They were at his side, changed into trunks and armed with beach towels before he'd put a period on the sentence.

He slathered them up with SPF 20 sunblock and made them sit on their towels for ten minutes while it dried. Seth calmly studied the waves, but Ethan was all over the towel, scratching at himself. "Ethan, stop digging," Russell said. "You got a live animal in there or something?"

"He's got bugs," Seth said, trying on Russell's prescription Ray Bans. "Whoa, Russell, you're blind."

"Hey, give me those."

Ethan took his hand out of his pants. "I do not, you booger. Can I help it if my leg itches?"

"Let's not call each other names." Russell pushed up the leg of Ethan's trunks and took a look at his thigh. "That's a bug bite. Leave it alone. Once you get in the salt water, you'll forget all about it. In the meanwhile, let's review the rules, shall we? Ethan?"

"Stay between this lifeguard stand—"

"Which is?"

"Number twenty-three, and that one, number

188

twenty-four."

"Very good. And what else, Seth?"

"Don't get separated."

"If by some chance you do?"

Seth sighed. "Walk straight in to the beach and find the number on the lifeguard station. Count back to where we were, then walk directly to your towel, and no talking to anyone because . . . because . . ." Seth looked up. "I forget the rest."

"Because perverts often wear normal people disguises." Russell checked his Shark watch. Nine minutes wasn't going to make or break down the chemicals in the sunscreen. "Okay, boys, let's hit the water."

Leashes already attached, they grabbed their Morey boogie boards (Christmas presents from Russell) and ran to the ocean, their tiny feet sinking into the wet sand, annoying the sand crabs. Russell loped after them, more than happy to spend the day in the whitewash, helping two lads learn the secrets of carving waves.

Seth needed only a push in the right direction. He'd mastered the beginning moves and was adept at floaters, going "over the falls" of smaller waves. He would spend all day attempting the "el rollo," an advanced move that required both skill and luck to gain entrance to the inside of the wave's tube. Even in the salt water grip of failure, Seth would have a good time. Ethan was still a hands-on beginner. Once again, Russell showed him how to lie flat and paddle with his arms. By now, Russell'd hoped to have him comfortable with a belly spin, but even a duck-dive in the whitewash made Ethan gasp and sometimes cry. Russell didn't want to say so to Margie, but it seemed like Ethan was maybe a little bit slow.

"You've got to pull the water toward your board, Ethan. Find a rhythm." Ethan smiled and dug his fingers in, letting the salt spray bathe his grin. "Look at me, Russell," he commanded. "I'm surfing like Dan Taylor!"

Thurfing! "Almost, little dude. Keep up the good work, next stop, Hawaii. The girls there don't wear any tops. Hubba, hubba."

"No way!"

"Yes, way. It's quite a sight, I'm telling you."

Seth rode by himself for an hour, then took his board in and set it on his towel. Russell was surprised to see him come high-stepping out toward his brother; he had the time-out figured for a pit stop, or a foray to the snack bar for gummy bears.

"Ethan's holding his board all wrong," he said with authority. "Let me show him how to do it."

Russell stepped aside, watching the two brothers maneuver the undersized orange board. Even with a sometimes-harridan for a mother and living in a crummy duplex, these boys had forged a lifelong bond. Ethan's face was fixed on following his brother's instructions. He wiped out constantly, then miraculously caught three feet of whitewash—possible proof of a benevolent God, Russell mused—and Seth cheered. Sometimes, in those sex-drenched nights early on in their relationship, or days like today, when the sun hit the water like it was polishing steel, Russell wished Margie hadn't had her tubal ligation after Ethan was born. Marriage—well, that was one terrifying exit that would keep him riding the freeway of love forever, but parenthood? He wouldn't have minded trying his hand. What kind of father lit farts for his sons and lied to their mother about taking naps? This kind, he said to himself, practicing Dr. Mapp's brand of medicine, silencing the inner voice that constantly reprimanded him. These boys deserve some guy time. Nowhere is it written they need to grow up believing every man in their life's going to spend their tennis shoe money in bars.

"Who wants a ride?" Russell hollered over the crashing water.

"Me! Me first!" Seth said. "I'm oldest!"

Ethan finished his latest mini-wipeout, spit up salt water, and looked crestfallen.

"Seth, Seth, Seth. You forgot youngest goes first. The younger you are, the harder it is to wait." Russell dragged them both ashore, wrapped them in dry towels and brushed the sand from his fullsized surfboard.

Out in the breakwater, he lifted Ethan atop his shoulders. Ethan screamed with joy as they caught the first wave. Russell's ears were still ringing as he dropped Ethan onshore and waited for Seth to climb aboard, then paddled them past the shorebreak. Here there weren't any swimmers to dodge, and they had a better chance of catching something decent, riding a little longer. The purported four-foot swell was barely up to three now, and in the next hour or so it would degenerate into chop. "Ready?" he asked his partner.

Seth nodded.

Russell lifted him by the armpits and held him tight as he got to his feet and gripped the waxy surface of the board. Then he parked the boy in front of him, facing forward, and the tough little eight year old proudly stood alone, his arms planing out at his sides to keep his balance. When the wave began to peter out, Russell picked him up and said into his ear, "After this, we'll blow up the high dive! Swim, Seth." And he threw him into the water.

Seth swam toward shore, almost crashing into Ethan, who couldn't bear being towel-bound any longer. "One more time, Russell!"

Russell plopped the kid on the board so he was lying flat, then paddled him around. "Okay, that's it. Time to get home and wash the sand out of our butt cracks before your mom arrives."

"No!"

"Next time, Ethan."

Ethan started to pout and thrash his legs. I don't want to wait for next time!"

Russell swung the board around so they were facing each other. "What's this? I thought we were mature men here, brothers in waves. There isn't going to be any crying, is there?"

Ethan began scratching his leg. His sunbleached crew cut was overlong, hedgehog-prickly, just the kind of hair other kids made fun of. Finally he swallowed his disappointment and said, "Okay, Russell. Next time."

On the way home, Ethan crashed hard into the wad of towels, slumped against Russell in the front seat of the Comet, snoring. From the back seat, Seth draped himself over the seatcovers and tuned in KROQ on the radio. Even as the head-banging music poured forth, Seth remained fixed, watching Pacific Coast Highway stretch out before them. Russell could take a hint. "Something on your mind?"

Seth looked down at his brother. "Gross. He's drooling on you."

"Who cares? He's asleep, and in my book that counts for an official nap, which means one less lie I have to tell your mother."

"His mosquito bite's gross. There's pus in it or

something."

"Seth, shall I pull the car over for a puke break?"

"Sorry."

They stopped at the light for Brookhurst. If Russell was going to see his sister, he'd turn left here, pass the sewage treatment plant, hang a roscoe on Victoria, then cut through the last of the county land and come out on South Burton, his street, which kind of ran west at that point.

"Russell?"

"That's my name, don't wear it out."

"Are you and my mom going to get married?"

Russell gripped the Comet's turquoise steering wheel and took a deep breath. "Marriage? Let's see. Isn't that where the wife locks a ball and chain around the husband's ankle, and there's no surfing, and he has to make birdhouses in the garage while she goes through his clothes and throws out anything comfortable?"

"Are you or not?"

"Did she tell you to ask me that?"

"No. I want to know."

He'd stalled just about all he could. "I don't think so, buddy. Your mom's a fine person. You guys are my main dudes. But I don't think I'm cut out for marriage, not with anybody."

Seth was silent for the remainder of the song. Next, some early Nirvana kicked in. "This guy at day camp told me Kurt Cobain shot himself in the head. Is that true?"

"Yeah. It's pretty stupid, but it's true."

"Why would somebody that cool shoot himself in the head?"

"Maybe because he took too many drugs, Seth. Cool people make stupid decisions, too. Promise me you won't ever get into that shit. It's a dead end street to a town with no beach and you can't go surfing."

Seth tickled a finger in his younger brother's hair until Ethan sleepily batted him away. "I won't if you don't stop being my friend."

Oh, God. Oh, God. This was what being a grownup got you, little moments like this one, gems to polish with the guilt cloth until you keeled over. It caused you to make decisions based on avoiding confrontation. Russell could not bring himself to add lies to the damage already done this boy. "I promise, Seth. Now sit down and put your seatbelt back on. We're cool, but I still don't want to take any chances with the crazy drivers out here."

The boy disappeared from view and Russell heard a small, compliant click.

Margie's Buick was in the driveway as they turned in. We're vulture sandwiches, Russell thought, get out the condiments. "Seth, leave all this stuff. I'll clean it up later." He gripped Ethan's shoulder. "Wake up, Ethan." Ethan didn't want to wake up, so he gently lifted him and carried him into the house.

Margie was sitting on the couch removing price tags from her purchases, dropping the plastic ties and marked-down tags into a small wastebasket decorated with black-and-white cows.

"Shh," Russell whispered as he passed by her, carrying Ethan into his room. Before he tucked him in bed, he brushed his sandy feet off into a wastebasket, then covered him lightly with the sheet.

Back in the living room, he said, "What a nap this guy's taking. Gotta be some kind of world's record. Ladies and gentlemen, Ethan Lomanto from the United

States, the gold medal for napping."

From her tight-lipped expression, he assumed jokes were out of the question. "Okay," he said. "Guilty as charged. Get out your Ginsu knife and flay me alive for taking these boys surfing."

"I specifically told you Ethan had a fever."

"Maybe a *slight* fever, Margie. Besides, salt water has healing properties, or haven't they covered that yet in nursing school?"

"Russell, that is total bullshit and you know it."

He stroked her arm. "I know. I suck. I'm wicked to the core. Lighten up, sweetie. It was a beautiful day and everyone got in some recreation. You find any bargains?"

She looked down at the blouses in her lap. "Two Liz Claibornes."

"They look kind of—"

"Kind of what?"

He swallowed. "Well, small, actually. But what do I know about sizes. I'm a guy—"

She made a disgusted sound. "They are small, Russell. They're size eight, and starting tomorrow morning, I'm going on Weight Watchers again, and this time I'm going to lose all this weight and become something you can be proud of." She looked up at him, her big brown eyes filling with tears.

He took her in his arms. "Don't talk like that. You're a good person, a great mother. You know how much I care about you."

Her breath came hot against his neck. "I'm fat and you don't want to marry me."

"You're not fat. I thought you knew how I felt about marriage."

She pulled out of his arms and stood up. "Sure. I

understand, Russell. Everything was going just fine between us until your sister's kid died and now it's like nobody gets to have a happy life, we all have to stand around and wring our hands for poor, poor Lainie!"

"That's cold, Margie."

From the other room, Ethan started to wail. Margie waited a minute, then huffed out her breath and stalked off to see to him.

Russell rubbed the skin between his eyebrows. It felt like someone had strapped a band of metal on him there and was tightening it mercilessly. High blood pressure? Some new allergy manifesting itself in his brain? Seth came over to where Russell was seated on the couch. He handed Russell the keys to the Comet. Crying and yelling resonated from the bedroom.

"I washed down the boards and put them in the trunk. You can go now."

"Seth, come here." Russell tried to get the boy to meet his eyes, but he wouldn't. Damn it, this whole business was beyond his control. Why did she always have to launch into the heavy shit in front of the boys?

Ethan stopped crying and Margie called out. "Russell, you want to come in here a minute?"

What else had he done wrong? Committed the felonious act of tucking sheets in upside down?

Margie pulled back the covers and showed him Ethan's torso.

Small, raised red spots were gathered in the warmest areas of his body. They resembled his itchy mosquito bite, but Russell had a feeling they couldn't all be bug bites. She lifted his arms to show him the same phenomenon taking place in his armpits.

"A sand rash. It'll go away with a shower and some aloe."

196

"This," Margie announced, "is chicken pox. 'An acute, contagious, eruptive disease, chiefly found in children.'"

Russell felt sympathetic itching erupt all over his body. "I'm sorry. Hey, wait a minute. Doesn't that disease have a really long incubation period?"

"Yes, but—"

"Then I'm off the hook. He would have gotten it anyway. Maybe the salt water hurried a few spots along, but he was scratching before we left the house. Ask Seth if you don't believe me."

Margie snapped the covers up over her miserable boy. "Now I have to call in to school, find some way to take care of him, probably lose my job. . . ."

Guilt racked Russell's bachelor soul. "Farmer owes me. I'll call him and trade hours."

Margie was looking out the small window at the brick of her neighbor's house. "Ethan should be in his own bed."

"So I'll come over here and watch him until you get home."

Margie looked at him evenly. He could tell she didn't quite know where next to point her anger. Finally she said, "Thanks."

Margie made them macaroni salad with the last of the mayonnaise and cooked up beef franks topped with chili and grated cheese. Ethan wanted only a few sips of 7-Up and to stay in bed.

She squirted yellow mustard on her hot dog bun. "Thank God he'll be over this before your grandfather's birthday party."

Russell hadn't yet decided with what he would decorate his buns, but it damn sure wasn't going to be that paint-like mustard. "You really want to go?"

She stopped squirting and began shoveling on relish. "Of course I do. Don't you want to go?"

"Don't be ridiculous," he lied. "Of course I want to go."

She got a faraway look on her face. "By then I should have lost at least ten pounds. I might even fit into one of those blouses. Which one do you like best, Russell? The black silk one or—" she lowered her voice suggestively, "the low-cut sexy red one?"

Seth let his knife clatter to his plate and got up to leave the table. Was there no hope for them to grow up normally? Would Dr. M live long enough to repair everyone foolish enough to come into contact with the Carpenter family?

"Either's going to look just great on you." Russell spun his fork around the salad, making a hole in the center. Mayonnaise—a high percentage of the population contracted salmonella from mayonnaise. He hardly trusted wieners either, what with the waste allowances for rat hairs and bone fragments, but for penance he dug in, grateful at least tonight there would be no more talk of marriage.

He called Lane at lunchtime, and was surprised he caught his sister home. "You're not working today?"

"There was a big hush-hush budget meeting downtown so they let us peons off early. I just walked in the door. Can you tell?"

Russell could hear the dogs barking in the background. "What's with the pooches?"

"They can't tell time. If I open the door and I'm wearing work clothes, that means it's got to be four o'clock, time for a W-A-L-K. We go through this every day. How blessed it must be to be born without long-term memory. For God's sake, Oddjob, settle down. There is *nothing* to bark at!"

The dogs continued to protest. "Listen, Lane, isn't there something you can do for chicken pox? This kid is scratching himself bloody."

"Poor little guy. I think it pretty much has to run its course. You could try an oatmeal bath."

"You mean, like Quaker with the Ben Franklin dude on the box?"

"No, Russell, it's medicinal. I remember the pharmacy with the medical rentals had it."

He cringed at the thought of all that mortal equipment they'd once rented. "I don't suppose I could prevail upon you to bring some over?"

His sister sighed. "Margie will flip out if she discovers I entered her house when she wasn't there."

"We don't have to tell her."

"What about Ethan?"

"He's so out of it he'll think you're Wonder Woman. His temperature's a hundred and one. Shouldn't I take him to the doctor or something?"

"Not unless it goes up to one hundred and three. In the meantime, read to him, that'll take his mind off the itching. I'll run over there now and leave the bag on the porch. Be sure and read the directions, and make sure the bath's only tepid, okay? And call me back if anything changes."

"Tepid. That's like, what, room temperature?"

"Yes. So it doesn't burn your wrist. By the way, Russell, have you ever had chicken pox?"

He flipped the phone cord smugly over his shoulder. "Well, that's a stupid question. I'm thirty-four-years old. Of course I have. Haven't I?"

CHAPTER 15

WALKIES

"WHAT WORRIES ME IS HOW GOOD I'M GETTING AT lying," Russell told Dr. Mapp from the edge of a truly uncomfortable chair. "I might have to get a little notebook to carry around so I can keep track of everything I say. Christ, what's the use? Margie's probably wise to me. I'm not that great a liar. I wonder if there is a hell? What do you think? Could this be Armageddon already and we just don't realize it?"

Dr. M tapped her stout pencil against her clipboard. "I'm interested in what *you* think, Russell."

Sometimes, when she was tired or bearing down, Dr. M rolled her *r*s. He couldn't decide if this was a remnant of a Swiss-German accent, some kind of formal Spanish, or simply an intimidating therapist-client tactic she'd mastered in medical school.

"You know, I've been coming here a long time. I'm wise to you, Dr. M. You're turning that question around on me on purpose. You do that all the time, you know. What's the deal here? Am I supposed to have all the answers? If so, why not have a therapy session by looking in the mirror and writing myself a check? I could do it while I was shaving. Save us both time. But wait, I have a beard. So I guess I need you after all. Listen, you're supposed to be the tour guide. Just this once, couldn't you tell me what you think? I swear, I'm throwing snowballs into space on this one." He slumped back in the uncomfortable chair, trying to look needy.

Dr. M looked down at her diamond ring for a long while, then she tilted her head back and nudged her glasses up her long, thin nose. "You know, Russell, I think it's time to discuss the concept of marriage. Why don't you tell me how you view the institution, not in general, but as in the case of yourself?"

"Marriage? That's easy. I don't. We're done. Next topic."

"Never?"

"Nope."

Dr. M wrote something on her clipboard. "And the reason for this is?"

He looked at her poster of Chagall's "I and My City," a painting he didn't understand. It reminded him of Lane's thought progressions—beautiful, fragmented little bits of craziness he only rarely understood. "I have a go-nowhere job, I'm addicted to my guitars, I'm losing my hair, and my genes are shot through with defective Carpenter heart DNA. My, what a prize package I'd make some lucky girl."

"I notice you say girl instead of woman. Why do you think that is?"

"Oh, probably continued proof of my immaturity."

"Immaturity?"

Russell shoved his hands into his pockets and fingered his Fender pick. "Why are we talking like this? I came here to feel better. It's been a week topped with chocolate-covered cherries. Trying to keep Ethan from scarring himself, Margie expecting me to fuck her lights out every night, my sister freaking out about my grandfather's birthday—and all I want to do is play a guitar I never got a chance to buy!"

"The Gretsch?"

"Of course the Gretsch!"

Dr. M smiled.

"What? You find my misery amusing? What

happened to compassion?"

"Russell, I don't mean to smile. Please continue. I'm smiling because I smell imminent breakthrough."

He watched in stunned silence as she rubbed her hands together, laced her fingers and, yes, he couldn't believe it, cracked her knuckles. "Really. I don't smell anything."

She lifted an eyebrow. "Clock's ticking. Can we get to work?"

"Work" meant hashing through all the marriages of which he possessed close personal knowledge. They started with his parents'. "The best times were nothing all that special, I guess. We'd go to the drive-in, watch *Planet of the Apes* and eat over-salted cold fried chicken and beg for Cokes. Or everyone'd watch Lane ride her pony in some rigged horse show, win a not terribly surprising bunch of ribbons, then we'd go out for peppermint ice cream after. Speaking of smells, I like how horses smell, but it'd take a great deal of money to get me astride one again. Did I ever show you the scar where that insane stallion my grandfather owns bit me?"

"Twice. The affection between your parents—lots of hugging, kissing, yes?"

A picture of his mother's cheek, slathered with makeup, offered to himself and his sister at bedtime flooded his brain. "My parents weren't all that demonstrative."

"With each other or with you children?"

"Both. Neither. Come on, Dr. M, that was a long time ago. I don't remember."

"And this absence of affection, did you miss it?"

"How could I miss something I never knew was supposed to be there?"

Dr. M wrote on her clipboard for five whole minutes,

202

by the clock in the Buddha's belly. "Your grandfather?" she said when she finished.

"Bop, now that's a whole different story. Talk about affection. Heart like a slot machine."

"That's an odd image."

Russell craned his memory back into the shadows of early childhood. Casa de Carpenter—they went there every weekend, kind of a substitute for Disneyland, this crazy stone and glass house sitting all alone in the newly dredged harbor. His grandma Alyce smelled like Jergen's hand lotion and chocolate chip cookies. He knew she favored him. She'd drive them to the Toy Chest and he could pick out something that cost five dollars while Lane only rated two-fifty.

"Well, at first it felt like being the star of my own TV show. Ladies and gentlemen, Russell's here! Let's give him a hand. Bake him some allergen-free cookies."

"And then later, when it wasn't?"

"Well, let's just say I missed the cookies."

Dr. M gave him her "straighten-up" look.

"Okay." His mind filled with a picture of Gloria cornering his grandfather in the kitchen, some Christmas or another. She had her leg wrapped around his waist and was rocking her pelvis against his button fly, right there under the recessed lighting, where anybody could walk in and where Russell had. His grandfather was honking her bare tit out the front of her black low-cut sweater and her nipple stood out pink as a pencil eraser. Russell was fifteen; his father was dead two years. On the spot, he developed an erection so demanding he hurried outside to smoke a joint on the dock in order to quiet things down. Helene was uninspiring, but Gloria made a lasting impression.

"My grandfather turns eighty next month. He's a

horndog. You know what that means, Dr. M?"

"I grasp the general concept."

"Do you think maybe I have a low sperm count? I can get by just fine doing it only once a week. Are men supposed to always fantasize during the act or is that sick behavior? You see—God, this is embarrassing—with Margie I shut my eyes, and Jesus, I can't believe I'm telling you this, it's the girl from the Guess jeans ad or some freckled checker who waited on me at Albertson's. Sometimes a week goes by I hardly even think about fucking, to tell you the truth."

"We've been through that topic before, Russell. I know all your concerns regarding your sex life. Tell me what you think of your sister's marriage."

"It's brick. The house the wolf couldn't blow down. Pardon the pathetic metaphor. I've read a few too many fairy tales this week."

"Do you really believe that, Russell, or is that the way you want to perceive their marriage?"

His stomach turned over and he worried Dr. M knew something he didn't. To buy time, he said, "Let me think a minute."

In the beginning, they were laying down solid brick, working in tandem. Nick could hardly stop smiling at his sister and Russell knew she was happy because she sang all the time. He imagined her singing through orgasms. Sex was part of it, it had to be, because in high school, whereas he'd kept his dealer busy scouting out nice grades of affordable pot, Lainie had sampled boyfriends' abilities in the sack. Then, after she married Nick and got knocked up, things only seemed to grow more solid between them, like all that work had been to lay the foundation for Spencer. *Unca Russell!* Spencer became the cotter pin of their lives—his, too, he guessed, because unclehood was endlessly entertaining and non-unclehood left pieces of his heart flapping like a giant tear in a tent. They had been talking about repeating the process, going for another baby when Spencer turned south of midnight, and since then, obviously no baby talk had taken place in the Carpenter-Clarke household. They slogged through the dark days, same as everyone else. But they were together, unlike most of the couples they met at that awful support group Lane swore she would never go back to. What did hold Nick and Lainie together, now that they'd lost their most precious cargo? Was it the pain of that wound, or was it company on the long trek out of it?

"I know they're not happy. I think we've all forgotten how to play that particular little number. All I know is it seems like they each found the right person. Each understands how the other thinks. There's respect. Lane doesn't bitch when Nick stays in the garage sanding wood until bedtime and he doesn't get upset when she cooks gourmet dog biscuits instead of his dinner. Hey, you think maybe somebody else could make me see this marriage deal in a different light? Probably not. There's a fundamental issue here involving decent women finding me attractive. And the whole Carpenter family heart thing. Or is that parataxical thinking? What do you think, Dr. M, any hope for me having a regular life?"

She smiled and pointed her pencil at the squinting, perpetually amused Buddha ticking on her bookshelf, where the books all had frightening, Latinate, multisyllabic titles. "I'm sorry, Russell, that's all the time we have for today. You'll have to come back next week to talk about this further."

What was the deal here? Was therapy some freaking

forty-five minute game show?

He was dreaming of the grade-school bullies again. They were eight years old, outfitted in three-piece Armani suits. No one but Russell found it strange they'd painted mustaches on their upper lips. "Trust me, these guys are wussies," he tried to explain to a small group of misfits, his friends, the boys who always sat under the acacia tree discussing fuel-injected engines.

The other geeky boys scattered like birdshot; Russell stood alone facing the horde of Huns. "Can we get this over with quickly?" he said. "Next period's science and I don't want to miss dissecting the cow heart."

Happily they complied, and he felt their blows fall on him like small fists of rain. Whoops—there went the cartilage in his nose. Pain was no stranger to his body. He may have been a wimp at physical education, but at least the science teacher liked him. She'd chosen him to make the first cut on the cow heart! Proudly he raised the scalpel and with his free hand wiped away the blood that was dripping down his face into the white enamel pan. Any minute he feared the honor would be taken from him, the teacher ordering him to the back of the classroom to wipe his face clean with one of those scratchy brown paper towels.

"Class, Russell's going to do a very special thing for us today," she said. "Let me tell you just what that special thing is. He's going to cut open his father's heart and show us what defect caused it to stop beating. That's right class, poor Russell has no father! Can everyone say, 'Poor Russell?' "

Poor Russell!

The bullies smirked and Russell woke up clutching a fistful of damp sheet. His clock read 2:21 A.M. and the phone was ringing. He lifted the receiver and whispered, "Hello?"

There was crying on the other end. "Lane?"

"Are you awake?"

"What's wrong? Nick get in a wreck or something?"

"Of course not," she sniffled. "He's a wonderful driver. He's never even gotten a speeding ticket. You remember that Hank Williams song, 'I Don't Care?' "

Russell rubbed the sleep from his eyes. His pulse was beating a little more normally now, but the image of the cow heart hadn't completely departed. "Not really."

"Yes, you do."

"Honest, Lane. I don't. Hum a few bars."

Lainie took a breath and started to sing, her voice catching on uneven sobs.

He remembered. Mr. Williams didn't care if tomorrow ever came. Neither did Lane. The perfect little fugue for late night ponderings. She sang all three verses. Even in the nightmare-sopped dark his sister had a voice that could light the light old Hank saw the night he took his final nap in the back of the rented Cadillac. Russell kept silent, sensing that whatever was bothering her, singing to him meant she was at some kind of turning point. When she finished the song, he said, "For a drug addict, old Hank could really put the pen to paper. Let me get dressed, I'll be right over."

"No, I'll drive over with the dogs and get you. I was making jelly and suddenly I just couldn't face another Ball jar twist cap. I feel like walking in the bluffs."

At two in the morning? "Leave Nick a note, Lane. He might wake up and wonder where you are."

"I'm not totally hopeless. I will."

"What kind of jelly, by the way?"

"Jalapeño."

"Am I allergic to that?"

"No. You're allergic to cherry tomato." She hung up the receiver so softly he hardly heard the click before the dial tone.

"We go out for walkies, after midnight," Russell sang in his best Barbara Woodhouse British tremolo, unleashing Shaky Jake in the darkness. "Chef Patsy Cline, her patsy of a brother, plus two very confused pooches."

Lane didn't laugh at his joke. In the moonlight her face looked like broken marble. The beauty there had been disassembled for all time. They walked to the edge of the cliffs and looked down toward the ocean. Far off in the distance, the lights from the Huntington Beach power plant shone through the fog, strange and garish as a carousel.

"Nick says I have to go to Bop's birthday party."

Russell wrapped the dog leashes over his hand. "It's not that big a deal, Lane."

"But that means I have to wear a dress and say hello to people and act like everything's okay."

"Everything is okay."

"Oh, Russell, how can you say that?"

"Because I'm an idiot. Idiots are optimistic. It's one of their noblest qualities."

Lane sat down in the dirt and hugged her knees. Russell sat down beside her. Soon the two dogs joined them, certain this human sitting activity involved the possibility of something edible. The four sat watching the night sky, feeling the dew settle in their clothing and fur.

"Nick wants to have another baby," Lane said softly. "He doesn't say it out loud, but I can tell what he's thinking."

Russell wanted her to have one, too. "What do you want?"

Lane petted Jake's neck where he'd flung himself across her lap. Somewhere in the background, out of sight, Russell could hear Oddjob digging.

"You know what I'd like most of all?" she said. "I'd like to find a really good recipe for sweet Mexican corn cake, like Grandma Alyce used to make. It must be some kind of trade secret, protected under penalty of death because I've checked a jillion Mexican cookbooks, but I can never find anything like it. I've sifted cornmeal and experimented with spices, but it never comes out right."

"You don't have to be able to make everything, Lane. Nowhere is it written that a few recipes can't stay secret."

"I know, but . . ."

Another baby—another crack at the Carpenter heart. She'd have better odds in Vegas. Russell couldn't think of anything else to do besides put his arm around her shoulders. He imagined Lane standing alone in her kitchen, suicidal over corncake failure.

"I wonder," his sister said, "if it's like certain words in Chinese, no one's allowed to write them down—it's considered bad form. I just don't know, Russell. But to tell you the truth, I think about that corncake all the time."

CHAPTER 16

MEMORY JEOPARDY

A THIRTY-YEAR-OLD BUILDING WAS A RARITY IN Southern California. Casa de Carpenter, with its odd angles and oxidized copper was even scarcer. As their Volvo neared the old house, Lainie felt the ghosts of thirty-four Christmases began to fire along her nerves.

"Maybe I'd better stop the car," Nick said. "My wife's smiling. Dare I hope for world peace? Or is that too much to ask?"

"There isn't and yes," Lainie said from the passenger seat as her husband pulled up to the already crowded curb.

"Come on, Lainie. Singing 'Happy Birthday' won't kill you."

She wondered what Nick would ask for next. A tap dance? Skywriting? "I'm here. You don't need to lecture me on the moral responsibilities of attending my grandfather's eightieth birthday party."

"Did it sound like I was lecturing?" Nick pocketed the keys in his khaki trousers. "I'm sorry. Maybe I enjoyed the smile for my own selfish reasons."

Lainie toed her way back into the black cowboy boots that had been too hot to keep on in the non-air conditioned Volvo and pushed her car door shut. She shot Nick her best manufactured grin, the same one she wore around the deep pockets at work and when dealing with County by-the-book bitches like Elizabeth Friedman. Sometimes she even hauled it out for her mother.

Nick sighed. "Oh, honey, what is it you need? You want me to tell you how great you look? Ripe—that's the only word for it. I could watch you walk in front of me all night, Elaine."

She stuck out her tongue and crossed her eyes. "We'll see how great everything looks after somebody gets drunk and starts throwing objets d'art. And they will."

"Try not to be nervous."

She felt her husband's hand press into the small of her back. This small act of possession never failed to undo her. She'd seen how women stared at Nick in public. They looked at her husband and suddenly it dawned on them how incredibly sexy stability could be, that little something they'd passed over all their lives in search of roosters sporting brighter plumage. Behind prematurely silvering hair and abundant laugh lines, this man would happily put his hand to raising another woman's children. He was a born negotiator possessing infinite patience. Even when his child died, he held up.

Though Nick seemed oblivious to his appeal, Lainie knew better. The hospital was flush with pretty young nurses and well-heeled female visitors coming and going. Nick, old butter-heart, might even fall for one of his patients, a woman he could help. She was trying her best to follow Russell's advice. So far this evening, that meant considering the effect the view of her behind had on her husband as she walked in front of him down the flagstone path.

There hadn't used to be a gate here. The original design of the house intended the flagstone walkway to gradually descend so that the surrounding wall rose from waist-level stone to shoulderder-height, creating the feeling of entering a fortress. About ten years ago, her grandfather had broken down and installed the gate to keep nosy passersby—and ex-wives—out. It was unlocked, so she and Nick meandered past the vanished corners and oxidizing blue copper roof to the redwood deck at the rear of the house, from which the party noise rose in decibel. It felt to Lainie like they were entering a ship, where at any moment the raised flag might just reveal a skull and crossbones.

A handful of well-dressed guests were sipping from champagne flutes, listening to the hired music, looking elegant and cool and problem-free. She didn't recognize anyone. Nick smiled and said hello to people while a twangy guitar and violin plunked out "Oceanfront Property." The song seemed made to order for this tarnish-free August afternoon. Caterers hurried plates and silverware from the kitchen to the rented tables. Her grandfather, the birthday boy, was nowhere in sight. His boat, *Shadow IV*, was tethered snugly in its mooring. She couldn't remember the last time anyone had sailed it. Sun dappled the bay water, casting dollar-sized circles on the greenish surface. Lainie put up her hand to shade her eyes and Nick pointed across the bay to where two college-aged kids were sponging down the foredeck of a shiny white sailboat.

"Nice looking boat," Nick said. "Brings back memories."

"It sure does." An endless string of memories, ranging from the child-self she had once been to believing that to sail a boat was to possess Olympian power. Then a brief sharp-edged snapshot of Spencer's small hand atop hers working the tiller. *Look at me, Mama! I'm the captain.* Similar boats bobbed at their moorings while custom-built homes hung over the water's edge, all part of some incredibly complicated beaded necklace stretched across the coastline, jewelry for those few who could afford it. "How long do we have to stay if he doesn't show up?"

Nick rubbed her arm. "He'll show up, Lainie. It's his party. Isn't that a perfect sunset?"

"Yes." He would show up. Act disrespectful, blow out his candles, and cause someone to cry. Soon it would be dusk. Running lights on passing boats would illuminate profiles of the houses and the people who stood outside on the decks, imbuing everything with a sense of endless summer. As a kid she'd stood for hours feeling the salt spray dry on her skin, crackling against her sunburn as she listened to the slow lap of the water.

When her dad died, Bop held a small reception here

following the graveside service. Mother wore a Chanel suit and made up the sandwich trays herself. Lainie could see that her mother was determined to get through the day without breaking down, that she felt it was her duty. Then Bop said, "Well, Meridel, the terms of Chuck's trust have left you a wealthy widow," and in the shocked silence that followed before her mother started to sob, the guests were privy to the true spirit of the Carpenter clan. The ear-piercing chug of boats motored by that day, spewing the sweet-awful odor of diesel fuel. The bare cement pilings where hand-shaped starfish once clung were winter-bare. Truth had come spearing through Lainie's heart, informing her that the only perfect thing to be found in Bop's harbor was the water. Daddy'd wanted cremation, his ashes scattered at sea, but Bop and her mother would have none of that. Why couldn't you visit the ocean as easily as a grave? she wanted to know, but they just looked at her as if the question was crazy.

I hope you didn't have your heart set on beans and wienies," Nick said, pointing to the caterers loading up the barbecue with lobster and skewered shrimp. Shellfish sizzled against the grill while one caterer painted them with butter and another transferred them to platters where they were immediately festooned with cilantro sprigs and bathed in salsa.

Nick took one of the waiting plates from its stack. "We could eat now if you're hungry."

"Could we wait? I want to see if Russell shows up."

"Lainie, your brother will be here if only to critique the guitarist's chord changes."

There were tiny, fingernail-sized orchids and wild ferns trailing from hanging baskets, and peach-colored satin ribbons decorating the deck in fanciful bows. She touched one. "I guess you're right. Wow, somebody sure went to a great deal of trouble with these decorations."

"Kind of a different look for your grandfather, wouldn't you say? More like a wedding reception than a birthday."

Bad joke, but it was as if the stone walls held themselves with renewed posture under the sprucing up. "Well, they're pretty flowers," she murmured.

Nick set the plate down and pocketed his hands, which was what he always did rather than start an argument.

Lainie bit her tongue. Her side ached slightly with the mid-cycle pain she sometimes got and tried to ignore. A waitress dressed in a gingham halter top and thigh-high denim handed each of them a glass of champagne, which Lainie accepted and Nick, uncharacteristically, downed in three quick successive sips before reaching for a second. He set his glass on a table and began kneading her shoulders.

Her black dress was eight years old, a Jonathan Martin her mother had bought her one Christmas. *Black never goes out of style,* Meridel insisted. Lainie'd worn it to Spencer's funeral, to three staff Christmas parties for the hospital, and now here it was again, the moderate hemline immortal, the spare lines calling attention to the fact that here stood one ex-mother who could still fit into her high school prom dress.

People she'd never seen before in her life were parking a thirty-foot Bayliner next to *Shadow IV* at her grandfather's slip, laughing and throwing lines to the concrete dock. She thought she spotted that icky reporter, but decided she was mistaken. Maybe Bop had gone swimming with a megaphone, inviting the entire Harbour. Rich people had well-dressed neighbors. Instant party guests—just add liquor. One by one they

214

came ashore, drinking Stoli on ice.

Nick finished her shoulder massage. "The category is nineteen seventy-nine, for a hundred dollars. The answer is, My earliest memory of this house."

He wanted to play Memory jeopardy, a game Russell had invented one New Year's when the cable television went out. She answered, "What is 'I shudder to think?'"

He laughed. "That question hardly qualifies. What is 'The summer before we got married, a barbecue, no special occasion—I believe wife Gloria presided over the affair—and what happened after one particular sailing trip I'll never forget.'"

"I don't win any imaginary money?"

"Not that easily. However, there may be a Daily Double. You and I'd spent the day sailing the little Laser. Actually, you sailed and I tried hard not to make an idiot out of myself by getting in your way. You were sunburned, here," he said, "and here," drawing a finger over the wings of her bare shoulders. "And every time you reached for something, white skin peeked out from under your bathing suit. We'd drunk a few beers before dinner and I was feeling awfully lucky having you sit on my lap. Your grandfather seared a side of beef and Gloria tried to fill everyone up on cheese and crackers. But we weren't the only guests. That interior decorator of hers was mincing around explaining what he was going to have to do to the casa in order to 'reclaim the downstairs from the old west.'" Nick laughed again, and shook his head. "That decorator sure pissed the old man off."

Lainie looked up. "I remember now! Bop threw him in the bay. But not his little pug dog. He was never unkind to animals, just people. How much is the bonus money?"

"No *dinero* for you yet. Later, what else happened?"

"I don't know. Something Bop said to you? Did he ask your intentions or say something so horrible you had to keep it from me all these years?"

Nick bent and nuzzled her neck where the fine hairs grew in an upward whorl toward her hastily assembled French twist. "Neither, and please remember to phrase your answer in the form of a question. While Gloria was crying, you showed me around the house, all the places you hid as a kid. Those secret spots kids manage to find that adults can't. Then you took me in the atrium, I shut the door behind us, and the paint was so new it stuck. You, me, and all those plants in temperature-controlled private humidity. One thing led to another and pretty soon I had your dress up around your waist."

They were in the midst of complete strangers, sipping birthday cheer, and here was Nick, discussing their sex life as blithely as the weather. Lainie blushed. "Jesus, Nick. A hundred and fifty years ago."

"Feels like yesterday to me. The atrium incident is one of my top ten favorite memories. On bad days, I haul it out and review every detail. My colleagues sit around the classroom nodding their heads at some new hospital regulation the administrators have thought up to make treatment plans more difficult, but not me. I'm twenty-eight years old again, about to score bigtime with my future wife."

She smiled and patted his hand. "You're a renaissance man, Nikolai. Too bad you don't have a queenly wife with the royal extended family you deserve."

"I much prefer the Carpenter clan with all their collective neuroses. There are definite perks."

"Well, if after all this time you can still find something perky in this drama, you're a magician."

"Your breasts come to mind."

"If Russell heard you talking like this he'd call you a horndog."

"Maybe I'm just a man in love with his wife."

Which was even scarier magic. The atrium incident. That was so like Nick to name it. He probably had it filed under its own DMS-IV numerical code. She remembered the dress, a summery cotton hippie calico print with little-girl smocking over her pre-childbirth breasts. It happened before the ice age, back when passion was immediate, so easily invoked all it took was the touch of a finger. No before-dinner drinks, no soft music, no deep concentration to blot out hospital scenes and bill worries that came flying at you the moment you shut your eyes, insisting you had no right to feel good in the midst of all this unfinished business. Memory Jeopardy was a dangerous game. *I'll take 1987 for $240,000, please. Answer: Red-beaded male infant, born 6:40 P.M. at Hoag Memorial Hospital. Question: And remember, this is the Daily Double! Who is, no, who was. . ."*

Here came her grandfather now, last one out of the party boat, half-sloshed on birthday cheer and lavish female attention, that angel-slandering cowboy hat fixed on his hard head. Lainie swallowed the last of her champagne. A third glass before food was asking for trouble, but oh, the comfortable haze it would deliver. Maybe she and Nick could sneak off to the atrium at some point, check to make sure the plants were watered, indulge in some light necking. Give him what you can, Russell had said. She could manage a few kisses for old time's sake. The night wouldn't be a total washout.

Nick, all manners, stepped forward with a grin to shake her grandfather's hand. "Charles Russell," he said. "Many happy returns of the day. Congratulations on reaching eighty."

"And I'm far from done reaching, son. Good-looking girl you got with you. Too bad you can't get her to smile." He pinched Lainie's cheek and rubbed his hands together. "Can't wait to get to the presents!" He passed by them and on to his other guests.

Under his breath, Nick said, "I knew we forgot something."

"No, we didn't," Lainie said. "I bought him a present."

"You did? What do you buy a man who has everything?"

"A case of drop-forged steel stud chains for that idiot horse of his. He'll have them all broken before the year's end."

Nick stared at her. "This from the woman who's always trying to get me to go riding with her."

"Well, it doesn't have to be on Tontito, obviously." She stopped the waitress and garnered another glass. She waved at her grandfather's attorney and the guests she didn't know. Let the evening blur. "Cheers," she said, to no one in particular and felt the carbonation enter her brain, each bubble a down pillow on which every troubling thought could rest a weary head.

CHAPTER 17

TEXAS CAVIAR

IF MEN GOT A VOTE, RUSSELL WOULD HAVE dressed Margie in something long and draped, maybe one of those tie-dyed, baggy pants outfits he sometimes saw displayed in the window of the import store across

218

from Red Lyzyrd. Something that announced: Here before you stands one big woman, but do not judge her by size alone. We're talking as large of heart as she is ample of body. Take her or leave her. That attitude would do Margie justice, but the trouble was, it wasn't anywhere near the truth. It was the way Margie *used* to be when he first met her, when she'd left Mr. Personality.

Back then, to fill up the gaps of time when Dad had the boys, she volunteered her time at the convalescent home. She delivered Meals on Wheels to shut-ins every Thursday, which was coordinated in the same hospital in which Dr. M's office was located. Russell had met Margie in the parking lot, fixed a flat tire for her, helped load up the trays of food, admired her smile, and asked her out. She was always hugging her boys like they had brought home those bumper stickers announcing they were Student of the Month. She was never thin, but thin never mattered to Russell. She looked good and she was easy-going; if the kids broke a dish, she got out the Krazy Glue.

Now her patience with the boys came in size petite extra small. She wore her red Liz Claiborne sale blouse like the lifeguard's flag announcing dangerous surf. Russell knew single-mothering was hard and he tried to help, but sometimes he swore her heart had sclerosed down to as narrow an opening as the grooves on an old 78 record.

All this speculation made for a pointless mind excursion, for when it came to clothing, men's opinions counted for naught. Still, he admired her pluck, that denim miniskirt and too-tight red blouse among a sea of careful Armani and Carole Little. What was he going to do? Dr. Mapp had advised him to wait until after the

219

party before telling her he wanted to end the relationship. He had breathed a large sigh of relief, because next to listening to late seventies music, confrontations with Margie were right up there on his list of favorite things *not* to do. Now that Ethan was well, however, the time was nearing. He scratched his neck and considered possible opening lines. *Margie, there comes a time . . .*

"There's your sister at the railing," Margie said. "I see she's wearing that same ratty old black dress. Things must be pretty tight if Nick can't even afford to buy her a new dress."

Russell nodded hello to the strangers on his left and kept walking. He wasn't about to reveal Lane's mountain of hospital debt to Margie. "Lane's never been a big shopper. I think she opens her closet and whatever falls on the floor, she wears."

Margie sniffed. "Well, that's not very smart. Men appreciate women who take care of themselves, fashion-wise."

"They do?"

"Why do you think I spent three weeks planning this outfit, finding just the right accessories, painting my nails to match my top?"

"I don't know."

"It's called *style*, Russell. Your sister could take a lesson."

Russell looked at Lane in the eternal black dress. "Her underwear isn't showing or anything. What's the problem?"

Margie sighed. "You just don't get it."

Maybe he was missing something, but it seemed like the only people who cared what women wore were other women. After that night in the bluffs, Russell doubted a new outfit would help his sister. He quit listening to Margie's commentary and checked out the band. They weren't half bad, especially the guitar player. Flatpicker, not an easy style. Whoa. Hold on. Damned if he wasn't playing a Gibson arch-top Super 400. Oh, the luck of encountering violin technology at a birthday party for the old man! The instrument looked to be in moderately good shape, only a few surface nicks on the soundboard. He wondered how many bottles of Korbel, currently making the rounds of all these strangers, could convince the lad to part with it. Could Russell come up with $3,000, which would be a steal of a price? However, considering the current state of his ATM balance, he wondered if this hired gun would go for as little as $400 as a deposit? Would Lane—who was coming this way—have any spare cash to loan? On all fronts, the weather looked doubtful.

Nick kissed Margie's cheek, and she smiled at him, her mascara and frosted green eye shadow leaving little metallic trails on her cheeks. Lane waved hi, and Russell wondered if his sister was thinking what he was thinking—that Margie's makeup looked like something out of an old "Star Trek" rerun, some chick Captain Kirk kisses just before she licks the salt off his body.

"Margie, how are your boys?" Lainie asked. "I was so glad to hear Ethan's feeling better."

"Ethan's fine."

"And Seth's probably growing like a weed. Is he in junior lifeguards this year?"

Margie rolled her eyes. "The teacher's making Seth repeat Slow Beginners for the third time. Until he jumps off the high dive, they won't pass him. I feel like climbing the ladder myself and giving the little toad a shove."

"I wouldn't advise it," Nick said. "Therapy costs more than swim lessons."

"I take him down to Huntington and he does just fine in the ocean," Russell said. "It's that pool business has him spooked. The kid can handle a bodyboard like Smokin' Dan Taylor. I don't see why he has to jump off some freakin' high dive to prove his manhood."

Margie made a face. "Russell always tries to make excuses for Seth, among others. He's so inconsistent."

"I am not. This is a perfectly logical question. And I've asked it before."

Lainie pointed up to the overhanging balcony of her grandfather's bedroom. "Russell, remember when we used to leap off that ledge into the bay? We were fearless, braver than lifeguards."

"We were knuckleheads. I can't believe neither of us broke our necks."

"How could we break our necks when we believed the water would always catch us?"

"I don't know. But the bay's too sludged up and shallow to try it now. You might not break your neck, but you'd land gonad-deep in some kind of toxic slime."

Lainie laughed.

Margie swung her champagne glass in a wide arc, meant to encompass the Carpenter compound. "Oh, quick, everybody stop talking while the twins go for a little hike down Memory Lane."

For a second, they did stop talking. Then Lainie, who'd been just about to say something, cast her eyes downward in that old search for reason to continue, and inside his chest wall, Russell's heart strained against several old scars. He pressed his lips together and watched Nick's fingers circle Lane's arm, delivering an almost invisible squeeze. The good doctor and his buck-up gesture, almost making things better.

Nick said, "They're setting out hors d'oeuvres on the table. Scampi, couple kinds of dip, it looks like. Can I get anybody a plate?"

Russell pinched the skin between his eyebrows. "Margie," he began.

"What?"

"Margie, there comes a time—"

"Kids!" Bop hollered from his entourage, who were clustered by the smoking barbecue. "Get your Carpenter butts on over here. Someone I want you to meet."

"What, Russell?" Margie said again, her brown eyes challenging.

"Later, and that's a promise." Russell lugged the awkwardness Margie'd flung out, a lunchbox full of lead pellets with which he wanted to smack her generously lipsticked mouth. His sister politely looked away, and the Nickster only wrinkled his forehead in clinical interest.

Dr. Mapp, Russell thought to himself, *I know I promised I'd wait, but wherever it is we're headed, I don't think the goddamn ice can get much thinner.*

This mismatched crew of relatives and unhappy lovers trotted across the redwood decking to wish newly eighty Grandfather Carpenter his happy birthday. Russell tried to keep an unobtrusive eye on the guitarist. Was he the kind of player who knew enough to wrap his instrument in felt? Exposure to sea air guaranteed warp, not to mention he was standing a little closer to the barbecue than was good for the finish.

"Miss Earlynn Sommers," Bop beamed, "these are my sorry grandchildren, Elaine and her husband, Nick, Russell and his friend, Margie."

Earlynn gave him a playful slap on his Hawaiian

shirt. His bola tie swung in protest. "Oh, Charles, they're not sorry at all. They're lovely young people. Stop your teasing."

Russell whispered to his sister, "Hasn't screwed her yet, but tonight may prove lucky."

"Shhh," Lainie said and shook the petite woman's hand.

Earlynn had dressed in nautical motif for the dockside party, navy epaulets at her shoulders, gold embroidered stars everywhere there was a square inch of spare material. Russell tried to figure out if she'd had plastic surgery, but up close there were fine wrinkles around her wide smile so he guessed not.

"I am so doggone glad to finally meet you all. Your grandpa here has told me your life stories. I swear, so much has happened to you all it's like reading the bonus issue of *Soap Opera Digest!* I can't hardly believe some of it. This crazy house, your papa cut down in his prime, that poor little boy's heart—" here she finally ran out of breath, simultaneously blushing plum beneath her face powder. "Good Lord, you all have got to forgive me. My tongue acts like a mutt dog sometimes, all eager and wagging, forgetting its manners."

Nick took the comment in stride, saying, "We're glad to meet you too, Miss Sommers. What do you think of the house?"

She visibly relaxed. "Just call me Earlynn, won't you?"

"Earlynn it is."

Good old Nick, Russell thought, diplomatic to all, the mannered and the mannerless alike. Russell shot Lane a look. She gave him a slow, wet-eyed wink, sad, but she was holding up. Meanwhile, Margie examined her fingernail polish.

"Oh, honey, I'm just a dyed blond nobody from Itty

224

Bitty, Texas."

Bop roared with laughter. "Can you believe it? She says stuff like that twenty-four hours a day."

"On the contrary," Lainie put in. "You must be somebody special if you've got my grandfather grinning like a horsetrader. The most we can ever wrangle out of him are a few smirks."

Bop's smile hardened. "Lainie, this here's my birthday. Be nice."

"I'm just making an observation. Tell me how that's not nice."

"Well, for starters it wouldn't kill you to lose the frown—"

"Everybody look here!" Earlynn scooped up a passing appetizer tray and offered it to them. "Texas caviar! Black-eyed peas, jalapeño peppers, and the sweetest Texas onion ever grown in hardscrabble dirt. You scoop it up on these cute little tiny tortillas we found at the supermarket. Cost a fortune, but oh well, you only live once and you can't take it with you, and if you do there's nothing fun to spend it on. Go on, try some. Those catering people had never even heard of it, can you imagine? I made this batch up myself and wrote the recipe down for them. It's a blue ribbon recipe. Not mine, but I been making it so long that it might as well be."

Russell eyed the oily bean mixture and thought it looked like a sure-fire fart inducer. If Bop got this Texas twister into the bedchamber he might be in for a bumpy ride.

"Of course, it can play hardball with the digestive track if you're not used to beans," Earlynn offered. "I mean, well, they are the musical fruit."

Margie scooped up a tortilla full. "Here's to making

225

music."

Oh God. Oh, God. What was this about? Was Margie thinking that two such ladies, united in their uniqueness, could form a bond against the blood Carpenters? In a pastiche of frosted eyeshadow and junior department outfits, stare them down until they broke? He had no time to ask, because just then Margie fumbled the whole caviar business down the neck of her red sale blouse. Russell turned to follow her shocked expression. Another party goer had arrived: Meridel LeVasseur Carpenter, his mother, stepped through the crowd. The only woman in his family who wouldn't politely pretend she liked Margie. To be fair, she hated anything female he'd hooked up with, but she hated Margie more openly than the others. *Russell, I think you can do better than* . . . She didn't have to finish the sentence; he knew what she wanted to say—*used children.*

"Due south," he said to Lainie, and swore he felt the prickles of dread travel his sister's spine.

"What's Mother doing here?"

"I invited her," Bop said. "You got a problem with that, little lady? It's a family party. She gave birth to you two. Much as I hate to admit it, that noble act makes her family."

Earlynn said, "Hush up, Mr. Crabby. Now who's not being nice?" She hooked Nick's arm in hers. "Nick, honey, I got a psychological question for you. Don't this Frank Lloyd Whatever house strike you as something a little boy might put together out of his Lincoln logs?"

Russell studied his mother looking over her adult children, assessing and measuring where another mother would have immediately gone to kissing and hugging. Her distinct disapproval—of his ponytail, his threadbare Gap jeans, the female baggage at his side—was palpable, even at fifty paces. Likewise, she seemed impressed neither with Earlynn's caviar nor her jaunty party garb, but no one except her children would ever pick up on that. Lainie seemed to just stand there, unwilling to accept what was happening. Russell scratched his neck. Whatever bug had bitten him must have had apple skins, raisins, and bee venom for lunch.

Meridel waved her hand in front of her face, as if the Southern California sunshine was unbearable compared to the cooler sea breezes of Carmel Valley. "Hello, everyone," she said, smiling brightly, her musical voice betraying nothing. "I came for a wedding. So where is it?"

"Right here, Meri, sweetie," Bop said, retrieving from Nick the woman who was on her way to being bride number four, stepgrandma number three, and God knew what else. "Soon as we get everyone fed and finish the birthday party business."

CHAPTER 18

OFF THE HIGH DIVE

HER GRANDFATHER AND HIS TEXAS HONEY, correction, make that *fiancée;* Margie with her abundant tactfulness; the waiter who slopped scampi appetizer across the sleeve of her mother's Adrienne Vittadini suit—those were minor irritations compared to the way Meridel Carpenter looked at her own daughter. When it came to Lainie, it didn't matter that she and Nick owned their house, albeit a small one in need of a magnitude of repairs that would have to wait until after

227

they paid off Spencer's bills, or that they had never once asked her for a loan to do either. No, Mother took one look at her daughter's flat abdomen and baptized her expression in grandmotherly disappointment.

Nick hadn't missed any of it. He took his mother-in-law's arm at the elbow and steered her toward the barbecued bounty. "You're looking great, Meridel. Come sit by me and tell me what's new in the northern state."

"In a minute, Nick. I want to say hello to my daughter."

"Mother," Lainie said, giving her a belated hug. "And a wedding. I don't know how many more surprises there can be tonight."

"Don't worry, Precious. *I'm* still single."

"Which we count as a loss for all mankind," Russell said as Margie dragged him away.

Meridel wasn't the kind of mother who had to pat her chinlength hair to assure herself it was in place. It was; she willed it so. She always looked great, but it was a surface achieved by constant polishing, the way sanding a marble statue produces a cold, silky texture. Seeing her always made Lainie feel sloppy, as if her hair needed washing. They sat down at one of the rented patio tables.

"Your grandfather called yesterday and insisted I fly down. All he would tell me was he'd met the woman of his dreams and there was going to be a wedding. She's kind of a different sort, don't you think? Elaine, you know, if you cut your hair just a wee bit shorter, your lovely cheekbones wouldn't be so hidden. Chin length—it's something to think about as you approach the close of your thirties. But the dress. Didn't I tell you it would be a classic?"

Lainie lifted her fork. She was only thirty-five. The lobster tasted like ground-up newsprint but eating was something to do. "Nice suit."

Meridel sighed. "Oh, I don't care much for red since Nancy Reagan wore it to death, but size four anything is getting just about impossible to find."

Margie glowered. Lainie thought she might stab Meridel in a minute or two more. Then Margie continued dipping her lobster in the tiny dishes of lemon butter. Russell didn't look capable of swallowing his own spit.

"Well, red looks terrific on you."

Her mother's eyes brightened. "Thank you, dear. Maybe we can work in a quick shopping trip before I go back and find one for you."

"I'm back at work now. It keeps me pretty busy."

Meridel's smile automatically emerged. "Cowboy boots with a dress. What a clever idea, darling. Did you come up with that all on your own or was it Marnie's idea?"

"Margie," Russell said, his plate still untouched. "Her name is Margie."

"Eat something, Russell. All this lovely seafood and you're letting it get cold. I'm so bad with names. Please forgive me, Margie."

"There's nothing to forgive, Mrs. Carpenter."

As they went about the business of emptying their plates, Lainie made an observation she hoped to remember to share with Dr. M. Her father had been a traditional horseman, equitation straight out of the pages of George Morris. Yet in his riding there had been a reciprocity between man and horse, not exactly a mutual understanding, but some deeper connection. Meridel could ride huntseat beautifully, clear four-foot

229

fences with inches to spare, but the moment she dismounted, she handed the horse to someone else to cool out, to sponge the lather from his tired back. But all that didn't necessarily mean she required a horse to ride. She'd never ask Margie to call her Meridel, unlike Earlynn, who wanted to be instant pals. She would simply smile just as she was doing now, holding the reins in a death grip in her manicured hands for the rest of the evening.

Earlynn came strutting out of the kitchen to the deck, a rectangular Pyrex dish of berry-studded Jell-O in her hands. "Banana-strawberry!" she announced. "Whoever wants a helping raise your hand!"

Her absolute favorite, Lainie figured. Now it would be his. No more of Alyce's recipes would be in that kitchen. The end had come for caramelizing crème brûlée crusts and New York-style cheesecake. Apple pie or peach cobbler, maybe, and thick slices of salted watermelon. From this moment forward, Bop's cuisine was taking a swift turn back toward the 1950s.

"A refill on your champagne, Miss?"

Lainie held out her glass.

I've had way too much champagne. And I may be walking a little crooked, but I'm still thinking straight, Lainie assured herself. *Oh Nick, where are you? You wanted smiles, I'm grinning like an idiot now. Can lobster swim in champagne?* She giggled, picturing the broiled crustacean afloat in her belly, his orange claws fording champagne seas. What were they to make of this ever-unfolding spectacle? Was her grandfather really planning to marry the Laundromat queen or had he hired her for the occasion, just to see how much he could annoy his grandchildren? Her mother's mouth

Even at that moment, realizing what could happen, she knew it was too late to do anything to stop the inevitable collision. Douching was a myth, Humphrey's Eleven, that homeopathic concoction she and her high school girlfriends used to down by the handfuls was ineffective, and prayer? Well, prayer only worked if you believed in it. Damn it all—why prolong certain agony if it meant only a handful of years you could pretend to be happy? Semen puddled between her thighs and he was still breathing hard against her breasts when she slid out from under him, more troubled now than she had been when she sought out the atrium as refuge.

"Elaine?"

Wordlessly, she extricated her dress from the cactus, felt for the label, turned it right side out, and slid it over her cooling body in the dim light. She couldn't find her underpants. Oh, the hell with them. It wasn't as if Bop's maid hadn't found lingerie in this room before. Nick sat cross-legged on the floor, his pants bunched around his ankles like a teenager caught in the act.

"I'm sorry. I couldn't help it."

"Don't say anything, Nick. We're not in high school. This isn't fifteen years ago, when we didn't know any better. What the hell were we thinking?" She shoved at the door until it gave, closed it behind her, realizing for the first time that she'd kept her boots on during the entire episode.

When she returned from the car with his gift, her grandfather was engaged in the less-dangerous process of opening his presents. Earlynn stood beside him, folding the wrapping paper neatly, as if she was planning to reuse it. Lainie set her present into the pile.

"From my grandson, Russell," Bop said, as he held up

235

the disc-shaped present wrapped in Red Lyzyrd's trademark fuchsia snakeskin paper. "He works at a record store. Anybody care to wager on what's inside?"

People laughed, and Lainie watched her brother shift his hands inside his pockets. Margie looked six miles beyond pissed. She was watching the waiters set up the plates and cups for coffee and eyeing the cake like it was the last friend she had on earth.

"You sure enough can't go wrong with Hank Williams," Bop said, chuckling, holding up what was undoubtedly a vintage pressing of "Mind Your Own Business." "That is, unless you mistakenly pick up one of his son Bocephus's sorry records. Thanks, boy."

"You're welcome, old man."

Despite their jesting, Russell looked relieved. His face was a little flushed, and he seemed to be scratching at the same place on his neck she saw him attacking earlier. Was that the hive? Maybe Nick was wrong; there was some hidden allergen in the food, like walnut dust. Ever since that last trip to the hospital when the ER doctor came out and screamed at Lainie that they'd almost waited too long, Russell carried prednisone at all times, and a syringe kit of antiserum in his glove compartment. If he kept up the scratching she'd go after it herself.

Lainie watched her grandfather be amused by a set of Jerry Garcia ties he would never wear and a book on western art he already owned, and admire a case of Remy Martin he would delight in emptying. Then he hefted her present and gave her a nod. It clanked. "Lainie-gal, how'd you guess I'd be in the market for the old ball and chain?"

Everyone laughed again, a little more drunkenly than before, and she watched her grandfather pry apart the

236

factory cardboard, exposing the chains. "I'll be damned. You think forged steel will hold back the beast?"

"What in the devil are those for?" Earlynn asked. "Some kind of crazy bedroom game? I hope you know I don't go in for that kinky business."

The guests found this hilarious, everyone except for Meridel. She had her pinched face turned downward where she could study her red pumps. Please, Lainie thought, tap them three times and go back home to Carmel, or Kansas, anywhere but here.

"These are for my unruly stallion, darling. Don't you worry. I'm talking horse, not fire hose. Now what have we got over here?" Bop set Lainie's box down alongside his other booty and lifted a small package among the unopened gifts. He handed it to Earlynn. "Guess you can't get married without the proper equipment."

"For me?" She tore open the box and let out a squeal. The diamond solitaire was pear-shaped, flawless, ungodly big to Lainie's eyes. It could have given birth to Dr. M's. It probably could have paid off Lainie's mortgage and Spencer's medical bills and still managed to twinkle a few leftover impressively sized carats.

Earlynn kissed Bop and let him slip it on her finger. It was an intimate moment, separate from the drunken party chatter and clinking glasses. They were alone there on the deck, promising to each other something that could never come true. At its best, Lainie thought, this is what love is all about. Wearing blinders and believing how you feel right now will make a difference later, when things are in chaos—and God knows, eventually they will be. She wondered if Nick was still sitting on the floor of the atrium, discussing the psychological ramifications of postcoital regret with the cactus brothers. She felt just horrible. What happened

happened mutually. She should have at least accepted his apology. But that pain in her side. *Don't think about it or you'll go crazy.*

Earlynn showed off her engagement ring proudly. Meridel exhibited the proper amount of interest; Margie did everything but take a jeweler's loupe out of her purse while Russell scratched his neck madly.

Are you okay? Lainie mouthed silently to her brother.

He mouthed back, *Are you?*

Bop stood up. "You ready to do the deed?"

Talkative Earlynn seemed to have progressed beyond speech to the study of diamonds. Bop helped her to his side and clasped her hand in his. The ship-feeling the house invoked made Lainie feel sentimental and forgetful, while the champagne in her bloodstream did its best to rock the deck. She thought back to her own wedding day. The nervous young minister with the high-pitched voice had to stop and wipe his sweaty face twice before they finished. Nick tickled her palm as he slid the gold band onto her finger. She had been so anxious to get to the next part, the rest of their lives.

One of her grandfather's neighbors pulled out his Universal Life Church minister's certificate and after everyone stopped laughing about the sanctity of that, started in on the ceremony.

At the "Dearly Beloved," Meridel looked somber and a little misty. Lainie knew why that was. After Dad had died, Meridel turned into a Wall Street-wise nun. She had a social life, but she didn't "date." She had been married once, to Chuck Carpenter, and believed that was her only definition. She collected antiques and shopped because those things were controllable; they didn't die on you. And it seemed like Russell would never get married, at least not to anything without a sound hole and chrome tuning pegs. Lainie's own marriage was rocky at best. Would it do any good to point out there was indeed sufficient reason for these two not to be joined in holy matrimony? That it wasn't fair anyone as mean as that man should get another chance at happiness?

Under her dress, Lainie felt a tiny trickle of semen run down the inside of her right leg. Why couldn't it all whoosh out of her like some great flood, for once, in a show of intelligence, why couldn't her body reject Nick's fluids? But no such luck, just that one excess drip. Her body felt ripe, a hormone-driven factory whose time clock was ticking loudly, bent on fulfilling biology, its globular cells already forming the mulberry-shaped morula, preparing for cleavage as certainly as her grandfather was promising only to cleave unto Earlynn.

"Do you take this woman . . ." the neighbor-turned-minister was asking, and Bop didn't even wait for the sentence's finish. He boomed out "Hell, yes!" like this was rodeo, not a marriage ceremony.

Lainie turned her face away from the happy couple. Behind her, smoothing down his corners, stood a penitent Nick. There were twin spots of dirt on his elbows and knees where he'd knelt on the atrium floor and the elastic of her white panties peeking out of his jacket pocket.

She couldn't help smiling. In front of her, stepgrandma number three showed off the ring's matching band of oh so many diamonds.

"Look at this thing!" she enthused to Lainie. "I ask you, is it the nuts or what?"

"It's the nuts," Lainie answered. "The absolute nuts."

"So, where you two lovebirds plannin' to honeymoon?" a voice boomed from the crowd.

Lainie craned her neck to see. Good Lord, it was MacLellan Henry, that nasty reporter Bop had been feuding with since time immemorial. He was still alive and still angry. What was he doing here—looking for Gloria? She watched her grandfather's face blanch with apprehension.

A camera flash went off. Out of instinct or habit, Lainie threw up a hand to shield her face.

Bop collected himself. "Welcome to Casa de Carpenter, Mac. Have some bubbly."

"Thanks. I believe I will."

More cameras flashed, and Lainie's stomach began to churn.

"I asked you a question, Carpenter."

Bop put up a hand of warning. "Ain't the time or place. Load up a plate of cake for yourself and tell your crew to do the same. That's a personal invitation."

But the old reporter wasn't going to be assuaged by mere foodstuffs. "Either you tell them or I will, Carpenter."

In the tension, Russell's itching seemed to have increased, and a sobering Lainie suddenly realized what Russell's problem might be. He'd undergone the proper period of incubation. Chicken pox was an equal opportunity virus.

Her grandfather sighed, and looked to his bride for advice.

Earlynn was none too pleased. "Charles, don't let this fancy pants writer stand here and threaten you. It's your life, your pocketbook, and our honeymoon. Tell that fancy pants what you told me. You been thinking about exercising your option to buy back Shadow Ranch and we're going to check things out. Alone."

So, Lainie thought, he had been saving the best for

last. He wanted to drop the bomb and drive off in a hail of rice. She'd heard her mother's gasp when he said Shadow. When it came to Bop, that gasp was the family's primal vocabulary. Now her mother started to cry, and Lainie moved closer, put her arm around her.

Bop removed his hat. He took hold of his new wife's hand like they were two school kids being accused of pilfering the milk money.

"Calm down, Meridel. Earlynn and I are going to see if we can't sell this white elephant of a house and maybe replant paradise down there on the Shadow, that's all." He swept an arm toward Casa de Carpenter. "Nobody comes here anymore. This is the first time I've had all my blood relations under the same roof in ten long years. It isn't like you'll miss it. And selling it won't touch you or the kids. My papers were drawn up a long time ago. You can still buy your little antiques."

Lainie felt ashamed for all of them.

Her grandfather turned to his assembled guests with his Robert Duvall grin. "Look at it this way. You'll always qualify for a ten percent discount on Shadow Ranch lemons."

CHAPTER 19

The Parking Lot

Los Angeles Times, Orange County Edition. Sunday, August 28, 1994. *Eric Lloyd Wright: A Third Generation of Organic Architects Seeks a Way of Life in the Southland* (first in a series on Southern California lifestyles). MacLellan Henry.

1994 may very well go down in the history books as

the year Mother Earth sent Southern Californians her most insistent warning. The 6.7 roll-and-shaker toppled structures that met or surpassed all state building requirements. When the dust cleared, Cal State Northridge was minus several classrooms, Santa Monica in flames, and there were dead to be buried. Eric Wright, grandson of the late architectural visionary Frank Lloyd, is at home in a double-wide trailer in our own Santa Monica mountains awaiting completion of his latest architectural design. Utilizing reinforced concrete and controversial sod roofing (see New Roofs for the Nineties, M8), Wright goes on record stating our fundamental building mistakes lie in our continual attempt to dominate nature rather than work with it, an echo of his noted grandfather's vision. Questioned about the earthquake, Wright elaborated: "Change can be viewed as catastrophic or informative. We can sit in the rubble or learn a new architecture."

The newlyweds spent their first married breakfast in bed enjoying separate halves of the same pink grapefruit. Bop watched Earlynn doctor up her coffee with Half & Half and honey until it was the color of a grocery store bag, then sop up two cups dunking halves of vending machine powdered sugar doughnuts. All that sugar and caffeine would have mired him in heart palpitations, but Earlynn was leaning over the counter applying her layers of makeup, singing along with the radio to "The Bluest Eyes in Texas."

Her voice brought to mind metal-taloned hens scratching gravel, but he loved her in spite of her singing voice. All night long they'd held on to each other, Earlynn in the pretty new negligee, him in sporty striped pajama bottoms, kissing and talking until they fell asleep. Starting today, they'd drive south into the back country to check on the Shadow property. During that time, Bop hoped to again catch a glimpse of that nightie and what lay underneath.

The photographs of the Wright boys revealed more than familial resemblance. Frank Lloyd's unique mixture of inquisitive and forbidding, son Lloyd sporting his father's wide-brimmed hat (almost a cowboy hat, Bop noted), and young Eric, who'd inherited the piercing eyes, elegant ears, and firmly set mouth. Aside from a few unfortunately placed adjectives, this article came close to respectable journalism. In fact, Bop so heartily approved that he decided to brave the swamp of voice mail and let Mr. Henry, the boorish uninvited guest who'd hoped to embarrass him at his wedding, know what he thought. His compliment would magnanimously bestow upon the hack a Christian forgiveness that ought to fan the flames but good.

He got the answering machine, No surprise there, but a man who couldn't answer his own phone once in a while deserved to have his chain yanked. "And a pleasant good morning to you, Mac the Hack. While I'm none too happy you crashed my wedding last night, I do think this Eric Wright piece is a crackerjack chunk of writing. Kind of surprised your editor would let you squirt out a story this intelligent. Probably had to sneak it through while he was out roller-blading, huh? Or maybe one of your little protégés helped. Guess there's hope for the *Times* after all."

Bop faked a full-bodied yawn into the receiver. "Catch that, Henry? The sound you just heard is one satiated lion stud emerging from his newlywed love den, and about to prowl off for more of the same. *Adios,* old friend. *Vaya con* all five W's. Have fun feeling up your computer keys."

Bop hung up the phone and watched Earlynn drop her robe to the floor and dress in her new outfit, which at its most fundamental layer involved a matched set of tiny peach-colored panties and lacy bra. Nice, firm behind. A dancer's body. *I do not deserve such incredible luck,* he said to himself, *but I damn sure intend to enjoy the show.*

"You'll see, Earlynn," Bop boasted as they took the freeway exit for Shadow, "this place might look a little run down, due to the fact that no one's been giving it proper care, but I'm telling you, it's the closest thing to paradise on earth you'll find in this part of the country. Rich earth—a man could grow whatever he wants in this soil. Little corn-tomato-zucchini garden, or enough lemons to service the southern state. Now the hills aren't dramatic like your San Bernardinos, but they sure enough felt like mountains to me as a kid. I used to ride my horse into town—town being a one-room grocery next to some unfinished train tracks! Oh, honey, what a time that was. There wasn't anywhere I couldn't go horseback. I never should have left this place. Think how decent those grandkids of mine might've turned out had their backyard been the Shadow."

He touched the brim of his weathered Resistol and waited for Earlynn to respond, but she was busy studying the maps spread out over her new Levi's. They'd gotten her slim-cut 501's dyed that dark blue denim that always smelled so sturdily American. In those jeans, sleeveless T-shirt, and her new Justin Ropers, she looked to Bop to be about fourteen years

244

old, the age when girls hit their first bloom. Russell would probably call that line of thinking an indication of being "dicked," but what did Russell know about being in love? He dated a witch who kept him on a choke chain.

"Make a right here," his bride said, pointing to where the asphalt road began to turn to dirt. "Eight miles, then another."

"Sugar, I *know* where the Shadow Ranch is. The map to it's in my blood. You don't have to tell me where to turn."

Earlynn folded up all the maps and then laced her hands across her lap. "Oh, I'm sure *nothing's* changed one teeny-tiny bit since you moved north. Go on, land the plane, Captain. Who cares if there's a runway under us?"

The temperature inside the cab of the truck had dropped forty degrees. "I miss, something here?"

Earlynn looked out the window, resting her chin on her fist.

"Talk at me, honey."

She huffed. "I don't know how you sliced the pie in your other three marriages, but listen here, this one's going to be a fifty-fifty deal all the way, including the crust and the whipped cream topping."

"Earlynn, what in hell are you talking about?"

"That means whoever's not driving the truck reads the maps!"

"What's wrong? You want me to buy you your own car? We could get you a nice little Mercedes, one of those two-seaters with a convertible top. Safe, smart lines, and excellent resale if you decide you want something else. It's a fact, the German automobile remains the only real excuse not to buy American.

However, I'd challenge them to a plumbing duel anytime. They might make good cars but they can't come up with a decent flush toilet to save their lives."

"Last thing I want is you buying me some German wind-up toy! Honestly, Charles. Maybe Elaine and Russell got a point. You think wagging your wallet's the answer to every problem."

"Then what can I buy you? You seem a little unhappy."

By way of answer to that question she gave him *the look*. They'd been married just short of one day.

Earlynn switched on the computerized Bose stereo, but rather than using his preset stations, she preferred manually twisting the tuner. Both directions offered only intermittent static. They were too far from civilization to find any Alan Jackson, the bleached-blond country singer who sent her sighing, looking as far away as Fort Worth, and biting her painted nails. The next real town they came to, he'd stop and buy her all the young fellow's CDs and tapes, hell, a life-size poster, too. Bop wondered if in their brief hours of wedded bliss, maybe Earlynn wasn't starting to regret his physical limitations.

"Charles! Stop the truck!"

He screeched on the brakes at once. "Please don't ask me to let you out, Earlynn. You're my wife. Anytime your heart desires, I'll let you tell me where to turn."

"Can't you see them?" she cried. "Over in that empty lot."

"See what?"

Three ordinary mule deer stood frozen in the middle of a field—if a field could consist of scrub, weeds, and litter. The deer stared uninterestedly at the truck while tramping down weeds searching for edibles. The smallest of the three, a fawn, was whipping his scrub brush of a tail back and forth over his tiny white butt. His wet black nose and eyes dominated his tan face, but the whole business was simply dwarfed by ears. Earlynn leaned across his lap, snapping pictures through the window with her throwaway camera. The feel of her body against his was such a comfort that Bop held back on what he wanted to say about the foolishness of shooting pictures through car windows.

"Isn't that little family just the most precious sight," Earlynn sighed, snapping off another shot.

It was of those point-and-pray type of cameras. Bop had carped a little when she bought it, but Earlynn made no bones, she didn't want any more lessons on his Nikon.

"Deer were plentiful on the Shadow," Bop said. "They're so hardy and common you'll find them today in suburbs where the few farsighted developers haven't ripped the shit out of the natural plants. Of course, plant flowers and deer take that gesture as permission to vary their palate. They'll peel bark off a tree in a fortnight, given the opportunity. Just about murder a grove."

"Enough history lessons, Charles. There's nothing common at all about them deer. That family having a snack together just thrills my heart."

"Family? Earlynn, they're animals."

"Shush up. Them deer are as precious to me as saving your damn harbor ducks is to you. That's all there is to it."

"Pardon me. My mistake." Whatever was troubling his new bride, they'd get it all ironed out tonight, when they checked into a nice, clean five-star hotel, took a whirlpool bath, and ordered a three-course supper—

when they began their real honeymoon. What about the Hotel Del Coronado? No reason why not. Given the economic woes politicians were trying to label a "recession," ought to be plenty of empty rooms available. Ocean breezes, elegant dining, Earlynn could shop till she dropped in one of the many boutiques. They could take the harbor cruise at dusk. Stroll on the sand, like lovers do. Or they could stay in bed and go where fate led them.

The deer bounded back into the scrub oaks. "You're right," he said, acquiescing. "That was a grade-A deer family. Remind me to send the deer people a check when we get home. Can we go now?"

Earlynn bestowed one of her sunny smiles on him and suddenly the dwindling day possessed hours of untilled hope. "Of course we can, Charles. I never said we couldn't."

A truck was still a truck. None of this yuppie four-by-four luxury for Bop Carpenter. Earlynn might not notice the twin I-beam suspension, the positraction rear axle, the seventeen-inch wheels sporting radial all-terrain tires set at load range E, the attendant leaf springs, but they crossed every mile of the last eight in relative comfort.

They stopped and got out to observe what was left of his old town. In Bop's gut a tiny ember of dread that no recognizable trace of the Shadow Ranch would remain began to smolder. When they came upon a god-awful creation gracing a hill near the center of what used to be his hometown, he felt the ember flare up and begin to glow.

To call the assemblage art was stretching things. It looked like a crazy man's combination plate of recycling:

concrete, broken glass, and leftover house paint mixed in with a goodly dash of Christian fear, all mushed up into the shape of a makeshift adobe mountain. Bop toed the material with his boot tip. The straw bits poked out from a twenty-foot diameter. It was a mud heart set into the hillside.

Earlynn backed up to get it all in her fifty millimeter lens. "Stand there, Charles. Let me get a picture of you alongside this whatever you call it."

Bop climbed to the top of the heart. From there he could see that the painted rocks almost as large as those outside Casa de Carpenter spelled out a message: "'God is Love. Jesus, a sinner, please come upon my body and into my heart.' John 3:16."

There was more religious nonsense on the other side. It looked like a Playdoh Noah's Ark in progress. So far, the artist had got around to a pair of poorly executed horses and some unidentifiable flying things that resembled pterodactyls. Behind the animals, turquoise mudwater was rising. Who would see all this besides crashing planes was beyond him. Topping the whole business was a cross made out of lengths of rebar, loosely wrapped in rawhide. Bop stood at the apex, catching his breath in the heat, one hand touching the leather cross for balance.

"Well, at least no one's using it to beat horses," he said as he carefully made his way down to the base of the sculpture.

"What's that, honey?" Earlynn asked.

"Nothing. Just trying to make some sense out of this rock pile. It's decorated up top and clear around to the other side in double-ugly. What kind of mind comes up with an eyesore like this? I sure enough don't remember anything like this around when the Shadow was going strong."

"Things change, Charles. You can stand there remembering or you can blaze a new path."

Her words triggered memories Bop didn't want to remember. "Look at this land, Earlynn. I mean took long and hard. I see nothing but potential here, waiting for someone to believe in it. Tell me what you see."

"The truth? A whole lot of empty space."

"Clear away this crap. Look harder."

Earlynn rubbed her hand across her camera. "Well, my Frank would take one look at all this open land and probably see it as opportunity to build up some fine brick homes. He's a wonder with brick, Frank is. Has this tall curvy brick fence runs the entire length of his property."

"I'm looking forward to meeting your boy real soon."

Earlynn bit her lip. "They're so busy I can't see them getting the time to come up here, actually."

"Then we'll zip down to Texas. It's a quick flight."

"I'm not much for airplane travel, Charles."

"Then we'll drive. You can read me the maps."

Earlynn frowned and tapped her camera case against her hip. "Tell you the truth, Frank's wife don't exactly wish to have anything to do with me."

"Why's that?"

"My past stripping don't go down good with her church friends."

"Earlynn, you're retired from all that."

"I'm afraid that can't erase it where she's concerned. Oh, I send them a Christmas card and I never forget the girls' birthdays, but—"

"How long's it been since you seen Frank?"

"Seven or eight years, I guess."

Bop sighed. "Then I'd say it's high time we corrected

the problem for Frank's wife and her narrow Christian outlook."

"Now, Charles, don't get all upset. The Sally Jessy thing probably tipped them over for good. People shut you out, after awhile you might as well stop knocking and keep the skin on your knuckles."

"They're not people, they're family."

She laughed.

"What's so funny?"

"Maybe Lainie is right. You might just try looking at it my way once and see if it fits, Charles. Think about it."

He'd stayed away from the Shadow property on purpose, believing that to look back at your past was to admit the present had defeated you. Standing on this land made him afraid that had come true. Seventy years ago, the town was so upscale it rated its own post office annex. They were on their way to becoming a part of the California whole. Wagon roads crisscrossed one another all the way to the top of the golden state and anytime they'd hook up the railroad. His father was well-known in town, respected. It was understood his only son would follow in his footsteps, blaze the path further, even if Charles I had to beat the boy to light the fire.

He remembered the day the old man had found an error with his recordkeeping, and made fifteen-year-old Charles turn the task over to one of the Mexicans. Then, in front of all the packers, he'd slapped his son's face. "This one's a dreamer," he said, and the Mexicans had stood quietly, waiting to go back to work. Humiliated, Bop had grabbed the nearest horse, a mare, and galloped her all the way up into the hills. He stayed away from the groves all day, watching the sky turn dusky, even though he knew he'd be in for a king-sized whipping. The mare caught a stone on the ride home. Even though he dismounted at once and pried it from her hoof, she was bruised and limping, so he hand-walked her home. Bop sponged down the sweat marks from her back, and after she was clean he planned to pack her hoof. His father had stepped out of the shadows, shotgun in hand. Bop kept on dipping the sponge in the bucket, rinsing the horse's back, saying nothing. His father jerked the halter from him and whipped the mare into a trot, lunging her in a circle, exposing her lameness. "More of your good work," he said, and led her out of Bop's sight.

He remembered the single report from the gun echoing in his bones, dropping the sponge into the bucket, walking blindly past the remaining horses into the house. It was the first time he'd traveled beyond tears to a rage, and he held on to that single shred of control tightly in the dark. He heard the screen door slam, and his father stop outside his bedroom door. His whole body went stiff, expecting the door to open and to feel the beating he deserved. But there was only the legacy of his words: "Disobedience reaps consequences."

His father's affliction lay dormant in his own blood. To keep it at bay, Bop had tried everything: wise investments, grandfatherly generosity, flapping opening his wallet as if his money could make a bandage.

Lainie's birthday gift—she thought he was so shallow he couldn't catch a hidden meaning, but she was underestimating her old grandpa—the stud chains weren't intended just for Tontito.

He breathed in the camphor tang of the eucalyptus trees, heard the shushing the branches made when the

252

afternoon breeze came up, saw himself whiling away afternoons poking through leaf piles, collecting those small, aromatic pods the trees dropped. It seemed as if his father could at any moment sternly order him over to muck the horses' corral, close his fingers on young Charles' shoulderblade until the nails bit in. He pictured his mother standing in the doorway, calling out, *Time to wash up for dinner. The only sound I want to hear is pump water running over dirty hands.*

She never knew the half of it.

They did better as a family at dinner. Fresh shelled peas, the hearty smell of cornbread steaming from the oven, so butter-rich it left a grease stain on your hand. How dare he not be grateful? He'd pick his mama a bunch of weeds, and she'd fawn all over them, set them up in a glass canning jar in the center of the table. They'd bow their heads, humbled in the face of such bounty. That was the Shadow he wanted to deliver to Earlynn. But here in the heat, studying those pictures locked inside his head, he knew he couldn't tell her lies.

Earlynn fanned her face with a handkerchief. "It must be a hundred degrees out here, Charles. Even the lizards have enough sense to take cover. Where's that little corner market you were telling me about? Let's get us each a cold soda and revive. I'm about done in."

They drove the quarter mile and parked under a meager oak beside the market. He hadn't been here in twenty-five years. The newly restored facade featured a small wooden sitting porch with two stools out front, but no one was using them, not even a tired-out stray dog. Swinging saloon-type doors provided a pretty clear indication there was no air conditioning inside. The market's advertisements were written chiefly in Spanish. *Chorizo Fresca para Mexicali—$2.99. Cubito de heilo! .99*

253

saco.

Earlynn pulled her reluctant husband inside. "Come on, sweetie, you'll fry out here."

It was as hot inside the store as out. Shelves in poorly fit corners held the staples of American life in the nineties: Tide detergent, Hostess cupcakes, *grande sacos de Cheetos,* box after box of sugary cereals, paper diapers ranging in sizes from newborn to ought-to-be-toilet-trained-by-now. From the red Coca Cola cooler in the rear of the store, Earlynn retrieved a tall bottle of strawberry pop with chips of ice still clinging to the heavy glass base. She set it on the counter and Bop glanced above the clerk's head to spy several dusty framed crate labels lining the wall. Besides the age of the soda cooler, it seemed the only trace of this town's past.

Bop pointed to the Shadow label. "That's from my daddy's ranch," he told the clerk.

The dark-skinned young man stared at him blankly.

"We grew lemons. *Cultivar limons. Señor* Carpenter. *Acordarsar de hacienda de la Sombra?"*

"Lo siento, Señor. No se."

The clerk, his white T-shirt rolled up at the sleeves, was no more than a boy. He couldn't be expected to remember history he wasn't around to experience firsthand. Earlynn worked her hand inside a jar of beef jerky on the counter, the extra spicy version. She placed five strips on the countertop, next to her soda.

Bop stared at her impending purchases. "Honey, you aren't really going to eat that."

"Why not? This here's about my favorite treat next to coffee on ice cream."

"But the havoc it'll play with your digestion! All those chemicals, the meat itself, good God, Earlynn, you're

254

inviting colonic disaster."

"Oh, let me alone. You're downright obsessed with other people's plumbing. When and if I have a problem, I'll let you know."

He touched a basket of apples on the counter. "Why not some fruit, honey?"

In response, she selected two more pieces of jerky, this time teriyaki flavor. She pointed one at him, its brown leather wagging like a dried-up dog tongue. "This body does all right on two basic food groups, meat and chocolate. How you manage all that citrus without a mouthful of cold sores is beyond me. Now hand over your wallet. Your last chance to get something cold to drink."

Reluctantly, he selected a can of so-called lemonade. Within the first sip, the lemon flavor was tainted almost beyond recognition by sugar and some other awful, biting aftertaste. They sat on the market's porch while she ingested one of those questionable strips of meat and drank from her pink drink. He set the can down at his feet. Not long after, a bee landed inside. Swimming or suicide, the bee couldn't seem to make up his mind. Bop left it propped upright in the store trash can on the porch so the bee could work the problem out for itself.

Further down the road from the market, the reason for Shadow's "Slab City" nickname became all too apparent. Like a yard sale gone berserk, patch after patch of hastily poured concrete driveways, on areas that might have otherwise made fine lots for single-family dwellings, sported aging RVs or rusted-out pickups. On the side of an old semi on blocks, someone had painted: *Welcome Slab City Singles. "Loners on Wheels" meets Wednesday nights. Dial CB channel 90 for more information.*

A few of the slabs might have been leftover from General Patton's days, when the military boys in nearby Camp Dunlop practiced desert warfare. But the others were recent, and serious proof of a lack of cement workers' skill. With no overall city plan, no one around to disapprove or fine you, it was as if the snowbirds and the homeless saw a good thing and set up camp.

"Even at my worst I did better than this," Earlynn said as she filed her thumbnail. "This is no way for folks to live."

Bop drove slowly so he could get the big picture. Beside an old "King O' the Road" Winnebago, a woman in sunglasses and faded shorts stood rewebbing aluminum lawn chairs. She was wearing a turban. Bad hair days or no hair days, he prayed Earlynn would never resort to wearing that. The woman stared back. Bop realized how he must look to them, a stranger driving a $40,000 dually truck when any one of these people would have been grateful for retread tires. The woman's unabashed hostility haunted him all the way down the road to the old packing plant. Her expression reminded him of the gorillas at the San Diego Zoo. Smarter than anyone gave them credit for, they looked back at you watching them eat, raise their children, attend bodily functions, and their attitudes took up residence in their memories. This was how mutations began, how genes went about invoking permanent change. Awareness tapped away at the existing DNA until it found a weak link, then a little something extra was encoded for future generations. It could start out simple: *Throw feces at camera-bearing humans.* Then, progress. *Hey, you know what? If we stand atop one another, maybe we can make it over these bars and kick some heinie.*

The packing plant wasn't there any longer, of course. They'd taken things north to San Diego proper shortly after the sale was final. Bop got a check every fiscal quarter; they built a new plant able to handle the labor with much fewer human hands. But he could make out the mirage of it in his mind, simply by tracing the scars in the earth. The flat land was nearly bare of trees. What ones had grown up were mere youngsters. He paced off the property.

"The lemons tumbled down a metal chute," he told Earlynn. "We'd hand sort, set aside the best to sell as gourmet, pack them according to size, and crate them up for shipping." A few feet away, he gestured. "Corral here, barn over there. Nice wood barn, none of that galvanized crap."

Earlynn dutifully inspected the scrub and trees, shuffling her Justins in the dirt. "I don't know what you want me to say, Charles. Somehow I pictured it with a lot more trees. Where's your lemon grove? All I seen so far is this eucalyptus."

Earlynn's pronunciation was all her own: *You-calla-petus.* He wouldn't have dreamed of correcting her, or of ever pronouncing the word differently in her presence. "Over this way." The ember in his belly had found a hot friend to pal up with. "Or at least it used to be."

The few trees remaining in the original grove were all past bearing. Leafless, chopped down to short trunks with a few half-severed limbs, the smooth bark was riddled with insect damage and graffiti. Whole rows of them like that—forgotten old soldiers—impotent, but not yet firewood. Over a ridge too far to walk to, stood newer trees planted in arcs, amply irrigated, leafing out in a healthy forest green. The dirt beneath them was as

257

neatly raked as a Japanese garden. "The McCormick trees," he told Earlynn, catching his breath.

"They for sale, too?"

"Everything's for sale if the price gets interesting enough."

They hiked back in silence.

All that remained of the hacienda was a few crumbling pieces of what once might have been brick chimney. As a condition of the sale, Bop should have insisted it be preserved. Maybe it wasn't a Frank Wright house, but it had been part of California's history. Even the foundation was gone. Time and progress had transformed his childhood town into an RV park for single seniors with broken hearts and rebuilt transmissions.

He wiped his face. "It was a fine house in its day. Wish I had photographs to show you. But over the years I'd get a wild hair about keeping a neat house, throw out boxes I hadn't opened. Hindsight, Earlynn. I'm telling you. That's what they ought to be teaching in the schools today."

She patted his arm. "You can't teach the young what you yourself don't understand until late in life. What with MTV and video games, I think they got their hands full just trying to get them kids to crack a book."

Here he was, behaving like there was no more important concern than his own sorry past, and Earlynn stood patiently waiting for him to come to his senses, five feet of wisdom in nice, tight blue jeans. "Now how did I get so lucky to find me such a smart, pretty wife?"

She smiled. "Just your time, I guess. You know, we should've invited Sally Jessy to our wedding. I'm going to have to write her a note card and tell her the news."

"You do that. Invite her out for a weekend sometime.

But not right now, okay?"

"All right, Charles. Whatever you say."

He took hold of his bride's pale shoulders, lifted her to her tiptoes and kissed her, here on the original site of the Shadow Ranch. He felt her tongue dart inside his mouth. Such an intrepid little kisser. She tasted of that crazy dried-up meat and pure sassy Earlynn, something he was starting to grow used to, to look forward to tasting. He kissed her back, hard as he dared. How he wanted to be able to give her more than a good kiss. She kept on saying the sex act didn't matter. It was the love between them that warmed her heart. But it sure as hell mattered to him. Love could take you only so far. Maybe that Osbon pump thing wasn't so awful an idea. He could hide it in the bathroom, excuse himself, say he needed to slap on after-shave, come out proud and able as any five-year-old stallion and service his mare. He gently closed his hand around her breast and she sighed, pulling him close. What could you do with sighs and memories? All that remained of his past was a handful of recollections and hot, bare dirt.

He thought of the *Times* piece Mac had penned. "Architecture in Harmony with Nature." In his mind's eye he saw a dwelling begin to assemble itself. It rode the hard crust of earth, stacked rocks into shelter, allowed light to shine into formerly dark places. Jackhammer those RV slabs into two-loot hunks, haul in cement, give his grandson-in-law a job building something real. Taliesin South? Taliesin North-of-the-Border? Likely the Wright heirs would look down on his borrowing against their famous titles. Whatever he built wouldn't be for him and Earlynn alone; it would pass on into Lainie and Russell's children. Suddenly between this dry patch and the woman in his arms, right here seemed like the perfect spot to remember how to dream.

"Come here." He sat down in the you-calla-petus leaves and pulled Earlynn down beside him. Before he pressed her back against the ground, he brushed away handfuls of the hard, green pods. Once she was by his side, he didn't want anything to distract her. She leaned on her arm, shyly watching him direct this concert.

Then, kissing her, he unbuttoned her fly and eased his hand inside the waistband of her silky panties. Even more than he wanted to build a new house, he wanted to make love to his wife. She looked at him, wide-eyed, a grin playing at the corners of her mouth.

"I want so damn bad to make you happy," he said, opening his heart to her. "Show me what you like."

They lay back resting, the skies of Shadow looking down upon the aftermath of their makeshift passion. The bottle of soda still contained a couple swallows of pink drink, but it was as warm to the touch as coffee. Earlynn nestled her head against his open shirt and raked her fingers through his chest hair.

"Sorry I got cranky on you in the truck, Charles. Marriage is an adjustment."

"Marriage to the damaged, anyway."

She gave his chest hair a sharp tug. "Stop that. Look at the progress we made so far. You call that damaged?"

She was talking about what had happened just now, and he agreed, but she was leaving out the part about his disability. Her cries reminded him of a baby coyote, ki-yiing his heart out some night when the full moon shone over his furry shoulder and the hunters were busy watching TV.

"It's just that I'm—"

"Say it, Earlynn. Don't hold back on account of hurting my feelings. I've got a problem that affects us both."

"I'm a very physical sort of woman," she finished, and paused, then whispered in his ear, "This here was just wonderful, Charles. You move your hand like a dancer."

Imagining her definition of dance and his fingers sporting peach feather fans, he laughed.

"If we could just exercise a little more. Something to raise a real sweat. It'd even be good for us, don't you think? Take square dance lessons, or go for walks every night? Maybe we could even think of getting me a horse."

"You really like riding, honey, or are you just trying to humor me?"

"I can hold my own. I could've been a rodeo queen if that no-good Wayne hadn't come into my life and robbed me of my girlhood."

"We can hunt him down with a private detective, I'll bitch-slap him around for you, show him who's the boss. Or I could set Mac Henry on his tail."

She giggled. "Old Wayne's probably turned into his own best punishment by now. Don't tell anybody, but when I was a new bride, I used to sneak into our neighbor's corral and ride his horses just holding onto the halter."

"I take back the offer of the car, darlin'. First thing we get back to the Harbour, I'm putting Ed Whistler to work finding you a nice little gelding."

"Why couldn't I have a mare?"

"A mare? Lord, Earlynn, why on earth would you want one of those? They go into season willy-nilly, spook at the wind, and the worst biters I've ever encountered are mares. I don't want you getting hurt. I

261

love you."

She tapped a fingernail against his cast. The thing had been on so long it had become a part of him, green fiberglass practically melded into his skin. He ought to cut it off himself, save the co-pay they'd charge him at the clinic.

"All right, I'd consider a mare. But it'd have to be a real quiet mare, with the transplanted brain of a gelding. Maybe we could find some vet willing to spay her. There's no more sorry business on earth than botched-up parturition, dead colts, or grief-stricken mares."

Earlynn began to pull the weeds one by one from his hair. "Charles, not everything to do with babies turns out terrible. It's true, sometimes they die, but not before they pack a whole lot of wisdom and joy into their young years. And you know what? Sometimes they live and thrive and even outlast you."

Already he could hear whinnying.

CHAPTER 20

NOSTALGIA, TECHNICALLY

"MORE VITAMIN C," MERIDEL INSISTED. "LINUS Pauling lived to almost one hundred and he ate the stuff by the handful. Honestly, Russell, you wouldn't be coming down with childhood diseases if you took your recommended daily allowances."

"Vitamin C gives Russell cold sores," Margie said.

"Nonsense. Cold sores are caused by a virus, actually, a different strain, but the same virus that causes chicken pox. Herpes complex, I believe. Perhaps you've heard of it?"

262

"Now why would that be, Mrs. Carpenter? Because I'm studying to be a nurse?"

Russell lay in bed wanting to die. There were two women in his tiny kitchen, each armed with sacks of groceries and sure-fire "cures." He wasn't hungry. Maybe they were. Vitamin C—give me a break—like Meridel had ever made them take One-a-Day after their dad died. The four food groups were "You kids are on your own tonight. Call out for a pizza," and the telephone numbers of two places that delivered. Besides, the idea of swallowing anything except maybe some Jonestown Kool-Aid was out of the question. There were chicken pox on the soles of his feet, between his toes, on the end of his love muscle, and one huge monster under his right shoulderblade, just the spot to interfere with lying down somewhat comfortably in any position.

He heard Margie relinquish her grocery sack to the table, which indicated she'd lost this round. She came into his bedroom and sat near his pillow, causing his secondhand mattress to sink to an all-time low. She bent down and kissed his forehead. "A hundred and three degrees," she pronounced.

"A hundred and three?" Russell felt panic shoot into every individual chicken pox. What was it Lane had said about fevers that high? "Shouldn't you use a thermometer to double-check?"

His mother called out from the kitchen. "What you need is a really nice broth, Russell. One made from scratch. I'm going to call the Chanteclair and see if they can make me some to go."

Margie frowned, her temperature-taking lips splaying out in displeasure.

Now his mother stood in the doorway, watching.

263

Hey, there were a couple spare inches of room—why not invite the band that had played at his grandfather's birthday party?

Meridel was not pleased with the sight of Margie on his bed. "I think I should drive Russell to the hospital. Surely Nick knows a virologist who can see him. I'll make some calls. There must be some kind of drug protocol for adult cases this severe. Would you like any help getting into your robe?"

"Mother, I don't own a robe."

"All he needs is rest," Margie interrupted. "I think he'd be able to sleep better if I took him over to my house."

"But dear, you have those two young boys."

"They go to day camp."

"Yes, and everyone knows children in public care pick up all manner of illness. Witness what's going on right here in this room."

"Ethan didn't get Russell sick on purpose."

"We all know that, dear. No one's blaming an innocent child. But really, what's the sense of putting Russell at risk for a secondary infection?"

Margie cut his mother a look that would have toppled a giant redwood, but Meridel only smiled sweetly, crossing the arms of her taupe raw silk cardigan. Today being her day off, Margie was wearing shorts and a T-shirt bearing the message Nurses Do It PRN.

"Hey," Russell croaked, "if anyone gives a damn about what I think, I can sleep fine in my own bed, I don't need to go to the doctor, and I'm not hungry. A little peace and quiet might help. Here's a novel idea. Why don't you both go out to lunch?"

The two most difficult women in his life were silenced by this unlikely proposition.

"I rarely eat lunch," Meridel said flatly. "But if Margie's hungry there's no reason for her to sit here. I'm delighted to play nursemaid to a son I hardly ever get to see."

Oh, God. Oh, God. Incipient cat fight right here in the sickroom. Claws out, snarls and lots of messy spitting at any moment. Russell pulled the sheet up over his face.

"Is the light bothering you?" Margie rushed to shut the casement window and pull the blinds. Now he was going to suffocate, too. He moaned beneath his sheet.

His mother said, "What is it, darling?"

He pulled the sheet down to his chin. "Now hear this. I want both of you, as kind as you're trying to be, to run out my front door and lock it behind you and throw the key in the ocean! I don't want pills, doctors, magic cures, pillow fluffing, to be read *Snow White*, to be fed Campbell's soup, a really nice broth, or any other womanly attention you can dream up to further annoy me. In fact, the only person I'd welcome with open arms is Dr. Jack Kevorkian. Please go away." He rolled painfully to his side.

"He's simply not himself," Meridel whispered.

Margie said, "I'm going to take his laundry and do it at my house."

Clearly miffed at Margie's one-upsmanship, his mother's voice lost some of its inherent musicality. "I hadn't given household chores any thought."

But Margie wasn't done yet. "Then don't."

All right, Margie, he dimly cheered.

Alone at last, Russell tried to lie motionless, not to breathe too deeply, not to think beyond the basic function of respiration. The mattress and box spring he'd inherited from Bop, rescued actually, when Bop dumped them, with the sheets still on, out front of Casa de Carpenter after deciding that ridding his home of Helene's evil spirit also required a new sleep set. Russell didn't mind a used mattress with a stormy history; sometimes he imagined it might bring him some luck. Bop always bought top of the line.

Russell's room was spare when it came to decor. He had a fire-engine-red secondhand dresser full of T-shirts and jeans. Rarely did he delve beyond the first layer of clothing; whatever existed below was anybody's guess. He only liked T-shirts that were white, off-white, pale gray, or light blue. Designs on them were okay, but on the back, not the front. Jeans all had to come from the Gap, pricey, but at least they stocked sizes that fit his bony hips. Margie wanted him to buy trendy clothes, baggy trousers that made him feel like he was impersonating a starving Father Guido Sarducci. A few compromises hung in his closet along with his one good jacket—tan corduroy, a gift from Lane thousands of years ago.

I'm getting just a wee bit tired of thinking about my wardrobe, he thought, and tried to imagine something easy on the ears—say Tom Petty and the Heartbreakers. But the notes swarmed like bees in his mind, crashing into each other, getting into stinger fights, sharping and flatting all over his aching brain. Envisioning tablature proved no better. Even well it took a certain amount of skewing your brain to read the strings sideways. Lately there was a lot about viruses in the newspaper. HIV, Ebola. Viruses were insidious. Bacteria fought fair. They colonized, sure, but gave you a chance to arm yourself for battle, plus delivered all those warnings, such as the telltale, last-chance red streak up a limb.

Bacteria fought like men. He figured viruses were female. They cut to the chase, raced straight for the nucleus of each cell, immediately set up a bar, and started serving drinks and free pretzels to all passersby. They told jokes about commitment and hee-hawed like a herd of drug-resistant donkeys.

He wasn't thirsty or hungry, but if some angel would just come along and open the window. Maybe in fresh air there existed a male antiviral breeze component. It was too bad that in order to allow that possibility to flow into his bedroom he would have to rise from the bed and maneuver not only the creaky blinds, but also the window. Much too much effort. If only I could sleep, he thought. He lay in his hot sheets and felt closer to tears than he'd been in years.

He thought of Dr. Kevorkian, that elderly, silver-haired gentleman. *It's you I like, not the clothes you wear—* wait, he was confusing him with Mr. Rogers, Ethan's last television holdout to babyhood.

Suicide had never been an option on Russell's personal checklist. "I'm going to kill myself" was a clever phrase to toss around, much like playing hacky-sack on the beach called attention to one's self, made you appear worldly and athletic. Lane's stint in the nut ward changed all that.

Nick had phoned him from the hospital. "Your sister's had a little breakdown," he said, and Russell had felt his heart lodge in his throat like a fishbone.

"Oh, God. Tell me she didn't cut herself."

"No, Russell, nothing like that. She kind of collapsed. I called your grandfather. We brought her here to see what they could do and before I knew it, your grandfather had signed her in to the psych ward."

"She'll never forgive Bop."

"Or me, it appears."

"Has she asked to see me?"

He remembered Nick's silence on the telephone connection, trying, he assumed, to hold it together and spare Russell's feelings. "Lainie's made it pretty clear she isn't really interested in talking to anybody in the family."

Russell remembered thinking, *Oh really? Well, the hell with that noise.* During visiting hours, he set up camp on a chair in the hallway outside her room, usually bringing two different guitars. He played his sad sister the most purposeful blues he could muster, from "The St. James' Infirmary Blues" to Peter Finger's "Hope and Memory" to the Mississippi Jook Band's "Dangerous Woman." Lane didn't respond, but no one came out and hit him over the head with a bedpan, either.

This went on for weeks, Dr. M coming and going, Russell playing his charity gig, her silence. After three weeks Russell had exhausted his repertoire. He was feeling a little fed up, so he settled on Willie Nelson's "Crazy," and played nonstop for three hours, making up his own lyrics as he went along: "Crazy. Lane, you're not the only one here going crazy. Crazy, hospital chow can't be much fun for you. They might call you crazy for crying, and us nuts for trying, but I'll never stop bugging yooooouuuuu. . . ."

When she threw her lunch tray at him, the whole staff applauded.

In and out of sleep, Russell contemplated the ramifications of suicide and insanity, the silence broken only by his partying nuclei. They were line-dancing. They were singing along with Lionel Ritchie. They were downing kamikazes much too fast for them to stay stomach-bound. He moaned loudly. How had Lane stood it, lying in bed all those weeks? He didn't want to be left alone in the airless tomb one more minute. As if in answer to his prayer, he felt a breath of air begin to stir the fevered stink of his room, and opened his eyes. It was dark outside. The window was open. There was someone sitting in a kitchen chair at the end of his bed. It was his sister.

"Lane?"

"Hello, Spot. See Spot dream. Wherever you were, I'd like to have been along for the ride. You were chatting up a storm."

His heart madly thumped its infected cells. "What was I saying?"

"Just a bunch of mumbo-jumbo about feeling crazy. Did you know Mother left you basil and cream cheese pâté, studded with walnuts?"

Russell tried to lick his cracked lips. "Trying to finish me off. Listen, Lane, would you mind finding me something to drink that doesn't hurt?"

"I think I can manage that."

He could smell something cool and sweet, feel freezer steam rising from beneath his nose.

"Lime Popsicles. I got root beer, too, in case you get bored."

"You're a fucking angel, Lane."

She leaned back on the chair until it tottered on two legs against the bedroom wall. "Oh, every once in a while. But I keep misplacing that gosh-darned halo. Today I found it under Oddjob's sleeping pillow. I think he was planning to trade it to the Rottweiler up the block for doggie treats."

"How did you get in?"

"Your door wasn't locked."

"Well, did you bring me anything else? Comic books? A surprise?"

"I picked up your mail, greedy guts. There's a new *Guitar Trader*. Want me to read you the classifieds?"

"No, it'll just depress me. Well, just check under Gretsch. No, nevermind. All right, just *glance* under Gretsch."

Lainie folded the newsprint magazine under the other mail. "I think maybe that can wait." She reached into her purse and retrieved a small sack. "Here's some free samples Nick scored for you. Zovirax cream, some pills. They said nothing really helps but these might give you a little relief."

"Thanks. How are the dogs?"

"Convinced I haven't walked them, but otherwise sound."

"Seen Dr. M lately?"

She sighed. "I go Friday to relive the birthday-wedding day-big announcement for her analysis. Can't wait to watch her underreact."

"That Bop. What a horndog. He can certainly find the ladies. Airline, that's what I'm renaming Earlynn. Airline to Paradise for eighty-year-old horndogs."

Lane laughed. "I admire her nerve. Offering Texas caviar to Margie."

"The cleaners can probably get the stain out."

"But not from her memory. Russell, do you think Bop means it about selling Casa de Carpenter and buying back Shadow Ranch?"

"I couldn't tell you."

"Think he's getting Alzheimer's?"

"Not a chance. He'd send out a posse on Old Timer's disease. Kick ass, take names, blow them all to smithereens with rhino bullets. I think he just wants to

270

go back to the farm and make peace before he buys it. Own the whole town this time. More people to tell what to do. Listen, let's try out that cream. I got a pox on my shoulder that feels like a volcano crater complete with lava."

"Do you want me to put it on for you?"

"No, I don't think you even want to look at it, Lane. It feels massive. And damp. Stuck to my pillow."

"I'm okay with gore. A homeless man came into Assistance today with a gangrenous foot, wondering if we could spare some Band-Aids. It took all morning, but I got him a ride to County. I'll use a Q-tip."

"Gangrenous? Was it that flesh-eating bacteria? Did you wash your hands? Don't tell me any more, okay?" He waited while she squeezed goo into the maverick pox. Pure flame touched bone, he was sure of it.

Lane waved her hand over the hot spot, trying to cool it.

Russell lay on his stomach, clutching his sweat-damp pillow beneath him. "This has me really worried," he started to say, then took time out to receive more chicken pox-lightning and moan.

His sister's face crumpled, as if she was experiencing the pain along with him. "As long as you don't eat any walnuts or get up while you still have a fever, you're going to get well, Russell."

"That does have me a trifle concerned. But I'm talking about Bop and Airline, selling the house. It's not the inheritance thing. I'd be surprised if there were two dimes left after the lawyers descend on Bop's estate."

"Then what?"

"Our mother. She thinks the house is a rock pile waiting to topple into the bay, but it's a *Frank Lloyd.* And, though that means more to her Merlot-sampling

271

friends than it does to her, she wants it in the family. Something she can point to and say, 'Oh, yes, my family's Frank Lloyd Wright. We deeded it to the Conservancy, but we still vacation there from time to time.' "

"She tries." Lainie lined up all the tubes of cream on Russell's bedside table. She opened the pill bottle and counted the pills. "You should take one of these," she said, and Russell studied the blue tablet she dropped into his spotted palm.

"Lane, could you say good-bye to that house?"

His sister placed a hand on her side, as if feeling for some hidden lump. "If I had to, I could say good-bye to almost anything. But that doesn't mean I'd want to."

"Will you tell Bop that?"

She looked at her brother. "Would you?"

He cleared his throat. "I think I'm getting chicken pox on the roof of my mouth, I swear to God. What's next? My remaining hair follicles?"

Lane brought the Sony in from the living room and set it atop the dresser. It hurt Russell's eyes to look at both the screen and the painted red dresser, so she thoughtfully draped the latter in a white sheet. Now it appeared that instead of a dresser, he kept his T-shirts in a shrouded bier, topped with a perfectly serviceable portable television featuring black and white "Cops" in search of American justice.

Lane was in the kitchen, sorting out the groceries Meridel had brought, when Margie returned, undoubtedly hoping to get to him before his mother.

"Russell? Are you awake?"

His sister stepped into view at the living room doorway. The house was so small that this also served as the bedroom doorway, a fulcrum on which the house centered. He could see Margie coming in from the front door, Lainie centered in her path.

"Hi, Margie. He's in there watching 'Cops,' big surprise."

Margie appeared momentarily stranded by the coffee table. "What are you doing here?"

"Throwing out stuff my mother brought over. She forgets about Russell's allergies. Of course, she hasn't had to drive him to the emergency room lately, and sit there waiting for the adrenaline shot to undo his Elephant Man impression. But I mean really, walnut pâté?"

Lane sounded nervous; she was blathering.

"You don't need to do that."

"I had a few hours free, so I thought—"

"Thought what, Elaine? That you'd come over here and play nursemaid to your baby brother? He's my boyfriend. It seems like you can't keep that fact straight in your head."

They'd moved out of sight now, but from a sickbed, a world could be assembled purely from sound: Lane folding a grocery sack, depositing it in the milk crate where Russell kept recyclables he intended to haul over to the college but rarely got around to. Then the cupboards opening, the small clicks and clacks as she began putting away all the nonpoisonous foodstuffs. Finally, her sigh punctuating the tension, her lowered voice, the speech weary.

"Margie, I don't know what it is you have against me. For three years I've tried to be your friend. I love your kids, and I want my brother to be happy. Is it so impossible to think of Russell having both a girlfriend *and* a family?"

273

Margie laughed. "Like you or anyone else in your family would ever accept me as part of the family. I know you don't like me."

Russell imagined Lane's reaction to this news flash. Lane was okay with confrontation. She remained cool. She shoved her hands into her pockets and planted her feet, even when it came to doctors telling her bad news or Bop trying to buy his way out of it. She wasn't the coward; he was.

"Margie, I invite you to dinner, to breakfast, walking the dogs, Fourth of July. Tell me what else I can do."

In retaliation, Margie set her sack down on the coffee table—a classic battle maneuver—the codependent Care package, spilling pills and ointments, undoubtedly literally identical twins of the medicine Lane had scored from Nick, but somehow more potent because they had been collected by Margie Lomanto, almost LVN.

"I'm the nurse, Elaine. What Russell needs is less noise and only one person to look after him. Go home to your husband. At least you have one of those to go home to."

At that Russell winced. Spencer's reedy voice ricocheted into his head: *Unca Russell, my chest hurts. . . .*

Lane came out of the kitchen and stood in the doorway. She pressed her lips together. She stood quiet a moment looking at her shoes—red hightop Converse she ordered from some catalog—then hooked her purse over her shoulder and turned to face him. He held the remote in hand, his thumb on Mute.

"Sorry," he said softly. "It's a problem I intend to address the moment I decide whether or not I'm going to live."

She nodded, but he could see the bewildered hurt in

her eyes. It all but spelled out Spencer's name in neon. "Good night, Russell. Feel better. I love you."

"Love you, too, Lane. My best to the Nickster and the pooches."

She cut a wide path around Margie on her way out the door.

Margie commandeered the kitchen, frying up some diet dinner-in-a-box that was designed to thaw in the microwave he didn't have. He could hear it spitting ice crystals all over the pan, and smell something vaguely Italian and lightly nauseating. He wanted another lime Popsicle; he wouldn't have minded a root beer. Yet if he asked for one, Margie would hammer at him until she found out Lane bought them, and then the headache he currently endured would be forced to don a size-small crown of thorns—and he wouldn't get to eat his Popsicle.

Margie had arranged her low-cal dinner on a plate, surrounded by cut-up cauliflower and carrots. These, he knew from experience, she was planning on dipping into exactly two level tablespoons of fat-free Ranch dressing. He listened to her crunch, her eating noise drowning out the sound of the television policemen's warning yells into the Nashville night. Someone wasn't dead after all, it was a something. Some rocket scientist had taken out a deer with a handgun. The cops were joking about having the carcass dressed out so they could enjoy drive-by, inner-city venison. Maybe it was time to outlaw handguns, Russell mused feverishly. He couldn't speak for the town of Harper, but he knew in his heart that it bothered him a whole lot more to hear of the deer getting lunched than any of the dirtbags on the show.

Margie washed up the dishes and tidied the

apartment without a word. He could tell she was lying low because of the altercation with his sister. Maybe she imagined that his particular herpes virus also contained a factor for amnesia. Well, she was about as dead wrong as the Tennessee deer. As soon as she came back in here, he planned to bring the subject up himself. But first, he'd rest a little. He closed his eyes, certain now that the grainy texture inside his eyelids were infant pox.

Margie was planning on spending the night! The slightest movement of sheet against his pitted, hive-struck body was agony and she wanted in there next to him. "Look," he said, when she began removing her jewelry and placing it on his dresser—a territorial gesture that always made him cringe—"I really don't think this is a good idea. Like you said this morning, I need quiet. I just want to be left alone in my misery. Where're the boys?"

"I left them with my neighbor so I could come take care of you."

"I'm fine. Go get those kids and put them in their own beds."

"You have a fever."

"So call me every hour on the hour and check."

"Russell, if I don't sit here and take care of you, you'll probably get up and go surfing."

He yanked the covers up. "It's not like I'm out scoping women, I have the flipping chicken pox. Quit treating me like a kid."

Margie wound her necklace around her index finger. "That's just like you, Russell, bringing up other women at a point where I'm feeling especially vulnerable."

"You're feeling vulnerable?"

"You know dieting makes me insecure."

276

"Oh, I see. Perhaps that explains why earlier you treated my sister so badly. Or don't you think reminding her of her dead kid was taking things a little far?"

Margie started to cry, but it wasn't sad-crying, it was wet rage, the snorting of something formidable that had been pushed to a primal corner, then poked with something hot and sharp.

Immediately, Russell regretted his inquiry. "Sorry. This isn't the time to get into something heavy."

"When is?"

"How about when I have a normal temperature?"

"So I have to wait until you get well to find out whatever terrible thing it is you have to say to me? That's fair?" She began putting her jewelry on again, pinning the earrings through her lobes, lining up necklaces so they fell in graduated loops across her breasts. "Say whatever you want to say to me right now."

He took a breath. "Okay, I will. You treat my sister like shit. I want you to cut it out."

She regarded him with half-lidded eyes. "And?"

"And so what if I want to sleep alone I'm sick. I don't want to have to be nice to anyone. I just want to lie here and do battle with my spots and my febrile cells."

"Don't you love me, Russell?"

His shoulder crater hee-hawed madly and he clutched sheet.

"Well, do you or not?"

"How can I answer that when I'm burning up with fever?"

She began to sob. Then she brought her fist down so hard on the mattress that the remote control flipped to the floor and broke in half, spilling its batteries.

Russell listened to Margie's sobs over the sound of the TV. It was a commercial for Ford, Lindsay Wagner

277

trying and failing to convince him that if only he'd shell out seventeen grand for a yellow Probe, fun times were assured. If it had been any other night but this one, he would have taken Margie in his arms and soothed her calm again. He was good at soothing, and Margie needed affection, maybe worse than anyone else he knew. Used to be he liked delivering it to her; he'd felt he had something of value to give. Not anymore. If he so much as patted her arm, she'd automatically assume the touch meant that everything was back on the rickety track from which they'd finally derailed. It only meant more miles endlessly circling the station in a town called This Will Never Work.

"Margie, you're not happy. You haven't been for a long while. Sometimes I get the feeling you'd like nothing better than to put me on restriction along with Ethan and Seth. That's not how adults who are supposed to love each other behave."

"Ethan and Seth!" she cried. "Don't you care about them?"

"You know I do. Those little surf monkeys are the best."

"Then you tell them we're breaking up. You explain it."

"Excuse me? We're breaking up?"

"Yes, Russell. It's Elaine or me, and obviously, you've made your choice."

He didn't answer. He was totally confused. Chicken pox had him squinting through fever and pain toward a very distant logic. Could one break up with a sister? Did you buy one of those quitclaim forms at the stationer's, take a reverse blood oath?

Meanwhile, Margie gathered up her groceries and slammed out the front door. Russell lay in the wake of her words wondering was that how people went about ending relationships? He was perplexed, compounded by the pain factor. He peered over the edge of the bed at the ruined remote. Countless times he'd dropped it from heights much greater than a bed, yet the sturdy plastic had stayed intact. He supposed there was some way to change the channels manually, but that tack necessitated upward mobility. He began a thorough examination of the problem, the only way he knew how, by creating a mental Roman numeral outline.

I. Desire

A. Getting out of bed

    1. advantages

      a. pick up remote; drag telephone to bed; mail on table contains Gretsch ads

      b. currently experiencing pressing desire to empty bladder

      c. Popsicles await!

    2. disadvantages

      a. remote appears beyond repair; phone miles from bed; once phone within reach, mandatory requirement to phone Dr. M, inform her of groundbreaking shit taking place

      b. fever may inhibit ability to negotiate proximity of toilet; possibility of humiliation factor looms

      c. freezer at least two continents away from toilet

B. Staying in bed

    1. advantages

      a. TV already on; don't have to call Dr. M; disappointment factor regarding guitars considerably lessened

  b. humiliation factor of adult incontinence kept private
  c. sugar supposedly responsible for dental caries; Popsicles remind me of Bop, a.k.a. horndog, yet married for fourth time, undoubtedly enjoying the fruits of matrimony while I am once again flying solo
 2. disadvantages
  a. currently enduring TV sitcom featuring three screaming women; staying with channel I will be forced towatch "Arsenio"
  b. urination question persists—urgently
  c. still want my fucking Popsicle
II. Wait. Duh, this hadn't worked in high school, so why expect it to work now?

He got dizzily to his feet and was immediately humbled by the pox. Half-crawling, he made it to the bathroom, became entirely exhausted by the act of urination and its equally tiring partner, aim. He pressed his cheek to the linoleum and studied the marriage of toilet to floor. Things were surprisingly clean down here. Porcelain possessed an inherent cleanliness rendered practically royal by soap and water. Of course, that was due to Margie's attention, not his, and at once he pictured her crying in her living room, cutting his photos into wastebasket-sized ribbons, and felt horrible. He tried to imagine what he might say to Seth, how what might be a relief for one guy might not necessarily be for another. If only everyone could just take five and enjoy a "quintessentially frozen confection." He crawled back to bed, dragging the phone by its cord and negotiated the mountain in front of him. El Capitan came to mind. Denali. Nothing purple and majestic, but a Sisyphean

280

climb he was incapable of scaling. He studied the tag sticking out from the mattress: *Do not remove under penalty of law.* Why was there no such rule book when it came to relationships? After resting a while, enduring more internal battering from his pox, he pressed his sister's number and got Nick.

"Russell? You all right?"

"All right. Such a simple phrase, really. So overused it could never hold its own in a copyright war."

"What's up, buddy?"

He thought of all those guitar builders who had their best designs stolen out from under them, their tricks of the trade incorporated under someone else's label. Thievery was an inherent part of American culture. In the nineties, they couldn't even corral a childhood disease like chicken pox. Margie had given him the gate. He was not all right. He was consulting dust burros with a broken remote, incapable of launching his own skinny butt back into bed, and Margie had left him.

"I hate to bother you, Nick, but I don't think I can hack staying alone tonight. Could one of you come over? Bring a sleeping bag? I think I'm getting worse."

God bless Lane. She brought the dogs. Oddjob required some scolding as to house rules, but Jake was psychic when it came to human pain. He nudged his head under Russell's hand, then folded up and slept by the side of his bed, right within reach. Nick steeped some ungodly smelling herbal tea he'd picked up from Mother's Health Foods. It stank like old vacuum cleaner bags, but Russell had to admit that after a few swallows his throat felt better. While he lay in bed, his sister and brother-in-law sat on pillows and they watched an old "Best of Saturday Night Live" rerun. John Belushi was dead.

Gilda, claimed by cancer. Some bangers in L.A. had tried to take Garrett Morris out with a handgun. All the new guys since the original cast sucked, except Martin Short's Ed Grimley character, captured here on videotape. Short had gotten so popular he quit the series almost as soon as he joined in order to make shitty movies. Well, at least Ed Grimley'd gotten his wish, the chance to appear on "Wheel of Fortune," shake Sajak's hand, ogle Vanna, and solve a few puzzles.

"I miss this show," Russell said.

"It's odd," Nick replied. "Do you realize we're reminiscing? None of us are in our fifties, and already there are a couple generations beneath us watching Ackroyd and Belushi sing 'Soul Man.'"

Lane smiled. "'What do you want for nothing—Rubber Biscuit?'"

"We watched 'Sturday Night' from day one," Russell put in. "Mother had no idea what we did after ten P.M. Lane usually fell asleep before the credits, but I hung in there till the end."

She said, "Why don't you try to sleep now?"

Russell shook his head no. "Can't. There's too much to think about. Margie broke up with me tonight. That alone's cause to pull an all-nighter, imagining how my life will change."

"Margie *what?*"

At the sound of Lane's high-pitched voice, Jake lifted his head and Oddjob barked until Nick shushed him.

"You heard me."

"Well," Nick said. "That's unexpected."

"Unexpected? Jesus, Nick," Russell said. "You sound like a therapist."

"I am a therapist—well, almost."

"Why do I always forget that?"

282

"Probably because I'm not your therapist."

"Yes, thank God I go to Dr. M. Imagine how awkward it would make my woodworking if you were my shrink. I'd get all nervous about the direction I was sanding, what it symbolized to chase the grain versus challenge it, choose joints and so forth."

Nick laughed.

Lane swirled the dregs of her tea in her cup, but didn't contribute to the discussion. Russell knew she was still keeping her own Dr. M visits a secret. He didn't approve, but would never give her away. "It's a problem—I mean an adjustment, as far as Margie and I are concerned, but Jesus, when I think of the kids. What do I do, Nick? I can't sue for custody of boys I didn't father. But I sure don't like the idea of never seeing them again."

"Just be cool, Russell. Treat the kids like you always have. Margie knows you're good for the boys."

"Margie might disagree."

"Men are such optimists," Lane said, in the process of picking burrs from Jake's thick tail.

Nick looked deep into Jake's eyes, received a wet canine kiss in return, and Russell felt most definitely that this dog-staring was because Nick recognized the inherent wisdom in his wife's words. "Saturday Night" signed off with the Not Ready for Prime Time Players waving into the camera and a requisite sound bite from the band. G. E. Smith, that ham of a lead guitarist, sure had a sweet deal going. Play two minutes before every commercial break once a week and get set for life.

"Well, one thing's for sure. Whatever happens, I can't come out of this feeling any worse than I do now."

They were all three quiet a moment, then the rustling of paper from the other room caught their attention.

Nick said, "Do you have a problem with mice?"

Russell listened. "I didn't think so."

The unmistakable sound of canine retching replaced the crackling paper noise. Lane got to her feet and ran into the kitchen. "Guess which four-legged creature polished off your basil and walnut pâté, Russell?"

Jake looked up at him, his conscience clean as new-fallen snow.

CHAPTER 21

THE HOME ECONOMICS DECATHLON

"I AM NOT PREGNANT," LAINIE MUTTERED TO herself as she unleashed her dogs so they might enjoy the late afternoon chasing elusive rabbits and digging for imaginary gophers. "I'm late. This is a fluke of body arithmetic, a momentary anomaly. Any second now that useless egg will drop like a cyanide pellet and everything will be fine. Oh, who am I kidding? I have no luck. Please, God, I'm not ready for this. Just about anything but this, okay?"

She looked up from her disjointed musings to discover Ruth Cranky Pony staring at her. Ruth was sitting in the dirt at the cliff edge of the bluffs, sobbing her heart out. She was a good, loud crier—Dr. M would have given this girl a gold star and five extra minutes on the Buddha clock. Of course Jake had to rush directly to the distressed girl; crying constituted a major disturbance in the universe as far as Jake was concerned. Which meant Lainie had to retrieve her dog and, in doing so, interact with Ruth. She spoke gently, not wishing to upset the girl any further. "Ruth?"

The dark-eyed teenager glanced away quickly. There was a pile of crumpled Kleenex at her side, and Oddjob raced in, snagged one, and triumphantly sped away with his prize clenched in his tiny rat-teeth.

Ruth and Lainie watched him go, a balding Pomeranian missile moving at warp speed. Between sobs, Ruth eked out, "Your dog is mental. That tissue's loaded with snot."

Lainie nodded. "Whatever winds Oddjob's clock is truly a mystery. We try to ignore him."

"Why have a dog you don't like?" Ruth asked, her sobs taming down to manageable beasts.

Lainie looked out over the Santa Ana river channel, where gulls circled the dark green muck that passed for the water and an egret stood out in ghostly, elegant silhouette. "He was my son's dog. I couldn't exactly kick him out when Spencer died. Besides, sometimes I like him."

"Give me a for instance."

"When he's sleeping and you can't tell where the bathroom rug stops and he starts. When he stands up on his hind legs like Nureyev, begging for bacon. And, of course, when he steals tissues and acts so thoroughly delighted with himself. Then I think, Okay, maybe I'll feed him one more week. Who knows? One morning we could wake up and he'll have changed into Lassie."

It seemed only Russell was good at making sad people laugh. All Lainie could do was watch Ruth blow her nose in another tissue. Ruth gathered the tissues up and bunched them into the pocket of her baggy jeans. Big jeans weren't a style issue with Ruth Cranky Pony. She was even thinner than Russell, which seemed odd, considering that Edna and the other Cranky Ponies tended toward the morbidly obese. Lainie prayed that aside from being born into life's most dysfunctional family, Ruth wasn't also bulimic.

"You want to walk with me awhile?" Lainie asked. "Sometimes walking helps. You put one foot in front of the other and pretty soon you're someplace else. I promise not to talk if you don't feel like it."

"You were talking to yourself a little while ago."

"I know. It's a really bad habit. I do it all the time."

"What were you saying?"

She could lie; Ruth wouldn't know. "That I am so a good sister."

Ruth made a sound of disgust in her throat. "Brothers. Let me guess, yours said you weren't."

"Not my brother. My brother's girlfriend. Well, she might not be his girlfriend anymore. She broke up with him three weeks ago. But they're still having these marathon phone debates. Daily. Which in my opinion defines relationship. He caught chicken pox and that seemed to tip the scales. Also, she's never liked me. None of those things are really connected, but they all bear heavily on the problem at hand."

"Girlfriend?"

Ruth had a long stride for such a skinny girl. Jake kept up no problem, but Lainie had to hustle and Oddjob was flat-out running. "Yeah."

"You mean that Large Marge who comes over to your house every once in a while and gives everyone in the entire neighborhood dirty looks?"

Lainie's jaw dropped.

Ruth was embarrassed. "Sorry. That wasn't very nice of me, was it? People, like my family, like to point out I'm not a very nice person. I mean, I don't even know her. But you have to admit she is kind of a porker."

Lainie slung her arm around Ruth's bony shoulders

for a moment. "Here," she said, pulling two pieces of watermelon-flavored gum from her pocket. "They're kind of stale, but they'll take your mind off whatever's bothering you."

Ruth chewed as they walked the circular quarter-mile trail that led past a stand of bamboo to the dogs' favorite stretch, a flat, sandy foot path that paralleled the river jetty. The only plants that grew here were the stiff, upright pampas grass, encouraged to spread by people who picked it to stuff in vases at home, and the lowly, bitter-tasting coyote melon. Riders often brought horses down here where there was room to gallop. Whenever they passed by, Lainie stood to the side of the path holding the dogs' collars, feeling Jake's heart race in some primal memory of a distant lifetime ago without leashes. Her heart too, felt similarly affected. Oddjob, not surprisingly, would simply stand his ground and bark, thoroughly pissed off that there were dogs so large suddenly polluting his universe. Today, only their hoofprints remained. Lainie fitted the tips of her red Converse hightops into the arc of the horseshoe imprints. What was new was that the formerly wild trail now was intersected by foot-high wooden sticks with florescent pink plastic ties on them. She stooped down to examine one. They reminded her of miniature red flags, like the lifeguards flew when riptides turned the ocean dangerous. She watched Jake expertly pee on one, then noticed it wasn't just the trail that was affected, there was a vast field of them before her, spreading out toward the river channel in a huge diamond-shape.

"What's all this?"

Ruth popped a fragrant, green bubble. "I think it's maybe where they're going to put in that soccer field."

"What soccer field? There's soccer fields over at

Balearic Center. There's soccer fields at Burton Elementary. This is a mandated wilderness area. How come I didn't hear about any soccer fields?"

Ruth shrugged. "Beats me. It was in the paper and stuff about six months ago."

But Lainie wasn't reading papers six months ago; she was in the hospital. She began pulling the stakes out as neatly as circus knives, loading up the bottom half of her oversized T-shirt. "Watch me get caught," she said. "I always get caught when I do illegal things. You don't have to help me if you don't want a police record, Ruth."

"Are you kidding?" Ruth began filling her own T-shirt. "If I had a police record, I could be popular."

"Is that what it takes these days?"

She screwed up her plain face and crossed her eyes. "Either that or you have to be born pretty."

"That old pretty business." Lainie smiled. "You just wait, Ruth. Go to your twentieth high school reunion and take a look at all those pretty girls who won't be friendly to you now. They'll be girdled into sequined gowns, troweling on the makeup, whispering about liposuction and life on Jenny Craig. And you'll be elegant and slim and still too good for town boys. Take my best friend Candace, for example. In high school she was just some geeky tall girl in a plaid skirt. A little hair bleach, a few years pass, she's beautiful."

Ruth didn't look too convinced. "Maybe."

Lainie put a little more shoulder into plucking stakes. "I can't believe those city council suits, sneaking this by the residents. Soccer field. Isn't there supposed to be an environmental impact report? Or some kind of ballot initiative? Did the statute of limitations run out on the Lukup Indian graveyards?" Silently, she wondered what would become of the meadowlarks, the burrowing owls. This was Harper's last wild place, not to mention her solace and the dogs' haven. When it was deeded to the city, it was with the understanding it would stay undeveloped. Like that would make a difference to anyone—Lainie, you are so naive, she said to herself. "I wonder what would happen if I chained myself to a tree, Ruth. They'd cut around me, wouldn't they? That's how it works. Pretty soon there's no trees except the ones they plant, and they didn't want to grow here in the first place." She stopped when she realized she was scaring the girl. "Sorry. It's really weird when adults get passionate about things, isn't it?"

Ruth shrugged again. She'd perfected the teenage I-could-care gesture. "I don't really think of you as an adult."

"Wow, thanks. That's about the nicest thing anyone's ever said to me."

"You're welcome."

The dogs trotted down the path, oblivious.

"What are you going to do with the sticks?" Ruth asked when they'd reached the trunk of the Volvo and Lainie started moving aside the baby clothes and toys to make room for the sticks.

"Send them to City Hall with a letter bomb," she answered. "Nobody develops these bluffs without asking."

"You sound like a cowboy."

Lainie imagined her grandfather in his threadbare Resistol, pulling his Robert Duvall face on perfect strangers, slipping a summons with that same friendly handshake. She looked enough like him that she wished she'd kept the hat for herself. "I wish I had a six gun, I'll tell you that. One bullet for every city council member."

Ruth stood at the car door looking pensive.

Lainie felt badly. She'd been so preoccupied with the stick gathering that she hadn't found a way to help Ruth feel better. "Not really, Ruth. I hate guns. Even water pistols. Listen," she said. "I'm going to make some bread when I get home. It's really hard work. You have to pound the dough out and it takes forever. But afterwards you get to eat it and it tastes great, way better than storebought. You could come along and help. That is, if you want to. Far be it from me to try to make anyone feel better. Especially in my kitchen."

Ruth opened the car door, shooed the dogs into the back seat, sat down and buckled her safety belt. "I don't mind helping," she said.

They drove the three blocks in silence until the stop at National and Burton. Ruth held Oddjob up to peer out the window at a gray cat preening itself on somebody's green lawn. "Behold, thine enemy," she said, and Oddjob seemed to wholeheartedly agree.

Lainie sprinkled the yeast over the brown sugar and hot water. "Watch, Ruth." The sugar sank to the bottom of the glass mixing bowl. They waited for the yeast granules to hitch a ride on the sugar and rise to the surface, exploding into the proofed cloud. It was a simple matter of chemistry, but every single time she did it Lainie swore it was magic.

"Wow," Ruth said. "How do you get them to do that?"

"Drop a Care package, they're more than happy to feast if you provide the correct environment." Her words felt weighted, sinking much deeper than reciting cookbook instructions. Her period was supposed to have

290

arrived days ago. When she could allow herself to think about that night in the atrium, she felt achy and terrified. Otherwise, it was one long case of continuous bewilderment. If she was pregnant, could she go through with it? Could she not go through with it? Heart, heart, heart. Her own beat out the nervous rhythm that by having another baby all she and Nick would be doing was repeating Spencer's dark history.

Ruth sniffed the empty yeast packet and made a face. "And this stinky gunk makes the bread rise?"

"That along with the flour and the kneading."

Ruth said, "My mom buys rye bread from the health food store. It takes about half an hour to chew one slice. And it has those awful seeds that get stuck in my brother's braces. They're all over the bathroom mirror from his flossing. Please tell me we aren't making rye bread."

"Don't worry. This is my grandmother's honey wheat recipe. No seeds. Brothers can be pretty unhygienic," Lainie said, handing Ruth her own bread board and the flour sack. "But eventually they get the idea. I really like my brother Russell. He's my best friend. Of course, Margie has a little problem with my feeling that way. Nobody else does, just her. Doesn't Aaron go to college next year?"

Ruth scowled. "Yes, the Westinghouse scholar won a free ride to the University of Montana at Missoula. Mr. Computer Science meets the great outdoors. Maybe if I'm lucky a bear will eat his brain."

"Montana seems like kind of a different place to go for computer science."

"Major duh," Ruth said. "UCLA offered him the same deal. But Los Angeles isn't far enough away that he can't fly home except for Christmas and Montana is.

My parents aren't real thrilled, but what can they say since he turned down the other scholarship without telling them?"

How Nick would love to be hearing this story, Lainie thought. It fit into all the textbook pie-charts. Lainie imaged that for every slice of the pie, a solution involving behavioral modifications and homework existed for everyone. Maybe it didn't always work, but the potential was there. "You have to stir the honey and margarine mixture in quickly, Ruth. Then start adding the flour in half-cupfuls, so the gluten mixes evenly. That's right. As soon as it has enough bulk, turn it out on this board."

Ruth turned her dough out on the floured board, and with Lainie's instruction, added scant cupfuls of flour to the sticky mess, which would eventually become a viable dough. In her grandmother's handwriting on the index cards, it said to fold the dough until it felt smooth and elastic, "like a baby's bottom," and Lainie stopped kneading for a moment to ponder those simple words. Bottoms were the business end of a baby for so long. First the doctor tapped him there to make him cry, then later on it was where they gave him shots. If someone stacked all the diapers a baby used in one room, how high that stack would reach. A baby's bottom—this was flour and water—adult Playdoh, nonsense. Ruth kneaded and slapped for all she was worth, and Lainie figured either she'd end up with one tough loaf sporting a tooth-cracking crust or a solid brick of sixteen-year-old brotherly hate.

"This the right way?" Ruth asked.

"Maybe just a little more gently."

"Sure." Ruth eased up. "You probably think I'm way stupid to be sitting in the bluffs crying over having the

292

smartest brother on earth."

Lainie shook her head no.

"Well, my parents find it unforgivable." She made her voice go high and whiny in a rather good imitation of Edna Cranky Pony. " 'Aaron is an *example*. Why can't you learn from him?' My teachers take roll and say my last name and expect me to be Madame Curie. And they keep after me all the time! 'Why is it Aaron gets As and you keep cranking out these crappy Bs and Cs?' "

"What do you tell them?"

"I tell my teachers I'm stupid. That Aaron inherited brains and I got the thick Karponi eyebrows. But my parents?" She smiled devilishly. "Them I tell nothing. Nothing at all. It drives them so crazy! My mother has this blue vein in her neck that throbs. It's completely great."

"And your dad?"

Ruth scratched an itch on her face, leaving a smear of whole wheat flour across her olive skin. "Whatever Mom says, he slithers behind it. The minute I turn eighteen, I'm gone."

"Where?"

"Aaron taught me one thing. Where doesn't matter. How far is the key. Maybe overseas. I could get a job. There's these flyers on the bulletin board in my French class. *Au Pair. Enchanté, mademoiselle.*"

When Ruth spoke French she got that faraway look Lainie felt when she rode horses that didn't throw her. "Traveling can be fun. I used to take trips with my grandmother a million years ago. She promised me that when I turned eighteen we'd tour Europe, see the castles and the Cotswolds. It didn't happen, but I got through a lot of hard times imagining that trip. Now we oil the bowl, turn the dough over, and let it rise for almost an

293

hour. You want a cup of tea or something while we wait?"

"Tea? I guess so."

She probably wanted Coke. Lainie didn't have Coke. She never let Spencer drink it, and Nick had a philosophical issue with soft drinks, saying "Why pay to drink something with no calories and artificial sweetener when you can have water for free?" Lainie tucked plastic wrap over the glass bowls. She set them in the oven to rise and boiled water for tea. She made Good Earth original, figuring sweetness and cinnamon would rehydrate the cried-out Ruth Cranky Pony. When she turned to hand Ruth her mug, she saw the girl was holding a framed picture of Spencer. It was a sterling silver sheriff's badge frame, a present from Bop in happier days.

"I remember your kid," Ruth said.

In Lainie's soul, thunder began to rumble across what had been a cloudless, summer-blue sky. "Oh? That's nice."

"No, I mean it. I was always hoping you'd ask me to baby-sit or something. I wondered if your house looked any different than ours on the inside. How come you never asked me?"

The summer sky turned navy blue, and yellow fingernails of lightning razed across it, crackling with heat. *Code Blue*, somebody yelled, then stage-whispered, *Nevemind, this one's history.*

Lainie cleared her throat. "He was sick a lot. I didn't really feel I could leave him with anybody."

In the awkward silence between them, Lainie stood without an umbrella, waiting for the downpour to drench her blind all the way to her bones. But it didn't happen. The sky pulsed dark, but the lightning fizzled

294

out and Ruth set the picture of Spencer down on the table and picked up her mug of tea.

"Does it?" Lainie forced herself to say.

"Does what?"

"Our house look any different from yours?"

"I like yours better," Ruth said, pointing to the few attempts Lainie'd made at decorating. "It's got all this light in it or something. Ours is dark. My mother collects china teacups and saucers. They're set out on this flimsy, three-legged antique table I always bump into. I'm so clumsy. My shoes are size ten-and a-half wide. Probably my hands are, too. So, are you going to have any more babies?"

Lainie's hand flew to her stomach beneath the kitchen table where they sat with their cooling mugs of tea. "I'm not sure."

"You should."

"Why do you say that?"

"Because I saw you and Mr. Clarke with Spencer. You let him fall down on the lawn, yell when he got mad, figure out for himself he wasn't supposed to pick up dog turds. That's the way parents should act, but they hardly ever do."

Ruth's face was shiny from the efforts of spanking bread dough, and her smart brown eyes glittered with leftover sorrow. For an instant, Lainie regretted asking her in, helping her make bread, talking, all of it. Though Nick would quietly applaud their communication, and Dr. M would have allowed a curt smile of approval to pass over her face, to a part of Lainie all this did was open up another avenue to hurt. Now she wouldn't be able to pass the Cranky Pony house without seeing Ruth bump those pathetic cups and hearing Edna sigh and imagining everyone chewing

295

that awful rye bread.

She got up from the table and went to the oven where the timer had only two minutes left before it dinged. "How long have we been sitting here? It's time to punch the dough down already."

She sent Ruth Cranky Pony home with a beautiful, aromatic round loaf of honey-wheat bread. They'd cut hatch marks in the crust with her good knife, then painted on a glaze of egg white, which glistened with just the right amount of shine and crackle. Actually, the loaf Ruth *believed* was hers was in truth Lainie's, risen to its full height, containing perfectly even-celled interior walls. She'd switched them when Ruth went to wash up in the bathroom. Ruth wouldn't be able to tell the difference as she cut it for the Cranky Ponies' dinner tonight. It wasn't a scholarship to Bear Country, Montana, but it was healthy and fresh, and required less flossing. She opened the front door for Ruth and prayed Edna wouldn't get all suspicious and make an issue over a loaf of bread.

In the arched doorway, Ruth hemmed and hawed.

"What's the matter?" Lainie asked.

"My mom's going to wonder about this bread. She doesn't exactly, well, like you."

"That's okay." Lainie gave her a one-armed shoulder hug—the kind of nonthreatening embrace that says, "We're sisters, and these aren't lies, they're creative alternatives." "Maybe you could tell her it' s something you did at school, for extra credit."

"The Home Economics decathlon!" Ruth said.

"Sure. Why not?"

Lainie wiped down the counters and returned the flour crock to the refrigerator. She washed the mixing bowls in hot water, her hands dreamily swishing through the suds while she hummed bits of old Hank Williams songs. Then she dried the bowls, nesting them one inside the other on the cluttered countertop, staring at their unblemished concentric circles.

She opened the mail. Without reading it, she put the statement from the hospital in its own special file, looping the metal prongs on the folder through the computer holes on the billing paper. The file was three inches thick now, a mountain into which she and Nick had chiseled one infinitesimal dent. If she were pregnant, people who knew about the bill would look at her belly and say, How dare that couple have another baby when they haven't even finished paying off the dead one.

CHAPTER 22

POST-YOGURT DRIVE-BY

NICK WAS AT HIS SEMINAR ON ARTISTIC temperament tonight. It was the latest thing for would-be therapists—trying to make sense of the artistic process. He wouldn't be back until late, and when he did get home he'd be sighing over all the new theories someone had thought up to complicate what he was still trying to memorize from his textbooks and journals. Being alone in the house wasn't so bad. Lainie counted herself the lucky owner of two security systems who barked and/or shedded at any strange noise, though they were currently lying in an unconscious heap on the tile, tail to nose, the yin and the yang of the canine kingdom.

She worried that her mother might show up. She

couldn't take a visit from Meridel tonight with that distant storm Ruth Cranky Pony hailed brewing offstage, ready if slightly encouraged, to grow into a monsoon. Whenever Lainie cried about Spencer in her mother's presence, Meridel got nervous. She might reach out and trace her finger along the rubber edge of Lainie's tennis shoe, maybe going so far as to tighten one of the loose ends of the bow in her laces before she chided her for being thirty-five and wearing red tennis shoes at all. Grief, as Dr. M explained, manifested itself differently in every person. When her dad had died, her mother's main emotional response seemed to be astonishment, as if Chuck's leaving had burdened her with two half-baked cakes and no proper cook to ice them. When Spencer died, she took a South American cruise and sent postcards from every port. Lainie had tried her best to find comfort in the pictures of endangered rainforest, her mother's presents of shell necklaces and *mola* throw pillows. To this day, the way her mother dealt with loss remained mysterious.

"I'm going to write the Harper City Council a letter," she told the dogs. They looked up, interested for a nanosecond, then sensing she wasn't discussing food, decided a better idea might be fitting in just one more nap before official bedtime.

She turned on Nick's old computer and typed, dismissing anything except the sight of crayon-orange earth-moving equipment scraping the bluffs down to level dirt, damning the history beneath them; the meadowlarks hovering above, homeless, yellow-breasted gospel singers.

When the doorbell rang an hour later, she thought, come on, Edna, let her keep the damn bread. But it wasn't Edna Cranky Pony, it was Candace, wearing a black halter-top dress and tiny round-lensed glasses, managing to look cool, dangerous and intellectual all at the same time.

"That's a new dress. Are you in love?"

Candace frowned. "I was, for about three hours. The pilot turned out to have a school boy-headmistress fantasy. I couldn't get into it. God, it smells wonderful in here."

"I made bread."

"Bread?"

"It was a tough day."

Candace handed the bouncing dogs each a peanut-butter dog biscuit from her purse, cut a slice of bread, then wandered over to the desk and read the Computer screen. " 'Dear Harper City Council Members, I respectfully protest your potential development of the Goat Hill wilderness area into a soccer field?' Lainie, what is this?"

"A letter to the council about developing the bluffs. They staked out a soccer field without telling anybody. I was just trying to check my spelling. What is the command for that again?"

"Control F2."

"Oh." Lainie laughed. "I was just space-barring, doing it line by line. Kind of faster your way, I'll bet. Don't read it. Well, read it and tell me what you think. The beginning is a little weak, but it gets better on page three."

"Page three?" It was Candace's turn to sigh. She wrote grant proposals for the community college. "Without a shocking opener this'll go on some semiliterate secretary's desk to be used as a coffee blotter. Here's how you start a letter you want an answer to, Lainie." She sat down and blazed her own letter over

Lainie's.

Dear Potential Heart Disease Victims (who happen to be obese white men all sporting mustaches): Would it really kill you to leave a foot of undeveloped dirt for owls and lizards? Must every inch of Harper feature a theme-oriented condominium complex? What exactly is your problem? Have you sat so long in your Jacuzzis sniffing your wallets that your *brains* have boiled away? Shame, shame, shame. What would your mothers say about boys who are never satisfied with their allowances?

Sincerely,
Lainie Carpenter-Clarke

"There," she said, slicing herself another chunk of the still-warm bread and slathering it with butter. She took a bite. "Good, but not your usual good. This crust's mean as wood shavings. Whatever you did to it, it's probably good for my colon."

Lainie laughed so hard she started to cry, big sobs coming out of nowhere.

Candace fed the last of her crusts to the dogs and took hold of Lainie's hands. "These aren't Spencer tears, are they?"

Between tearful gasps, Lainie shook her head no.

"And Nicky's not boinking nurses?"

"Of course not." She took a breath. "Hand me the tissues."

Candace pushed the box her way. "Is mean old Margie making snide remarks again?"

"No."

"Your mother?"

Lainie wadded the Kleenex into her fist. "Busy

bugging Russell."

"My poor, dearest Russell. One of these days, when Margie tires of earth and returns to her native planet, I must see to his needs." She folded Lainie into a hug. "Come here. Oh my God, there's only one thing left I can think of that could get you this upset. Don't lie to me. How late?"

Lainie's heart fluttered. "A week."

"A week!" Candace let go, sliced more bread and began eating again. "Missing your period a week, the reason might be you ate something weird, or scared yourself driving in traffic on the 405. You are not officially allowed to start to panic or fantasize until it's been at least a month. Then you may rail, pull hair, blame condom failure, jump rope for twelve hours, worry a little, and idly consider names. Get a grip, girlfriend. What you need is fat-free frozen yogurt covered with hot fudge. *Andale,* pooches, ice cream run."

The dogs began leaping in happy anticipation.

Lainie stared at her friend. "Candace, you never stop eating. How do you stay so thin?"

She smiled. "Well, it helps if you take the aerobic approach to *everything.*"

Candace's car was every single woman's dream—a silver convertible Mazda Miata. It looked great parked under the pine tree on Lainie's front lawn, but even greater when Candace was driving it, the tape deck blaring Michel Doucet and Beausoliel, her eyes a total mystery behind her Ray Bans. However, beneath the hood of the car things were held together with bobby pins and favors from the mechanics she sometimes dated. The Miata was too small for both dogs and Lainie, so they opted for the dependable Volvo. Candace insisted on driving. The trunk full of stolen sticks rattled at every stop, as if the vampires on the Harper City Council ought to be feeling at least a slight ache in their otherwise bloodless hearts.

Lainie leaned back against the head rest and watched her hometown pass by the open window. They turned left on 19th, passed the pawn shop and *carniceria*, the fish taco place, the Smart and Final Iris outlet, which sold bulk food, not flowers. Across from it was the DMV, where you had to make an appointment to schedule an appointment, and next to that, the tower condos where the seniors lived. Right around the first of the year, two elders coming back from the breakfast special at McDonald's had gotten lunched by a driver who swore the sun was in his eyes. It was directly on the way to the Public Assistance offices, so Lainie had to drive over the spray-painted body outlines in the street. Across from the tower was the really good Mexican food place where you could eat lunch for three bucks. Candace liked to flirt with the handsome order taker, but she hadn't yet scored a date.

Further down, Triangle Square, surely the least pertinent name for a minimall ever to smudge California. Russell often referred to it as Rectangle Oblong, which he thought made about as much sense. Its sole purpose seemed to be to cram eight movie theaters into the space of one, to open upscale restaurants only to watch them close when no one could afford to eat there, and to provide the strangest setup for underground parking ever conceived. Wise people parked across the street, where at least you could confirm you were at sea level. Lainie touched her flat stomach and wondered for the jillionth time that hour—impending cramp or businesslike mitosis?

"I'll have a killer chocolate with Heath bits," Candace

302

said at the yogurt counter, "and my friend here will have her usual pistachio without cashews."

The dogs stared in the store window longingly while a security guard tried to get close enough to take information off their licenses.

Lainie took her dish in hand. "I think my dogs are about to get arrested."

"If there was a Ph.D. in worrying, you'd have tenure."

"Candace, dog tickets cost *people* money."

"They rarely issue tickets for a first offense. I'll take care of it."

Lainie watched her friend slow dance up to the man, her long legs exuding something so promising that every man who met her wanted to check them out. She leaned close to whisper something. Then she stepped back and licked her chocolate yogurt suggestively, smiling as the man hurried away.

"What did you say to him, Candace? People still get very weird about rabies, you know. Killing dogs and dissecting their brains. Tell me you didn't infer that Oddjob has rabies."

"Did I mention rabies?"

"Meridel's right. You are a bad influence."

"I'd hate to think of you spending all your nights space-barring through protest letters for excitement. Think how boring your life would be without my badness."

"I do. Every day."

The late September night was cool. They sat under the heat lamps and listened to a guitarist with an open case sporting few coin offerings murder Neil Young's repertoire.

"This guy doesn't look old enough to have heard of Neil Young, let alone master the major chord progressions," Candace said. "Where do they find these twerps? Russell can play circles around this guy."

"Triangles, too."

"Possibly even rectangles." Candace threw her half-finished yogurt into the trash can. "No chocolate for doggies, sorry." She yawned. "Can I spend the night on your couch? I'm too tired to drive home. I have an early meeting at school with the marble shooters from administration. Oh, how I despise all this pre-semester bullshit. I have to wear pantyhose and not swear at anybody and listen to Judith Smartass talk about every 'really good chicken sandwich' she discovered on her pathetic vacations to America's foodparks. It's all just such a waste of time. I'm the only one who does any real work. Please, please say I can sleep over. We can stay up late and paint our toenails. Or go to bed early like good girls and whisper until Meridel shushes us. Don't fret, I'll be gone before you and Nick are up, my towel folded neatly on the towel bar."

Candace always promised to be gone before they got up. But usually she came in the bedroom at six and bounced on their double bed and got the dogs hyped until everyone woke up, when she promptly started asking what Lainie was making for breakfast. She liked French toast, but she also enjoyed leftover pasta. "You can always spend the night," Lainie said. "Just deposit a check on the silver tray when you go."

"Hmm. A check might bounce. How about I leave you my earrings?"

"Earrings are okay, too."

"Then it's a deal. Listen, you want to stop at Sav-On and get a Fact-Plus on the way home?"

"A fact what?"

Candace sighed. "It's a pregnancy test, Lainie. I buy

them by the case."

"You do not."

"Shame on you for doubting your best friend's word. We can drive to my house and look in the bathroom cupboard. I can perform a Fact-Plus in my sleep."

Candace lived in a trendy part of Belmont Shore, twenty-five minutes away. "I believe you, I just don't want to." Lainie threw her empty yogurt cup in the trash next to Candace's. She looked up at the night sky and wondered where her grandfather and Earlynn were this very moment. On the Shadow Ranch, tucked into bedrolls, slathering Deep Woods Off onto their leathery skin, or checking into some five-star hotel where the maid turned down the sheets on your bed? "What's the big hurry finding out? If it happened, then it's already true. I'll just wait a little longer and see if I throw up or something. Then deal with it."

Candace peered over her glasses. "That's a breathtaking display of logic, Elaine. No one else could possibly grasp what you're saying but me. You realize that, don't you?" She punched her friend in the arm and they hugged. "Let's buzz Russell on the way home, what do you say?"

"Well, I wouldn't say no."

They parked the Volvo behind Russell's Comet and Candace walked in the front door without knocking. Margie was there. So was Meridel. Apparently it was some rerun of early childhood. Meridel had always mothered Russell in a way she never did for Lainie. Neither looked thrilled to see Candace's bright and smiling face.

"Kiss me, you faker," she said to Russell, who sat looking pale and hairy-legged in his workshirt and shorts at the kitchen table. She plopped down in his lap and planted a wet kiss on his cheek, then began to unbutton his shirt. "Okay, big guy. Show me some scars."

Meridel looked like she was about to take up smoking again, but Margie was already smoking. Lainie tried to think of something innocuous to say to them, some small phrase that wouldn't cause either to immolate in the small kitchen. *Mother, that's a lovely pants suit. Margie, how are Seth and Ethan?* Did she ever ask anything else?

Candace turned to Margie. "Looks like you guys made up. I've got to tell you, I'm a little disappointed. Here I was planning to set my cap for this younger man and ask him to allow me the gift of bearing his children. Now I have to go back to my lonely single life and return all those cute maternity smocks. What else could I possibly do with fat clothes?" Her eyes flashed wickedly at Lainie.

Lainie threw her a glare and pulled her away from where she was sprawled across her brother. "Candace doesn't know it, but we have to go now. The dogs are in the car. They need air. Glad to see you're feeling better, Russell. Nice to see you, Margie. You, too, Mother. 'Bye, everyone. Candace, we are going now."

Meridel walked them out past the hedge of morning glories.

At the car door, Candace balked. "Lainie, I wasn't done provoking Margie yet. I had a bunch more provokes in my bow that I wanted to shoot her way. Have you always been such a rotten spoil-sport or is this a recent development?"

"More?" Lainie sputtered. "Sitting on his lap probably has a half-life of fifty years."

Meridel sighed and folded her arms across her chest. "The two of you."

Lainie felt instantaneous guilt yoke her neck. "The two of us *what?*"

Meridel lifted a single eyebrow. "From day one, you two just loved to stir the pot, especially where Russell was concerned."

"Stir the what?" Candace said.

"Now don't play innocent with me, missy. I know what you're up to. And whether you young ladies are aware of it or not, I happen to be sacrificing important social occasions. I almost had her out the door tonight at dinner. Sushi and chopsticks. Russell adores sushi."

Lainie said, "Mother, that's cruel. I can't work chopsticks very well myself."

"Then maybe you should practice."

"Is there any left over?" Candace asked. "I adore sushi, too."

"I'll fix you a tuna sandwich when we get home," Lainie said, wrestling the keys from her.

Her mother looked so pretty, standing underneath the streetlamp, the sulfur-yellow glow illuminating her tiny figure against Russell's fence of morning glories, shut up for the night as tight as kitchen cabinets. "Be assured, I'm not leaving town until that breakup is as absolute as the Berlin Wall coming down."

"Let me know if you need any help," Candace said. "As usual you're looking great, Meridel. Younger than ever. You know, someday we have to sit down and find a way to get you to spill your beauty secrets. Think of it as a legacy, Lainie and me your pot-stirring understudies."

Lainie watched her mother's careful smile and the dismissive wave as she turned back toward Russell's own

307

private drama. She thought, okay, I can understand everything going on here. Candace and Mother are each acting within their prescribed roles. Nothing overtly polemical, just regular life as we've been trained to live it. But I can't morally support the sushi move; sushi makes a legitimate meal but not everyone can stomach raw fish. And no way is Candace getting involved with Russell. That's a joke. Besides, if she were my sister-in-law and they had children—if there was a chance that anybody as thin as Candace could even *produce* fertile eggs—everything would change, wouldn't it? She drove the block and a half to her dark house, Candace laughing, chanting "sushi" the entire way.

"Up. This is my bed, not yours."

"Nicky," Candace whined. "There's room for everyone."

"Don't Nicky me. I have twelve new theories to memorize and I am not in the mood for a group nap. Out. And take that shedding fleabag with you."

Candace reluctantly exited the double bed where she had been sleeping alongside Lainie and trudged off in the direction of the couch carrying Oddjob in her arms. "Marry me," she said sleepily to the dog, her voice echoing down the hallway. "I'd never kick you out of bed for hair loss."

Nick punched his pillow three times before he settled into it. "Lainie?"

"What?" she asked sleepily.

"My entire side of the bed smells like Obsession."

Candace was pouring coffee, dressed in Nick's robe, when he came into the kitchen the next morning.

"You wear too much perfume."

she whispered. "You cannot throw up a week after missing your period."

Queasily, Lainie corrected her. "Starting today, we're heading into week two."

CHAPTER 23

FIVE THINGS

THE TWO SISTERS PARKED IN LAINIE'S OFFICE could not have been much more than nine or ten, but already they were old hands at the system, possessing the hard-bitten dignity of survivors. Their thrift-shop dresses clothed their bodies but remained miles adrift from their souls. Instead of the cheek-and-shine common to girls their age, these two had turned all that light inward to guard what was left of their lives.

"Hello there," Lainie said, and the older one—eleven, twelve?—stared back at her so accusingly Lainie had to look away to get her bearings.

"Our case worker went to the bathroom. We didn't touch nothing." Her voice was as raspy as a barmaid's.

Lainie looked around her office, which consisted of a desk, three chairs and a framed poster of Georgia O'Keeffe's "Ladder to the Moon." "Nothing much here worth touching, is there?"

The older girl didn't smile, but her younger sister did. She held one of those spool devices used to weave long snakes of yarn. Lainie hadn't seen one since her days at elementary school. It had five nails hammered into the top of the spool around which to twine the yarn. A tongue of acrylic purple stuck out the back of the spool, and the girl's stubby fingers trailed yarn over and around

311

those nails in constant motion. Wherever the sisters went next, some adult would undoubtedly yank it away because of the inherent weapon potential of those five nails. Lainie had crayons and a drawing pad in her bottom desk drawer, but these girls had left crayons back in the stone age.

She picked up their file from her desk but didn't open it. "Would you girls like to walk down to our lunchroom? There's a machine there with chips and pretzels. My treat."

"I like pretzels," the younger one said. She got right up, but when her sister gave her skirt a tweak she sat back down.

"Becky," she hissed, "we're supposed to sit here."

"It's okay," Lainie said. "I promise. We're only going down the hall. Your caseworker can see us from there."

All Lainie was supposed to do was kill some time with them, fill out their intake and initial referral forms, then shuttle them off with the caseworker to where ever they were going to live temporarily. They'd go to Sunshine House if they'd been abused in some way. Abuse—what a quiet-sounding word for what some of those kids endured. Or maybe they'd used up their time slot there already and were entering into the foster care swamp. If Casa Esperanza was on the itinerary, they would at least be with their mom. Lainie didn't need to read their file to decipher the reason they stuck so close together. Intuitively, the older girl sensed there was a better-than-average chance they might end this day in separate domiciles.

But of course, Lainie read it anyway. And just like choking on her toothpaste this morning with Candace, her throat glued itself shut. Vending machine pretzels were not nurturing foodstuffs, they were ropes disguised nonlitigious prose. Lainie wound a strand of hair around her thumb and index finger and pulled hard in order to feel something real, something other than this great hollow tunnel opening up inside her.

In the old days, before she understood the situation between Bop and Mac Henry, she thought Mr. Henry was nice. He'd show up at the stables when she was riding Banjo Man and lean over the fence rail, sometimes taking her photograph, sometimes just standing there telling her she handled a horse so well she could be a trick rider for western movies. What aspiring Annie Oakley didn't appreciate hearing that? He bought her rainbow-flavored Sno-Cones, or bags of pretzels like the ones she'd bought the sisters Randi Lee and Becky. When he asked questions about her grandfather, Lainie answered without hesitation; people impressed with her grandfather's philanthropic deeds were always telling her how wonderful he was. Grandpa Bop was a king who presided over the ocean his waterfront castle abutted. He sailed single-handedly from here to Catalina Island. Where anybody else tired after a lap, he swam for a mile. Like a magnet draws iron filings, legal-sized clams thrust themselves upward to meet his clamming fork. If you got a foot caught in kelp, Bop untangled it for you. If you cried, he wiped your tears with a faded bandanna, gave you a hug, and made you a glass of Carpenter punch. Best of all, he understood about loving horses. He had given her Banjo Man, a perfect pony who nickered in delight just hearing her footsteps. Oh, the shivery feel of Banjo Man's tongue against her palm as she slipped him sugar cubes! Bop, on the magic scale, he outdid Merlin.

At first, her parents had hidden the articles from her, but there was always someone at school who showed

her. All that money, the parties, the crazy big house—
he made an easy target for middle-class rage. *Your
grandpa's a bigamist!* some kid had informed her. She
remembered looking the word up in the classroom
dictionary, thumping that kid in the nose for lying,
getting in trouble with a teacher who couldn't fathom
Elaine Carpenter acting up. Now these pictures in a
new article filled with the same old meanness. It was all
starting up again, and Mac Henry had made Spencer a
part of it. Their family history turning ugly in as public
a way as possible, so cretins like Elizabeth Friedman
could guffaw at Carpenter family life over a bowl of
morning granola. Maybe Lainie should have punched
her in the nose. She would have gotten fired, but at least
her semi-career would end in a blaze of good-guy
gunfire.

"Spencer," Lainie whispered, running her hand over
his newsprint face. "My boy. I'm sorry they dragged you
into this." She looked down at her fingers, surprised.
Tangled in them were long strands of hair she'd
somehow pulled out of her scalp without feeling a thing.
She folded the newspaper into the trash and opened the
file into which she was supposed to log morning
visitors. The sisters were already gone, their baby
brother having escaped out the only exit he was shown.
Lainie closed the file and pictured the bluffs.

She wished she were there now with her dogs, taking
a walk that might go on forever. Right this minute some
city worker was probably earning his hourly wage
hammering stakes back into the ground, and her letter,
well, thank God at least she'd never mailed that joke of
words arranged on paper. Candace had the right idea,
get right in people's faces, but it took someone like Mac
Henry or her grandfather if you wanted to stir up a real

316

storm. Soon her bluffs would be filled with soccer enthusiasts and the dogs would have to go back on leash. The meadowlarks would fly to what was left of Riverside County to hunt out a meadow in which to sing. The owls could try Oregon—owls were having luck up there recently. Well, if she really needed something to feel bad about, there was always her overdue period. Halfway to day eight, either she had fully launched into paranoia or was starting to notice incredibly premature secondary symptoms.

Enough of this. If she broke down and cried, that provided one more piece of evidence that she wasn't coping. She was on the time clock now, and that was that. She threw her hair into the trash on top of the pretzel bags and made her way back to her office, touching the walls for balance. Vertigo, it was one way to navigate your life.

Fifteen minutes before she was to go home, Irene tapped at her open office door. "Lainie? Got a minute?"

"Sure. But you know I can't stay late if there's someone coming through to process. I have my— appointment." Irene knew she went to Dr. M, but Lainie didn't run around announcing it.

Irene smiled too widely for this to be about a client and shut the door behind her, She sat down on one of the empty chairs and faced Lainie. Her boss reminded Lainie of what Candace might look like in twenty years, a little less glamour, but the don't-mess-with me foundation intact down to each individual brick. She took no lip from people like Elizabeth Friedman. Once, when Irene prevented Liz from ousting a battered wife from Casa Esperanza for a positive drug test, Lainie had overheard her say, "Elizabeth, I have news for you. Life is not some spelling bee you lost in the fifth grade. You do not win a ribbon this time. Live with it." Yea, Irene. If Mac Henry had written such trash about Irene's family, she would have filleted his butt and served it at the Lion's Fair Fish Fry.

"So. How are you doing, Lainie?"

The question seemed innocuous, even fair. Depending on how full various halfway houses were, everyone around here was "not-fine" at certain times of the day. It was a running joke. "Why, I'm fine, Irene. As fine as any of us are dealing with the unsolvable problems of our unshockable universe."

Irene nodded sympathetically. "Those little girls this morning—they didn't upset you?"

"Upset me?" Lainie laughed nervously.

"Their file is pretty brutal. I should have warned you. But listen, I made a few calls, and there's a good chance Mrs. Lewis will have space for them both by the end of next week."

Mrs. Lewis was a local saint who raised desert tortoises in her back yard. Her house was decorated in Early American turtle statuary, Sierra Club posters, and stuffed terrapin. If you had to go to foster care, scoring the Turtle Lady was Christmas.

Lainie blew out a breath. "That's good. Sibs need to stay together. Look, just because I had a little breakdown doesn't mean I can't handle child abuse. I mean, this is my job, for Christ's sake. She's not the first ten-year-old to come through this office with gonorrhea."

"You're right." Irene looked at the linoleum. Then she looked up at Lainie. "Please don't let me be the one to have to break this to you. Have you seen the article in today's paper?"

318

Lainie felt her skin start to prickle. "I've seen it. Mac Henry's nursed a grudge against my grandfather since day one. I can't do anything about what's already done."

Irene touched her arm. "Of course you can't, sweetie. I just wanted to say I'm sorry about it. And don't think I missed what Friedman said to you in the lunch room. Consider her ass grass and me one relentless lawnmower in eternal pursuit."

Lainie laughed politely. But you read every word of that article first, didn't you, she wanted to ask her. "We're friends, Irene, aren't we?"

"Of course we are."

"Then why are you so nervous? What's going on? What don't you want to tell me?"

Irene crossed her arms in front of her chest. "You're looking kind of worn out again, Lainie. Are you getting enough rest?"

"I stayed up late last night. I'll be fine by Monday."

"You know, there are certain aspects of my job I could do without."

Her boss was looking everywhere but at her, as if she knew Lainie could read the deeper truth in her eyes. "Am I fired?"

"Not fired, per se. But I have to let you go."

Lainie was quiet a moment. "Let me get this straight. I work for you for five years, during which time I don't steal paper clips. I do pretty good, considering what I have to work with. My kid has the bad luck to die and I have a teensy bit of a breakdown. Not unexpected, even forgivable, considering the circumstances. So I get help, which isn't supposed to count against you, hell, even our insurance plan says that. Three months ago I come back to work, not because I salivate like Pavlov's dogs thinking of the pitiful programs available for the people

319

who pass through this office looking for some kind of salvation, but because I have a mountain of bills to pay. Some aging journalist with a grudge digs up a few family skeletons and parades them across today's newspaper because he was short on drive-by shootings to report and *now* I'm looking so tired I'd better leave my job? Is that all of it, Irene? Did I leave anything out?"

Irene rubbed at a cigarette burn on the chair next to her. The chairs were so old that at one time they'd sat in a building that allowed smoking. "I never said any of that. I'm sorry you think that would be the reason. It's fallout from the budget meeting. Last one hired, first one fired. As ridiculous as that sounds, those are my orders."

It seemed pretty clear Irene was being nudged hard herself, by somebody a few rungs higher on the ladder, and Lainie tried hard to rack her brain for someone she might have insulted.

"Does this have anything to do with Judy Casey's great big teakwood desk in the downtown office? Or maybe Dan Alexander striving hard to make that hundred grand a year he pulls down attending meetings and sampling doughnuts appear worth everybody's while?"

"Nope. I'm just the skunk who drew the lucky job of messenger. Kill me quickly and we'll both feel better."

Lainie sat back in her chair. "And if I let you live?"

"Then we chalk this up to budgetary concerns and I spend the rest of my life feeling lower than a rock in a dog turd."

Lainie gripped her pencil and wondered how Russell would handle this. Quit and be done with it, play some blues, circle the want ads when his checkbook balance dipped to two figures? Maybe she should call Candace, eat more frozen yogurt, take her up on that home pregnancy test. All she felt was injustice firing through her veins and the profound embarrassment of being told to leave a place where she knew she did good work.

"It's nothing personal."

Lainie's gooseflesh electrified. This was really happening. "Maybe I can get a job working at a burger joint. I hear some of them hire the handicapped."

"I'm sorry. This is the last thing I want. But somehow what I want never seems to be at the top of the list."

"Well, I know how that goes." Lainie looked around her office, her gaze coming to rest on the pile of intake reports she was planning to file next week. "Those papers," she said, and Irene gathered them up into her hands.

"Someone else can finish them. Take off now and I'll see that you get your two weeks' severance."

"But I'm not full time. Severance is only for full timers."

"I think I can manage that much."

Sure, but what about the——sisters? Or whichever kids came through here next? Who would put quarters into the pretzel machine and sit with them while Elizabeth Friedman plotted to send them to separate foster care hells?

Irene started to give her a hug, then began to cry quietly into Lainie's hair. Lainie wanted to, but couldn't make herself hug back. She patted Irene's back woodenly and watched her go back to her office. Then she stared at her poster on the wall. People always raved about Georgia O'Keeffe, what a visionary the woman was, as if she had sprung up in the middle of Ghost Ranch, New Mexico, like some night-blooming cactus, certain of every brushstroke. But the rumors were she had been sexually molested by her father and her brother, and her route to those paintings had been like ten thousand miles of bad road ending in blindness. Some days, when the children and women who passed through her office made Becky and Randi Lee look like debutantes, all Lainie could do was stare into that picture and keep on trying.

She took it down from the wall and cleaned out her desk. Then she drove to the hospital, because after all, it was Friday, and Dr. M was waiting with man-sized Kleenex and the ticking Buddha, her spiritual timekeeper.

CHAPTER 24

STIR-FRY WITH FORTUNATE RAT

OUTSIDE DR. M'S OFFICE, LAINIE SAW RUSSELL unhappily exiting his hour. Friday wasn't Russell's regular day. What was he doing here?

"Chastened down to my skeletal remains, that's how I feel!" he stated rather loudly into the open doorway of the office, his left foot still technically inside. "Between chicken pox and Margie and sleazy reporters, I wonder if I have any blood left. Listen, we can't be done here."

MacLellan Henry's article must have upset him plenty for him to change his schedule. Or perhaps it was the aftermath of the sushi maneuver. "Russell?"

"Hey, Lane. Canceled your subscription to the *Times* yet? Listen, I need a few minutes of your hour. We're talking ten, tops. I'm not done. Please?"

"No."

"Okay, five minutes. Look, this is all in the family. Can't I just come in with you?"

"No, you can't come in with me," she said, positioning herself to overtake the doorway. "I need every single one of these fifty-five minutes to myself. This has been a wretched day. I lost my job, Russell. As in no notice, no paycheck, no duh." She looked down at the picture she was still carrying. Was she planning to hang a Georgia O'Keeffe in Dr. M's office?

"We'll firebomb them later. Two minutes." He ducked into the office and shut the door behind him.

Lainie stamped her foot and leaned against the wall, staring down at the homemade ladder in the poster. When she got tired of looking at that, she checked the time on her watch. Two minutes wasted already. She imagined those minutes ticking themselves by in triple time, the same as when she'd sat on Spencer's hospital bed willing them to slow down. They juxtaposed oddly with the slow waste of "rest" time as she foundered in the hospital bed upstairs seven months ago. People like Russell, who rarely wore a watch, couldn't possibly understand the loss of time. Maybe Bop could explain it to him if he wasn't too busy honeymooning Earlynn. Damn it all! This was her hour. Russell was leaving if she had to pry him loose herself. She knocked on the door. "Russell? Do you hear me? Russell! Dr. M! Open this door or I'm going to start yelling."

When Nick walked up, Lainie was too leveled by the day's events to try to hide, or even make up a flimsy story as to why she was standing outside the office of one of his colleagues holding a dead painter's reproduction of one possible idea of heaven.

Her husband stood there in his white coat with his picture ID snapped on the pocket, the perpetual

323

textbook tucked under his arm. "Were you looking for me?"

She bit her lip. "No, I was waiting to see my therapist. Don't worry, it's for the last time."

"You're seeing Annie Mapp? For how long?"

"Oh, just until she pronounces me sane. But don't worry. We can't afford it after today, so I'll be amazingly cured. I got fired, Nick. Some big butt in administration informed Irene my ten bucks an hour would balance their two-million dollar budget. Then Irene said it looked like I needed a rest anyway, all of which more accurately translates to 'You're fired.' I've never been fired before. I'd rather get a speeding ticket every day of my life than feel like this again."

He put his arms around her, hugging both her and the framed poster. Anyone walking by might think she had given him an ultimatum: Love me, love my art, or hit the road. "Well, that's too bad. Annie's a good therapist, Lainie. If you think she's helping you, we'll find some way to afford it."

"How? Send Oddjob out on landscaping assignments?"

He kissed the top of her head and held her by the upper arms. "We'll find something. Did you see the *Times* article?"

"Could anybody have missed it?"

"Well, nobody in psych did. This day will go down in history. Don't worry about your job. You can find another one. I know you don't believe it, but you're stronger than I am."

Lainie looked at him, stunned. Why did people—especially people who knew better—always say that? I am not strong! she wanted to scream. I am the same woman they tied down to a white bed and kept all the letter. What on earth is inside that box?"

Mailed her letter? Well, of course, why not? Could this day, preordained by a cosmic force with a sick sense of humor, possibly end any differently? "A rodent."

"A what?"

"White rat." Said rat scurried around his new universe while the dogs stood by tensed, much too interested for this to work as even a temporary solution. "Mother, relax. I'm going to walk down to the neighbors and see if they want to take it off my hands. Please, just sit. He can't possibly get out of the box. Make yourself a cup of coffee or something. Ginseng tea. A slug of Scotch. When I get back, I'll wash my hands thoroughly and explain everything to you."

"Elaine, here our family is in shambles and you're playing with mice—"

"I said *rat,* not mouse. There is a big difference." Lainie shut the door on her.

Wisteria Street at sunset—children hollering, racing around a street where all traffic slowed for the business of play. Skateboard wheels clacking down the sidewalk. Bikes pulling brodies. Girls with Barbies trading those fingernail-sized high-heeled shoes and talking in falsetto voices. Somebody's boom box pumping rap music. *Yo, yo baby, wanna take you for a good time. . . .* The Fuentes tribe intercepted her before she'd gotten past their driveway.

"Please, please," they chanted. "Give it to us!"

"Your mother will kill me."

They danced up and down, pulling at the box. "No, he'll make a fine companion for Hector!"

"Who's Hector?"

"Our guinea pig! He gets lonesome all by himself."

Lainie opened the box and they quieted, taking turns

331

stroking the rat with careful fingertips. She didn't know if the two species were remotely fraternal, but she let the kids carry the box inside. Uté would let them keep it until they could con a classroom teacher. She watched the herd of children racing through the dark, their whole lives ahead of them with acres of time to mature into messed-up adults who got themselves accidentally pregnant and paid money to ventilate on a therapist's couch. "*Adios*, rat. Count your blessings."

Lainie watched her husband closely over dinner. He'd behaved very coolly when he walked in the door, as if it was completely normal on Fridays to discover his wife had been hiding her therapy visits from him, for her to get fired, to find his mother-in-law talking back to the television newscasters as if they needed her unique slant to realize they were reporting the facts all wrong. Perhaps Dr. M had given him a lecture. Maybe the discovery had come as a relief. Maybe it *wasn't* a surprise and when you were a shrink-to-be the patient confidentiality boundaries blurred. Or it could have something to do with the shock of finding three actual related food courses set on the plate before him. The possibilities seemed endless.

"So, Meridel, did you get anywhere with the Russell and Margie situation?" Nick asked as he blew on his Udon noodles before chopsticking them into his mouth.

Meridel twirled an empty chopstick. "Whatever sense I try to talk into Russell *she* undoes at night in b-e-d."

"I told you they would eventually start having sex," Nick kidded.

"Oh, hush up," Meridel said irritably. "I had to give it a try. I guess Dear Abby's right. Keep your nose out of your children's business."

ghost."

"Shall I total your bill?"

"Appreciate it. Throw it on my credit card and I'll catch the receipt on our way down."

Bop left the lobby in search of Earlynn, who, wet hair or not, wasn't sipping coffee in their room. She wasn't in the gift shop either, though the moment she woke this morning she'd announced she wanted two copies of *The Legend of Kate Morgan,* "one to remember our honeymoon by," as if some poor rejected woman's murder made a romantic keepsake, the other to send to her Texas gal-pal, Smokey the Bare.

Bop's irritation toward journalist Henry spat at the edges of his pot, disorienting him for a moment as he made his way back downstairs. He mentally reviewed his blessings. From Sally Jessy to his arms, he was good and married to his petite, platinum blond telephone sweetheart. It was time to head on home. They needed to sell a boat nobody ever sailed, call somebody about patching up the seedier aspects of the house, give it a coat of presale eyewash, then go about getting it listed with the county's hungriest available realtor. He'd come to the conclusion that putting a bid on the Shadow property—step one, was the right thing to do. Given its location and architectural notoriety, selling Casa de Carpenter should present no problem.

Of course, south of the belt buckle, he still couldn't whip his steed into a halfway decent trot, but in the last few weeks between here and souvenir-shopping in Tijuana, he'd learned how to make his bride somewhat happy in the sheets. From reporters to grandkids, let them say what they wanted. The perpetually dopey grin that greeted him in the shaving mirror was about the business of the heart, that hopeful pump, and nothing else.

Bop turned the corner and spotted Earlynn staring out over one of the hotel's balconies toward the glittering Pacific. She rubbed her arms, maybe feeling a little chilly here in the shadow of that great body of water. He hated to disturb her. Was she pondering the heartbroken ghost, or imagining how whales found each other and fell in love in all that ocean? Or was she reviewing some hard time in her previous life? No-good son of hers shutting the door on her like that—children just loved sitting there in judgment, grandkids, too.

If it were possible, he'd sneak back to the room, fetch her red sweater, tuck it over her shoulders, and drift away quiet as Kate Morgan. But real people hadn't ghostly luxuries. Real people took the circumstances that lay before them and made the best of things, even if it meant being arrested for justifiable assault committed on an aging journalist.

He took a deep breath, visualized a mental picture to urge his blood pressure down: autumn on the Shadow. The you-calla-petus scent came stinging through the cold air a little more sharply, clearing the sinuses. The horses turned shaggy-coated and sleepy, started voluntarily going into the barn at night, nickered in welcome when there was enough money for regular oats. Lemons hung green on the trees, gathering their juice the same way the profits—

"Charles!" Earlynn shot an arrow through his reverie.

"Hell's bells, honey, you about stopped my heart. What is it?"

She thrust a *Horsetrader* newspaper toward him. "I found us a prospect to check out up in Carlsbad. You mind going home a day early? I already called and warned the sellers we might drop by. Well, I sort of hinted we'd more than might drop by. They got a trailer, too, and she's regular on her vaccines."

His single-minded wife. He pinched the skin between his brows. "Tell me *she's* not an Arab."

Earlynn made that little click of impatience in her throat.

"Good God, she's dish-faced as a teacup, and no doubt a proven breeder."

"Why don't you just wait and be pleasantly surprised?"

He patted his heart. "Sugar, you get to be my age, it takes an earthquake of eight or higher."

Earlynn delivered him one of her tell-nothing grins and damn if he didn't just melt. "Right now you look too pretty for me to get mad about whatever kind of horse it is. And you know that, don't you?"

"I don't know nothing except how much I love you, Charles."

"Then how about my mid-morning kiss?"

"Well, it is your husbandly right. Take it if you want it so bad."

He embraced her. She was up on tip-toe, her breasts so full and warm against his chest his brain fogged up like a sauna. "Shoot. Forgot the hair dryer. Hope I'm not getting Old Timer's."

"Oh, I'll just wear a scarf. Beginning to feel like a Russian peasant woman, but I'm getting used to them."

He twisted his faxes into a roll and stuck them into his back pocket. "Did I tell you today how much I love you?"

"Not since grapefruit. I was beginning to wonder."

The hell with those twenty-something honeymooners next door howling all night. He and Earlynn could hold their own just fine by kissing—with a little judicious touching applied here and there.

Now and then, between the dull green freeway ice plant and the weeds, a hardy golden California poppy lifted its copper head to paint the landscape. The state flower was staging a comeback, and if they quit planting all this nonnative frou-frou, it might just start an army. "How about those flowers?" he said.

"Charles, I don't have time for flowers just now, I am concentrating on my driving."

Earlynn was tending wheel. To Bop fell the task of reading the maps atop cramped knees, the seat pulled close to accommodate Earlynn's short legs. He was being a good boy, holding back on all the "history lessons" he might have given her regarding the changes in the land since the old days.

"Left off the next off ramp. Look for Stockbridge Road. The mailbox'll say Smith Horse Farm."

At the exit, Earlynn rolled her window down, took a deep breath, and wrinkled her nose. "Horse manure."

"Honey, that's perfume."

She clicked on the turn signal and headed due east.

It wasn't much in the way of a horse farm. From the looks of the single-wide, no-color mobile home and the rickety wire-and-post corral, this was a family operation operating at subsistence level, capable of turning out maybe three or four horses a year, depending on how much they could afford in the way of prenatal veterinary care. Horses had less than a fifty percent rate of successful babymaking—one large reason Bop felt loath to get involved in this mess—but starved mares dumped only two kinds of babies: dead and weak.

"Did you know that only the Chinese panda fares worse with offspring than the horse, Earlynn? Animals

342

grieve, same as people. That's proven fact. Sometimes the loss of a foal will drive a mare clean out of her head."

"Hush, Charles. When her time comes, my mare's going to have her pickles and ice cream and shots and a healthy baby."

"I'm telling you, you're pressing Carpenter family luck. Factor our history in, she'll probably twin. Twinning's not a double-your-money thing with horses. Generally, both die."

"Now you listen here, Mr. Smarty Know-It-All Gloom-and-Doom. I did grow up in Texas, where there's one or two horses, and God knows how, but I managed to learn a few facts about them before I turned into a brainless woman good for nothing but making your supper."

All his internal organs cringed simultaneously. "Please tell me that isn't some kind of feminist jabber dangled just to make me bite some trick bait. If so, you can spare the poor worm, let me out, and I'll walk home."

Earlynn gave his thigh a little pinch. "It's a get-down-off-your-hobby-horse warning. And I'd like to see you walk home from here. Imagine how grateful you'd be to see me. I could maybe get two horses out of it."

She threw the truck into park like a hired hand. Her little legs dangled a good two feet above earth when she opened the car door. He hurried around the truck to catch her, should she suddenly decide help was an acceptable alternative to falling on her keester, but by the time he got there she was safely down, already three strides ahead of him.

"You the lady called about the horse?" a dark-haired little girl called from the fence railing. "I can ride her for you if you want. We don't got a saddle but I'm good at

343

bareback."

The girl was thin and dark-haired, some Mexican to her, but also a goodly measure of white mutt, Bop decided. Her sweatshirt looked secondhand, and as far as the jeans went, too much ankle showed, but however poor she might be living, she was rich in loving those horses. Nosing around the corral, a rangy bay and a fleabitten gray hovered near enough to her that it was clear she didn't live here friendless.

"What's your name, honey?"

"Deborah."

"Where's your daddy, Deborah?" Earlynn asked. "Sure, we want to watch you ride the mare, but I'd also like to talk to your daddy in case I decide to buy her."

Deborah's smile instantly departed. "Well, he's . . . he got a job this morning, so he ain't here right now."

"He didn't say nothing about a job when I called." Earlynn rested her hands on the top rail of the fence. "What kind of job does your daddy do, Deb honey? Construction? Does he hire out for ranch work? Handyman?"

Deborah turned her face away. "See that white horse in the pipe stall? She's our brood mare. Throws great color. But she ain't for sale. The one for sale's around back. I'll get her."

She leaped off the fence, all lean agility and youth, but Bop couldn't miss the heaviness in her step—she didn't want to part with that horse anymore than she'd want to wake up having grown a second nose. Was the mare a quarter horse? The bay horse looked to be mostly quarter. It wasn't that Bop minded the California quarter so much, but he'd rather call some folks he knew in El Paso who still bred them with decent bone girth.

A Leopard Appy was too much good fortune to hope

344

for. Some Bureau of Land Management jughead with Mustang in her? Well, even Mustang was preferable to Arab. Crazy hotbloods—only thing you could train them to do was have accidents.

Bop stepped gingerly through somebody's idea of mucking. Apparently, whoever was in charge of the stall cleaning scraped whatever lay in the rake's widest path to the edges and let it mound up like ever-growing foothills. Lord, he wanted that rake in his hands now, to start in taking care of the problem himself. Ahead of him, Earlynn had made a friend in young Deborah. As he listened to their laughter, and saw their hands brush, he regretted not meeting Earlynn fifty years earlier, when they could have combined their blood to create their own fine stock.

"Wait here," Deborah said, and Earlynn hung back by the fence.

Bop waited a moment, then said in a low voice, "This place isn't even third-rate, Earlynn. Why don't we go on home and let Ed Whistler make a few calls, find you exactly what you want?"

She turned her face to him, and in the sunlight he could see a spot on her cheek where the makeup wasn't doing its job. "Let me guess. You want to buy me a German horse with a built-in CD stereo and power everything. Or maybe this here is what Sally Jessy calls one of them 'control issues.' The horse can only be worth your dollar if you pick it out. Am I getting warm?"

He threw up his hands. "North Pole! Me, I got no control issues. We'll buy you whatever you want. Glue on hooves, if it makes you happy."

Earlynn laughed, and then the girl came back leading a tall black and white nervous-looking pinto, sixteen hands and a maybe little finger's worth higher. Overo and a Medicine Hat to boot—showy, but Bop's horseman's eye began assessing angles and measurements before he let his saliva glands kick in over the startling black and white splashes. Color breeds had that weakness to melanoma, a definite minus, and mares, well, Earlynn was over her head. He hadn't even seen her ride yet, and this mare looked young, three or four on the outside. He'd have to take a look in her mouth to tell for sure, call out a vet who wasn't in anybody's pocket, X-ray the legs, hope for the best.

"She's pretty," he said to Earlynn. "But you know what they say: Pretty is as pretty does."

"Oh, you just hush. This is a fine horse."

Behind them the mobile home door slapped at its hinges and a man in filthy jeans came weaving out. He licked his palms and smoothed them over dirty blond hair that needed cutting. "Got a trailer for sale, too," he said loudly, in the tone reserved for those who drank hard liquor well before nine in the morning. "Nice oak floor. Put it in myself."

Bop knew exactly how to handle drunks trying to conduct business deals. You slowed things way down, inquired nonchalantly, gave no promise or urgency to your voice, kept everything deliberately understated. Eventually the drunk would fall down at your feet, belly up, and you'd save a bundle. "Nice looking girl you got there. Your daughter?"

The man squinted. "Yeah."

"She got a mother?"

"Someplace or another. If she don't care for the way I run things, let her find another wallet, that's what I say."

Bop pursed his lips. "I've always felt women deserved to be treated like fine horseflesh myself. Manicures, flowers, as much affection as a man can humanly dish out. How much you asking for the mare?"

The man tried to put one foot up on a dead potted plant, stepped down hard, then recovered his footing. "Fifteen hundred."

Even Deborah looked surprised. Bop waited a second, opened his mouth, but before he could start negotiations, Earlynn popped in.

"What are you, some kind of highway robber? Look at that mare's coat! Why, how much would it have dented your Jack Daniel's budget to feed her a handful of vitamins? And while you're at it, why don't you try trimming the hooves of all these horses? It don't take a balanced checkbook to learn how to measure and file. Even I could do it. *If* I like the mare, and if the vet tells me it's financially sound to fall in love with her, and there's no guarantees either'll happen, I'll give you six hundred American dollars, out of which I expect you to buy this lovely young daughter of yours a new pair of jeans and two Sunday dresses. Now you just get yourself back inside that trailer, drink a pot of coffee while I ride this horse, wash your face, change your filthy pants, and cool your jets."

The man stood there stunned, his jeans so creased with dirt no amount of scrubbing would get the stains out. They were testament to his chosen way of life. Earlynn clapped her hands. "Go on, now. Do as I say. Shoo."

Deborah waited until her father had gone back inside the trailer before she asked Earlynn, "Are you married?"

Bop had the answer to that. "Damn straight she is."

"Oh."

"Oh is right." And he sat there scratching his head in gelded wonder while Earlynn buddied up to the mare,

347

cooing and touching her legs, checking for faults. Damn if she didn't bring to mind Lainie all those years back, when Chuck was still alive to argue with and little Spencer's passing was so far off in the future and everything felt so fat with profit he wanted to buy every citizen of the world a spotted horse. Deborah looked like she could use one right now. His eyes unexplainably stung. Goddamn allergies. The ways things were going, it might be wise if he got up to check out the mythical oak flooring in the trailer.

CHAPTER 26

A KINDER, GENTLER BUFFALO BILL

HENRY FORD HAD PLANNED HIS BIG TRUCKS TO withstand much. Unfortunately, he'd overlooked three-year-old pinto mares dead certain that trailering constituted grounds for a rodeo event. Bop had his pick of laments, starting from purchasing the horse on down to the present state of his tailgate. When they emerged from the other side of this nightmare, the Ford dealership would have a field day with his wallet.

The trailer hitch had broken at the seam and come off the ball and was repeatedly slamming into the tailgate, basically humping a fist-sized hole into the deep ocean blue and leaf green of his custom paint job. He'd become aware of the problem somewhere around San Clemente. The damage already done outweighed stopping; the only logical path was forward. The hole might widen, but taking that wild mare out of the trailer on the side of the freeway was asking for pure mayhem. Bop drove on, listening to Alan Jackson wail about loving all night while a rapt Earlynn filed her nails.

His bones were still rattling as they parked in front of Ed Whistler's office. A *little case of trailer jitters*, Earlynn called the equine kicking and screaming they'd endured since Carlsbad. That explanation might hold for the simple-minded. Now she was hard at work convincing Eddie Whistler to bend his stable rules when it came to turning her horse loose short of the seven-day quarantine. She wasn't going to win. Nobody won nothing off Ed that he didn't beat you out of later. But he had to admit, the woman had a serious jaw on her.

"Bat your baby blues all you want, Mrs. Carpenter," Ed said over the sound of the ringing phone on his beat-up desk. "Stable policy is we shut all newcomers up for a week in a nice, big, comfortable box stall."

"How much is that going to cost me?"

"Including cookies and *agua*, twenty reasonable dollars a day."

"Robber! I know for a fact them pipe stalls go for half that."

"It's only one week, ma'am. During which time your mare gets herself room service via Alejo himself, who'll keep a special eye out for any medical problems that might arise. By today's standards, that's an unbeatable deal. So unload her if you want, but right into stall nine and nowhere else."

"For goodness' sake, Mr. Whistler, it's not like she's carrying tuberculosis. And may I point out we didn't cross any state lines?"

"Point away. I ain't about to budge on what's worked just dandy for twenty-five years."

Earlynn scratched her new mare's butt through the trailer door while Bop watched her work on his old friend like a carnival shill.

349

"Look at her. Don't you think she's just the prettiest thing?"

"All horses, with the exception of your husband's, are pretty."

"Watch your mouth, Ed."

"Woman asked me a question, Charles. You saying I should lie?"

Earlynn continued. "Tell me how something this pretty could have a communicative disease."

Adios to the more commonly accepted "communicable," Bop thought. Depending on the length of their marriage, Earlynn might just re-tool the entire language.

"Pretty or parrot-faced, horses don't carry the TB, ma'am, But they're sure enough prone to strangles and Potomac fever and an assortment of other snot-producing diseases that spread about as bad as the graffiti those gang boys feel compelled to spray paint over any flat surface they can find around here. Why, first thing every Monday morning I got to send Alejo out to cover it all when what he ought to be doing is scraping up horse buns and mending fences. I tell you, I don't know who's more fed up with that particular chore, me or him, and we need a new problem like I need five or six new hemorrhoids."

"What is it with you and Charles about that particular area of the anatomy? I swear, y'all are behind-obsessed. Here I just want to ride a little bit, three or four times around the arena isn't asking for the moon."

Ed cut her off. "Honey, Lady Di goes into the stall until she clears a vet check and seven days pass. Or if you'd rather, she can bunk down into that pitiful excuse for a trailer till Christmas. By the way, nice-looking gash in your tailgate, Charles. I didn't know a truck could be taken advantage of in that particular way. Where'd you two come across that piece of litter? Ensenada?"

Bop shuffled his feet, embarrassed, upset all over again that the first dent in his truck had to be such a dramatic one. "Came with the mare, Ed. Another bargain we just couldn't pass up. Don't suppose I could talk you into selling it for me."

"In your wildest dreams. If you want, you can tip it into my Dumpster. Just have Alejo bury it good under plenty of manure. I don't want the trash collectors laughing themselves to death."

"Back into the trailer?" Earlynn said, her needle still stuck in the groove. "Mr. Whistler, when it comes to choices, you sure are stingy."

"I'm an old man. I can't see wasting breath to argue when I'm right. You heard my terms. By the way, it's all right if you want to call me Ed."

"If I call you anything it should be by your true name, Mussolini. Where else *can* I put her but in your stall?"

"Well, ma'am, be that as it may, and I got an ex-wife might agree with you, your husband's got himself a barn-sized house. How about setting the mare up in a spare bedroom?"

"Ha, ha, ha. Everyone around here fancies himself Jack Benny." Earlynn turned to Bop, mouth primly fixed, eyes wet and pleading.

He shook his head. "Oh, no. Don't start in giving me the cow eyes, darlin'. You got your way five times already today. Anyway, Ed's right. You're beat, Earlynn. Give up."

The trailer bucked, metal fighting hooves, hooves winning. "Oh, all right. But it doesn't hardly seem fair I just bought her and I don't get to ride her."

351

During the lengthy stall debate, Alejo had steadily scraped a path toward the office, stopping every few minutes to fill up his wheelbarrow, listening.

"Maybe we should get the vet out," Bop said after the first try of moving the mare, which was unsuccessful. "Pop her with some Ace Promazine."

"*Calmada,*" Alejo crooned to the horse, who snapped her baby teeth at his wrist, just missing connecting by scant inches as he backed her out of the trailer. Then, prodded by Alejo's able fingers, she swung her piebald Medicine Hat face into the direction he wanted her to go, caught her first glimpse of the fat flake of alfalfa awaiting her in stall nine and decided life was definitely better here than in her rickety Carlsbad digs. Suddenly entering box stalls was as fine an idea as beating shit out of the trailer had been. Alejo closed the hasp on the door, sighed wearily, and brushed his hands off on his jeans. He fixed his gaze on Bop. "*Chiflado.*"

"Hey. Don't be cussing me and *don't* be giving me the evil eye, either."

"Another wild horse, Señor Bop? A mare?"

"I can hire a trainer."

Alejo waited until Earlynn was out of earshot. "*Y otra mujer?*"

"*Sí*, Mr. Alejo. As you enjoy pointing out to me so often, life goes on. Either you get with the program, or you sit around watching 'Murder, She Wrote' on the television, trying to act surprised. Earlynn may not be perfect, but I'm keeping warm at night."

Alejo smiled, his teeth white against a newly grown mustache. "Nights after my work is finish, I think about life, since thinking don't cost, you know? Tontito. All it takes is a man would sharpen his knife and make one cut, zip, zip, throw both troubles to the dogs. But not

352

Señor Bop, the brave man who must have his stallion. Brave men lead short lives."

This impromptu speech caused Ed to depart his desk chair and venture out into the sunshine and study the two men conversing alongside the now empty trailer. "Tell you what, Aristotle, if it's within the realm of possibility, perhaps you could set aside explaining the rules of life to Mr. Carpenter and help us move this eyesore somewhere dark. I'll lay down odds he'll give it to you to sell so long as he never has to set eyes on it again. Ought to be enough scrap aluminum on that heap to fill your wallet with pin money."

Alejo looked skeptical. "Couldn't sell that trailer to Satan."

Meanwhile, only steps away, Earlynn crooned to her mare over the half-gate of the box stall. The mare was ignoring her in favor of filling her gut as quickly as possible with decent grade hay.

Ed Whistler pointed a thumb at them. "That sight puts me in mind of a certain young lady your horse threw in the marsh a couple months back."

"She break anything?"

"Nah, Lainie's tougher than you are."

"Shut up, Whistler."

"My, you're the surly one today, aren't you?" Ed raised his voice so Earlynn could hear. "You go on and ride any of the rent string horses you care to, Mrs. Carpenter. With the exception of your husband's Tontito, all our horses here are easy. Him I'd steer clear of."

"Mr. Whistler, may I use the facilities?"

Ed pointed to the plastic johns over by the entrance.

Any other woman would have crossed her legs and waited for civilization, but Earlynn stomped off to the

Porta-pottie, her head held high. Bop said, "Thanks a bunch, Ed. Now she'll make it her business to ride Mr. T or die trying. My luck, I'll get to be a widower twice."

Ed went back into his office where the phone was still jangling, but apparently not enough that he felt like answering. He shoved aside paperwork and made room for lunch, foil-wrapped homemade tamales retrieved from a Styrofoam cooler. Bop stood watching. Ed said, "I sincerely doubt that in a contest between herself and that horse, your wife'd sacrifice so much as one inch."

Bop looked at the stable hand, who leaned on his rake in the doorway, studying the earth beneath the tines. "And you, Mr. Alejo?"

"*Verdad?* Could go either way."

Earlynn dropped him off at home and sped out of the driveway in his ruined truck with directions to the nearest tack shop. Forget good strong halters and the essentials, that mare would have a pinafore for every day of the week when Earlynn finished shopping. Bop unlocked the entrance to Casa de Carpenter, the redwood doors creaking as portentously as if he were entering Vortigern's tower. In the foyer, a small rock stood in his pathway, fallen from the overhang. It was a reminder that time, with its incessant hammers, never took a lunch break.

Be that as it may, as Nick had so kindly pointed out to him, he had more pressing concerns. It sounded manageable enough: Get Mac Henry off the family. But he couldn't exactly buy off a journalist *and* build his new house, although the idea of being able to reassign Henry to printing good news for a change was sorely tempting. What he wanted to do was saddle up Earlynn's mare and gallop her dancing hooves over the man's hands—cowboy justice—but these days actual justice made for instant martyrdom, and the son of a bitch would probably end up tapping out stories with his teeth and winning another Pulitzer. Bop fixed a pitcherful of Carpenter punch, located the Yellow Pages, and took them and the cordless outside to call realtors.

"Well, hello there, Mrs. Tortellini. How is Orange County's number-one real estate saleslady doing today?" He waited while she corrected his pronunciation.

"No, ma'am, I was not aware your name was pronounced differently. I'm genuinely sorry if I offended. Listen. How'd you like an exclusive listing to Huntington Harbour's Gem of the Waterfront? Well, I'm speaking of the Carpenter house, ma'am, surely that rings a realtor's loudest bell.

"Maybe the reason you never heard of it might have a little bit to do with it was undoubtedly built before a young lady like you was ushered into this world. Let's just set us a frame of reference then, shall we? Mr. Frank Wright.

"No, he doesn't work for the Irvine Company, he's a dead architect. No, ma'am. That isn't some kind of sick joke at all, it's a sad fact attesting to human mortality striking the great as well as the meek. I guess a young lady such as yourself might not be able to fit mortality or Mr. Wright into your frame of reference after all. However, it does bear greatly on this listing. Tell you what, why don't you spend a few days at the library and give me a call back?

"No, ma'am, I surely do not intend any disrespect, but it seems to me that any skirt who can afford a half page ad to advertise herself as Orange County's premier real estate agent might make it her business to know more

355

than her almighty cup size when it comes to goddamn architecture of merit. Hello? Hello?"

Goddamn cheap phones. He ought to sue Sony for criminal intent and let the settlement buy him the Shadow property.

The sight of water was supposed to be calming, particularly when all around you the world was filled with half-wits and youngsters ignorant of how the past indeed impacted on the sorry state of present-day affairs. The bay was opaque, a light film of oil glistening rainbow colors on its greenish surface. It occurred to him that viewed from above, perhaps not as high up as heaven, but somewhere between that supposed dwelling and earth, they all probably looked like spoiled rotten children floating their toys in a dirty little wading pool.

Then, lo and behold, far in the distance like a symbol of hope, four harbor ducks appeared, small, taupe, aquatic dots paddling his way. He quickly glanced up to the Englishwoman's patio, where behind the glass sea wall, she lay draped in her typical long sleeves and girl trousers, beneath an umbrella sporting the name of some British pub shading her from every single ray of California sunshine.

Why did she want to live in California when she could haunt a dozen gloomy places in Gray Britain? He couldn't be absolutely sure without binoculars, but it looked like she might just have a plastic sack of bread on that little end table next to her fancy chaise lounge. His heart raced like a losing horse, and he hurried inside to get his cameras, the bag of lenses, and hopefully end this wretched day by striking a single blow for the good guys.

356

CHAPTER 27

SEARCHING FOR STEVE EARLE

OCTOBER SURF HELD ITS OWN PARTICULAR SORT OF charm, none of which was lost on C. Russell Carpenter IV The combination of bright sun, warm air temperature, and chilly water brought to mind the past joys of cutting high school to surf alongside the longboarders, those old dudes who parlayed fun into successful business, forever avoiding the dreaded sentence of a "regular life." Now the age they had been, Russell noted that his own life was far from regular. Ordinary maybe, disappointing, certainly, but far from regular. The slight constriction squirming in his chest was not the ticking of the mortal Carpenter heart, but rather a partnership of sentiment and memory—recalling wave-carving in an era when fear had not yet tainted the sport.

Last winter, Mark Foo had bought the farm at Maverick's Beach in Half-Moon Bay. On shore witnesses said Foo'd never even stood up. A wave from all hell had simply tucked him in its curl like one of Lane's jellyroll cakes and spat out his body an hour later. Maverick's was full of underground caves. At least the guy died doing what he loved.

Californians took the Pacific for granted. Sneaker waves like that one were out there, just waiting for a chance to get ambitious. Russell took nothing for granted since Spencer died. In all things he believed it paid to err on the side of caution.

The pretty young lady next to him astride the Jamaican Style surfboard had a rope-thick braid of black

357

hair reaching down her back nearly to butt-crack level, though it was hard to judge since that particular piece of anatomy was covered by a wet suit. Hang summer and string bikinis, Russell thought, give me cool fall surfer girls any day. Yes indeed, the intrigue of what lies beneath neoprene will do me just fine. Of course beyond the promising view, he expected a gold wedding band on her ring finger and some dork on the sand waiting for her to tire of this childish pursuit and go home and make his breakfast if not his bed. Just for the moment, however, to float in the brine, pretend Mark Foo was still among them, and imagine that girl's ringless finger seemed pretty rewarding.

"Nice waves today," he hollered, performing a little Dr. M homework. *Russell, I want you to make conversation with three women per day. And remember, in this situation, your sister and Candace do not count as women.* Wouldn't Lane and the Miata queen be surprised to hear that?

The surfer girl was generous with spare smiles. Old Hey-Bop-a-Re-Bop would have known what to say next. He'd've asked her out for breakfast, let rip some obscure historical bullshit about the land on which the restaurant sat, then talked her into a sheet inspection of his king-sized Sealy Posturpedic. She would have hung on his broken arm like the cast the old coot kept replacing with newer and more offensive colors. Nick kept saying somebody ought to get Bop to a real orthopedist one of these days, quit settling for those Jerky Boys with the Doc-in-the-Box diagnoses. But Bop wrote his own rules, always had, always would, even though it looked like the Airline to Paradise might prove capable of besting him in a dogfight. I have a stepgrand-mother who eats Cheetos and Coke for breakfast, Russell thought.

Russell considered his options: death by sneaker wave or a foray into the Wonderful World of Women? He sent the girl an I'm cool, just-handling-things-here-on-my-wave smile, but Enrico Suave he wasn't. His impersonation netted him a mouthful of saltwater.

"You okay over there?"

He coughed and tried to nod offhandedly. She knelt and began paddling to catch her wave. It was a pretty decent wave, and normally he would have followed suit, but ocean etiquette insisted that surfers trade off. He rode his board over the falls watching the girl take it into shore, all the while hacking up diatoms and pasteurized *e. coli* from the sewage treatment runoff. She had to be married.

Women—why was it all the beautiful ones were bolted to slugs? They managed their husbands' faults by marathon eating, shopping, or trying to ride men like harnessed pigs. Exceptions occurred, certainly, crazy gourmet cooks like his sister and the platinum Candace *(not* women in this case), but bottom line, what was a beautiful woman but a potential Margie in the rough? She had been gone from his life a little over a month now. There was a definite empty space. How odd it felt not to have her on the beach waiting to feed him a picnic, or her two boys here beside him in the water, warming up this fine surf on boogie boards. He missed trying out all the new jokes he heard at work on the lads. *Wussell, my turn now! Will you light a fart for us? Russell? Are you and my mom gonna get married?*

Some days the memories of their conversations rang in his head like schizo voices. Try as they might, they could not make the relationship work. He'd come to see that what he loved about Margie was the mother in her,

359

not the potential partner she could have been. Margie was adamant—she didn't want him fraternizing with the boys if they weren't a couple—it was too "confusing." Those boys were smart, smart enough to realize the valuable bargaining chip they'd become to their mother. During these manipulation sessions Margie generally spent lots of time with them, charged new clothes for them on her MasterCard, and for short periods transformed into a hypervigilant mother. Well, if they bagged that clown lamp in the process, it wouldn't be a total loss.

Pero de otra manera, Margie could be right. When she found her next boyfriend—and Russell knew she would, someone as devoted as Margie would forge a bond with another man sooner or later—Seth and Ethan would have to work all that history into perspective. Russell would be remanded to a corner of the duplex's closet, right along with the abandoned platform shoes Margie predicted would change styles forever.

The tide had changed. The waves were crappy. Enough of this briny wool-gathering. He cleared his throat and caught his last ride of the morning. He'd get to work early, earn some dollars he could stick in his mattress, wait for life to offer up something interesting upon which to spend them—single, wetsuit-clad girls, Gretsch guitar bargains, screaming good discounts on Ferraris.

On shore he set his board down in the sand and found his Ray Bans, put them on and blinked away salt as his world came into focus. In many ways, Huntington looked like a town hastily nailed together following a hurricane. Gone forever were the true beach definitions, such as the Golden Bear, where such musical greats as bluesmeister Albert King once performed. Jack's

Surfboards, above which Farmer had resided for twelve years in obscure, low-rent happiness, was now a godawful mess of neon, for-lease banners, and some kind of fabbo postmodern decorative edging. The city planners were a powerful lot, capable of erasing architecture the same way women bore down on men's hearts. Someday they'd win their various battles against Casa de Carpenter and Bop would have two choices: homogenize or tear the sucker down. If he didn't sell it first.

Imagining that crazy house belonging to another family, Russell felt the same way he did when Lane had sat him down as a kid and once and for all debunked the Santa myth. All she'd said was, *Look, Russell, you're my brother and I love you. So don't hate me for telling you that Christmas business is a load of crap. Dad is the one who puts the presents under the tree. And while we're on the subject, don't you think maybe the reason that kid keeps throwing you in the ivy might have something to do with the fact that you wrote your science report on reindeer?* A high-speed drill engaged, carving the Holland tunnel right through his little-boy heart, providing easy access for the women who would later travel through his life.

He rolled up his towel, stuck his board under his arm, scratched one of his more memorable pox scars, and trudged through quicksand to the Comet. In the parking lot, the wetsuit girl was strapping her board to a mountain bike. He'd expected an attitude, a BMW, a boyfriend. Instead, she smiled at him.

For a moment he stood there stunned, rehearsing all possible rebuffs his opening lines might evoke. She'd never go for someone who was, as Candace had once so lovingly referred to him, "Cute, like Leon Russell with a bald spot." The wedding band was probably at home in her jewelry box, so chock-full of diamonds she didn't want to take a chance of losing it to the ocean.

"Nice bike," he said. "Give you good mileage?"

The girl looked at him blankly. "It's a *bike*."

"And that was a joke. Feel free to laugh anytime."

Her smile turned uncertain. "Are you, like, talking to me?"

"Well, I'm trying. I would have done it earlier, but it took me this long to cough up all that water."

Now she laughed. It was a generic, I-kind-of-get-this laugh.

Russell pressed on. "That wasn't a joke. Look, let me just put this as simply as possible, so if I'm completely off-base, which in all probability is the case, we can keep the level of embarrassment to a discreet minimum. I mean really, it's a big beach. What are the chances of us encountering each other again?"

She twisted her green handlebar grips. "We've surfed alongside each other a bunch of times. This is just the first time you've noticed me."

Russell looked skyward and pointed. "He's up there, you know. Some great big bearded dude yanking all our strings and having a rather good laugh over all this. He's enjoying it."

"Excuse me? Who's enjoying what?"

"The Great Whomever. Mr. Funny. He Who Invented Humans with Which to Toy. Nevermind. Somehow I kind of doubt I'd miss seeing you given the opportunity. Unless of course there was a tsunami distracting my attention."

She laughed, putting a little more heart into it this time. "You never could see past those kids. Where are your boys today? With their mom or something?"

Russell shook his head. "Yeah. Turned out they

weren't mine. It's a long story. Long enough to last through breakfast, if you're interested."

"Thanks, but I don't eat breakfast. Also, I have a girlfriend."

"Sure. That's cool."

"Well, see you around sometime." She put her slim right foot to the pedal and then she was gone, leaving Russell's hopes of heterosexual bliss behind.

Red Lyzyrd Vynyl was empty except for the homeless guy listening at the headphone station, swaying back and forth hypnotically like one of those bored horses at Bop's stables. He was fragrant, uniformly grimy, and totally into whatever music he'd cued up. Well, everyone deserved a harmonic fix now and again. Music could heal in a major way. Russell often wished he had an IV of Bessie Smith running directly into his own aorta. How sad to think that if not for Red Lyzyrd, the homeless guy would only get his music by overhearing various offensively loud car stereos. After he left, the Lysol spray would tidy things up. Not asking him to move on fell under what Dr. M would call having a "charitable heart," a heart that frequently got you into trouble being too generous—yet another Carpenter defect. Oh, screw Dr. M. She got to work in a nice little office and get paid a jillion dollars an hour; her expenses were Kleenex and short-term memory.

Farmer leaned over the counter where he was studying *Rolling Stone*. There was a photo of Courtney Love on the front cover. The throes of wealthy widowhood did not appear entirely uncomfortable.

"Dude," Russell said. "Watch over the register while I try my sister again, okay?"

Farmer looked up and scanned the aisles, seeing only

the homeless guy. "Like we're swamped, Russell. Like today will be the great profit tip over for Red Lyzyrd. Whatever."

Russell punched up her number. Lane certainly was holding those five minutes of Dr. M time against him. Sunday breakfasts were canceled; she hadn't suggested walkies in so long he imagined Shaky Jake and O.J. keeping track by scratching lines in the doghouse walls. Strange, Lane had never been all that great at holding a grudge; no, Olympic grudge-holding was Margie's event. Lane's was metaphoric recipes, reliving their grandfather's past injustices and holding inside her all those unsung notes. The phone rang and rang, a sound so lonely Russell wondered if it might someday replace train whistles in country-and-western music.

Farmer said, "Just leave her a message and hang up. It's like you're weaving a hair shirt to go with your wool underwear."

Russell tucked the receiver under his chin. "I already left her a message. Either she was unimpressed, which given my level of wit, is unlikely, or she's still really pissed. Wish I could figure out what about."

"They say you should never end a sentence in a preposition."

"They also say hard work pays off, Farmer. And a penny saved is a penny earned, and love means never having to say you're sorry. They sit around thinking shit like that up meant to greatly confuse us and they are successful."

"Mercy." Farmer held up his hand. "But consider, Russell. Maybe she's just preoccupied, not mad."

Russell got the answering machine beep. "Hello, Jake. Woof, Woof, Hand Job. Lane, I know you're there. In fact, I can hear you breathing. It's a 'Star Trek' kind of

364

thing, reverse polarity or whatever Captain Picard called it. Not only can I hear your breathing, I can see you as well. You're standing in front of the sink washing dishes because the sound of my voice causes you to break out in guilt hives, so you're thinking, Why not fake a household chore to prove I really am too busy to answer the phone? To hell with the dishes, Lane. Just pick up and talk to me. Look, I'm trying to figure out some way to return your five minutes to you, but you have to help me out here. You want a guitar? Would that do it? Which one?"

He heard a small click followed by what might be two sets of dog toenails clicking across Mexican paver tiles. He gave Farmer a thumbs-up. "Lane?"

"I don't get hives," she said, and hung up the phone.

"So," Farmer asked, turning pages. "What did she say?"

"That she doesn't get hives."

"Which could be construed as progress," Farmer told him. "A sister immune to urticaria is better than no sister at all."

"Oh, suffer me the wisdom of an only child. This is some kind of test case for the Navajo code talkers and we both know it. Nevermind. I think I'll inventory aisle four before we close tonight."

"Strange Brew hasn't changed that much. I'll wager we've the same eighty-five records there that we had before summer. Why bother?"

Russell held up Farmer's magazine. Under the tank top, Courtney had her high beams on, Russell hated himself for thinking it, but he wouldn't mind delivering Courtney some bodily comfort. "For one thing, you happen to be researching the industry. For another, Dr. M insists that busy hands produce endorphins. I pay her enough I have to try whatever she tells me at least once."

In front of them, the homeless guy swayed to his music.

That night, Russell switched off the TV set and checked the dehumidifier inside his workroom, which was set to maintain a relative humidity of forty percent. Why had he put the task of repairing the Rancher off so long? Well, for one thing, the wrecked back of his favorite ax made for a succinct visual aid, a faithful partner for grief. Three years and coming up on four. *Unca Russ? I can't breathe. Where's Mama? Can you play me "Here Come Santy Claus"?. . .*

Between Margie, his mother, and the mighty herpes complex, he'd somehow managed to sneak a few moments to glue in new linings and rout the binding channel. Now he could insert the strips and start sanding for finish. The only thing square to the world on a guitar were its sides. Everything else had to index off them. If done incorrectly, a blind man would notice. As his father had drilled into him twenty-five years ago, sloppy work was *not* better than no work at all. You did every job before you as if God himself was going to evaluate it.

Once the binding was affixed, he could contemplate the satisfying act of spraying nitro cellulose lacquer on fiddleback flame maple. The binding choices before him were three: mother-of-jackknife, mother-of-bowling-ball, or the infinitely more rare and precious mother-of-toilet-seat. His purist's soul convinced him the factory way, upholding tradition, was the only proper way, so mother-of-toilet-seat it was.

I'm doing this for you, Lane, he said to himself as he pulled up his dust mask and started to work. All those

366

years back, his sister had looked out for him. Even when it wasn't cool to like your brother, she hadn't tried to hide her affection. Her kindness had cemented her to him in a way that—let's face it, maybe Margie had a point—wasn't your typical sibling closeness. Lane had tried as hard with Margie as he had. The fact remained, kidless or not, cooking weird dishes or weeping and tied down to that bed in the hospital, he loved his sister, and he couldn't feel really comfortable until he'd set things straight with her. When he finished, he was going to walk over to her house, knock on the door, and do just that.

He wondered if the repaired Gretsch would mutate into a different animal. Once the bindings were glued in, ear against the instrument's body, he could test the tap-tone, running a fingernail across the bare wood. In the violence and grief of Spencer's passing, it might lose its original personality, tightening up, relying on defense mechanisms not unlike his own. Nothing ever stayed the same—he didn't need Dr. M to do her hundred-dollar-an-hour song and dance to understand that particular homily.

He heard his front door open and froze. Margie?

"Russell? Are you in here or not?"

How strange to hear Candace's voice. He set down the guitar and covered it with flannel. "I'm in here."

"Good. Just stay where you are and shut your eyes. I'm coming in. With a present."

Russell stood in the doorway to the guitar room. "Candace, you walk in here, hand me a maimed carburetor, you walk out holding self-same carburetor. I am not fixing your car again."

"Will you just be quiet and do as I say?"

"Okay." He shut his eyes, expecting anything but

367

what Candace put into his hand. It had been a very long while, but he recognized the unmistakable feel of a petite, firm female breast, its erect nipple slipping between his fingertips as if specifically designed for the digital experience. Interesting things were happening all over his body. "Well, this is definitely not a carburetor. Can I open my eyes?"

"No, you may not. I want you to listen closely. Then we'll negotiate."

In Russell's hand lay the warm breast of his sister's best friend. All his shallow breathing and variously engorged parts weren't putting much stock in that history. There was a definite tear between mind and body. "Candace, this is nuts. I'm opening my eyes.

"Don't you dare."

He heard her take a hit off her clove cigarette and step back. The silky feeling was suddenly absent from his fingers, the whole episode possibly imagined. Childhood diseases unlocking old doors and the ghosts of a nephew's voice asking for favors he could not return—he wondered if 764 South Burton rested atop an ancient Lukup Indian burial ground, if his house was the scene of some timeless moral transgression that needed to be put right.

Candace cleared her throat. "Inventory. I'm taller than you, and short of surgical leg reduction on my part, I'm afraid there's nothing we can do about that. Consider David Bowie and Iman. She's heads taller than Major Sam. I'm a year older, too, but what's a year if we live to be, say, eighty? I know, your mother despises me and I'll probably age like a rotten banana, but I do have a Master's degree, and I am so adept at raising money for the college I imagine I can roust enough nickels to keep us both fed. Here's the deal.

Spencer wrecked all of us for a childless existence. You know he did. It put Lainie in the hospital and she's still a wreck. For Christ's sake, the solution to all this pain is so incredibly simple it's been staring us right in the face all this time. You have viable sperm; I have dozens of eggs just sitting there in the carton going to no particular use. Every month, they drop inside me like quarters in a slot machine."

Her voice softened to a whisper. "Can't we do something about that, Russell? Make our own wonderful, crazy child? It's not like the experience would be unpleasant for you or me. And look what we'd be gaining. Our own little baby."

Russell opened his eyes. His heart was behaving like a spastic nail gun, firing pins in boards over every window so neither of them could escape. He wanted to touch the top of his head, make sure it was still affixed to his skull, that it hadn't blown off in some kind of mental orgasm. Candace stood before him in her French blue jeans, probably size 000, her white blouse unbuttoned, no bra, the breast he'd fondled half hidden now by an empty pocket. He smelled grapefruit juice and vodka; she'd been drinking Greyhounds. It was the perfect libation for this lanky racehorse.

"I have crappy DNA. Lane's proven that. Besides, we're not in love."

She buttoned her shirt, "Maybe you're not. But you could catch up."

"Excuse me?"

"I want you, Russell. I've thought about it since third grade. Since way before you knew what to do with a boner. Desire is related to love. I want a baby, too. I'll share it with you. I'll even saddle it with Charles Russell Carpenter the fifth if it's a boy. Think how happy it

would make your grandfather. Service me and you'l
fulfill your biological destiny, maybe get another trus
fund in the bargain."

"Well," Russell said, feeling her slim fingers touch hi:
hips as she brushed away sawdust. "This is darnec
romantic."

"Maybe not right now," Candace said. "I'll concede
that. But just you wait."

CHAPTER 28

LEMON-SQUEEZING DADDY

IN THIS DREAM OF ALL DREAMS, RUSSELL WA:
fearless, athletic, tall, sporting a full head of luxuriou:
hair. He was Fabio with an Oxford education. A sex)
jazz quartet provided inspiring background music
Cigarette smoke that mysteriously did not cause him tc
sneeze imparted a sleepy, sexual haze. From far off, a
female voice assured him this was absolutely her *las.*
clove cigarette, this one was just for celebration, anc
from now on, only clean California air was welcome ir
her lungs.

Fine with him. Everything was fine. In fact, it was sc
fine, that suddenly a new town motto was instantl)
born—*Welcome to Harper, California, the Just Fine Towr*
Where Everything Is Just Fine. Best of all—and this part
was real—Candace with the magic, flexible, endlessly-
rolling hips was straddling his pelvis.

Russell reached up a hand, encircling half ol
Candace's waist. He slid his fingers down to that
intriguing indentation at the base of her spine where het
secret tattoo nestled in the dark hollow under his

370

thumb. The dice-shaped I-Ching characters proclaimed creativity and abundance, apt reflections of her bedroom abilities. Everyone warned how drug abuse and alcoholic binges destroyed brain cells but underestimated the debilitating power of intercourse. Like an avalanche, Russell felt himself falling from the crumbling ledge of orgasm into sleep. Actually, it felt like jumping to his death off the rim of the Grand Canyon.

"Russell?"

"Ummm." When he'd come inside her, he felt like one of those Japanese high-speed trains roaring at over two hundred miles an hour, a great blurry missile filled with the indistinct faces of the future population. Power. Cargo. Transport. Grace by design. But the train was no longer affixed to a track. It was airborne, headed past Bright Angel Falls into the rocky maw of one of the world's seven wonders, oblivious to the permanence of death, willing to trade all life's pleasures for a wee nap. A few abandoned freight cars rested atop his eyes.

She kissed his nose and he felt the soft brush of a breast, a nifty bonus. "Wake up. I like to talk afterwards. We've got decisions to make, a game plan to formulate. Not about childbirth. I want every legal drug available and knowing how you feel about pain, we'll try to get you some, too. Russell? You're not asleep, are you? Poor baby, did I wear you out?"

Feathers. Cotton. Pillow—that was what he had crash-landed into. Imagine, a flock of generous geese had donated their feathers just for him. He wanted to cry for the denuded birds, to give them money and guitars in exchange for providing comfort upon which to rest an entirely empty postcoital skull. But he was just too tired. Candace bent forward and gently nipped her teeth along one of his nipples. A minor nerve bundle flared in appreciation. He couldn't clearly identify which nipple was being attended, but there was a fifty-fifty chance of getting it right.

"Russell," she growled in his ear, nipping the lobe, too, a little less lightly than she had the nipple. "Wake up."

Adios, possum sleep. Attention, brain cells. "I think you blew out my entire IQ. Open a window, woman. Feed me protein. I'm blind."

"Put on your glasses. The way you're behaving, anyone might think this was your first time."

He groped for the bedstand and heard the glasses fall to the floor. She leaned over him to pick them up. Myopia had advantages: up close, pert bosoms gently grazing his face, the high breasts a woman was willing to ruin forever to nurse his offspring. Pretty cheekbones and white-blond hair, lipstick smeared up and down the length of his body. *Childbirth*. The word rang clinical and cold, a linguistic alarm clock. This unforeseen interlude had been an astonishing amount of fun, but the baby thing had to be some kind of joke.

"Candace."

"Yes, my little love muscle?"

"Tell me the truth. You're on some kind of scavenger hunt, aren't you? What else is on your list? Your own Ford dealership?"

She was putting on lipstick without using a mirror, getting it right. Women's priorities baffled him.

"I've never been more serious in my life. As we speak, your little swimmers are finning their way toward my bait box. Think of it, Russell, this great marathon taking place inside me, leg one of a nine-month triathlon. Aren't you excited?"

372

Her rather incredible muscles tweaked him pleasantly. The baby business was as difficult to imagine as a Beatles' reunion. "You really think we could do this once and get it right?"

Candace nodded. "Stranger things have happened." She patted her firm belly. "And if they didn't, I have other eggs we can try. Any one of them might get to wear the Carpenter crown. I can't believe this. I am thirty-five years old and finally I know what to do with my eggs." Claret-lipped once again, she set her lipstick tube down on his chest and ran her fingers through her cropped hair. "Do you think I'll really have to stop bleaching my roots while I'm with child? That's what all the books say you're supposed to do."

The lipstick tube was chrome, cold against his skin, the shape of a large-caliber bullet. "Can we get back to the baby thing for a moment, clarify?"

"What's to clarify? We've entered into a partnership, Russell. Start saving your mad money so we can buy cool baby furniture. I don't want any of that pastel bunny crap. With her first breath, our child is going to reach far beyond bunnies. Besides, theoretically, bright colors stimulate babies' imaginations and we don't want a dull one. Now *mothers* could probably do with pastel shades, such as a soft Valium yellow, but our child is going to thrive in a stimulating environment filled with Cajun music and the words of the great poets and the wisdom of contemporary philosophers. In fact, we'll read to her each night from the *Utne Reader*. When she comes of age, we'll arrange a marriage to Bill Gates's son."

"Does he have kids?"

"He will. Nobody wants that much cash going to strangers. I suppose I could settle for a Danish modern

373

crib, but what would be amazing is if you'd make something out of that wood in your little guitar room."

"Excuse me? I make *little* guitars with that wood."

"Okay, we'll explain that to our daughter when she's sleeping in a dresser drawer. Sweetie, Daddy was unable to sacrifice any of his good wood to make your bed. But don't feel bad. His ratty old socks work quite well as a pillow, don't they?"

Russell grimaced. "Could you hold off on the guilt at least until my afterglow fades?"

She bent forward and gave him a wet, snaky kiss he wanted never to end. It was a Jesus kiss, covering great distances to resurrect what she'd earlier crucified. "Next time you go out, buy more wood."

"Okay." He'd rob the Bank of America, too, if Candace needed dimes. Just ask.

As they disconnected, Russell heard a small pop of their bodies reluctantly separating, like a dud firecracker. The lipstick rolled down his body and lodged next to his skinny butt, chilly as an ice cube. He stared at his recently freed equipment, his poor brain-dead soldier lying there like it had spent sixteen months sawing down the walls of a tiger cage only to take its first free step directly onto a landmine. Never once with Margie had his body felt this drained, so purposefully used. This wasn't "getting laid." Not in a jillion years could what had just transpired be reduced to something as simple as mutual sexual entertainment. This coupling, partnership, investment—whatever you called it—was important shit going down. He ought to be on the horn to Dr. M., free-associating like an banshee at her answering machine.

He might be in the process of becoming a dad at this very moment. His heart beat wildly at the idea of his

374

own issue forming inside his sister's best friend. Lane would not be pleased. What if it inherited the Carpenter heart? Nah, he couldn't see Candace allowing such a betrayal to take place. Guerrilla Mother, she'd earn her degree in obstetrics before the end of gestation, deliver the baby herself, immediately set it aside to do the Buns of Steel videotape.

Oh my God—he'd have to *marry* her. That was what normal people did when they discovered they were about to produce a baby. The word alone inspired the old fight-or-flight response. But he'd based bachelorhood on imagined life with Margie, watching her grow crankier by the day. Marriage with a tall, skinny, sexually uninhibited, unnatural blond might just prove to be a whole other ballgame. What was the etiquette here? Should he propose now, wait for a confirmed pregnancy, or just throw her in the back seat of the Comet and drive to Harper City Hall, quick, before she came to her senses? Of course, a baby wasn't any assurance Candace would tender him her heart. Or that his own would be able to contain such a wild thing. Maybe the best he could hope for was the baby connecting them like a solid link in a goofy charm bracelet.

"Russell, I'm hungry. You want anything?"

"Maybe a brain cell transfusion."

"Sorry, Sweetie. I'm afraid we emptied that particular jar."

He listened while she rummaged in his refrigerator, wondering if anything was left in there besides that old box of oatmeal and some molding cheese. Unlikely. He was taking what few meals he ate these days out—a fish taco now and again at Wahoo's, a Dr. Carlos vegetarian burrito from *Los Primos*—order one of those suckers and

375

you felt full for a week.

"I'm calling out for Chinese, Russell. Szechwan bean curd and Moo Shu Chicken. How are you with MSG?"

His skin prickled at the very sound. "We fight and lose."

"Okay. They make it both ways. I think I'll take a shower. Listen for the delivery guy, okay?"

"Okay. Whatever."

She peeked her head around the door jamb. "You want to shower with me? It's not common knowledge but I'm equally agile on sea as I am on land."

Intriguing as watersports sounded, he wanted to lie in his bed and savor things, rescue his logical though patterns from the soup of sexual satisfaction. "I'm paralyzed, Candace. There's been major large-motor damage due to testosterone depletion. Otherwise would be in there swimming in a heartbeat."

She laughed and it echoed in his bathroom, a trapped momentary music. It reminded him of the sound he sometimes coaxed out of the National, bright, spangled notes of bodily triumph. He heard the plumbing groan to a start in an effort to please her.

In his cooling sheets, Russell felt a great sadness creep over him, tinting all this wonderful sex and astonishing change of events a shade of dark blue. His sister was still ticked off at him, Spencer was still dead, and Margie's boys were back with their original father figure, Mr. Personality. For the first time in a very long while, he missed his dad, and wished Chuck Carpenter was still alive. He could certainly use some mature male advice about now, and his grandfather, riding first class on the Airline to Paradise, was no help.

"You know," Candace said, chopsticking her way to the

376

tastier tidbits, "we have a lot more in common than just our impending child."

Russell stared at her full and generous mouth, thinking that the next time he kissed it, he was going to take his sweet time about doing so. Happiness didn't come along that often. At best, it was a tricky state of being. Happiness was interested in late-model sports cars, not balding guitarists who drove aging Comets. "How's that, Candace?"

"Lainie's mad at me, too. She won't return my calls or answer the door. Nicky says she'll grow out of it, but I think your sister is an adolescent mule."

"Well, she's definitely equine," Russell said. "Me, I can understand. I stole five minutes from her. Wrecked her life. But you're her best pal. You guys have been in it together since you mastered twosies at jacks. What did you ever do wrong besides insult my mother and tell my grandfather you deserved your own Carpenter trust fund?"

Candace shrugged, her lovely breasts lifting and lowering in a muscular spasm that his ratty bath towel failed to stand up to. Oh my. Another place to memorize. He might just have to set down his chopsticks and tackle the Continental Divide.

"Just this stupid thing about a letter I mailed." She yanked the towel back up. "Quit staring at my bosom."

"I'm sorry, but it's rather nice to look at."

"Well, thanks. Personally, I think Lainie's headed for the hospital again."

Goose bumps pebbled Russell's shoulders. "Lane's not crazy anymore, she's just noticeably different."

"Yep, she's different." Candace grinned. "Maybe more *different* than you know."

"She cooks and walks dogs and talks to herself. She

just won't talk to us. What's so different?"

"Let's approach this like a math problem, Russell. One step of the equation at a time. Take the food thing. Guess what she was making last time I came over. Come on, I dare you. Guess."

He thought of the Fourth of July Jell-O wienie. "Anatomically correct mashed potatoes?"

"No, she had the entire sink filled up with *cucumbers* pickling in brine. *Brine*, Russell. They put lye in that. What's it going to do to the sink? Or how about Nick's stomach lining? You know he'll try to eat all the pickles. He tries so hard. Who could eat a sinkful? And it's not like we're headed into nuclear winter, desperate for dills. No one outside of Cedar Rapids *makes* pickles, Russell. Why does she waste the time when she could just drive to the market and have her pick?"

He chewed a dice-shaped chunk of fiery tofu and gave that some thought. "I think it's a process thing, Candace. Everything Lane makes, she's more interested in getting through the process successfully than the end product. Kind of understandable, given what happened with Spence."

Candace's pretty post-shower face scrunched up. He could tell she wanted to cry, but wouldn't. Candace probably hadn't squirted out more than five tears over her entire lifetime, four of them when she was an infant. She pasted her best smile over the sadness. "Russell, I hope our baby inherits your little gift for insight."

"Little? What's with the 'little' business? Did you know you have a preponderance for using that word in connection with me?"

"I do?" She set down the chopsticks and fingered his member. "I'll damn sure never use it in connection with my chum here. Talk about gifted." Hurriedly, she set

378

containers on the floor and pushed him back against the pillows.

"Yikes. Shouldn't we wait until our food hits bottom before we go shaking it around?"

"I think the food will be fine."

His body was a flesh runway and Candace eyed him like a 757. He lay there imagining all manner of aerial transportation metaphors while she cleared the bed and swooped down, making him ridiculously happy, much happier than he thought any Carpenter male deserved to be.

"About the letter thing. Did you mail it or not?"

"They must get thirty-five million letters a day down there at City Hall. They can't have time to read them all, in fact, given some of the recent county fund investments, it's questionable that they're literate."

"You did mail it."

Candace sighed. "Yep. You want a fortune cookie?"

"Today's good fortune is just about all I can handle."

He lifted an arm and Candace snuggled close, still chewing her cookie, folding her long legs against him, exhaling deeply. She pulled his arm around her, commandeered a corner of pillow and fluffed the covers over them both.

She was staying the night! Russell smiled. "Comfy there, big girl?"

"Isn't this the best?"

"Isn't what the best? Our full stomachs? My second bout with postorgasmic exhaustion? Our Ann Landers-sanctioned snuggling?"

"Any and all of the above. And don't forget this, Russell. The satisfaction of a job well done. By two people who love each other."

379

"Come on, Candace. I'll throw my lot in with the baby idea for now. I find it an interesting concept. But you sitting there and saying you love me—"

"I do love you, Russell. I've always loved you, you idiot. You love me, too. In our own seasoned ways we love each other."

Russell found it difficult to concentrate while sword-fighting sleep. Sleep laughed heartily at his pathetic sword, folding it up like recyclable cardboard. "How do you know you love me?"

"My mirror."

"I beg your pardon?"

She licked his ear. "I stand there and look at myself every morning and take inventory of my life. I tell myself, 'You have a good job, Candace. A best friend who will eventually come to her senses and forgive you and, secretly, you love Russell Carpenter, your best friend's brother. You used to steal his marbles. He taught you how to smoke pot and then told you you needed to quit doing it. Every good first thing in your life happened with or because of Russell Carpenter.'"

"You say this every day?"

"Russell, how simple-minded can we be? All of this other stuff was just waiting. We were being the complete and total dunce caps, looking for it in Margies and Ferraris and dating services and more bars over the last seventeen years than are probably in business today. Everywhere but here, where it was waiting all along. Love doesn't happen the same way for everyone—roses and proposals and fevers. Some of us just get this, and we're still lucky." She trailed a hand down his belly.

It felt great. But Russell couldn't quite bring himself to stick more than a toe in this lake just yet. Simplicity had a dark side, it practiced fake-outs, plus, it palled around with happiness. Once in session with Dr. M, she'd told him to relax and enjoy life, stop behaving as if the wolf was just outside the door.

Oh, he's there all right, he'd told Dr. M, and a shiver had run down his vertebrae one by one, racing stair steps to gloom. *I set out kibble for him every night, pat him on the skull, respect the fact that I am prey and he's a predator. That's about as relaxed as I can get.* The possibility that this instantaneous lover-parenthood perspective could graft onto the trunk of his heretofore spindly life seemed considerable.

Candace fell asleep on his left shoulder. While his arm went quietly numb under the weight of the sexpot who wanted to bear him a child, he realized in a way what Candace'd said was true; he did love her. They'd grown up loving each other, grateful for each other's company. It hadn't been a burn-the-clothes-off-your-body, movies-type of love—at least up until now. He had loved her like he did Lane, but more exalted, as if she was so much too good for him he'd never pictured her in partner terms.

Loving Candace: She was passionate about guitars, she danced on tables, and she seemed shamelessly compatible with his penis. She liked kids. She'd written more in Spencer's baby book than Lane had. Suddenly, he pictured Seth and Ethan lying in their beds, the crappy clown lamp glowing primary colors over their trusting little faces. Without a second thought, he was betraying those two wonderful boys. Well, it wasn't their fault God had screwed up the paternity thing.

Say—wonder of wonders—Candace married him. Could he be comfortable being surprised by her the rest of his life? He mentally reviewed his grandfather's relationships, his parents', Lane's. What family history

381

all this thinking made. Maybe they were fashioning a team from capables who'd sat the bench all those seasons—the uncrowned princesses, the too-short basketball forwards, the nerds-turned-heroes. The upshot of it was, Lane couldn't hold the door shut indefinitely—not against the two of them—and definitely not against a potential threesome. He felt sleepily jubilant. If they'd made a baby from all this tussling, well, pour some gravy on top of some very comfortable mashed potatoes, set a cucumber along the side.

He listened to Candace's breathing, soft purposeful snores, a woman taking her rest seriously, aware that the days ahead held hard work and morning sickness. Who would have thought the amazing act of love could so elevate a relationship? Here they lay, poised on the precipice of a brand-new venture, together, in his grandfather's cast-off bed.

CHAPTER 29

AS YOU REAP, SO SHALL YOU SOW

"IF YOU COULD OPEN YOUR LEGS A LITTLE WIDER, please."

Lainie took a deep breath. "Sure." The alcohol stink of the exam room made her recoil. Back when she was in the hospital following her "breakdown," they sent a massive Samoan phlebotomist to draw her blood so they could check out her daily levels of chemical craziness. He never spoke, just tied her off like a junkie, patted the crook of her elbow, and sank his needle home. She was in restraints the first time, howling, certain she'd never see her kitchen or dogs again. That needle plowing her flesh was the closest she'd ever felt to rape.

All these months since her release, the thought of having to go back in the hospital had kept her toeing the emotional line, fibbing about her darkest thoughts to Dr. M, out-and-out lying to her husband. She'd assumed it was a question of keeping her worries balanced, but by tucking them into their respective pockets, all she'd done was encourage them to form a committee.

Eyes clamped shut, she felt the pressure of the doctor's finger against her cervix and conjured up the ghost of Dr. M's hand. Dr. M's diamond could cut through anything. Lainie'd lain down on this table voluntarily. She *wasn't* going back to the hospital, even though it was right next door. She quieted her breathing. Over the alcohol smell she caught the faint whiff of expensive men's cologne.

"Nurse, you want to hold Mrs. Clarke's hand? I think she's having a little trouble relaxing for us."

Lainie didn't like this hairy-armed blond doctor. He looked like Sandy's kid brother on the old TV show "Flipper." Bud, the one with a lisp. She knew Dr. Rabinath, the kindly East Indian woman who'd delivered Spencer—and attended his funeral—was away. Her replacement, Dr. Stewart, seemed so fresh from his residency that when he smiled Lainie thought she saw the shadows of braces on his teeth.

He was humming, as if every pregnancy was routine, wanted, guaranteed payment against his student loan. She opened one eye and peeked as a latex-gloved hand gently pressed her knees apart for a third time. He had a friendly face, but he was way too young. He wore glasses like Russell's. Russell thought she was still mad at him. She wasn't mad at anyone, she was terrified, terrified of being pregnant and of what everyone would think.

"Are you just about finished?"

He smiled and shook his head no. "Why don't you imagine you're on a dream vacation? That helps most women relax."

She shut her eyes. At least he'd stopped humming.

"The knee?"

"Sorry." Lainie moved it out an inch and the voice bent back to work. There in the doctor's stirrups while she waited for the chill of speculum to bisect her most private parts, between the peaks of her bare knees where the sheet had fallen away, lay the primal female landscape: the top of a man's head. Unfortunately, this sandy-headed stranger wasn't entertaining her to orgasm, he was looking interestedly into the results of one.

Lainie thought about where she might go if there was a virgin MasterCard in her back pocket instead of disposable paper between her and the pebbly Naugahyde exam table. She peeked again. The top of his strawberry-blond head looked like a sand dune. She imagined posing her childhood Breyer horse collection there—a makeshift Assateague Island, where Misty and Sea Star were born. She'd always wanted to see those sand dunes, but nowadays you had to be a biologist or a photographer for *National Geographic*.

As broke as she was, it hardly made sense to lie here imagining dream vacations, but she knew where she'd like to escape to—Nantucket Island, Massachusetts. Rent a bicycle with a wicker basket and a bell, stuff Oddjob inside, tie Jake's leash to the handlebars and ride out to the lighthouse on Great Point.

She'd been there once with Grandma Alyce. When Lainie was twelve, they'd flown first class in their good suits and gloves from Los Angeles to Boston, wiping their travel-weary wrists with linen towels dampened in hot water by stewardesses who had kindness to burn. They'd landed in Boston, taken the train to Hyannis, then a ferry ride over to the island. It seemed to grow out of the foggy jade-colored Atlantic all at once, bustling to life with tourists dragging luggage and cargo trucks unloading crates of fresh produce from the mainland. They stood on the cobblestone street waiting for the shuttle to the Wauwinet Hotel. Halfway to Great Point, this stately mansion with the trellis-climbing roses and tame rabbits grazing on the lawn stood like a testament to civilized human endurance. Their room was New England elegance—hard beds, fine linen, cut crystal, a tub long enough to lie all the way down in and stare up through the water's surface.

"Are you and Bop going to get a divorce?" Lainie asked that night, as a water taxi motored them on a sunset cruise past the homes of founding families, people born as wealthy as her grandfather had strived to become.

Grandma Alyce tipped her flute of complimentary champagne. "Where did you hear that word?"

"This girl at school. Her parents got one, and now she has to decide who to live with."

"With *whom* she wishes to live. Divorce is only acceptable under a very few circumstances, Elaine. People who divorce develop a stain on their characters. Remember that. They can be interesting people to know, but they can never recapture the class they've lost. The real test of human grace is enduring difficult times."

That night they turned in the soft sheets, moonligh pouring in through the windows, the sound of the wate humming in the distance. In the morning, the larges basket of flowers Lainie'd ever seen arrived for Grandma Alyce with an apology from Bop. Lainie started to repack her suitcase.

Grandma Alyce stopped her with a manicured hand and a wink. "We'll stay a few more days, teach him lesson," she said, folding the card between her fingers Alyce bought herself an authentic Nantucket lighthouse ship basket purse with a scrimshaw whale on the lid She walked Lainie up and down the beach and took her photograph next to a lighthouse. Then, on a night fligh through the dark skies, they flew back home to California. Bop was there at the airport to greet them turtle-eyed, penitent, all loving hugs, as if he possessed no bite whatsoever. It wasn't too long after tha Grandma Alyce started to forget who everyone was.

Lainie felt the pinch of the speculum release. "Well?" she said to the sand dune. "Don't keep me in suspense The test was wrong, wasn't it? A false positive."

"No, I don't think so. But your uterus is a bit more enlarged than I expected. You might be further along than you think."

"Impossible. Contraception is my religion. If I'n pregnant, it happened August twenty-fourth. Or after. kind of lost my faith when my period failed to arrive."

"In any case, I'd like you to have blood drawn at the lab."

She thought of the Samoan with his greer dishwasher basket of test tubes and cringed. "They didn't take blood last time. Isn't pee in a cup enough?"

He snapped off his gloves and threw them on the chrome tray along with the other scary obstetrica

386

would narc on her, but she had to put them back. Otherwise, Ruth, a teenager, might end up shouldering the blame.

Impending winter revealed its Janus face in the formerly brown summer grasses. Rain and sun greened everything up, making it look more like springtime than late fall. The wild anise vibrated a lime green. Puddles formed and, boom, three or four ducks flew in and set up house. These weren't seasons, they were mood swings of a state that needed Dr. M, or at the very least, a Prozac suppository shoved up one of its major fault lines.

Besides worrying about the newspaper, she was holding Russell and Candace at arm's length. It was a question of emotional distance or the psych ward, plain and simple. While Candace kept her secret, she also chased the *P* word relentlessly. Russell obsessed over her five Dr. M minutes until she told him, *What do you want me to say? Yes, I blame you for Nick finding out I was seeing Dr. M? Fine, then. I do.* She didn't, really. Nick's big confession that he'd known all along she was seeing Dr. M made Lainie ashamed of herself. Did Russell know that Nick knew? Did Candace? Did everyone? Pretense at every turn, like some shoddily written whodunit—here Nick was reading books that explained what was wrong with his wife, but he was powerless to fix her. If she was a broken drawer, he had the tools right there in the garage. *How long have you known?* she asked him one night in bed as they lay sleepless under a full moon that punctured the curtains. He pretended to be asleep, but she could tell he was faking even before she pinched him. His final answer: *Hospitals are pretty small worlds.* Well, she still had one secret.

Lainie'd spotted Russell in the parking lot of

Albertson's this very morning, walking toward the Comet carrying a sack of groceries. Russell, up before eight, whistling some top-forty love song. There were flowers sticking out the top of the grocery bag. Russell was allergic as hell to flowers. And Candace's message machine said something about "a permanent vacation" while in the background, Clifton Chenier belted out "Mama Told Papa."

To O.J. and Jake, reinserting stakes into the muddy earth constituted canine adventure. To Lainie, marking off that diamond may have been reparation for a crime, but it felt more like the end of the trail. As she pounded them in and retied the fluorescent plastic ribbons, she apologized to the coyote melon the bulldozers would tear out of the dirt, the burrowing owls who wouldn't be born next spring, the stink bugs who bottomed-up and shot warnings each time her red tennis shoes invaded their territory. Tears scored her cheeks at the idea of the empty fields altering, at losing her boy, at being able to do nothing to stop the damn planet from continuing its calloused spin. In her mind, this dirt had been sacred, a place resonating with the quiet echoes of those ancient Indians who'd scattered shell fragments. They'd tended milk goats—she'd found a skull fragment with the little horn attached. Raised children—she imagined Spencer racing his bike over hummocks, getting airborne. Shivering at the slither of a garter snake against his palms. Eventually, he'd take a girl up here, giving up his jacket just so he might glean a few more minutes alone with her, providing the opportunity for that first kiss.

She didn't need Dr. M to tell her to give up, let all this go. She was thirty-five years old, a grown up. She just needed someone to tell her how to let the ghosts go.

She tamped stakes until she'd managed a crooked recreation of the soccer plan. When she stood up and brushed her muddy hands against her jeans, a policeman in a yellow slicker was writing her a ticket for having two dogs off leash. Through several previous narrow misses, she knew it would cost her at least fifty dollars—the equivalent of one visit to Dr. M. That wouldn't have been so bad, but this particular policeman did not appear to be a ticket-quota kind of officer. He tore it off his pad and handed it to her. She watched the paper pucker and as raindrops battered it in her fingers.

"You want to tell me what you were doing down there with the stakes?"

Lainie fired back with a question of her own. "Can you tell me why it's legal to help destroy a natural habitat, but not to take steps to protect it? No, I guess you can't. You also probably won't arrest me for putting the damn stakes back, but morally you should."

He failed, as had so many others before him, to grasp her unique form of logic. "Ma'am? Let's take a little walk."

At least it had stopped raining. The policeman stood there ranking her out by the side of his car. He flipped his citation book open and shut over and over, as if ultimately the decision whether or not to write her another ticket lay in the whim of how the pages landed. "Trespassing is a violation of the California Penal code."

"I wasn't trespassing, I was walking my dogs."

He pointed at the posted No Trespassing signs down near the stakes. "I assume you can read?"

Jerk. He kept trying to kick loose the mud from his tall boots, but it was too wet to let go. He looked like a clumsy folk dancer who couldn't even manage the solo steps. Ruth Cranky Pony, Lainie thought, you just had to pick today to start going to classes, being a good girl. Together, we might have gotten the best of this guy.

"Officer, I was putting the stakes back. You want criminal intent, go talk to the city planners about their soccer field."

"Young lady, your attitude is going a long way toward making me reconsider."

Lainie watched her tennis shoe toe sink a little hole in the mud. Oddjob immediately started investigating possible gopher potential. Clots of mud splattered her jeans as he tried to dig his way past the water. "I just—"

He held up a hand. "Not another word."

She watched him silently mouth each word as he wrote out the second ticket and wondered who had taught him to read. They hadn't done a very good job. The handcuffs hanging from his belt were shiny chrome, dry under his slicker. Like Russell's Boy Scout ax, the cuffs looked important. But they were so big and clunky they'd probably slide off her small wrists onto her hands.

"Here you go," he said and handed her the second citation. "This one will cost you one hundred and fifty dollars. The other one's only fifty. You want to challenge them in court, I'll be delighted to show up and explain things to the judge."

"That's a lot of money."

"Yes, ma'am, it is. But it takes three weeks for them to arrive in the mail, so there's time for you to figure out a way to scrounge up the fines."

Russell would have said something clever—*Have yourself a real special day, Sheriff Hemorrhoids; by God, these bluffs are finally safe from the likes of me!* Lainie just stared at her new ticket for disturbing the peace and wanted to cry.

Home, dry in her house, she stepped out of her wet shoes and thought about calling her brother to borrow the money to pay the tickets. Russell was familiar with coming to her rescue, but he was poor. She couldn't ask her mother for money without anticipating a permanent shopping relationship in exchange. Dr. M gave her a big enough discount as it was and Candace, some best friend, was never home. That left Nick. He might just throw up his hands and sign her back into the hospital.

Lainie dialed Russell, but there was no answer. For one feeble moment, she considered selling plasma at the blood bank downtown. She'd heard from clients at Assistance that they gave you twenty dollars a pint, but you could only donate once a week and pregnant women might not qualify. Over a month's time, eighty dollars still didn't add up to two hundred. The idea of another needle made her so woozy she sat down at the kitchen table and ate half a row of saltines. She put her head between her knees and watched Jake stare up at her, his furry, damp shoulders quivering with concern. "I'll live," she told them. "That's the trouble here. We're all going to live."

She heard crackling, paper rustling, and lifted her head to check out the noise. She bumped her head on the table edge and caught sight of Oddjob racing down the hall with the waxed paper, trailing broken crackers. She rubbed the sore place on her head and decided to call her grandfather. People backed into a corner didn't have a great deal of choices.

"Hello? Carpenter residence. This here's Earlynn speaking."

Stepgrandmother? Mrs. Carpenter? What did she call the woman? With Bop's other wives, it was easy to say

393

Gloria and Helene and be done with it. Earlynn was more the type who'd want to be called nana or gran. "Um, this is Elaine. I'm in a little bit of a tight spot. I wondered if you might be able to convince my grandfather to"—she squinted her eyes shut and said the words in a hurry—"lend me two hundred dollars and try not to give me a lecture because I was only trying to stand up for my convictions, which happens to be something he taught me."

"There, there. You poor baby. Slow down and tell Earlynn everything."

"Maybe I should tell my grandfather first."

"Well, honey, he isn't here right now. He's off yelling at the Ford dealership about painting over some weensy little dent I put in his truck. It's something to keep the man busy, I suppose. Guess you're stuck telling me or waiting on him to get back."

"Look, I don't mean to be rude, but it's difficult to ask to borrow money from Bop let alone tell—"

"A stranger?" Earlynn said, finishing Lainie's sentence.

"I didn't say that."

"No, no. I understand. Well, then. Let's get you started on knowing me better. I've been a Christian since I was ten years old. I love the color peach, cannot get me enough of it. I wear Dr. Scholl's inserts on account of heel spurs from dancing too many years in high-heels. My favorite food is chocolate cake and my second favorite is coffee. I like dogs better than cats, and I think they should get rid of all these racy cop shows and put 'Mayberry RFD' back on television. How's that?"

Lainie smiled into the receiver. "My favorite color is blue."

394

"Would that be a deep, dark, purple, night-sky blue?"

"Yes."

"I knew it! I had you figured for that dusky blue the minute I saw you at our wedding. I used to be a blue person, once upon a time, all dreamy and thoughtful. Had me a closet full of blue clothes. Lately however, I find the autumn shades go farther to keep my spirits high. You ought to give them a try sometime. Now tell me why you need money and maybe we won't have to involve your grandpa at all."

The cop's smug smile flashed in front of her eyes. "To pay some tickets before Nick finds out. One's an environmental crime involving stakes and soccer fields, but they're being nice and only charging me with disturbing the peace. Still, that costs a hundred and fifty dollars. Second, I was caught walking my dogs off leash. Which is fifty dollars more. Which adds up to two hundred dollars more than I've got."

"Disturbing the what?" Earlynn squawked. "My advice, let them throw you in a cell and we'll hire a lawyer and embarrass the pudding out of those cops. Imagine, arresting a young lady out walking her dogs. What's the world come to?"

"I can't afford the luxury of jail, not to mention hiring the lawyer. Tomorrow morning I have to be at the gynecologist's bright and early to have a sonogram."

"Don't do it if you don't want to, honey. Them doctors'll run every test in the book if you let them. They're test fiends. They start talking tests, walk away. To listen to your grandpa talk, lemon juice'll cure anything from corns to emphysema."

"They say I have to. To know for sure."

"Know what for sure?"

"Things."

"Like whether or not your doctor can afford a fancy summer vacation?"

"Not exactly."

"Well, better spell it out, Elaine. You're getting me worried."

"Whether my loins are spawning a tumor or a baby, I assume."

"Oh, my goodness. I see."

Lainie felt her hackles lift. "Do you, Earlynn? Can you or anybody else really understand that maybe, just maybe, I don't want to love anything ever again that can just up and die on me without warning?"

Earlynn was quiet a few moments. "Yes, sugar, I can. In fact, I might be the only one in your family who can truly sympathize with that particular set of feelings since I have history in that area. But that's no subject for telephones, it's a face-to-face kind of talk we can have someday if you're interested. I know y'all think I waltzed in here and married your grandfather for his fat wallet. I know how people are. Think college education and fancy clothes give a person soul. I say bull. His money's more trouble than it's worth. Why, I could be happy living in a trailer court, taking my Tuesday night chances playing bingo. TV dinners do me just fine. I don't mind taking the bus places."

Lainie held the receiver out from her face and stared at it. This woman buys her makeup at the Tammy Faye counter, here I am spilling my guts to her on the phone in hopes she'll front me two hundred dollars and she's telling me to take the bus?

"Thanks, Earlynn. I think maybe I'll just go get in my car, rob an ATM machine. Or write a bad check."

"Hold on, Elaine. Wipe your nose on your sleeve and sit tight. Your grandpa, bless his grumpy old heart, rented me the cutest little Jeep you ever saw so I wouldn't have to sit around careless until that truck's fixed. Well, I think it's darling. You'll have to give me your opinion. I have only got to drive it to the store so far and the cupboards here are pretty well stocked up. Let's make today the day we have that talk."

Lainie stared at her stocking feet, so damp she was leaving wet footprints on the tiles. "I've already taken up your time on the phone."

"It's mine to fritter away as I see fit. Go sit outside in the sun and wait for me. Get a little vitamin D on you before it turns completely winter. No sense breathing air-conditioning when God give us the real thing. Now give me directions."

Lainie recited the street names, saw the long drive down Pacific Coast Highway unroll, ocean on one side, high rise condos and oil derricks on the other.

"Got it. I'll honk when I get there. Bye, bye now."

She was out front pulling weeds when Earlynn drove up. Thanks to the rain-soaked earth, it was basically lift and drop in the mounting pile. Her cactus stood green and tall, unadorned. The snails were having some sort of nearby convention, but they knew better than to expect an easy meal among the spines. Lainie leaned back on her knees and wiped her mud-covered fingers on her jeans.

"Ooo-ooh, baby, baby!" Earlynn wailed from the driver's side of her pink Jeep Renegade. She waved at Lainie and switched off the radio. "I love that song so bad I have to sing along whenever it comes on. Here. I picked us up a couple of forty-ounce Thirstbusters on my way over. Got to have my daily Coke. Your grandpa favors that lemon punch, but to tell you the truth it gives me mouth sores."

Lainie accepted the bucket of soda. "Thanks."

"You're welcome. You know, California isn't all that it's cracked up to be. I was beginning to think a girl had to go clear back to Texas to find any real excitement. Hearing about your secret tickets is the most exciting thing to happen to me since I married your grandpa."

Lainie stared at stepgrandmother number three, who was dressed in a white jumpsuit festooned with tiny red and gold embroidered hearts. Factor in the pink Jeep, she looked like a geriatric Cupid. "That is a great car."

Earlynn smiled and shut the driver's door. "You think?"

"As little as I can help it, but occasionally. Come on inside. My house is a mess, but there's nothing new about that."

"Oh, hush. Your house is darling. Now who is this handsome fellow?"

"Jake." The old shepherd-mutt wagged his tail and welcomed Earlynn into the house.

"He's your dog, I can tell."

She told Earlynn all of it—the hate letter Candace might or might not have mailed, the possible Mac Henry element that could evolve from it, she and Nick in the atrium, how late she was, the pee test coming up positive, how on hearing about the abnormal blood test results she felt it absolutely necessary to return the stakes before the impending sonogram dictated her future. "Here I try to do one honest thing," she said softly, "and for my trouble I get a police record. If Nick finds out—"

"Nonsense," Earlynn said. "If he's any kind of man at all, that'll only make you more interesting to him."

"You think?"

"Sugar, I *know*."

Earlynn sat cross-legged on the couch and calmly sucked her Thirstbuster. Jake lay near Lainie's feet and didn't tremble once. Earlynn said uh-huh in all the right places. Oddjob came flying in the dog door from his eternal task of digging up the yard, took one look at Earlynn, stopped in the middle of a bark and fell in love.

"He'll wreck your clothes," Lainie warned.

"That's all right. They're wash and wear," Earlynn crooned as Oddjob stood on his hind legs biting at her dangly bracelets. "Aren't you just the cutest little boy? Come here and see Earlynn."

Oddjob rolled over on the tile and showed her his cracker-filled belly, where great patches of hair were missing. Earlynn scooped him up and he settled into her lap as if he expected satin ribbons and nail polish, that both would go a long way toward revealing his hidden elegance. Lainie and Jake looked on, amazed.

Earlynn scratched Oddjob's ears. "You know Elaine, I buried a son, too."

"I'm sorry."

"Me, too. I'd like to tell you what I learned from that day. My own mother stood by me all through the service." Earlynn set down her drink. "Maybe it was the first time I felt like she approved of anything I did, helping me get through the ordeal without breaking down. Such a tough day. Then soon as the preacher was done talking, the dirt shoveled in, she took me by the arm and told me the Lord had finally answered her prayers. Imagine, her own grandson, okay, retarded and sometimes a burden, but all those years she'd wished him dead, like as his grandma that would be the best gift she could hope for."

Lainie wondered how Earlynn's boy had died, the

extent of his retardation, all those questions a fellow mother asked in her heart but couldn't say out loud "That must have crushed you."

"Flatter than roadkill. After that, a lot of time went by where we didn't speak two words. Then she died. It was just me and Carol left, and Carol never gave a hoot about having a mother, she was so busy having all the men. I have another son, but to this day, I miss my Dewayne as sharp as the day he passed over. I see something reminds me of him, my arms just ache. But I truly regret not forgiving Mama. She was a dried-up old busybody who never had one nice thing to say about anyone, but she was still my mother. Like it or not, there's a bond."

Lainie nodded. "I know you're right. But that doesn't make it an easy concept to apply to real life."

"You have to try."

"I will. Just let me get my feet under me. Pay off those tickets. See what the sonogram has to offer." Earlynn's gaze was so direct, Lainie wanted to run away hide under the bed where Oddjob kept his stash of stolen items. "Where's your other son?"

"Frank?" Earlynn waved a hand. "He don't speak to me. Of course, that can't prove I was a bad mother. I've made my peace with what I did for a living even if nobody else has. The way I see it, stripping's between me and my maker and nobody else. A girl can't go around clinging to the past. It'll drown you same as hugging a stone."

Lainie reached out and petted Oddjob. He growled. She took her hand back and Oddjob went back to his wheezing, glassy-eyed, blissed-out state on Earlynn's knees. "I'm sorry you lost your son. Frank's an idiot. I think you'd make a terrific mother."

"I could say the same for you."

Touché. "Just answer me one thing if you can, Earlynn. What's the point of loving, if you end up hurting so much it lands you in the crazy ward?"

Earlynn cocked her head and stared out the French doors to the plum tree. There was one maverick blossom on the end of the spiky branches that was not about to wait for spring. "I don't know if there is one. But I happen to harbor a king-size respect for craziness. All those street people passersby try to ignore, shoot, I'll give them a dollar if I have it to spare. Whenever I see somebody crying in public, I hand them a Kleenex." Earlynn set Oddjob beside her on the couch. "Watch out, I might just steal this little cutie and take him home with me."

If only Jake possessed the power of language, Lainie thought, we'd be hearing the Martin Luther King of dog speeches. "Maybe you should. He hasn't been very happy since Spencer died."

From Lainie's kitchen, Earlynn said, "A day this stressful calls for coffee and ice cream." She opened the silverware drawer as if the old stucco shoebox was her childhood home. "Lie down on the couch and put your feet up. You've had a hard day. Me, I got nothing but time to burn until that stinky Ed Whistler grants me permission to ride my mare. At first he said one week, now it's been almost a month! She has an allergy, not TB. Where do you keep your coffee?"

"In the freezer. The filters are in the cupboard next to the sink. Bop bought you a horse?"

Earlynn set down the bowl and looked at Lainie, doe-eyed as she nervously scooped out Albertson's vanilla. "I had to let him buy me something, honey. He was about to start handing out stock certificates to strangers. Now

401

listen here, Elaine. Your grandpa is loaded. I know it's none of my beeswax, but why won't you let him pay off that hospital bill and have yourself a life?"

Lainie stared into the bowl Earlynn handed to her. Her grandfather's wife had sprinkled coffee grounds over the ice cream. It reminded her of the dirt Oddjob tracked in on the paver tiles. Was she supposed to eat it? "It's our bill, our responsibility. That's how I was brought up."

"Baloney. You're as hardheaded as he is. Let him pay it. You got your whole married lives to worry about, you don't need to drag along saddled to some everlasting debt. Go on, eat that ice cream. Stir in the coffee and it'll perk up your spirits. You got a needle and thread laying around here anywhere?"

Lainie obediently took a tiny spoonful. The coffee grounds crunched in her teeth, but it wasn't altogether unpleasant a taste or sensation. "In the junk drawer. Did you lose a button? There's an old baby food jar of buttons in there."

"Nope, my buttons are all on tight. I want to try something I haven't tried in maybe twenty-five years, back when my daughter-in-law used to think speaking to me wouldn't land her in Hades. Lie back down, pull up your shirt and be still."

From a two-foot length of thread, Earlynn dangled a needle over Lainie's bare belly. Lainie thought she detected a slight swell to her abdomen that hadn't been there the day before. "What are we doing? Planning how best to sew up my navel?"

Earlynn laughed. "Shoot. You made me move my hand. Now I have to start all over." She stilled the needle, then seemingly of its own volition, it began to slowly twirl, first right to left, then back and forth reminding Lainie of the Ouija board sessions she and Candace had knee-to-knee back in junior high school. "Hmm," Earlynn said. "That's odd."

Lainie thought, what could be odder than coffee grounds on ice cream, our collective life stories, and the needle-and-thread thing?

Earlynn took a bite of her ice cream, sighing. "This needle trick of my grandma's is supposed to predict the baby's sex. If it goes back and forth, that indicates a boy child, the other way, a girl. On you, it's all katty-vampus."

"I guess tumors don't have a sex."

Earlynn pulled Lainie's shirt back down and gave her shoulder a squeeze. "You don't have a tumor in there, you got a big healthy baby growing. But things won't stay that way unless you eat more and relax. You look about half-starved. Well, I made up my mind. I've decided to lend you the money."

Relief flooded through her. "Thanks. I'm not sure when I can pay you back. As soon as I find a job, I'll make out a payment schedule."

"I'm in no hurry for the money. But I might want something else."

Lainie set her spoon down. She felt all her money-trouble relief begin to dissipate. "You wouldn't tell anybody about the sonogram?"

"Of course not, honey. Provided you let me come with you and hold your hand." Earlynn winked and spooned up the last of her ice cream. "Otherwise, I intend to rat you out first chance I get."

Lainie knew she meant it. A stepgrandmother who wasn't above blackmail had entered her life. From one glossy peach fingernail, the silver needle dangled on a length of blue thread.

CHAPTER 30

HORSES, HORSES

TODAY OF ALL DAYS, NICK LINGERED IN THE kitchen, watching the rain pelt the window, acting so generally unenthusiastic about leaving for work that Lainie wondered if her husband might be coming down with a cold. She sat at the table peeling the crust from her wheat toast, watching him. Outside, Oddjob raced in muddy circles while within the shelter of the eaves Jake relieved himself in a gentlemanly arc on the cracked cement.

"What are your plans for the day?" Nick asked.

Lainie set the toast on her plate. Her plans? Race to the bank the second the sonogram was over and cash Earlynn's check, which rested securely in the bill compartment of her wallet. "Oh, the usual. Fill out applications, call places I sent my résumé last week. General prayer." She sipped her second glass of water and checked her watch. Nineteen minutes until the appointment. If he didn't leave soon, she'd be late.

"We're not doing great, but we're not out on the street yet."

"It was a joke, Nick. Somebody will hire me. I really, truly almost believe that."

"Reggie Joe called."

"Oh?" Reggie Joe was his old boss, back in the days when business meant chisels and mallets, mahogany and lead-based lacquer, not cognitive theories, hospital corridors, and endless textbooks. Nick came home at six every evening and sat on the couch reading Spencer *Cars and Trucks and Things That Go*. It could have happened

404

n a prehistoric era. "What did he want?"

"He offered me some finish work on a local craftsman-era house. I was thinking I might say yes."

"What else could you cut back on, Nick? Sleeping?"

"It's craftsman era. That kind of work doesn't come along very often."

He set down his cup and picked up his gray canvas jacket. He'd had it forever. When he slid his arms inside the sleeves, she remembered their first camping trip at Montaña de Oro state park. Nick all nervous she wouldn't like the campsite—pit toilets and no showers tested a relationship. The short downhill hike from the tent to miles of rocky tidepools. She couldn't believe her luck. Somehow, in all her years of dating idiots, she'd stumbled upon a man who got a thrill watching brown pelicans traverse the shoreline.

He folded down his collar. "Why don't I meet you for lunch?"

Sonogram, bank, money order for the tickets, Carlynn. "Lunch?"

He looked at her, surprised. "You know, that big snack people have in the middle of the day? You could meet me in the hospital cafeteria, or across the street at the deli."

"I thought you used your lunch hour to study."

He looked out the window again. Oddjob hauled a fallen branch from the plum tree to the patio and was alternately gnawing on it and hacking up shredded bark. Weariness hung on her husband's shoulders like a caul. "I suppose I should."

"Nick?"

"Yeah?"

"Do you hate what you're doing so much that you maybe don't want to become a shrink?"

405

He shrugged, keeping his mouth impassive, just like Dr. M, proving he'd mastered at least one shrink technique.

Lainie set her water glass down. She wished she could tell him everything, that by tipping her cornucopia o worries his way she wouldn't add to his burden. "You know, it would be just fine with me if you wanted to go back to being a woodworker. I kind of liked being married to somebody who smelled like cedar sawdust al the time."

He smiled, came over to her and gave her a kiss. She tasted coffee and a hard-working male resilience. The force of the withheld truths inside her nearly made he choke.

"I can try it another day. Let you know."

"Promise you will?"

"Sure. We'll talk about it tonight."

"I'll make you a real dinner. Whatever you want Spago meat loaf? Name it."

"Something bland. My stomach's tense."

It was probably from eating all those pickles she'c made. Lainie watched Jake follow him to the door, wag his tail hopefully, then as he patted his head good-bye turn and retreat. Routine—another effort to keep the wild randomness at bay. She heard his car engine stal twice before it caught.

The telephone rang and she picked it up. "Hello?"

"Can you believe this? Your grandfather went ou bought me a phone for the jeep. It plugs right into the cigarette lighter. You get a craving, you can call anybod anywhere. I'm telling you, Elaine, let Charles pay of that hospital bill. He's about to drive me to the nu house talking electronic gadgets. Now he wants to buy me a computer. What am I going to do with computer? Testosterone overdose, that's his problem. Whoops, your husband just now drove by so I guess the coast's clear. Get your slicker on, honey. I'm just around the block."

"Okay, Mrs. Clarke," the technician said, wielding the microphone above her belly. "Here we go."

Lainie couldn't speak. Sixteen ounces of water sloshed uncomfortably inside her bladder. She nodded and a glob of chilly bluish gel squirted onto her stomach, causing her to shiver down to her very core.

Earlynn stood at the head of the table, her hand in Lainie's, squeezing. "Hang in there, honey. At least there's no needles."

"We'll begin with an initial deep sweep of this quadrant. Look up at the screen if you care to watch. The ATL-HDI three-thousand is our latest model. We're very excited about its capabilities."

Earlynn said, "Hah. Reminds me of a computer."

"Similar technology."

Lainie cleared her throat. "With this thing, could you, hypothetically speaking, see a baby's heart?"

"Depending on the stage of development, sure. Our old machine was strictly gray-scale globby dots. With the ATL, we can zoom in, introduce color. Our printouts rival Kodak."

Globby dots or not, the picture on the monitor screen was a mystery. It reminded Lainie of the space capsule that changed every kid's dream of becoming an astronaut from fantasy to actual career choice. For awhile, Russell had astronomical intentions. Then he discovered his fear of flying and the furthest he got was buying a car named Comet. The monitor picture looked like the cramped interior of the Mercury capsule.

She glanced at the technician's name tag—Jennifer Olds, RT, Radiology/Ultrasound. Lainie wished she'd finished college. With an LCSW in hand, she'd be giving Elizabeth Friedman a run for her bitchiness, arranging for siblings to stay together instead of gritting her teeth so she didn't pee all over the exam table. Face it, she told herself, Nick doesn't want to be a shrink. He misses the wood. If had a job, he could do what he wanted.

"Elaine, look at that," Earlynn said.

On the monitor screen, the arc-shaped gray smear sharpened up. Inside the gray gravy, white flecks floated, a sheen of bubbles, as if they were scanning an over-aerated aquarium, but this was her body and they weren't looking for fish. "I don't see anything."

The technician's face remained impassive as various blobs floated in and out of view.

"Well, I'm relieved," Earlynn said. "All night I worried I might upchuck looking at your internal body parts, but this here's as interesting as that PBS television your grandpa favors."

"Does everything look all right in there?"

"Sugar, I'm not a nurse. Well, how about it, Miss Olds?"

The technician clicked a set of buttons and superimposed graphs across the screen. "The radiologist reads the scans. He'll call Dr. Stewart and explain everything to you."

"They have to say that on account of lawyers," Earlynn offered. "All it really means is two bills'll arrive in your mailbox."

Lainie felt her breathing accelerate. She had to pee so badly she ached. Given how often she did this, the technician had to know more than she was saying. On the monitor, something dark infiltrated the space

408

capsule. A white teardrop-shape fluttered. No, it was more the shape of a caterpillar.

"If that's a tumor, I'll eat my car phone," Earlynn said. "Come on now, lady. My granddaughter here's just about petrified she's growing a tumor. Surely it won't cost you your job to identify that blob on the screen there as a baby."

"It appears to be a viable fetus."

Lainie started to cry.

"See what you've done?" Earlynn said. "Come on, we're all women here. We all of us in this room have bled and worried at certain times of the month. Have mercy. We aren't asking you for anything more than the basics."

On the monitor, the pod-shape once again floated into view. The technician pointed. "These are limb buds. This is the spinal column. There is the heart."

Lainie counted four potential arm-or-leg buds, then, like a starfish, it seemed to sprout a fifth. "What's that?"

The technician's face didn't waver. "Your doctor will discuss the details with you."

The definition was so poor it could have been wadded up Kleenex. Tumors, Lainie was convinced. Growing at warp-speed. Cloning.

Miss Olds printed out three views. "Try not to worry, Mrs. Clarke."

Earlynn leaned down and pressed her cheek next to Lainie's. It was as damp as her own and Lainie felt their tears mingle. Earlynn said hoarsely, "I'm no specialist, but I recognize a baby when I see one."

"With three arms?"

"Well, honey, I don't know. Maybe that was its little shadow."

They both looked at the technician, who folded the towel she'd wiped Lainie's belly dry with into a hamper

409

marked *Sterilize*. "You're seeing your doctor later today?"

"Not until Monday. Can I pee now?"

She pointed to the door. "Restroom's right through there. After the radiologist checks your films, you're free to go."

Lainie sat down on the toilet in the bathroom, rested her elbows on her knees, and cried. The phantom ache remained, undeniable as that fifth limb. She was not growing a future John Glenn. Just some unidentified, aberrant astronaut whose sex she had not thought to question. Monday—the adolescent doctor Dr. Stewart. Maybe it was too early to pronounce the octopus child viable, or maybe with the help of the ADL—whatever they already knew, but such information fell under a category lab techs weren't allowed to reveal. She knew what to do with a tumor—cut the sucker out, slash and burn like her great-grandfather had the brush on the Shadow Ranch. That cocoon inside the black pod wasn't terminal in the standard way, but maybe in another way, it was just as doomed.

Lainie could tell that the silence on the drive home was about to kill Earlynn. When she dropped her off in her driveway, she said, "Honey, tell everyone at once. It'll go easier on you. I think a family dinner is in order. Settle the old scores with your grandpa. He'll be so tickled, he'll probably buy you your own car phone. Then you and me can call each other and discuss important stuff like the traffic on the freeway and how many runs we got in our nylons. How about I pick up some groceries and meet you back here this afternoon?"

Lainie smoothed the sonogram printout in her hand. "It doesn't look like a baby. I wonder if they'll say I

410

should have an abortion."

"Do you believe in that?"

"I always thought so, at least for other people. It never seemed like a question I'd have to ask myself."

Earlynn took hold of her hands and rubbed hard. "You really think them doctors'd let you go today without fifty-seven more tests if they suspected something terrible wrong?"

"How should I know? They're doctors, not mothers."

Earlynn sighed. "True. Well, until Monday, all you have to be is patient. Now people got to eat, so what should we fix for dinner? Some kind of roast or my tuna and potato chip casserole? Actually, I use Durkee onions instead of chips. People swear by it."

"I don't know. At this point, you know my grandfather's preferences better than I do."

Earlynn's car phone began to twitter. "Hear that? Probably the only call I'll ever get is him testing it out. I think I won't answer just to fret him a little, let him get his money's worth. Never wanted the darn thing in the first place. Ask your brother to join us."

"Russell?"

"You got another brother I don't know about?"

Lainie laughed. "Nope, just the one."

"Good. More Carpenters I'm not sure I could handle."

Earlynn tooted her horn as she drove away, the pink Jeep the brightest thing to hit Wisteria Street since the July Fourth California candle. Lainie envisioned the Jeep merging into traffic on South Burton, then Pacific Coast Highway, as the Lexuses and Infinitis of Orange County swerved to allow Earlynn passage, her country radio station thinning out in the sea breezes.

I am as guilty of making fun of her as Jimmy Carter was

411

lusting after other women in his heart, Lainie thought as she stood in her driveway. *Yet for some reason, the woman likes me. She called me her granddaughter.*

She drove to Earlynn's bank, cashed the check, tucked the bills into her wallet. As soon as she paid off the tickets, maybe she'd start to feel normal, whatever normal was anymore. She called the hospital and canceled Dr. M. She couldn't sit on the feel-better couch *gratis* with two hundred dollars in her wallet. Better to lie and tell the receptionist she had a cold.

Roast chicken. Mashed potatoes. Baby green peas. Crescent rolls. And lemon pie. The lemon pie would have to be last minute and store-bought. Somehow that seemed appropriate for this awkward family reunion. She picked up the telephone and called her brother.

"Russell?" she said the moment she heard the phone pick up. "I figured it out. Five minutes amounts to three hundred seconds of time that I might have spent staring off into space or picking my nose. Come for dinner. Bop and Airline are coming, too. Not my first choice in dinner companions, but hey, I needed the money, which is a long story I'll bore you with sometime when I am not free-floating in massive crisis or surrounded by relatives. Actually, Earlynn isn't all that bad, once you get to know her."

"Hello, Lainie."

"Candace?"

"Do I count as family?"

Across the room, Oddjob was performing the stealth maneuver, inching toward Jake's food dish. "Of course. What are you doing over at Russell's?"

"Oh, we're just working on a little project together. When we get a little further along into it, we'll tell you

412

ıll about it. What should I bring?"

Jake growled and Oddjob whined as if he'd been ınjustly attacked. Lainie'd never fallen for his ransparent small-dog politics, but Earlynn would cave ight in. Clearly, Oddjob was rehearsing for a larger vent. "Just bring Russell. And whatever guitar he leems appropriate for such an occasion. By the way, I :alled you a bunch of times. Your answering machine nust be messed up."

"I've kind of been out a lot. Lainie?"

"What?"

"I'm really sorry about mailing the letter."

"Forget it. It's been so long I'm sure someone threw it ıway."

"Am I still your friend?"

Lainie's heart flopped the same way the caterpillar-)ctopus-five limbed baby did on the ATL monitor. Life vas simply too short to hate anyone. "Of course you're :till my friend."

"Good. Now, speaking of friends. Have you heard rom your *other* friend? You know, the one who always 1elped get you out of gym class? Visits once a month? Dresses in red. Has she come by?"

Lainie sighed. "Just come to dinner, Candace."

CHAPTER 31

BIG BROTHERS

ʀUSSELL WAITED ON THE SIDEWALK ACROSS THE :treet from Harper Elementary, worrying that standing 1ere, related to no one, he presented the profile of a)otential child molester. The yellow Blue Bird buses

413

were parked out front, idling. The bus drivers had all finished their cigarettes and waited in their seats, one hand on the door levers. Each and every weekday there wasn't a phony-baloney school holiday, these guys transported sixty small bodies safely from home to learning and back again. Russell had ridden the bus until he realized only geeks did that and got himself a bike. He liked the smell of the bus exhaust. Maybe he should have become a driver. No, drivers didn't get paid enough for how awful the kids behaved. Spit wad fights, all those spilled leftover lunches, stepping in A-B-C gum. But driving a bus was responsible. What was he responsible for besides perpetuating sixties music? Well, for one thing, breaking Seth and Ethan Lomanto's hearts.

He leaned back against some lady's well-tended planter and felt a pulled muscle yelp in his lower back. It appeared that the bedroom queen was constructed out of libido and elastic. Candace hadn't missed a period yet. He tried to assure her as she sat there disappointed in the bathroom, there was always next month and it was certainly painless to keep trying. Meanwhile, he was becoming washboard-trim in the abdomen area,

Play me something to fall asleep by, Russell, Candace often begged him. He'd sit cross-legged in the bed and play her "Summertime"—a jazzy, simple adult lullaby, even though it was winter now. But lullabies weren't enough. *Russell, let's put your name in to do a solo act at Triangle Square.*

Play in public? Why?

Because I want to stand up and tell everyone this talented man is the father of my children.

We're going to do this more than once?

Take a good long look, Russell. Lying in your bed is a

414

*typical only child. You remember what I was up to in high
school? Well, none of that stopped until I met you. This
baby's going to have siblings.*

Siblings, as in plural?

*Come here, Russell. Stop talking. You talk too much. You
think too much, too. Feel this. Isn't that nice? Now lean
down here. Yes. Do me this way. Oh, my god, that feels
incredible.*

Sometimes, after they'd done the deed, as they lay
wrapped in his comforter and she snuggled up beside
him, her short platinum hair right under his fingertips,
her big girl voice going on about nothing in particular,
he'd wonder about the magnitude of what they were
doing. Was orgasm the antithesis of rational thought?
Were sperm little tadpoles set on autopilot? Did they
race to the egg because they were born to the task, or
did reaching it constitute the biggest orgasm of all?
Then it would hit him and he'd freak—it's been over a
month and she hasn't hit the road.

At their last session, he'd come right out and asked
Dr. M what she thought of the baby thing. The most
she'd offered was, *Russell, we're not talking about you two
getting a puppy.* But he could tell she was kind of jazzed
that a pretty, smart girl had said she loved him. Then
she brought up a topic they rarely discussed: his father.
For no particular reason, Russell had started to cry, and
Dr. M seemed so impressed she set aside her clipboard
to listen. *I was thirteen years old when my father checked
out,* he told Dr. M. *I cut school that day, surfed some great
waves, smoked a doobie with my friend Mark, and
hitchhiked home to find out my father was taking the great
dirt nap.* Dr. M said sooner or later he was going to
make peace with what happened. Since it was going on
twenty-two years, Russell kind of doubted it.

The only thing in his life that felt taller than his fixation with Candace was how hard it was not seeing Margie's boys. He wondered how Ethan was doing in first grade. First grade was when you had to start printing your name on the papers. No name, no grade. The initial taste of failure. They started pulling that responsibility crap and boys were first to get nailed. He wondered whether or not Seth had to do book reports yet. Heinous stuff, trying to finish some girly book think up how to say you didn't hate it in twenty-five words or more. Did Margie still let them use their boogie boards? Indian summer was over, but now and then a sunny day poked its head through the winter sky. Maybe surfing was a casualty of the broken relationship, something the boys missed so much they tried not to think about it.

"Russell?" Margie had pulled up beside him in the battered Buick. "Is that you?"

"Margie. Hey, nice to see you. Did you know you're parked by a fire hydrant?"

She frowned. "Maybe I don't plan to be parked here long enough to care. What are you doing here anyway?"

"What's it look like I'm doing here?"

"Loitering."

He was grateful to have the old lady's planter to fall into if need be. "I wanted to see the boys. Talk with them. If it's okay with you."

"What did you want to tell them? How great your new girlfriend is?"

He shoved his hands into his jacket pockets. He could feel a cellophane-wrapped condom, something he wouldn't be needing anytime soon lurking in there among the lint. "Just see how they were doing, maybe set up a date for surfing. That is, if it ever warms up again. It's been pretty cold this week, hasn't it?"

Margie got out of the Buick and slammed the door. Car needed a new muffler, and her paint job constituted metallic dandruff. She'd lost some weight. Her nurse's uniform didn't really show it, but he knew her body so well he noticed. As she stood by him, he realized she was about the same height as Candace. "You look good, Margie."

"Shut up and go stand over there," she said.

"Why? It's a free sidewalk."

"The boys see us standing together, they'll take it the wrong way."

"You're right." He reluctantly abandoned the planter and walked about three feet further. "Listen, think it would be all right if I gave them a ride home?"

"That's even worse than us standing together letting them think we're a couple."

"I'm not going to tell them anything negative about you. I kind of hoped we could still remain buddies, that I could be there for them to lean on in case of . . ." His voice trailed off.

"In case of what, Russell? They need to write a paper on a record store? They hit puberty and suddenly decide their life's ambition is to become a guitar hoarder?"

He slapped his sore thigh. "Yeah, that's it exactly, Margie. I want to tell them what incredible fuck-ups adults are so they can grow up not expecting anything but disappointment from every man who beds their mother."

She set her mouth in the old familiar hard line.

"Look, we tried. I'm sorry it didn't work out with us. I wish we could be friends. Your kids are still great kids. We agree on that, right? I like them. They like me. Just like Barney the dinosaur, only I'm real. They haven't

417

grown out of me yet."

"They will."

"You're right. I know I'm nothing special. Maybe it's asking too much, but I just want to be in their lives a little while longer."

"That's not fair, Russell."

The school gate opened and children began rushing to cars and lining up for the buses. The kids swung book bags and clanked lunch boxes against each other, hollered out loud with the incomparable taste of freedom. The chilly air seemed to swirl around their growing bodies in an invisible embrace, causing Russell to experience a lump-in-the-throat kind of reaction at his own someday-future fatherhood. He spotted Seth in the crowd, admired the boy's studied coolness as he searched for a glimpse of his mother, then on confirmation, pretended not to notice. When he saw Russell alongside her, the boy did an unadorned doubletake. Russell lifted a finger to say hello. All coolness was suspended as Seth hopped on one foot waiting for the crossing guard to blow his whistle. He raced off the curb and ran across the asphalt. A few kids behind him, Ethan carried a four-foot long construction paper surfboard.

He stopped in the middle of the crosswalk. "Wussell! You came back!"

Russell's heart felt as insubstantial as that construction paper. Any minute now, the organ would rip in two and be carried away in the wind.

Margie crouched down, arms open to receive her charges. They ran right past her, tackling Russell to the sidewalk. "Easy," he said. "Go give your mom a hug. Then if she says it's okay, maybe we'll go out for a Coke."

418

She held them fast to her body, their faces mashed against her belly, a place where she'd grown each baby hoping he would be the son to cement her failing marriage. Russell thought the boys endured her affection rather good-naturedly, considering the looks other kids were giving them. He stared into the old lady's planter for a few minutes, giving Margie some privacy. Finally Margie gave him a tired smile. Silently she mouthed the words, *Just this one time. Say good-bye, Russell.* He nodded.

"One Coke, Russell. Then you bring them straight home."

"They're fine boys," he said, thinking if he'd set out to do so, he couldn't have come up with anything more Bop-like than that particular phrase.

"Wussell? Can I have a quarter for Mortal Kombat?"

"A whole quarter? Man, Ethan, you must think I'm a bank." He emptied his pockets and changed all his dollar bills into quarters. "Go forth. Be Scorpion. Annihilate Sub-Zero. Throw a dagger into that nut-freezing bastard and flame him with morning breath. Show no mercy."

Seth scoffed. "If you really want to win the game, pick Kano. Kano's part robot. His flying ax nails anything. When it hits the guy in the chest, all this blood squirts out of his heart. That's cool. Ethan, you're so lame, you'll probably pick Sonya."

"Will not."

"Will too. I can't believe they let chicks into Mortal Kombat. Wrecks the whole game."

"Here's an idea, Seth. How about we let Ethan pick whoever he wants? Here's some quarters for you. Go find a chick-free game and leave your brother alone."

Seth jingled his handful of coins. "You want to play me in Killer Instinct?"

"Prepared to die, are you?"

"Start digging your grave, Carpenter."

"You're the one who'll be needing a headstone, dude."

They passed a bank of phone booths. Seth said, "Hey Russell, want to give Forest Lawn a call before we start?"

"Pal, you're cruising for the bruise of a lifetime."

Russell dropped the quarters into the slots. He knew this game. It was a complete retrace, with virtual characters and dropped-in scenes filmed from real life. He didn't play it that often since it cost seventy-five cents and he figured thirty-four year olds shouldn't regularly be spending seventy-five cents on video games. Two could play. The point, if video games had a point, was to kill everyone, a male dream some guys never grew out of. Seth chose Glacier, the block-of-ice guy who steamed around creating piles of frozen ground for his adversary to slip on. Russell chose Pyro, basically the same guy, but his arsenal was fireballs and lakes of flames.

Russell flipped his controls and tried not to give Seth any slack. The kid stayed quiet, his face stern. They played hard. Russell got in a few righteous hits, then Seth bore down and froze him, Pyro hunched over and fell to the ground. Flames shot out of his head. "There go my brains. You beat me, you weasel."

Seth nodded and took a breath. The way the game worked, his moment of glory consisted of a close-up of Glacier, the words *Supreme Victor* flashing across the screen, then the computer assumed the character of Sabrewolf. Seth lasted two or three seconds before *You Lose* flashed across the screen.

420

Russell lifted more quarters from his pocket. "Want to go again?"

Seth shook his head no and slapped one of the controls. "This game is gay."

So that was what they were teaching in school. "It's hard, lad."

Seth slid back into their booth and nursed his Coke. All around them, games spat out soundtracks and pool balls clacked. Margie would flip out if she knew he'd taken them to a pool hall. Women didn't understand places like these had the best video games.

Seth said, "Russell, how does a guy know if he's a queer?"

"If you mean homosexual, I'm not really sure. Probably one day you wake up and realize you like guys. That tatas don't ring your chimes or something real basic. But anybody queer is more likely a guy who's misunderstood and lonely."

Seth nodded. "Then Ethan is probably just queer."

"Good Lord, Seth, he's in first grade. You were in first grade not too long ago. You forget how hard it was or what?"

Seth made a face. "Maybe I could go live with my dad."

Russell freaked—Mr. Personality laying a hand on this boy was unthinkable. "Why would you want to do that?"

"I don't know. Sometimes I just feel like I don't belong with her."

Margie—a woman he had tried to love, but only ended up letting down. He remembered their final break-up scene. It had taken place in the parking lot of Red Lyzyrd Vynyl, their cars nose to nose, since Margie's battery was dead and Russell always carried

421

jumper cables. The traffic sped by on Newport Boulevard and Margie let him have it for every single crime known to man. It wasn't a conversation, it was more akin to verbal stoning. Several times the idea of interrupting her, explaining his side occurred to him, but in his heart Russell knew that would only make things worse. He let her rail, and when the diatribe finally died, she was sobbing. He unhooked the cables, gave her a hug, and she slapped his face. *Her.* Would his own child someday talk like that about Candace? Try it, he'd whip his ass. No, he wouldn't. He'd never been able to hit anyone. He was the ivy king of the elementary school. He'd walk a league around a potential confrontation. What made him think he could start being tough now?

"Seth, I felt the same way after my dad croaked. There I was, captive in a house full of females, Sonyas, all of them. My mother, my sister. We're talking makeup, perfume, monthly mysteries, lots of crying. And you know how I feel about crying. I did a lot of stupid crap trying to keep myself separate. After awhile, I discovered my sister was halfway decent and we got to be friends. She hates me right now, but it'll blow over. It's kind of great having somebody related to you as your friend. They have to be nice to you on major holidays. Plus, if they croak first, they'll leave you money."

"What about your mom?"

Russell sighed. "Boys are supposed to think their moms are weird. It keeps them from turning queer."

"Do you got another girlfriend?"

"Yeah, buddy, I do."

"What's her name?"

"Candace."

"That's a stupid name. What's she look like?"

422

"Tall. Skinny. Dyed blond hair."

"She got big hooters?"

Russell smiled. "Nah, they're small but decent. Good legs, though. Can't be dating any girt with piano legs. Your mom's got good legs."

Seth nodded like that was important to him, too. "You going to marry her?"

Whoa. *Déjà vu.* He hoped another case of chicken pox wasn't going to follow this line of conversation. "I might."

"Why? You said married guys had to make birdhouses. No surfing. My mom won't let us surf anymore. She says it's dangerous. I'm never getting married."

Jesus, the kid was writing an article for the *Times!* A junior Mac Henry, sporting Coke dribble down his chin. Russell tapped his Coke cup and felt the beads of moisture chill his knuckles. "Surfing is not dangerous." He thought of Mark Foo and wished he hadn't. "Babies need a dad, Seth. If we have one, I want to be married."

Seth's mouth dropped open. "So, does that mean you can't be my friend anymore?"

Russell reached across the table and touched the boy's hand. "Of course not. I'm always going to be your friend."

"Liar." Seth jerked his hand away. "Why'd you bring us here?"

"I thought we could play some games. Catch up. It's been a while."

"You could play games with Candy ass."

Russell leaned back in the sticky booth. He took a deep breath and slowly released it before he answered. "Well, Seth, for one thing, I'm going to teach you how to call me collect, so if you ever, anytime of the day or night, need a friend, you can do it without needing a quarter. And for another, I know this'll sound queer, but I missed your ugly face."

Seth stared into his Coke cup, selected a piece of ice, and chucked it at Russell.

Russell picked it out of his hair and set it on a napkin. "Thanks, I think we both needed that."

Ethan came running back to the table, his lower lip trembling, and slid into the booth.

"What's wrong, Ethan?"

His face screwed up and the first-grader looked about to cry. "I picked Kano like Seth told me."

"And?"

"Sonya killed him."

Seth gave his brother a push out of the booth. "You dweeb, where's your quarters? Let me show you how to whip the chick."

Russell watched the brothers concentrate in front of the video game. Seth coached Ethan patiently. He let him in on the secrets, the codes, the tricks other nasty kids would hold back. They were a team. Russell smiled. They were going to be fine. Just fine. Just fine brothers in the Just fine town of Harper, California, where everything, everything except the aching gap these two boys left in his Carpenter heart, was Just fine.

Russell dropped the boys at Margie's and drove around, aimlessly at first, then finding himself headed in that direction, toward the cemetery. He thought about the river Styx from mythology, a jillion years ago, when elementary school had slipped for a few minutes and been interesting. He remembered that peasants were supposed to give the ferry driver money in order to be carried across. He had a few leftover quarters in his pocket, but the gate tender in the cemetery where his grandmother, father, and nephew were buried only asked to see his driver's license.

He could understand why Lane went off about the sycamore tree Bop had planted. It was tall and healthy while what it shaded was obviously not. He parked the Comet, got out, and stood at the gravesites. The last time he'd been here was when they buried Spencer. "Hey, buddy," he said aloud to the smiling brass angel on the boy's grave. "I think about you every day."

Then he nodded to his grandmother, thankful he'd known her in an era when it was grandmotherly to bake cookies and favor your grandson. He wondered if he might get Alzheimer's, too, and if Candace would take care of him, wipe up his drool, or just send him out on his surfboard into a rip tide. Nervously, he checked out his father's headstone.

Charles Russell Carpenter III
Born May 30, 1935
Died November 4, 1973

He couldn't remember what he looked like, but he clearly recalled his smile. It was as pure as the looks on Margie's boys' faces when they caught a wave. With his dad, it usually came about as a result of Russell understanding his math homework, or Lane voluntarily removing her eye makeup. But Russell remembered seeing that smile whenever he'd walk over to the high school to meet him, and catch him tutoring some rocket scientist who was failing Algebra I for the fourth time.

He guessed his father's life, however short, had been fairly satisfying. As satisfying as it could be for a man married to an antique hound, with two teenagers believing every piece of advice he handed down was bogus and annoying. As difficult as it must have been to have Bop and all his money sitting in judgment of him, Chuck was a good teacher. When he died, the school held an assembly.

"We're doing okay here," he told his father. "Things are in a bit of a twist right this second with Lane and all, but you know what? I have this gut feeling it's all going to work out."

Even though it would undoubtedly give him a rash, Russell sat and pulled up the weeds around the three graves. He brushed the leaves out of the lettering on the plaques, squirted out a few girly tears, threw a quarter at the ferry tender, and drove on home.

CHAPTER 32

A *REALLY* GOOD RECIPE FOR CORN CAKE

NICK WAS IN THE SHOWER WHEN LAINIE GOT home from walking the dogs. To avoid repeat disasters, she'd taken them to the park on Canyon, where they stayed nervously on her heels, moving as jerkily as needles on emotional barometers. This constituted normal behavior for Jake, but for Oddjob to have developed a sense of his surroundings larger than whatever he might destroy bespoke major change. She filled their supper dishes and went into the bathroom. Her bladder still ached a little from the sonogram.

"We're having company for dinner," she said above the running water to the shadowy figure behind the steamed-up door. "My grandfather and his wife, plus Candace and Russell. You don't have to dress up, but prepare for significant weirdness."

Nick turned off the water and stood there dripping.

She could see him reach up and pinch the bridge of his nose, wondering if he'd heard her correctly, or if maybe his workday hadn't yet ended.

Lainie handed him a purple towel over the top of the shower door. "Here."

"Thanks."

Nick opened the door and stepped out, the frayed towel cinched around his waist. His hair stuck out crazily in all directions. "Dinner with the family?"

"It was either that or a rerun of 'Star Trek.' "

He stood at the sink and shaved the two little strips of hair that grew high up on his cheekbones. "Are we celebrating something I forgot or just asking for general trouble?"

Lainie looked at her shoes, the white rubber toes stained green from grass clippings. "Maybe a little of both."

Nick set down his razor. "Well? Care to elucidate?"

"Get dressed. Let's take a walk, Nick."

The dogs were ecstatic at the change in routine and grateful to be back on the familiar ground of their bluffs. Nick threw a stick for Oddjob and the dog clenched it in his tiny jaws, shaking the life out of it as he ran.

"Do you remember when your pal Ernie discovered he was sterile? How freaked he was, figuring he'd spent over twenty years and a lot of money employing all manner of birth control?"

Nick nodded. "Poor Ernie. He thought life began and ended with viable sperm. I suppose that's true on a literal level."

Lainie stopped at the cliff edge where she'd found Ruth Cranky Pony crying that day, which seemed to

427

have happened years before. She crouched down and petted both dogs for support. Nick looked at her, puzzled, and she felt her heart pounding. "Well, let's just say that you'll probably never fall victim to Ernie's dilemma."

Nick took the stick away from Oddjob, sat down next to her, and began trailing the stick in the dirt and weeds. "Which is why you were so upset with me the night of your grandfather's birthday party."

She could not yet meet his eyes. His feet she could look at. Under his tennis shoes and socks, she knew there were long, elegant toes and high arches. Spencer's feet had been exact replicas, but on a smaller scale. Inside her, the three-armed baby was growing God knew what kind of feet. "Well, that was three months ago."

"Yes, it was." Nick dug deeper with the stick. "Exactly what subject are we dancing the hokey-pokey around, Elaine? Might it be pregnancy?"

"What makes you say that?"

"I've lived with you twelve years. I know your cycle. The pale blue box under the sink is gathering dust. Is there some reason I always seem to be the last one you confide in?"

She held up a hand. "Hear me out. I had a sonogram today. Earlynn came along. Don't be angry. She pretty much blackmailed me into taking her. I know how full your plate is, Nick. I know you don't like your work right now and the last thing you need is another burden. This is hard for me to tell you. But already it looks like things might not be okay down there. That's why they made me have the test. Everyone's being tight-lipped and way too cheerful."

He gave her the therapist face. "When will you know

something definite?"

"Monday. I was going to spare you until then."

"What changed your mind?"

"Do you really think I could tell anyone else before I old you? Are we that far gone?"

Nick's mouth stayed impassive. He scraped at the lirt, unearthed something, and brushed away the dust. He showed her his outstretched palm, inside which ested a fossilized horse tooth. "Hunter's luck," he said, and they grabbed for each other, holding on for a long, quiet time, during which Lainie decided if their marriage had survived losing one son, a defective baby probably wasn't going to end it either.

"I want to come with you on Monday."

She sniffled into his neck. "You'd better. In fact, for the rest of my life, there's hardly anything I can think of that I want to do without you."

He tucked the horse tooth into her jeans pocket. "Just tell me one thing, Elaine."

She breathed in the clean soap smell of her husband, grassy dog paws, the undeniable stink of her own fear. "Okay."

"How long have you suspected?"

She pulled away and rested her elbows on her knees. "Well, there are two answers. One is long and convoluted, overripe with denial. The other's pretty straightforward."

"Let's go with straightforward."

"Ever since that night in the atrium when you came inside me, I had this sinking feeling our grace time had ended. That the gods had hunkered down waiting for us—me, anyway—long enough. We were supposed to be done grieving, and they decided enough was enough." She bit her lower lip. "Guess maybe they went a little overboard if this baby turns out to be more defective than Spencer."

Nick pulled her to her feet and they stood together looking out over the cliffs toward the ocean. He tilted her chin up. If his face could hold any more worry Lainie sure didn't see how. "What the hell are we all about, Lainie?"

She shook her head. "I don't know, honey. I don't know anything more than what happens from moment to moment."

"I hate my job."

"Then quit."

His shoulders began to shake and she held him fast wishing there were a window of time for them to step through together and sob their aching hearts clean. Crying wouldn't change things. Crying was the tip of the slippery glacier upon which they floated their tenuous lives. Time, from the Buddha belly clock to Monday, that was the real culprit. There was never enough to get everything done, or else these obese polar-bear-shaped chunks of it floated by, slow and goofy and good for nothing but regret while you lay there tied to a hospital bed. Maybe it was the wrong kind of time, ticking fortissimo, moving so fast you wanted to reach out and snap the hands from the clock, throw them high and far away into another time zone.

"Whatever happens," Nick said, "remember that I love you."

She rubbed her hands over his shoulders, trying to warm them both up. "I love you, too."

"Would anybody mind if I said a blessing out loud to give thanks for this food?" Earlynn had changed clothes for supper, into a yellow satin exercise suit replete with gold-trimmed jacket and eyeshadow to match.

"Heap on the blessings," Candace said. "Whatever bounces off the food might splash on us."

Russell shrugged and toyed with his fork. After her news, Lainie saw the depression land on him hard. She figured he'd push the chicken under his mashed potatoes the same way he did after their dad died. Her grandfather folded his hands, trying to look pious over his pissed-off-at-the-universe attitude. He simply did not know what to do when he could not fix something with money or bluster. At least he'd finally gotten that stupid cast off his arm. He carried around a rubber ball to flex the muscles, and she could see Jake eyeing it. Nick rested his head in his hands, looking as if prayer would be a most welcome medicine.

Earlynn squinted her eyes shut like a kid making a birthday wish. "Lord, we thank you for this food, though I am afraid I might have cooked the bird dry. Everyone seems to like lumpy potatoes, no worry there. Elaine has done a wonderful job with the peas and whoever made this pie at Albertson's, well, bless her heart, too, won't you? Your bounty is a wonderful thing, and don't think we aren't grateful to receive it. But as for your overall plan, I am having some trouble accepting your will. Have you cleaned the wax from your almighty ears in recent days? Are you looking out for this family? I have to wonder. We are some of us rag-tag and all of us stubborn, but deep down we are good people who could use a break. Amen to that." She opened her eyes. "That's it unless somebody has something else to add."

Russell cleared his throat and drank some water. Candace stared at Lainie, her lower lip trembling. "Are you sure you don't have any vodka?"

"Young lady," Bop said, "you could do a lot worse than have a glass of Carpenter punch. Citrus—"

"Enough with your citrus cure-all!" Earlynn shouted.

"Well, it wouldn't kill her to grow her hair a little longer, too," Bop added.

They sat at the table staring at their full plates.

Russell got up and fetched his guitar case. He set it on the couch and opened the latches. From the flannel he retrieved his Western Orange Gretsch Rancher and set it on his thigh. "I fixed it," he said to no one in particular. "It took a great deal of patience to find the correct wood and I had a little trouble initially with the bindings, but it's done. I haven't really played anything on it yet. Haven't felt like it. But if nobody minds, I feel like playing something now."

"That's a great idea!" Earlynn said with entirely too much enthusiasm.

Lainie thought, prayer, music, a meal with an actual course for every food group, not to mention a real family to enjoy it, should any of them find themselves capable of swallowing—it was the first normal thing to take place inside her house since before Spencer got sick.

Russell played "The Tiger Rag," a silly song he used to annoy her with as a kid. Its lyrics were simple: "Hold that tiger, hold that tiger," each phrase punctuated with a raspberry, or if abdominal luck was with him, a fart.

Lainie started laughing first. She laughed so hard tears ran down her cheeks and her ribs ached. Her family stared at her, speechless over their full plates and worries. She tried to catch her breath, to gain control long enough to explain to them, *Come on, we'll die of boredom trying to be this serious and sad until Monday. If the baby is doomed, at least he will have had this one night where all of us gave up and into the fact that these things are*

432

ut of our worldly control, but every time she got one word out, she'd start laughing again.

She could see the fear in their eyes, them assessing her, wondering if these wild mood swings indicated she needed transporting back to the hospital. Still, she didn't stop until she got the hiccups, and then somebody, Earlynn or Candace, got up and started patting her on the back.

Dr. Stewart entered the exam room sporting his Flipper grin, rolling a machine that looked neither familiar nor pleasant. "Nice to meet you, Mr. Clarke," he said, shaking Nick's hand. "Glad you're here today."

He winked at Elaine and she felt ancient, her life wrinkly at the edges in a way this young Dr. Kildare was still a decade from experiencing. "I trust the sonogram wasn't too unpleasant."

"You try holding your pee for an hour and then being told absolutely nothing."

He laughed. "Those radiologists, they're a quirky bunch. Relax, I'll explain everything to you both as soon as I've done my exam."

He lifted her gown and listened to her belly with his stethoscope. Lainie shivered every time the chrome circle pressed against her skin.

"I'm going to use the Doptone now," he said, pulling the machine on its wheeled cart to the exam table. "It's a little like the sonogram, but for listening, so please be very quiet."

He turned some dials and switches, then ran the handheld transducer over her belly, first on one side, then the other. Suddenly the room was filled with the sound of galloping hooves.

"Zebras," Lainie said.

433

He gave her a half-smile. "No, horses. And there ar‹
two of them. One here," and he ran the instrument ove›
her right side, where the galloping noise was th‹
strongest. When he switched sides, she and Nick hear‹
the same kind of noise repeated over there. "Your othe›
little monkey was behind the first one on the sono›
They do that sometimes, early on, hide behind eacl
other. With two, it can cause the HCG to pea‹
abnormally high, so that explains your blood work. Bu
I repeat, they're both horses, and they look as good a›
they sound. Do either of you have any questions fo›
me?"

Nick shook his head as if clearing away an attic'›
worth of cobwebs. He laughed softly, and Laini‹
watched her husband's face empty of the worry he'‹
carried for months. He grinned, reached out, an‹
stroked her hand and she clasped it in hers, hard.

"If it won't bother them," she said, "could you play i›
again?"

The young doctor happily complied. "Once mor›
then, for posterity."

Lainie rested her head against Nick's hand, listening›
Hold that tiger. Yes, and hold that one, too. Hold ther›
both.

CHAPTER 33

FOUND ON ROAD DEAD

THE INTREPID REALTOR WHO'D COME FOR A LOOK›
see flicked a nicotine-stained thumbnail across th›
redwood walls of Casa de Carpenter and said, "Tack u‹
some decorative mirror. Big rooms, tall ceilings. That›

434

what buyers are after these days. That and closet space. They don't give a damn about foundations or termites, but they want closets big enough to park an elephant."

Decorative mirror—Bop was itching to deliver him a lecture on architectural purity, partner this fellow up with the duck-murdering Englishwoman, toss him and his gold blazer into the bay, but Earlynn would pitch a fit if he got himself in any more newspaper stories. He thanked him for his time and showed him the door.

The Conservancy people must have had a direct line to that Spaghetti realtor woman. For days now they'd been calling, asking if the rumor he was putting Casa de Carpenter on the market was true. There was no end of committees to which they wanted him to answer. Their endless numbers reminded him of the stinking Iranians sending children in to draw the enemy's fire. He'd come to a sobering conclusion: Casa de Carpenter was in no condition to put on the market.

As the telephone rang again, he pondered the state of the world. Lainie was pregnant, but the question of the baby's heart persisted. The vet had telephoned to tell them Earlynn's mare was coughing again and no way would he approve the quarantine lift. Russell's new girlfriend was a vast improvement over the old one, but that Candace was smart-mouthed and way too familiar with their family secrets. It would be difficult to get her to side with him in any skirmish. Maybe Mac Henry had fashioned a set of Carpenter voodoo dolls. He picked up the ringing receiver wearily and said "Hello?"

"How are you faring with attempt number four at wedded bliss? Has your retired stripper run for the hills yet, or are you still at the choosing attorneys stage?"

Speak of the devil. "All I'm trying to do is sell a house, Mr. Hemingway. Say, why don't you buy Casa

435

de Carpenter? I'm sure Gloria would feel right at home here."

"Oh, we're just fine in our condo, Carpenter."

Bop said, "It's been a long while since the telephone delivered me any good news. Maybe I should pull this instrument out of the wall and sever telecommunications permanently."

"But then you'd miss my reality updates, old man."

"Now there's a case of the pot calling the kettle black. Well, let's have it. What's so important you took time out from reporting earth-shattering news to the masses?"

"This isn't exactly something you want within earshot of any of my fellow scribes."

The reporter's voice sounded unusually solemn. Probably a trick. "Mac, cloak-and-dagger went out with Mickey Spillane. Just tell me over the phone."

"Charles?" The reporter's voice had dropped a full register. "Can you meet me at the coffee place a block north of the *Times* around twelve-thirty? I promise it will be worth your while."

"Well, it so happens I'll be in the area picking up some parts for my truck. All I can say is this better be worth something."

"Trust me, Carpenter."

"In a pig's eye." Bop hung up.

The grease monkey behind the parts counter went after him while he was waiting for the computer to spit out the receipt on the new tailgate. "Sir, allow me to take this opportunity to alert you to an unadvertised service special. Miracle Shield. It's not for the run-of-the-mill Ford customer, in fact, we only recommend it to valued customers such as yourself who purchase superior ehicles. Utilizing polymer formula and the highest uality ingredients available, Miracle Shield protects our vehicle from weather-induced oxidation, omething I'm afraid we all have to worry about living 1 the coastal air, not to mention UV gloss-reduction, or he invisible toxicity of air pollution. For eighty-nine ollars and ninety-nine—"

Bop flexed all his patience muscles twice. He couldn't ecide which component of air pollution was thicker— xhaust fumes or lies. He wouldn't trust these clowns vith a water hose. "It's a truck, son. And I wouldn't let ou slop that garbage on it if I was an old woman who nly motored once a week to the supermarket."

"Sir, may I speak frankly? I think you're making a iistake."

This red-headed stepchild was working his way up ie corporate ladder to the respectable position of the onscienceless guy who strong-armed young couples ito loans they couldn't afford. "Tell me something. Vhat's your commission on this crap? Twenty bucks? hirty? I'm curious how you sleep at night after onvincing housewives on budgets to fall for these orporate tall tales."

"Sir, you're about to miss out the opportunity of a fetime."

"Son, I'm eighty. However much more lifetime I got ft, I imagine I can do without this particular pportunity. Let me tell you a funny thing about missed hances. You lose one every day. Wait a while, another ill commence along. No guarantee it'll be the right ne, of course, but right up to the end, life offers you no nd to choices."

The young man's uniform shirt showed the eginnings of sweat stains. "Ford's studies reflect a documented twenty-percent increase in resale on cars—and trucks—coated with Miracle Shield."

Bop cocked his head. "I ain't planning on selling Hell, I might even decide I want to get buried in it How's it going to look to future archaeologists if they dig up a rotting skeleton in a truck with a perfect pain job? Why, they might get the idea we were a society that valued our cars more than our dead."

"We include a complimentary customer maintenance kit with each service contract. The need for waxing i entirely eliminated."

He patted the young man's shoulder and grabbed hi receipt. "Nice try. Probably the next old lady walk through here will lay right down for you."

He pulled into the parking lot of Starbucks, the newes Harper journalists' watering hole. Instead of bourbon the reporters, many of whom he doubted were of lega age to partake of alcohol, wired up on imported java Mac sat at a corner table, stirring some white frou-frou into his paper cup. He smiled, which Bop did no consider a good sign, and gestured to him to sit down "Can I get you a latte?"

"Mac, I don't know what the hell a latte is and I'n sure I don't want to. If they got it, I'll take a glass o orange juice. If they don't, my whistle will get through this dry."

"Well, then, let's get straight to the point."

"That's my preference."

Henry reached into his briefcase and handed Bop ar envelope. Its return address was the community college Inside, a smart-ass letter from Lainie lambasted the Harper City Council members, cast doubt on thei masculinity and generally begged in wild-woman

438

ashion for them to leave her precious bluffs alone. Bop thought of Lainie's face at dinner when she explained the problem with her blood tests, the sonogram. His granddaughter was holding together with spider's web. How'd you come by this?"

"I told you, I have friends in high places. Sounds like your granddaughter's got a wild hair over this soccer field project."

Bop pursed his lips. "She's intelligent enough to recognize greed. First Amendment entitles her to state her views."

"Which is the core of the journalistic approach, Mr. Carpenter. Our code, if you will."

"Call it what you like, it's still an invasion of people's lives." Bop nonchalantly folded the letter into his breast pocket. "She's still a little fragile from losing her boy. I'm sure a wise fellow such as yourself recognizes shakiness in a woman."

Allusions to Gloria's mental state usually tweaked Henry good; today the reporter seemed implacable. "Which is why I'm showing the letter to you versus penning a nice juicy feature."

Bop blew out a breath. Taking the letter wouldn't solve anything; Mac Henry had copy machines galore back at the *Times*. Two could play at this dirty game, but today he felt every one of those eighty years, and if Lainie lost another baby, he knew he would lose something, too. "Let's cut to the chase. How much will keeping this letter hushed cost me?"

Mac Henry didn't bat an eyelash. He stirred his fancy coffee drink, tasted the stick, peered out the window, and then looked back at his old rival. "For some reason, Gloria misses waking up to that damn horse painting in our bedroom. Myself, I can't fathom the love for a beast when cars, airplanes, and trains abound. Still, dedicate my life to keeping my wife amused."

Gloria in possession of his Maynard Dixon—Bop' teeth ached at the thought. "Let me get this straight You expect me to hand over my best painting to kee Mrs. Crazy from losing a wink of sleep? Mac, you nee to have a long talk with my headshrinker son-in-law."

Mac Henry frowned, making a great pretense o weighing a difficult decision. "As a professional, consider every possibility before I act. Including whethe having set a precedent, I owe my readership anothe story in my series on Southern California lifestyles. Jus now I was picturing a headline: 'Third- Generatio Carpenter's Tragic Fall: Losing the Grip on Reality. Sidebar on nervous breakdowns, which of course, woul naturally segue into past queries of your treatment o several wives. By the by, Charles. Speaking of wives Are you aware just how interesting a past your brid claims? Does the name 'Early Summer' ring any bells So many potential routes there to explore."

Bop kept his gaze level. "It's a damn good thing fo you I don't own a gun."

Henry stared back. "The pen is mightier than th sword."

"Fine. Whatever. When you're through lashing m with old sayings, we can step outside and go to fists What the hell is it with you, Mac? You find your ow family so goddamn boring you got to go after mine?"

"When Gloria's happy, I'm happy."

"Well, then stuff a Gold Card in each of her hand and give her a bunch of orgasms. She'll be delirious."

"Watch it, Carpenter."

Who did Mac think he was kidding? This had to d with Gloria being unable to negotiate the Dixon as par

440

of the original divorce settlement, a thorn that stuck her side so painfully she'd dragged the proceedings out an extra three months. She didn't want the painting she wanted his balls on a bed of Beluga caviar.

Mac sat there patient as a house cat, waiting for the inevitable cave-in.

Bop looked at him and said, "So many yuppies in this place it turns my stomach. I'll get back to you."

"Do."

Grandchildren. Great-grandchildren. Bop had envisioned his last years as smooth sailing—reveling in the high points of their lives with none of the responsibility of directing them out of trouble. Seemed like no matter how much wisdom he tried to bestow upon them, they had to do things their own bullheaded way. He drove the side streets of Harper mulling over Mac's blackmail. Russell's hovel was looking in particularly ill repair these days, the hedge of morning glories suffering from some kind of leaf-blackening fungus. He was so busy strumming Kumbaya on his guitar he probably didn't notice.

Maybe it was a discussion they'd never had during Chuck's lifetime, but like an unspoken promise, Bop intended to do right by his son's children. *I failed you, Chuck, but I won't fail them.* Thing was, he hadn't expected them to stay children this far into their thirties.

He turned down Wisteria and slowed to permit a tribe of children to finish their game of catch. Lainie's house didn't look that bad from the outside. It was what they called a "starter," but come on, after eleven years of marriage, those two ought to be locked into something nicer, building equity, planning for the future. Her driveway was empty. She was probably out looking for a

441

job when she ought to be resting.

He turned the corner and headed up to the bluffs sh
was so crazy about that she wrote that nutty letter. H
parked by the cutoff telephone poles and got out of hi
car.

Couldn't ask for a nicer afternoon. Clear enough tha
the humpback of Catalina island was visible. Plenty o
sparkling ocean water in between here and there
California winter had no conscience—dreary one day
sunny the next. The last rain had left a pond-size(
puddle, and somebody's golden retriever was splashin;
in it, following his breed's instinct. In the distance Bo)
could hear a woman calling out, "Simma! Come bac]
here!" but the golden was having way too much fun t(
mind.

Idly, he wondered if this pond forming every yea
constituted a wetlands. Holler wetlands in this county
you could foil the most well-intentioned constructior
plan. It was the reason they couldn't go hog-wild an(
build up the Bolsa Chica wetlands that ran alongsid(
Whistler's Stables.

He walked along the dirt path worn into the tabletoj
mesa by many sets of feet, human and animal, and
somewhere in this dirt, his own great-grandson'
footprints were included. It wasn't much in the way of ;
park, all dirt and weeds and a few birds, but for som(
reason Lainie cherished it. What a funny girl she'(
grown up to be. No huge ambitions: motherhood, ;
quiet husband, part-time jobs, and a kitchen to suppor
her cooking obsessions kept her happy. Maybe he was a
guilty of foisting ambitions on them as they were o
blaming him for life's injustices.

From the cliff's edge he looked down on the
haphazardly set stakes for the impending soccer field

442

he source of his granddaughter's pain. She needed the comfort of arms—her son's, her daddy's. Chuck. How green the grass would be at the cemetery right now. He'd never missed a visit, but what had those visits accomplished? Where he was needed was *outside* those gates. The living were depending on him, as patriarch of the tribe, to right the wrongs.

Everything he owned, even the happiness he felt with Carlynn, he'd trade it all to take a walk with Chuck right now, develop a plan to help Lainie together. He tried envisioning things from Chuck's point of view, what he'd do, given the circumstances. Bop stood a long time at the cliff's edge, watching turkey buzzards scout field mice as they soared overhead in lazy circles. He heard the warning cries of ground squirrels and spotted one well-fed jackrabbit standing so still he nearly blended into the brush.

He didn't need to build himself a second home in Shadow anymore than Harper needed a soccer field to which there would be no clear parking access without destroying this wild place. Maybe he couldn't sell Casa de Carpenter, but he could damn straight do something about preventing his granddaughter's tears. It would take money and lawyers and some hard pushing, but he believed he could do something to stop the development. Friends in high places—lo and behold, it seemed like for once in his life, Mac Henry might be half-right about something.

He made the call on his brand new car phone, staring at Lainie's bluffs.

"MacLellan Henry. Features."

"You want the painting? Here's my end of it, Henry. No stories on any and all Carpenters, past, present or future."

"Old man, who taught you to dream? P. T Barnum?"

"Anything of worth I taught myself. No more stories."

Mac Henry laughed long and hard. "For a demand that large, I expect regular invitations to your Christmas and birthday parties, and for you to be extremely nice to my wife until you buy the farm."

He had the weasel now. "With luck, you'll make five parties, and one of them will be my funeral."

"Not to worry, Charles. The painting will sustain me long after you're gone."

Letting the Dixon go suddenly seemed as easy as loving Earlynn. Bop started to laugh. "Thought you had me, didn't you, expecting I'd hang a painting above my granddaughter's happiness?"

"Let's just say I was curious, if push came to shove which you'd choose."

"Unlike you, Henry, I'd do anything for my grandkids. Family is what this life is all about."

"Hold on a minute—do I hear violins?"

Bop grinned. "Oh, they're playing, all right. But it takes a clean conscience to hear that kind of music. Something you sadly lack and always will, my pencil-pushing amigo."

PART FOUR

REBIRTH

Long stormy spring time, wet contentious April,
winter chilling the very lap of May, but at length,
the season of summer does come.
　　　　　—THOMAS CARLYLE, *CHARTISM*, 1839

CHAPTER 34

STARGAZING

FROM THE PEACE AND QUIET OF HIS BEDROOM TO full-bore Henry Mancini, Bop's silence was shattered by Earlynn's announcement: "Ladies and gentlemen, may I present a little Early Summer?"

He looked up from his king-size bed to see his wife of nearly a year dance out of their walk-in closet, totally nude. In front of her body she fluttered a peach-colored fan he'd never seen before. From behind, another trembled over her trim bottom. What in the devil! They'd been up twenty-four hours straight, worrying on Lainie in the labor room, but all that was over now. Lainie was fine, full of stitches but fine, and it was time for everyone to get some sleep.

Earlynn sashayed the dyed feathers around her naked body as she danced closer, her smile elfin. She let the wispy feather ends drop a few inches to momentarily reveal a swell of a breast. In the background, the theme from the Pink Panther soared from the stereo. Bop started to smile. "Honey?"

She ground her hips toward his question, the fans spreading like twin peacock tails and he caught a glimpse of gold lamé G-string. At no time was any one body part exposed; Earlynn was that good at keeping up the intrigue. He folded his hands behind his head and watched her pretty legs bowing, catching sight of skin in between feathers. Maybe this wasn't heaven, but it was right next door.

She smiled and looked directly into his eyes, a loving

wife who had bared all for total strangers in order to feed and raise two kids on her own. She'd been made to feel bad about stripping by that no-good Bible-thumping son of hers. Now, with the new great-grand-babies to celebrate, she was staging a private comeback just for him. It made him want to cry.

She leapt athletically onto the mattress, dancing from foot to foot back and forth over his prone body. He reached up and took hold of the arch of her foot. "Come on down here, sugar."

She swatted him with a fan. "Charles, I wasn't finished! I still had my finale to show you."

"Come on down anyway. I got a little finale of my own here you might want to take a look at."

"You what?"

He chuckled. "That's right. Ladies and gentlemen, appears we have a dog that will hunt."

Earlynn squealed as he directed her hand to what stirred beneath his robe. "You see, Charles? I told you we just needed to be patient."

"Earlynn, we've been overly patient. I think it was those dance moves of yours got me going again. Well, don't let's aim our hopes too high. We'll just take it slow, see what happens."

Earlynn fell on him, kissing, abandoning the fans. In her arms, it all started to come back to him, easy as riding a horse. What went where, how good it felt to get this close to another human being, how moving into each other made so much sense when the rest of the world had lost its mind. She crooned in his ear and he slid his body on top of hers. Pretty soon, he was out of breath, staring up at the top of his head from the inside out, spent.

"Thank you," he said, later on. Earlynn shushed him.

447

She gathered up her fans, gave one last bump-and-grind, kissed him on the forehead, and disappeared into the john. Soon he could hear her awful singing voice and the sound of the tub filling. This was what most people called regular life.

He stared up at the ceiling. He'd missed the talk shows for so long now that Phil, Oprah, Montel, Sally Jessy, Geraldo, and Ricki might have come and gone along with their guests. He wondered what today's theme had been. Whether Geraldo, got punched, or if anybody had started to fall in love the way he had the first time he spotted Earlynn. *I am in my sixtieth dee-cad and proud of it.. . .*

It appeared the ceiling could use a coat of paint. Undoubtedly some special Conservancy-approved unlocatable paint, but first came puttying over the cracks that every California earthquake seemed to widen. Aw, who cared about cracks or paint when two brand-new Carpenter issue (okay, Carpenter-Clarke), a boy and a girl, were sleeping wrapped tight as tamales in their hospital blankets? The day he thought never would come had arrived. He was a great-grandfather again twice over.

For the first time in a mess of years, he didn't have one single worry. Russell hadn't managed to knock up that skinny smart-ass who stood half a head taller than him, but Bop could tell he was giving the task his all. He needed to convince those two to marry. Marriage, no matter how outdated it sounded, built a foundation beneath a couple. It was there to catch you when the almighty excrement encountered the Casablanca fan. It had kept Elaine and Nick going.

Lainie was recovering in her private hospital bed down the hall from healthy twins with perfect hearts.

448

according to the neonatal cardiologist he'd hired to check them out. Her operation would leave a scar, but hell's bells, scars were outward proof of human survival, something to be proud of and reason to celebrate.

Bop knew she'd be furious when she discovered he'd paid off her bill at Children's. A second go-round at motherhood might soften her heart, but it wouldn't eliminate her bullheaded Carpenter nature. Well, whatever flak his granddaughter strafed his way, he could handle it. He'd told the girl in receivables, "Next time she sends in a payment, how about we divert it to a college fund?" She didn't seem too keen on the legal aspects involved, but Bop hadn't given up hope.

Lainie's babies weren't going to be the only additions. The vet had telephoned to let them know Earlynn's mare was officially bred, a blessed event Bop was hardly looking forward to. But, if Carpenters could change their luck, maybe Tio Tonto's offspring might skip over the madness and deliver something rideable. If Russell'd hurry up with the war effort, this could go down as the most fecund Carpenter summer on record.

He stared at the blank wall where the Maynard Dixon used to hang. Those twenty brilliant flashes of oil painted horseflesh striding across the shadows of the Nevada desert toward a sun-dazzled mesa led by a gray stallion now hung on Mac Henry's wall. They'd made an even trade: art for Mac keeping Lainie's letter, good name, and mental-health status out of the fish wrapper. Bop expected a nugget of resentment to fire up like gallstone pain, but now as he thought of how Henry had manipulated him, he pasted the wrinkled, brand-new faces of those two tiny babies over the anger and felt peaceful instead.

In 1927, when Dixon put brush to canvas to

immortalize "Wild Horses of Nevada," Charles Russell Carpenter II was thirteen years old, only seven short years from fatherhood, though he didn't have a clue that was coming. That same year Lindy took off for Paris in the Spirit of St. Louis and Coolidge declined renomination. Good for him—the presidency was a helluva crappy job. Babe Ruth hit sixty home runs, television was invented, and Charles Russell Carpenter senior took his son out behind the barn and made him watch while he shot a mare whose only crime was getting old. All that malarkey about life being simpler in the old days was a load of horsepucky. No matter what era you got dropped down into, life boiled down to three basic issues: loving your way through hurt, surviving the hurt to hope, and holding out hope that something you did with your time here on earth made a little bit of difference in the grand scheme of things.

Once his life had included rows of lemon trees, watching the weather, hiring bodies to help pack fruit, trying to steal a few minutes a day to ride a horse. Then along came Alyce, Chuck, the grandkids, a whole bunch of money, and what seemed like a quarter-century of sorrow. Given the scope of eighty years, all that didn't seem terribly unfair. Earlynn had come to him, of all things, via the television. They'd courted over Pacific Bell, saved a drunk's life, and love tumbled into Bop's once-empty heart like lucky dice in a casino cup.

His feisty Texas stripper had healed the family, enabled Bop to love again, and in this very bed, hoisted Old Glory. But more than recent successful bedroom activity, Earlynn had traveled into the lives of all the Carpenters, performing a wizardry more healing than angioplasty.

He imagined his own heart, the dark, booming drum

of muscle beating in his chest. He'd been pretty damn lucky when whoever handed them out gave him this one. It kept a steady rhythm, like some great old daddy of a tree, the father of an entire grove. Underneath, a knot of liferoots spoke to each individual tree in the grove, and wanted like hell to pass on history, but lately had come to understand the other trees would have to wise up by themselves.

He was ready to die now. Feeling peaceful, a little tired, Bop got up and dressed in his Levi's and favorite shirt, the Hawaiian one with the leis and tiny airplanes. He tied his shoes. As much as he would have enjoyed sticking around to watch those babies grow up, he knew asking for any more time was pushing celestial luck. He imagined hooking up in the afterlife with Alyce and Chuck, feeding carrots to all his old horses, watching Spencer come running toward him. *Bop! Bop, come see my pony, Banjo.* . . . How interesting it was to feel so uninvolved with your own demise. To accept that your earthly work was completed. Just to open your arms and go.

He turned his head and waited for whatever was coming—the long uninterrupted sleep or the beckoning light.

"Charles! Charles Russell!"

Whoa, these angels had strident voices. Maybe he'd wait a while before answering to see if any nicer ones happened along.

"Charles Russell Carpenter the second, put in your damn hearing aid and wake up!"

Maybe it wasn't an angel.

"I said, telephone! You have a call."

There were telephones in heaven? Or—they'd warned

451

him about this—was he in that other place?

He blinked, his world coming slowly into focus. A peach-colored pillow slip, ironed with a crease. Fieldstone walls for which Frank Lloyd Wright was famous. Well, this wasn't so bad, if he could just figure out where to yank the phone cord. He looked up. No gilded wings, no pristine clouds. A too-short ceiling that needed paint? Wait just a minute here. "Earlynn? Sugar? You calling me?"

She appeared in the doorway. "Only for the fourth time. Mr. Henry's on the phone. Better pick up and see what he wants before you get him mad all over again and the grandkids in an uproar. You know, we've got more to think about now that those babies have arrived. Responsibilities. . . She went back out the door, muttering.

Bop jammed a hearing aid into his ear and fumbled for the bedside receiver. "Hey, Mac. I was taking a little nap and had the strangest dream that just this second turned into a nightmare. You decide my painting isn't enough, you want my wife, too?"

"Don't tempt me, old man. Nope, I'm calling about a little item that came over my modem."

Bop let out a sigh. "Don't even start. I just now got to where I can imagine letting go of the Shadow. You get me all stirred up again, Earlynn'll come after me with a fry pan."

"Okay. I won't tell you."

Bop waited a half-second before he changed his mind. "Please don't tell me the Indians won the ruling to turn it into a dump."

Henry laughed. "Authorities say you should be kind to your elders, so consider this my one random act of niceness."

"Listen here, Mr. One Year Behind Me. If I were you, I wouldn't get on so high and mighty a horse. It might just turn out to be your funeral I attend. Whatever, don't keep me hanging. If I'm so old I might die any minute, it damn straight ain't going to be with my ear pasted to this torture device."

Mac Henry cleared his throat and began to read. "'The town of Shadow was purchased for one point four million dollars by the Southern Diegueño Indian tribe for development as a gambling casino.' How do you like those lemons?"

"I'd say that's your typical Southern California thought process in a nutshell. Hurry up, everybody line their pockets and when you need a piece of fruit, get ready to pay triple for it 'cause out of state produce costs money to get shipped back here."

"I guess the only lemons down that way will show up on the slots."

"Thanks, Henry. You're a real brick."

"A brick through your fancy windows, just as you are to me, my friend. By the way, about that painting, Bop."

"Oh, Lord. Don't tell me. Gloria sold it at a garage sale."

"No, it's right here in our boudoir. Did I tell you it picks up the color of the drapes? I guess that western crap's hot right now. However, Gloria wants to sell it."

"You don't say."

"In fact," Henry went on, "she thinks we should retire, possibly take ourselves on a long cruise with the profits."

"Mr. and Mrs. Mac Henry take the ocean air? Dare I hope this means you'd exit the poison pen business?"

"Well, journalism is my life's work, but if the price is right, I suppose I can afford a short hiatus."

Bop wanted that painting back so badly he could taste oil and turpentine. Calmly, he said, "I'd caution you to be extremely fair concerning price, Señor Pulitzer. Old men can fight dirty, too."

Mac Henry laughed. "I've been thinking of trying my hand at a full-length book of fiction, Mr. Carpenter. Big family saga sort. What do you think?"

"I'm the first to applaud ambition at any age, Mac, but I'd cast my vote with the cruise. Nothing all that interesting to write about. People are into television these days."

"Well, let me think the price aspect over. I'll get back to you."

Bop smiled. "I'll be here. I believe you have the number."

MacLellan Henry rang off and Bop replaced the receiver in the telephone's cradle. He got up from the bed and walked out on the balcony to watch the sunset. Years back, Lainie and Russell used to leap off the railing into the water. They thought they were clever fooling him, but Bop knew exactly what they were up to. He'd gone so far as to measure the depth of the water and calculate how far those dives could safely take them. Crazy kids. He took a deep breath. The sky was a rich purple-dark, striped orange at the horizon, the dusky warm air a little fishy. He stood alone watching as the wind lifted the "For Sale" sign taped to *Shadow IV* and sent it spinning like a cheap kite into the bay. It floated on the surface and three harbor ducks paddled over to investigate. He shot a glance to the nasty Englishwoman's house, but it was blessedly dark, as it had been for weeks. Maybe she'd moved away.

He smiled to himself, imagining his granddaughter's reaction the first time she felt well enough to take a

454

walk in her precious bluffs. Lately she'd been preoccupied with the pregnancy, but eventually she'd return to her old habits, and when she did she was in for a king-hell surprise. He'd done a little something that just might qualify as his one selfless act of redemption, an act of which Miss Lainie had to approve. With his smart lawyer, expert environmental testimony, and photographs from the Harper Historical Society, Charles Russell Carpenter II had taken on City Hall in secret, the same way those clowns had made the soccer field decision. It had cost him, but what better way to spend your cash than having a hand in creating a half-mile of natural preserve for future generations to enjoy?

As soon as he started laying out the plan, the Harper Council suits began to see what a magnanimous trade-off this chunk of land could be to them in terms of any future development they wanted to accomplish elsewhere. In fact, it made them look so good that corporate jump-ons quickly threw down much of the necessary cash, but Bop Carpenter made certain the sand dune planting was all his.

The dune planting consisted of forty yards of sand, beach grass, and California poppies. Nothing monumental, but it beat the tar out of a brass angel. The out-of-the-way plaque was small and tasteful; Carlynn had helped him with the wording. It hung beneath the informational sign explaining what plants grew there—sand verbena, seacliff buckwheat, beach evening primrose—and what kinds of reptiles and bird life a lucky passerby might hope to encounter.

The Spencer Clarke Memorial Sand Dune
Look closely in the sand. People are not the only ones who have beachcombed this area. Can you see evidence

that a southern alligator lizard has walked before you, or the tracks of two gulls as they rummaged for breakfast?

Do you see where a cottontail rabbit was chased by a nighttime predator? The number of characters and plots is almost endless in the story of life on a sand dune.

Dogs Welcome. No leashes necessary.

There was no responsible party listed. Lainie was a Carpenter. She'd figure it out.

After awhile, Earlynn came out and stood next to him, wiping her hands on a yellow dishtowel. A recently groomed Oddjob jumped at her feet, hoping for her attention. Earlynn was wearing her "Kissing don't last, good cookin' do" apron. Bop marveled there was a woman left in the world who would don an apron for him.

"Supper's almost ready," she said. "Nothing fancy, just my tuna casserole. Lord, I can't stop smiling, thinking about those beautiful babies. However, I am sorry Elaine had to undergo that painful Caesar's Selection. She will need my help when she gets home. I'm already planning out meals to take over." She grinned. "Charles Russell, it appears our quiver is blessedly full."

"Amen to that." He kissed the top of her head and held her close, feeling the warmth of her skin, remembering being inside her, smelling her woman smells, all lotion and garlic and lemon and mystery. Then he added, "I love you, Grandma."

"That's *Great*-grandma to you, Buster."

"Pardon my mistake."

"I will this time." She kissed him on the mouth, slipped him the tongue.

He laughed. Charles Russell Carpenter II raised a fist

456

o the night sky, where either one brave star or a passing
et winked a moment of brightness through the inky
lue. *Got what I wished for*, he said to himself, and stood
olding onto his wife, looking heavenward long after
he dot was gone.

CHAPTER 35

THE FAT LADY SINGS

AINIE CARPENTER CLARKE SAT UPRIGHT IN HER
atio swing, naked from the waist up, her breasts
eaking, a sleeping baby cradled in each arm. She
eached across the picnic table into a jar, extracted and
it into one of the pickles she'd put up six months ago.
*So what? It's my backyard. Let people think I'm nuts, sitting
ere eating pickles half-nude. As Earlynn says, going crazy
roves you have a heart so big it can swing both ways.* With
er big toe, she pushed against the cement, making the
wing go back and forth lightly, creating a little breeze
to counteract the summer heat. A sleepy Jake lay at her
feet. He was busy these days, guarding the babies from
harm. Occasional thumps punctuated the silence as the
plum tree dropped ripe fruit. Moonlight shone down on
the patio creating intriguing shadows.

Months ago, Oddjob had gone home with Earlynn
under the guise of a grooming appointment and liked
Casa de Carpenter so well he decided to stay. That
seemed pretty much okay with everyone, Jake in
particular. Lainie imagined Spencer himself would have
approved of the love match that had developed between
his dog and the step-great-grandmother he never knew.

Across from her, Nick was fast asleep in the

Adirondack chair, his legs splayed out, one work boo untied. What with the babies' birth and going back tc his old job, her husband hadn't slept well for the las couple weeks. Since he started doing woodwork again he came home exhausted, but it was good-tired, from real work. He wasn't talking about psychology, finishing his clinical hours, any of that. Neither was she. This summer they were just taking things day by day, oi more truthfully, hour by hour, as dictated by the twins Her twenty hours of labor had ended in surgery. The incision still ached, but she was feeling way too lucky tc permit scars to enter into this equation. She needed help to get up and had to hold a pillow across her belly to walk, but these two healthy bundles in her arms were proof her luck had definitely changed.

Jake woofed, and a moment later, the gate opened. Her brother came down the brick walkway, carrying a guitar case. "Jesus," he said, "I can see your tits. Hey, they look different."

She pulled one of the baby blankets up over herself. "I know. They grew. But alas, it's only from the milk. The minute these bandits decide to wean themselves, I'll be left holding empty sacks."

"So, keep having babies."

"Let's just see how we do with these two, Mr. Daddy. When's the wedding?"

Russell sighed. "Stop it. You have any idea how nervous it makes me when you call me that? I think I just broke out in a hive."

"I love how nervous it makes you. Get used to it, Russell. I fully intend to rub in your impending fatherhood at every opportunity."

"Well, ease up for the moment, okay? What's with the Nickster? He looks unconscious."

"He fell asleep in the middle of a sentence, poor guy. Let him enjoy the quiet because it won't last. Where's Candace?"

"Aaron Brothers' framing sale. She's having her Fact Plus test triple matted and framed."

"Very funny."

"You think I'm kidding?"

Lainie laughed and her daughter gave a tiny yawn. Her hands uncurled like starfish and her face was angelic in sleep. Her new son looked so much like his brother it was as if somebody up there decided Spencer deserved a second chance and poured his features directly into this baby

Russell sat down next to her and ran a finger across the baby's cheek. The baby turned and his mouth made sucking motions, the automatic responses kicking in. Russell said, "Doesn't it hurt when he, they, you know, suck on you?"

"A little. But it feels right, too."

"Could I hold him?"

"Whenever you want." Lainie handed the baby over.

Russell looked down at his nephew. "Jeez, Lane. It's totally uncanny. He looks so much like—"

"I know. You don't have to say anything."

"Thought of any names yet?"

"Nick suggested Mortise and Tenon, but it's probably that Bop has him working so hard on Casa de Carpenter he can't think of anything but wood."

"Yeah, the old gomer's a slave-driver." Russell handed the baby back. "Well, you have to call them something, even if it's just Pork and Beans."

Secretly, she'd decided on names, but was waiting to tell Nick before anyone else. Her daughter she would call Alyce Earlynn, after the grandmothers who had

459

taught her so much. Her son, she was going to name after her brother and husband, Russell Nicholas, because Nick didn't like junior names. She planned to call him Rusty.

"You know," Russell said, looking up. "Mother's probably jetting through the sky now that the messy business of giving birth is over. She's going to descend any minute and wreck your life."

Lainie nodded, thinking it might be all right for once, Meridel holding her grandbabies, focusing on them instead of herself and Russell. "Well, it was nice while it lasted."

Her brother bent down to open his guitar case, revealing the Rancher, shiny as her newborns, and Lainie felt a pang of sorrow flicker inside her heart, then burn out like a shooting star. Shooting stars weren't stars at all, they were minute particles of dust, the friction of their descent causing the blaze as they entered the atmosphere.

"Are you sure my playing won't wake them up?"

"Russell, they have to get used to it. Besides, this is the only present I ever wanted. Thanks to Bop and Earlynn, I have two strollers and two million diapers and two of everything else I could ever possibly need. Just play."

He began to execute chord changes softly, dinking around, not headed in any particular direction. Lainie had helped her brother build his repertoire. She knew every segue he chose a moment before he got there. That was the way with twins; they developed senses single births missed out on. They felt one another's pain, they blurred the boundaries, they bonded so deep and eternal that sometimes outsiders found it hard to accept their kind of loving.

460

Lainie kissed her babies' heads, inhaling the jasmine-sweet scent of their newness, the gift of their health on this fine summer evening when nothing was wrong, and everything was right. Then she heard Russell make the shift into Melvin Endsley's "Singing the Blues."

These were not the blues, they were the peach shades of hopefulness. They were prayers set against the panic of randomness, human messages headed heavenward to those who had left and would always be missed. She closed her eyes. Hugging her children, she opened her mouth, felt her heart burst into her throat, and then, at last, she began to sing.

Dear Reader:

I hope you enjoyed reading this Large Print book. If you are interested in reading other Beeler Large Print titles, ask your librarian or write to me at

Thomas T. Beeler, *Publisher*
Post Office Box 659
Hampton Falls, New Hampshire 03844

You can also call me at 1-800-251-8726 and I will send you my latest catalogue.

Audrey Lesko and I choose the titles I publish in Large Print. Our aim is to provide good books by outstanding authors—books we both enjoyed reading and liked well enough to want to share. We warmly welcome any suggestions for new titles and authors.

Sincerely,